The Infernal Gate Trilogy

Part I

Invasion

By
Joshua Cloud

Cover and Internal Art
Ade Faisal Haq

"Fallen Giant"
Jason Johnson

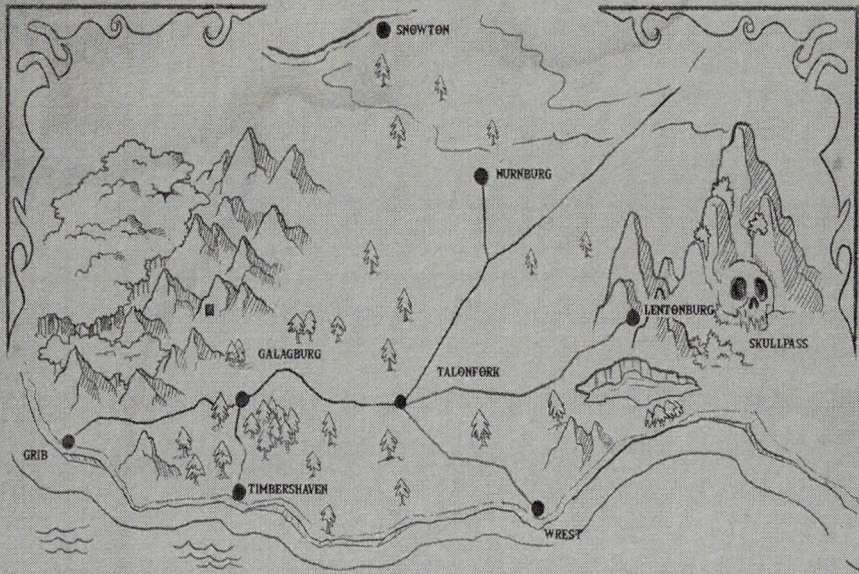

SNOWTON

NURNBURG

LENTONBURG

SKULLPASS

GALAGBURG

TALONFORK

GRIB

TIMBERSHAVEN

WREST

N

STRAIT
OF
KOLLUNE

GAERNIA/
PEORN

VALENCIA

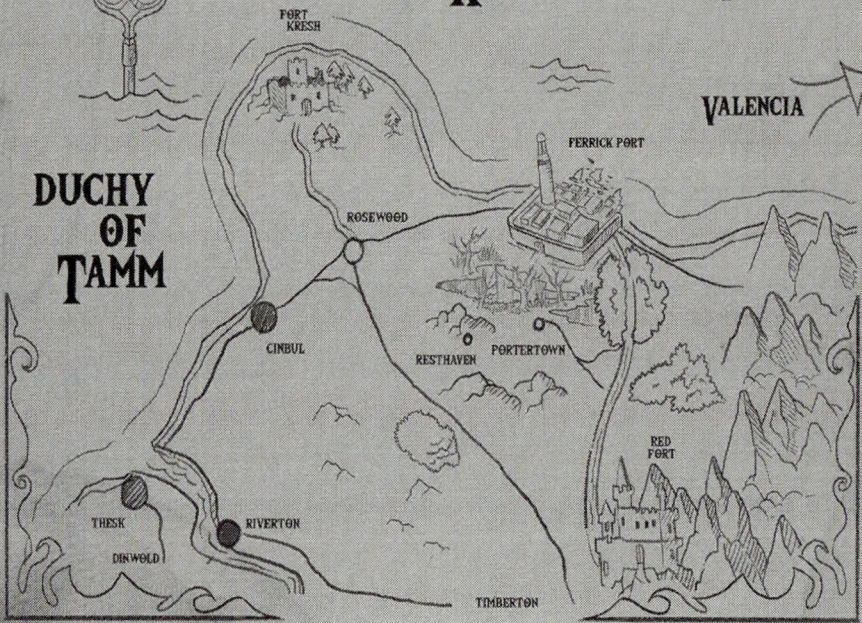

FORT
KRESH

FERRICK PORT

DUCHY
OF
TAMM

ROSEWOOD

CINBUL

RESTHAVEN

PORTERTOWN

RED
FORT

THESK

RIVERTON

DINWOLD

TIMBERTON

ISBN 9781687829924

Theo,
I truly hope you enjoy this read inspired by the magical world of dungeons and dragons.

Happy Christmas

Ty
xxx

Dedicated to

My wife Jennifer
And my four sons
Tristan, Lancelot, David and Kayden

I raise my sword to you all.

Moonlight filtered between thick clouds, and the moist smell of rain clung to the air. A dark clad figure glided through the vacant dock-ward and treated his surroundings as if he were watched from every window. The lone figure constantly glanced back over his shoulder. He stayed as close as possible to the buildings while he darted from one warehouse to the next.

Ahead in the darkness, the figure spied a tiny light. A short stocky cloaked man puffed on a long brown pipe which produced a near imperceptible glow. Before making any moves toward his prey, the watcher observed the building that the lone smoker protected with little regard.

The structure was a large, two-story warehouse, no different from the buildings on either side of it. Dark paint hid its weathered features. Large windows, spread out at regular intervals, dotted both stories. Facing the street, the warehouse had two sliding doors large enough to permit access to loaded wagons or carts. The side where the guardian stood had two windows and a lone door.

The observer moved in closer to get a better look at this 'guard'. The smoker took a long drag on his pipe and the light revealed a small spider tattoo on his cheek. Confident that this was a legitimate target and that there was no additional and immediate danger, the assassin easily skirted the shadows and flanked the unwitting cultist. A flash of blade and the gurgle of blood preceded the soft thump of the body as it was discarded further back in the shadows.

Satisfied with his kill, the cut-throat made a sweep of the windows and doors. From within one window, the deadly scout took note of another guard making rounds. Careful not to alert the patrolman to his presence, the figure retreated to the shadows where he retrieved a small roll-pouch and a silver disc from his black-dyed pack. The disc he tossed to the ground and incanted two simple words under his breath.

Ignoring that the disc grew and swirled into a silver mist, the figure knelt at the door and unrolled the leather pouch which revealed an assortment of lock-picks and tiny vials. He inspected the locking mechanism, decided on some choice tools and went to work on securing entry.

Behind him, the silver mist glowed and undulated. Three figures appeared, and then they stepped out of it as if through a door. The first, a young man clad in thick brown padded armor and who wielded two broad swords, knelt beside the assassin and whispered. The assassin nodded an acknowledgement and the crook-nosed warrior turned to his other two companions. His eyes were enough to command them to take up positions on either side of the door.

The next figure to come through the mist was a female half-elf. She kept her long black hair in a bun and wore tight fitting shirt and hose. Their burgundy hue hugged every curve of her toned body and her leather boots ran up nearly the entire length of her legs. She carried a short curved blade in one hand that made her look more the melee fighting type than the sorceress she was. Before taking her position, she leaned down to the lock-pick. "Are you certain this is the place Ryven?" she whispered.

Ryven only responded, "Arachnid," and continued to work on the lock.

The last to come through the mist was the largest. He was a full foot taller than the warrior and had the head and tail of a lizard and skin scaled red and orange. He resembled more a wingless dragon than that of his humanoid kind, the lizardmen. This one was clad in plate armor. He tried to muffle much of its clanking with a large winter cloak and tie straps on his legs and arms. In one hand, he held a spiked mace; the other wielded a large circular steel shield. Around his broad red-scaled neck, the lizardman wore a necklace adorned with a dangling silver sword, the holy symbol of Chess, goddess of combat.

The warrior sidled up alongside the last arrival with a whispered command, "Rassakk, let's let Ryven and Daria take the point. We'd just slow them down anyway."

Rassakk gave what only could be construed as a smile and replied, "You are the bosssss, Aerik."

Ryven popped the lock and spun next to Daria. He kept low to the ground so she could take aim above his head.

Aerik stepped out and gave a great kick to the door. It burst open and nearly flew off its hinges. Shafts of burning green light sprang from Daria's outstretched hand and impacted the earlier patrolman square in the chest. He barely had time to register surprise before he crumpled to the ground in a heap.

The group filed in and Daria and Ryven, almost at a run, spread out in what had to be an office. They quickly covered the ground to the far door, and seeing no danger beyond, disappeared through it and down a hall. Aerik stopped briefly, snatched a handful of papers from the desk and shoved them into a belt pouch as he and Rassakk jogged after the other two.

Aerik was pleased with the speed and efficiency of Ryven and Daria. The romance that brewed between the two fed their tenacity and desire to keep each other safe. The leader of this small group worried at first it would be a hindrance to their mission, but that thought was quickly dispelled the first time they encountered a cell of cultists. Aerik smiled as he passed another two dead bodies. He hadn't even heard them get attacked.

Rassakk, a priest of Chess was also fond of the pair. He admired their skill in combat, and even though they did not worship Chess, they honored her with their actions. This was a vile cult who worshiped a disgusting worm devil. This band of friends had already rooted out and destroyed three cells previous, finding sacrificed victims and depraved rites performed. Each time though had pointed to something even more nefarious. It appeared the cult was trying to bring their dark lord to this plane of existence. This was something Rassakk could not stand for. Thanks be to Chess for the companionship he had earned.

Daria and Ryven worked in tandem, alternating between their targets as the cultists made themselves available. The couple each possessed magic, either innate or through device, that enabled them to make 'hops' through space. Ryven was a little more restricted in that he required shadows to bridge the space he teleported through. Daria, on the other hand, had an additional advantage of staying invisible the first half second she materialized in a spot. She had usually already unleashed her deadly magics before there was an opportunity to see her.

Their path resembled a deadly dance, and the looks on their faces betrayed not only their determination, but also the enjoyment they took in devastating yet another evil cult. The pair continued through the whole of the bottom floor of the warehouse. When they were certain there would be no surprise visits from additional cultists, they wound their way to a set of stairs that lead down to the 'basement'; basement was code for secret temple.

Rassakk and Aerik took the first stairs they found up. The plan did not involve cultists of Codrugon flanking them in the final fight or to escape to bring back reinforcements. Meticulously, the two went from door to door in search of prey.

A good number of cultist guards were housed in the upper floor. The hallways gave a distinct advantage to the warrior and the priest as they fought them. There was no room to outmaneuver the attackers, and the cultists had to fight them straight on.

Aerik and his blades moved as one. Even when two cultists would attack side-by-side, Aerik was able to parry and attack them simultaneously. He usually cut them down faster than they could advance.

Rassakk on the other hand liked to give the enemy the chance to swing. His large shield would block their blows and his menacing stare instilled despair in his foe. With the restricted space, he had to thrust with his spiked mace. He possessed such strength that even this unwieldy attack collapsed his enemy's skull in a single motion.

When Rassakk and Aerik had cleared the upstairs, they worked their way down to find their companions. The warrior and priest caught up with Ryven and Daria downstairs at a large pair of oaken double doors that stood as the entrance to the secret temple.

"The doors are unlocked," Ryven noted aloud and put his pick roll-pouch back, "and this looks like the battle we have been looking forward to. Daria and I didn't want you to feel left out."

Even as Ryven spoke, they could all hear deep chanting come from the other side of the doors. Rassakk pulled a symbol from has pack. It was larger, yet identical to the one he wore around his neck. He spoke some words the others could not understand. The symbol, the priest and then his companions took on a warm white glow.

Aerik spoke, "This is it. We've plotted and planned. Now let's put it to action. You know your rolls. Be safe. And Bayoric watch over you." He looked over to Rassakk who removed the last binder strap from his armor. With the lizardman's nod, Aerik put a shoulder to one of the doors and forced his way in.

The room beyond was large and hot. Braziers were spread generously around the perimeter and cast a warm red hue on the stone walls. The far wall had what looked like the only other entrance, a single closed wooden door. Near the center of the room and off to the right of where the double doors opened, a sacrificial altar sat. Blood dripped down from the lifeless body of a nude female. Behind the altar, a man clad in a red robe stood, his sleeves rolled up to reveal several tattoos of insects on each forearm. The man's head was shaved clean except for a pinch of hair on his chin. His eyes bulged out of their sockets and he reveled in his debauchery.

The cultist priest was flanked on either side by two alert bodyguards. Each wore black padded armor with dirty bone helmets in the shape of twisted insect heads. More intimidating were the twin forked short spears they wielded and their spiked gauntlets, blood-caked from use.

In addition, a dozen cultists, half nude and slathered in blood swayed around a summoning circle and chanted the ritual's requisite magic. They dragged their knives down their arms, breasts or legs and fed their blood to the circle as evil pulsated in tune to their chants.

The two bodyguards reacted immediately to the open door and Rassakk knocked away one of their spears with his shield as it lanced to where Aerik stood. Aerik stepped in and met the second bodyguard who had charged across the room. Steel on steel rang out and alerted the remaining cultist that something other than the ritual took place.

Methodically, Daria took aim at the swaying cultists and let loose with volleys of green fire. Each, in turn, ignited as her magical blasts unerringly impacted them. She slowly edged her way into the room and to the left for better target acquisition.

The cultist priest realized the strain this combat put on the ritual and redoubled his efforts to speed up and conclude the rite. His two guards had engaged the enemy at the door and effectively blocked line of site to the spell caster.

Ryven stepped into the room and immediately drew bead on the priest at the altar. He assessed how easy it would be to tumble between the combatants or bank a dagger off the ceiling, but decided on the tried and true. He kissed his ring and disappeared back in the shadow of the door.

The assassin reappeared standing in the priest's shadow, dagger out. Ryven wrapped his arm around the priest's forehead and delivered three rapid thrusts with his dagger to his victim's side, under the ribcage. The cultist squirmed to no avail and immediately began spitting up blood. Then Ryven's knife found the priest's throat and drove itself to the hilt. The cultist priest's body fell forward somersaulting over the altar into the ritual circle. There it ignited in a black flame.

Their leader slain, the remaining participants, bodyguards included, panicked. Aerik cut down the guards as fast as they could turn away to run. One bloody cultist made it to the far door, only to be brained by Rassakk's spiked mace. His morning star had, by divine magic, flown across the room and pierced the skull of the routed. Grey force bolts finished the last cultist as he tried to rise and escape.

Aerik gave a congratulatory slap to Rassakk's back. "Check yourselves," he commanded.

Ryven and Daria were more interested in making sure the cultists were finished and only acknowledged with curt "Fine"s.

Rassakk circled the room to make sure there were no surprises waiting for them. Midway around, he stopped. His head cocked as he intently listened for something he hoped he had not just heard. Then his red-orange scales paled to a yellowish hue. He hissed out, "Over here......"

The other companions, once at his side, immediately heard the same chanting he did. It was coming from beyond the wall.

Daria joined her index fingers and thumbs into a triangle and, with a quick incantation, released a spell of revealing. A purplish glow outlined a large secret door before them.

"This isn't over," Aerik vocalized, but didn't have to. Ryven had already found the mechanism that would open the secret door.

Weapons out, Aerik gave the nod. Ryven slid the stone portal to the side and revealed a secondary summoning hall. The smell of sweat and burned wax accompanied the dull repetition of the chanting from within.

Larger than its preceding ritual chamber, this room's floor was built deeper and covered more than double the length and width of the first. The large space was illuminated by a glowing silver ring of liquid in its center and from candles placed at regular intervals in wall nooks. The candles had bled down to their stumps and signified the time the ceremony had already taken. Six wide pillars surrounded the mercurial ring, all adorned with bas relief of screaming humanoid faces and twisted insect forms. Across the ceiling, three arching beams with features mirroring the pillars, spanned the width of the room.

Occupants busied themselves near the dais and magic circle. Like the first room, several disciples of Codrugon swayed, chanted and bled themselves into the lighted ring, oblivious to their surroundings. Behind each stood an insect-masked figure, dagger raised for the climax of the ritual. Bronze double doors stood at

7

either side of the room, each guarded by a half dozen armored warriors with the familiar double-pronged spear and spiked gauntlets.

A dais, formed from the smooth flat stone and elevated by a natural grey stair, dominated the floor beyond the silver ring. Behind the dais, a large hexagonal shape, crafted from timbers or slate, had been molded into the wall and outlined a dark, pulsating greenish light. A lone red-robed figure stood between the dais and miasmic wall. His head was shaved and displayed a tattoo of a centipede that circled twice around his skull. The priest's gaze locked upon an open leather-bound tome propped upon the dais, and he incanted phrases of power from it. Each word caused the light behind him to coalesce and give solid form to a gateway between this place and a most infernal one beyond.

A stone landing and stairs led down from the secret door and hugged the wall to the right. Ryven entered through the narrow doorway and melded with the shadows. His attention was fully upon the central figure. Aerik and Rassakk were not so easily concealable, and as they entered, a guard called out an alarm.

Like the first room, central figures continued their evil rite while the armored figures moved to intercept. A half dozen javelins launched through the air at the group on the stairs and were deflected by a magical shield conjured by Daria.

"FAZRADIA!" the central figured boomed. The sickly green swirls behind him vented a foul stench and sulfurous smoke.

Aerik launched himself off the landing to the left to divert the cult's attention away from Ryven. The guards from the left of the room took the bait and moved as one to engage him.

The guards from the right might have done the same except that Rassakk slammed down from the center of the stairs. The bunch turned to face steel and was greeted with fire. Rassakk let loose a breath of flame that swept back and forth over the stunned group. For some, only a burning, gurgled scream escaped as they died. Two were able to back out of the swath of fire, blistered skin and singed hair their reward for survival. With trepidation, they moved to the new threat.

Green fire lanced from above as Daria unerringly reduced Aerik's opponent count by two.

Ryven found his spot and disappeared.

"ZYNTHA-KOR!" the central figure shrilled. One by one, the dagger-clad cultists brought their blades down. Haphazardly, they stabbed the bloody victims in front of them. A cacophony of screams resounded. The mist gave shape to dark and alien forms.

"Stop the blood-letting!" Aerik, who was fully occupied by the remaining guards barked. He parried then dropped one attacker to his knees with a well-placed thrust to the gut. Aerik let his next swing be deflected into a decapitating swipe and sent the kneeling cultist low.

Rassakk shield-bashed an opponent. The force of his swing lifted and launched the cultist back several feet. The second cultist's sword clanged off Rassakk's breast plate. A swing of the priest's morning star brought the second guard's arm down. At that moment, the lizard's large jaws found the soft supple neck of the cultist, and like a hungry crocodile, he shook violently until the head hung to the body only by a few muscles and sinew. Bloodlust had overcome the draconian cousin.

Daria, aware of their time constraints, switched to a more encompassing offensive. Her fingers crackled and lightning streaked to her first target. The insect-masked cultist lit up revealing his insides, at first as if a light shone brightly from within, then again with an explosion of innards that sprayed the immediate area. The lightning continued to his victim and to each of the adjacent pairs of cultists. Within moments, one quarter of the circle was littered with dead bodies and gore.

Ryven appeared in the shadow of the priest, their backs to the gate-way. The assassin failed to notice the figure drop down from the ceiling behind him as he brought his dagger up for the killing strike. His own arm was stayed by an icy-cold steel grip. "You are not the only one who can use the shadows as a weapon." a breath that smelled of death whispered in his ear. With that, the black clad figure wrapped its other arm around Ryven and they ascended to the arch in the ceiling where the creature disemboweled its hapless prey.

"ARITHRAX-FAZRADIA!" the high priest bellowed. He beamed at his accomplishment as the gate behind him solidified into a putrescent, contorting tunnel that linked to his patron's realm. The blood-bath in the center of the chamber ended. Either by their own hand or Daria's, the sacrificial cultists completed their task. The creatures in the gate stirred and then parted for one behind to come through. A dozen cultist guards burst through the door closest to Rassakk and moved to engage him.

Aerik was pinned by his opponents. One more of the guards fell to a skull-splitting swing, but the last two pressed him into the corner. Aware of how dire the unfolding situation was going to end, Aerik made a desperate plea to his companions, "Daria, Ryven, Rassakk! Focus on the high priest!"

Blood dripped down from the ceiling, Ryven's only answer to Aerik's call.

Rassakk launched a glowing holy lance, formed from the air, at the high priest and turned his attention to the newly arrived reinforcements. The cultist leader batted his conjured weapon aside as if it were a fly. Ignoring the ineffectiveness of his attack, the lizardman opened up his melee with a deep swing of his morning star. The momentum felled the two front guards. The others fanned out to gain flanking advantages.

Daria was the first to realize Ryven was missing. She scanned the room and only supposed he was setting up some shadow strike. The sorceress directed her full attention on the central figure. First she delivered her 'fingers of emerald fire'. Although they penetrated his defenses, the missiles had little effect. The High Priest squared off with her, robes singed from her spell. Next the sorceress let loose with 'lightning's loving embrace'. This one knocked him on his backside. The electrical arc caught two of Rassakk's opponents in its rebound. *All the better,* she thought. Confident she had found her spell, Daria incanted a second time. The high priest found his footing just as the spell reached him. His hands came up as if in fear, but magical force stopped her lightning and forced the spell's effects back upon her. The sorceress barely had time to scream as her insides boiled and exploded back toward the stair.

From the gate stepped a monstrosity. It's scarred black chitinous armor plating betrayed years of fighting enemies of Codrugon. The creature's head was a cross between a rhinoceros beetle and dragon and had large, fly-like eyes. It's carapaced thorax sat upon four thick, armored segmented legs and each of its two pairs of arms were crossed as it strode into the summoning chamber. A large double-bladed battle axe was sheathed on the thing's back while it surveyed the battle.

Aerik and Rassakk recovered quickly from Daria's unseemly demise. The tides of combat brought them back-to-back. Aerik still clung to his professional training and surgically attacked his foes. Tears streamed down his face at their loss. Rassakk was in a full rage. Wisps of fire escaped his nostrils, and every attack from his morning star was accompanied by a guttural cry and overcompensated swings.

Backed by its insect-like followers, the giant insect monstrosity moved with confidence toward the two trapped heroes. The priest fell in step and the undead dweller from above also dropped down into cadence.

Seeing hope dwindling fast, Aerik whispered back to his ally. With Rassakk's nod of understanding, Aerik slid down between the legs of one of the two guards he had cornered and disemboweled him as he came up. The warrior then used the wall to spring over the second while Rassakk hurled his mace into the face of the distracted cultist.

All in the same motion, Rassakk braced to receive the airborne Aerik and then launched him over his own head toward the oncoming foes. Aerik righted himself for a death-strike. The speed and reach of the insect warlord's axe was too great and Aerik was split in two. His insides showered the enemy, his blades clanged to the ground.

Tendrils of icy blackness snaked from the high priest's fingers and enveloped the lizardman who reached to recover his mace. As consciousness escaped him, the last thing he heard was the guttural voice of the demon-invader, "Let the draconian live. He shall be our very first prisoner. Bring the slave back to our master's realm for indoctrination…"

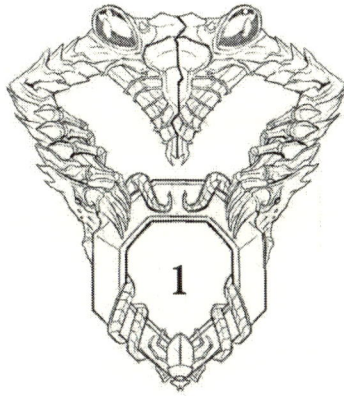

1

It was mid-morning on a small farm near the village of Resthaven. This farm, home to a family of four, had no barns or miles of fenced fields, but it was quiet and generally undisturbed. Three pigs that wallowed in a small pen made the most noise throughout the day. Birds sang the praises of the rising sun, and laundry was already hung from an early morning wash. Two boys played outside the home. These boys were adventuresome, or at least they liked to think so. Each day, they would travel to the outskirts of the farm and, with stick in hand, trek to the farthest reaches of the lands to do battle with the forces of evil. This usually ended up being a fence post or tree.

Tristan was the elder of the two, just having turned fifteen. He stood a good shoulder's length taller than his younger sibling. His brown eyes had strength in them and he always looked out for Lancelot, even if the monsters and villains were not really alive. Whenever there was action, he would call his brother to arms, and they would scream out their charge as they bound to meet their enemies.

At thirteen, Lancelot was the loyal bodyguard. He always looked to and fro to ensure that there were no actual creatures nearby, but this always translated into him finding something to chop at with his wooden saber. Lancelot was of fairer complexion.

He spent more of his younger years at his mother's side before Tristan enticed him to join his ranks in the fight against evil.

This day, their father had taken a wagon of corn to the village square. He would sell or trade all day and would not return until nightfall. With their chores finished, the two had all day to fight and explore. Tristan suggested that they investigate the dragon cave near the stream on the south side of the fields. Lancelot insisted that they stock their provisions before such a long and perilous journey. And mother had just finished with some baking.

Back in the house, Sarauna, the boys' mother, had some treats in store for her sons when they spilled through the front door. "Wipe your feet," she scolded even though she couldn't keep from smiling. The two boys could instantly smell the sweets that she had so laboriously prepared. Bread twists with candied tops issued a fragrance that challenged their self-control. Lancelot already had one in each hand, eating from his left. "Save some for the cave," Tristan ordered. Lancelot immediately stowed his meal in a small leather pouch he kept looped to his belt.

After stocking water and bread, Tristan went to his room and fetched his carving knife. His stick would be his sword, but he kept the dagger for anything real. Sarauna came to his bedroom with two ears of corn. "Put these in your pack. I know you and your brother are probably just going to eat the bread, but I want you to eat something else too." Tristan replied that he would. Then, with a bow, he excused himself from the 'castle'. Lancelot mimicked his actions and bound out the door after him.

Outside the farmhouse was large and expansive, and it took the boys several minutes to reach their destination. A stream cut a path across the southern border of the property, and eventually down the side of a hill. It left a rocky ladder which the boys used to get to their final destination. A small cave, hidden by berry bushes sat atop a small, flat plateau where the stream bent away and further down the hill.

The whole area smelled of the ripe berries, and the boys picked and ate them on their hike down the side of the hill. Lancelot went first to ensure the safety of his liege. Although the rocks were wet and slippery from the splashing stream, they navigated the path deftly and swiftly. When they reached the flat area before the cave, each drew their sword from their belt and prepared to enter.

The cave opening itself was not large, possibly three feet at its widest, and stretched a few yards back and then up into the hill. There it abruptly ended. The two had been here a hundred times before, but each time, they imagined a different, horrible enemy lying in wait from within.

This time was different. Tristan looked inside from the entrance. It was dark, and the dripping of water near the back of the cave gave off a hollow echo. Something else inside stirred. Lancelot heard the shuffling sound first, and put his hand on Tristan's shoulder to give him pause. The younger brother moved in front to protect his liege from whatever threat lie within, and with his stick in hand, crawled into the cave. Tristan watched in amazement as his brother actually went in to face the danger.

Not wanting to appear the coward, Tristan drew the knife that his father had given to him and proceeded into the cave mouth. Just as he had done so, Lancelot forced passed him in a panic. "It's an axe-beast!" he screamed as he pushed his way past. He leapt to his feet and ran down the steep embankment of the hill. Tristan's heart jumped as he heard the shuffling from within grow closer.

Trusting Lancelot implicitly, Tristan exited the cave post-haste and scrambled down after his brother. Of course, young boys' excited minds can get the better of them, and shortly after the rout, but long before the boys could ever come back to investigate, a chicken emerged from the cave and worked its way up the hill back to its roost.

Tristan and Lancelot fled down the hill and followed the natural path the stream cut. After the cave, the hill leveled out somewhat which allowed them to run even faster. "Are you certain it was an axe-beast?" Tristan asked between labored breaths. He had already caught up with Lancelot and had already started to pass him.

"Are you kidding?" his brother replied. "I can't believe it could even fit in the cave. It was so big!"

Tristan urged Lancelot to keep up and began running faster. "I hope it's not fast. And I really hope it's not after us," he said looking back. He noticed a horrified look on Lancelot's face, but it did not register until too late.

Tristan turned to face forward and had the wind knocked out of him as he slammed headlong into a real monster. The impact bounced him backwards and he landed square on his hind quarters. Lancelot skidded to a halt and then took his version of a warrior's stance with his wooden stick raised to strike. Tristan recovered and looked up at what had put him down with such force.

Standing before the boys was a creature, nearly six feet in height, but hunched slightly and with huge girth. Its skin was green and oily, and its black matted hair came down about its shoulders and covered the right side of its grimy face. Beads of sweat trickled down its cheek and a long tongue came out of its tusked mouth to lick at the salty trails. All black eyes stared intently at the two boys, itself somewhat stunned at this encounter. Its arms hung down at its side, and strapped to its belt was no stick, but a large, gleaming scimitar.

Tristan scrambled back to his feet and brandished his knife defensively to ward the creature away. The green beast just stood there, then cocked its head. A small smile played across its face as it eyed the meager weapon and children before it. The thing, clad in black leather armor, blood-caked from many years of use, took a step forward. The boys turned to run, and with a speed the belied its stature, the green-skinned monstrosity reached out and grabbed each of them by the scruffs of their necks. Tristan reacted boldly and cut the creature's arm twice with the blade of his knife. He screamed, "Let go of me you oversized rotten apple!" It shook him quite violently and he dropped the dagger into the grass. The grip did not slacken though, and the beast dragged Tristan behind him, Lancelot under its other arm.

Both boys squirmed and writhed to escape from its grasp, but to no avail. It only grunted what could be some kind of amusement and then stalked off along the ridge of the hill in the direction of its original heading. Tristan twisted so he could communicate with

Lancelot, but his brother's face was smothered in the creature's side. Tristan felt every rock and bump as he was dragged along, and after what seemed forever, the creature stopped.

It slung both boys into a pile in front of it and then found a seat on a nearby rock. It propped its arms in the shape of inverted C's and rested its hands on its knees. It displayed that same grin as it watched the boys collect themselves. Lancelot was the first to get to his feet and stepped forward. "I'm going to kill you, you filthy orc." He raised his right fist and prepared to charge at it, but was stopped by Tristan's command, "Wait!" Lancelot looked quizzically back at his brother and Tristan continued, "If he wanted to kill us, he could have done it back near the stream." His gaze shifted over to where the orc sat. "Why did you bring us here? What are your intentions? Our father will come looking for us. He will find you."

After studying them for some time, it responded. Its voice was very guttural and deep. Tristan could barely tell it was talking, and had thought that it was clearing its throat. "What are your names?" it asked. Both brothers were taken aback. First, that the thing would answer them. Second, that it could talk at all. Tristan stood and dusted himself off. "I am Tristan, son of Amroth. The warrior before you is my brother, Lancelot." Having forgot his company was an orc, Lancelot bowed at his introduction, then turned beet red when he realized what he had done.

"I'm Trazk." the orc nearly laughed. "And I won't kill you. In fact, I just saved your life." The boys looked both surprised and incredulous.

"How is that?" Tristan asked. "Is this some ploy to get us to jump happily into your stew pot?"

This time the orc did laugh. It was hard to differentiate this from his speaking. "First off, I don't eat humans. At least not as boney as you two. Second, I myself was running from a great evil. Greater even than I. It has been sweeping through from the west, out of the mountains somewhere, and has newly arrived in this kingdom. When I saw you two, dumb and deer eyed, I took pity on you and brought you with me. This is as far as I carry you though. So if you want to live, you will run on your own feet."

"What is this evil?" Lancelot asked, "What will become of mother and papa?"

For the first time, the orc took on a dour and serious disposition. "It is called the hive. Our shamans believe them to be demons. They look like tall armored insects. Some have six, some eight arms. They have tusks, or rather mandibles, larger than mine that can slice your head off in one bite. As for your parents... I suspect they are already dead. The hive is relentless. Everything it encounters it kills and then takes."

"We need to go back for them!" Lancelot exclaimed, and he tried to brush past Trazk, but the orc grabbed him by his elbow and spun him around.

"You cannot return that way. You will die." Lancelot tried to pull away, but Trazk's grip was a vice, and what little compassion the orc had, he showed by not letting go.

"I fear the orc is right," Tristan said as tears welled up. "Can we travel with you? As much as we play warriors and wizards, neither of those are we."

"I will take you with me. But you will do as I say. I have little patience for things that may get me killed. Can either of you hunt?"

Lancelot answered, "Tristan is the best with a bow. He can hit rabbits and squirrels from so far away, you have to strain your eyes just to see em."

"When I find a bow, you are our hunter Tristan." Trazk finished. He got up from his rock and started off in the direction that they had been running.

Lancelot paused, and for a moment, he could not decide if he would follow the orc or his instincts to go back for his parents. As Tristan fell in behind Trazk, Lancelot bowed his head in a quick prayer for his mother and father and took off at a jog to catch up.

The hills were thickly overgrown with biting shrubs and tall, broadleaf trees. As the three traveled into the early evening, the rolling dips gave way to steadier flat ground and into open high grass fields. A burning smell permeated the air, and behind the travelers, columns of smoke rose from numerous places near where their journey had started. This time, both boys gave prayers for the safety of their family.

A short number of hours later, the sun finally dipped down behind the hills and darkness overtook the land. Trazk had slowed the group to a near crawl for the last hour as he scouted around for a good place to camp. When he had found what he thought was suitable, he had the boys collect as much wood and debris as they could while he cleared everything away in the small circle of their camp.

"Lay those branches and leaves around the camp," he said to Tristan, who had returned with an armful of leaves and wood. "Pile it around where I have marked the boundary."

"Why aren't we using this to make a fire? It gets pretty cold at night," Tristan queried.

"Because we are not going to give ourselves away to the hive or anything else while we sleep. I would set watch, but we are tired from running all day, and one weapon is not going to protect us all if we are ambushed anyway. The dry leaves and twigs are an alarm. It will not give us much time, but maybe one or more of us can get away if the camp is attacked."

Lancelot came into the camp and immediately started following Tristan's lead, padding the perimeter with his find. "Why are we not using this to make a fire?" he asked.

Tristan answered, "We are. Can't you see? After its all ready, Trazk is going to have us get in the middle here, and cook us for his supper."

Trazk and Tristan laughed. Lancelot was not amused.

When the camp was finished, Trazk, who already sat comfortably, dug through his pack and retrieved dried meats and his flask of water. He passed a bit to each of the boys and then ate some himself. Silently they ate, then after some wordless contemplation, each found his way to sleep. They all slept restlessly.

By the time the boys awoke, Trazk had already been up for some time and returned the camp to its natural look. He had just finished covering their most recent tracks and studied the landscape as if it would reveal some deep secret. When the orc saw that the two boys were fully awake, he beckoned them to where he stood. "I am going to travel south from here. It takes me away from the human settlement to the north, and the human farms to the east. If you like, you can travel with me. I do not think those humans have much time. Or you can try to warn them before the hive gets there."

Lancelot looked to Tristan and shrugged. "I wouldn't mind going with Trazk," he said. "He seems to know what he is doing."

"Yeah," Tristan replied, "but we have a duty to get to Porterstown and warn them. It's the right thing to do."

"You are right." Lancelot was already walking.

Trazk grabbed him by his shoulder and turned him. "Your settlement is that way," he pointed.

"Right. Thanks for saving us Trazk. I wish we could do something to repay you. I am very grateful."

Tristan chimed in, "We are both very grateful for your help. And I am sorry we cannot travel with you. We have a duty to…."

"You do right by your kind, boy." Trazk cut him off. He watched as the two boys plodded north, the weight of the world on their shoulders.

2

Clouds darkened the skies, and the early morning cold nipped at the boys as they plodded north toward Porterstown. Neither talked for several hours. Tristan led them through winding trails. Lancelot kept his head down and just watched where his brother walked. He tried to step into each of Tristan's prints, for no other reason than to entertain himself on his uneventful journey.

Tristan kept replaying the events from the day before in his head. He wondered what happened to his mom. It was possible that his dad was safe, for he may not have returned from the village before their home was attacked. Of course, it was possible that the whole village was destroyed and everyone in it. That fear kept creeping back into his thoughts.

By noon, the boys reached a road that Lancelot immediately recognized as running between Porterstown and the Hetch Farm. When not with Tristan, Lancelot liked to spend time with his friend Arden Hetch, a tall and lanky boy of twelve who loved to fish and hike. "Arden lives down that way." Lancelot pointed and shared with his brother.

"We can't go that way though," Tristan thoughtfully mused. "We risk running into the hive."

"What if the orc was lying to us? What if it's orcs lighting the fires and killing? It could be some sick joke of his to have brought us

here. He could be back there right now plundering our house."
Lancelot chose not to use Trazk's name. He wanted to depersonalize
himself from the orc in case his thought could be true. He kind of
liked Trazk, but didn't know anything about him.

"Doesn't matter. We have to get to Porterstown and warn them
none-the-less. If it is orcs or demons, the danger to everyone
remains the same."

"That is true. We should hurry."

The two boys started to jog along the road but found they were
tired from their ordeal. They also found the hard packed road to
their dislike and spent most of the time walking along the side of
the road in the grass. The softer dirt was easier on their feet, but
slowed them down. A deer startled the pair when it leapt across the
road. Then the realization that they had not eaten since the night
before sank in. Lancelot's stomach reminded them with a loud
churn.

"I could sure use some of mom's cooking," Lancelot answered
his growl. With a slap across the back of his younger brother's head,
Tristan answered, "Yeah. Maybe if we had only put some of those
bread sticks into your leather pouch, we could be eating right now."

"Oh, yeah." Lancelot retrieved the bread and passed some to
his brother. "Didn't you put some corn in your pack?" He narrowed
his eyes at Tristan.

"Oh, yeah," Tristan said coyly.

With spirits a little lighter and stomachs a little fuller, the two
traveled alongside the road while they played guessing games and
imagined what actual adventuring would be like. Tristan often
pointed to things off in the distance and they attempted to guess
what the objects were. Most of the time, they determined that the
splotches and far off dots must be huge dragons or waltzing giants.
Their minds slipped back to their fantasy play, as it was much
easier than dealing with this reality.

Their pace slowed to a crawl, and by nightfall, they felt as if
they were not moving at all. Tristan began to mimic the actions of
Trazk from the night before. He was looking for a suitable place to
camp when Lancelot pointed out the lights from Porterstown not

far ahead.

They found that they had some run left in them and sprinted nearly the rest of the way to the walled town's outer gate.

To Tristan and Lancelot, Porterstown was massive. From the outside, they could only see the taller buildings, some of which were three stories high, surrounded by a wooden palisade that was nearly ten feet high. The road led right up to two reinforced gates. Each was flanked by a small watch tower. Lanterns hung in each tower and illuminated the road right below them. Shadows moved within the tower tops, and when the two boys had come to within twenty paces of the gate, a voice rang out from above.

"What business could two young boys have this late in the night? State your names."

Tristan stepped forward and bowed. "I am Tristan, son of Amroth. This…" pointing to his brother, "is my younger brother Lancelot. We hail from outside of the village Resthaven. I am here to warn you that Porterstown is in danger." He started to choke up at the thought of his parents being dead, and the voice took that opportunity to interject.

"Resthaven is pretty far. Two days walk from here I believe. What danger could Resthaven have that would be threatening our…modest town?" The voice dripped with sarcasm that even Tristan understood.

"There are demons coming this way!" Lancelot yelled out for his brother. "There isn't much time. They are sweeping across the land!"

Surprised, the voice asked, "Demons?! How many?" The sarcasm was still there, but the voice was a little unsure at such a bold statement in the middle of the night.

"I don't know," Lancelot answered.

"What do you mean you don't know? What do they look like?"

"Well, I think they look like insects, but I didn't see them. Trazk, an orc told us what they were."

Now the voice seemed to get a little irritated, "Let me get this straight. You come here to warn us of demons you have no proof exist because you were told by an orc…that isn't here…. Who put you up to this? Was it Barnek? Your joke was pretty good. You can come in now…. Open the gate."

As the gate creaked to life and begun to swing open, Tristan tried to recover for his brother, "Good sir, my brother is dead serious about the matter of the demons. We did not see them ourselves, but we did see pillars of smoke and ash above the trees by where we live. We did meet an orc, and although he did not kill us, and in fact did help us, he was an orc to be sure. Please take us at our word and let us speak with someone who will listen."

The voice was both entertained and annoyed. It said with an incredulous laugh, "Seek out Sir Brell. He resides at the Scorpion's Sting Tavern. Easy to find. Once you enter the gate here, take your first left and follow the street for about two hundred paces. The tavern will be the only building alight."

With that, the voice dropped to a dull unintelligible whisper, directed at yet another unseen figure in the tower. Tristan and Lancelot walked through the gate and took the prescribed left. The gate creaked shut behind them. They both jumped when it fully closed and a large draw bar crashed down to secure it.

As the two walked down the street, the moon penetrated through the clouds and cast a white glow over the buildings and street. Light escaped from windows and the brothers caught an occasional glimpse of someone revealed behind half open curtains or shutters. The streets were quiet except for the distant chirping of grasshoppers and the dim buzz of flying insects.

As the mysterious voice at the gate had said, the tavern they sought was fully alight. When the boys approached the building, they heard laughter and boisterous conversation from within. Two wide wooden steps led up to the entrance. A sign hung over the door and a lantern hung from a metal pole above that. Painted on the sign was a dark green scorpion's tail and stinger.

As they walked into the two story building, Lancelot nearly tripped over the body of a sleeping man who was lying near the front door. The man slept restively and was mumbling in his slumber. Tristan opened the door to the tavern and was immediately assailed with light and noise. Nearly twenty patrons were inside. The room was filled with drinking, dancing, singing, laughing, and talking. A large woman, her auburn hair up and disheveled, moved from table to table and either took orders or dropped drinks off for thirsty townsfolk.

Tristan and Lancelot were hardly noticed as they entered. The lack of attention was rather unnerving, and Tristan had to work to get the bartender's attention. "Excuse me sir. Can you help us?"

"What will you be having?" the skinny, beady-eyed man asked. He scratched the back of his neck, all the while he tried to seem interested while he kept an ear to a conversation in another part of his tavern.

"Actually, my brother and I need help. There are demons coming to town and our parents may have been killed back in Resthaven." Tristan had a hard time not saying it all at once.

"Boy, you look too young for grog, but you sure talk like you've been in it all day."

"Sir, I don't drink...grog... and I am very serious. The man at the gate sent us here to find Sir Brell."

At that, the barkeep laughed, "Brell? Oh, I am sorry good sir. Your mission must be of great importance." He had on his face an expression of mock concern. "Sir Brell stands guard outside these very doors. It is possible that he is asleep at this time, since he has had a full day of saving damsels and killing brigands."

Tristan looked puzzled and Lancelot followed him as he hesitantly moved back toward the front door. The barkeep watched them with amusement as they walked out.

On the porch, the boys stood over the sleeping man. From his looks, he had been on the out and out for some time. His long grey hair was dirty and unkempt. On top, he was bald. He had a mustache and goatee beard, but that needed some dire attention. His face and neck were dirty from what looked like months of dust and wear with no bath. Lancelot bent over and shook the sleeping man. "Sir Brell, please help us." The man did not stir.

"Shake him a little harder," Tristan ordered.

A more violent jerk brought the man's eyes open. He smelled of dirt and urine. "Sir," Lancelot continued, "we need your help against demons."

The man's eyes opened wider. "Hmm? Demons? Help me up." His speech was slightly slurred.

Tristan came around to the other side of the man, and the two boys hoisted him up. Brell was unsteady at best. He continued to slur, "You need to help me back to my house. I'll help you fight the demons."

Tristan shot a glance over to Lancelot, and the younger brother understood that they had been had by the voice at the gate. Angry, the two boys continued to help the man, not out of need, but more of respect for an elder.

Helping Brell was not easy at all. The man stumbled at almost every corner, and he continually gave the wrong directions. Carrying him was even worse. Brell was sweaty and the newly added smell of vomit and ale issued from his body and breath. Tristan tried to estimate how old Brell was. It was hard to tell if all the lines on his face were from age, sun, alcohol or a combination of the three.

Even though Brell was missing some of his faculties, he did show a keen interest in the demons. He asked what they looked like, how many there were, and where they had come from. Of course, none of the answers could be addressed with any certainty, but that did not deter his probing.

The thick clouds obscured the moonlight and it became even more difficult to navigate the streets. Eventually, by what Tristan could only believe was a miracle, Brell stopped them at the entrance to a small building. Its wooden walls were dilapidated and worn and the front door was partially off of its hinges. "This is my home," Brell chimed. "Get me inside so I can armor up."

With looks of incredulity, the two boys walked Brell to the door. Once there, it took great effort for Lancelot to force the door open. When it finally gave, the two nearly dragged Brell in and propped him up against a wall. Lancelot then fumbled in the dark to get a candle lit. With a little light, they were able to navigate the small home. Brell, they got into a chair. Then the boys made toward the front door. "Look," Brell's voice stopped them. "I know I'm a drunk, but I can help."

Tristan turned, "I'm sorry sir. But the man at the front gate sent us to you as a cruel joke I'm certain. We need to be going to find help."

"I can help. I just need to get thinking straight so I can get my armor on and help you boys out. Can't have demons wandering around."

"You don't understand sir," Tristan replied. "There are so many demons that one person is not going to stop them. We thought maybe you were in charge of this town and could help to rally some kind of army. I am sorry to say, but you are just one drunk man that we found sleeping in his own piss." Again the boys turned to leave.

"Please," Brell pleaded. "If nothing else, it looks as if you have nowhere to stay. You could stay here. Let me just clear away the stuff in the spare room and you both can sleep on the bed in there." The ale in him started to wear off, and Brell, even aged, started to take on the demeanor of someone who at least once, had authority and charisma about him.

The boys were indeed penniless and had not thought about where they would stay or how they would take care of themselves. "We could stay, just to make sure he is okay," Lancelot conceded.

After a moment, Tristan agreed. They helped Brell to clear the years of piled junk from the bed in his spare room and then helped the old man to change into cleaner clothes. While searching for something for him to wear, Lancelot found a pristine suit of armor neatly piled in the corner. While everything around it had collected dust from the years of disuse, the armor still shone as if it were just made. He waited until Brell was long asleep before confiding his find to Tristan.

Tristan replied with an insight of his own, "I noticed when we were changing Brell that he wore a symbol on his necklace. It was the same symbol mother kept in her bedside drawer." The two spent the rest of their waking hour trying to decipher the significance of their discoveries. Sleep overcame them before they could come up with any answers.

Sometime in the middle of the night, Tristan thought he woke to chanting and a light blue glow emanating from the other room, but took it as a dream and went back to sleep.

The boys woke to frantic knocking on the front door. They heard Brell talking to someone in the other room, and then heard him open the front door. Panicked voices made their hearts jump. Lancelot was the first out of the bed. He still had his shirt half over his head as he went into the other room to investigate.

There were already two townspeople seated in the front room. One was a young boy, maybe eight or so. He had been crying for some time and his eyes were red from it. What had to be his mother sat beside him. She also had been crying, but anxiously watched as Brell, clad in the armor found earlier, let three more people into his home. It was light outside, but still early. The three new visitors included a tall, dark haired man and two teenage boys. The man looked disheveled as if he had recently woke. His hair was unkempt like the beard on his face. The man had a dour look about him and he carried a blacksmith's hammer in his hand. The older of the two boys bled from his arm or shoulder. His white shirt was crimson red from his right elbow to his chest. Everyone looked scared and confused.

Brell continued the conversation that he had at the door, "Miss Gray here says that there is something attacking the town? How many are there? Which direction are they attacking from?" At the mention of the attack, the woman, Miss Gray, began to tremble.

The dark-haired man looked nervously to the two teen aged boys then responded hesitantly, "I think we are being attacked by giant insects or something. They look like ants that are standing on two legs. They wield swords and axes in their remaining four arms…legs…arms. Anyway, one of them threw this which cut Jerrod's arm." He motioned for the older boy to step forward. "Son, show Sir Brell your arm."

Tristan walked into the room as the man produced an object from within his shirt. It looked like three black bladed daggers attached to a central, circular handle. The whole thing looked like a horrific triangular killing device. It had both dried and wet blood on its blades.

Brell seemed less interested in the weapon than the deep gashes in the boys arm. He asked if the boy felt a pain in his stomach which was answered in the affirmative. "I bet the insects looked less like ants and more like praying mantises." The recognition in the man's eyes said that Brell knew what he was talking about. "And you have been poisoned," he directed at the boy. The boy looked terrified as Brell continued, "And… these are not demons." A collective sigh of relief was let out until Brell spoke further. "They are the spawn of devils."

The teenage boy with the wound to his arm started to convulse. Saliva frothed at his mouth and his father had to catch him as he buckled over. In one motion, Brell swept the debris from his dining table. "On here," he said. The father laid his son onto the table while Brell rolled up his sleeves. His eyes and hands gave off a slight blue glow as he began whispering unintelligible words.

Brell passed his hands over the boy's exposed stomach. Lancelot could see that black vein-like lines covered the boy and even pulsed. Brell's voice found a rhythmic chant and his hands glowed a deeper blue. As he continued, the veins on the boy's stomach receded and eventually dissipated altogether. Brell visibly sweat.

The dark-haired man grabbed Brell's arms with both his hands. "Thank you sir Brell…."

Brell interrupted, "My work is not yet finished." And then he moved his attention to the wounded arm. Although he chanted, whatever it was he said was different. Even the glow he gave off had a more white fuzz to it than blue. With each passing moment, the wounds closed up. Even the boy's ripped shirt looked partially mended, and the blood appeared to fade from the white.

"Now I am finished," Brell gasped. He stumbled a bit, and Lancelot caught him and guided him to a chair before he could fall.

Lancelot and Tristan were both impressed and astonished that this man could do what he just did. The others in the room took it all in as if this were an everyday occurrence, or at least their faith in his abilities were restored at the site of his miracle. "How did you do that?" Tristan asked dumbfounded.

Tired, Brell answered with a sigh, "I used to be somebody….before I was a drunk. I was a demon slayer. My talents, like others, were to be used by the great churches. I have been to Hell, more than once. This work is taxing at this age." He reclined some as if he were about to take a nap, and fiddled with the necklace on its chain.

"What is that necklace?" Lancelot asked.

"It is a symbol of my faith."

"I don't mean to be disrespectful or none-such," the dark-haired man interrupted, "but the devils are coming this way." He stood at the window and looked out through the closed drapes. Urine filtered down his pant leg.

"Step back from the window," Sir Brell commanded with a whisper. Sleep, however involuntarily, was going to overcome him. "The wards will keep them out. Demons and devils alike." Then he was gone.

The sounds of screams emanated from all around the house. At first, sword against sword could be heard, but that was quickly silenced, and only the screams came after. The more audible it became outside, the closer the occupants of Brell's home huddled around Brell.

Smoke from a nearby fire soured the air. "Sir Brell said to stay back from the window," Miss Gray warned Tristan. He was at the window and stared out the small crack where the drapes met the wall.

"The building across the street is burning." He ignored her. "Those things are big. And there are lots of them." He watched them further. "You can sense how evil they are just by looking at them."

A woman outside and very near screamed. Tristan briefly saw her come into view as one of the devil spawn dragged her between the two buildings across the street. Helpless, he watched as her feet disappeared into the shadow of the buildings, then he heard what sounded like a muffled cry and a gurgle. The creature reappeared, crimson ichor covered its limbs and torso. It moved off to the right in the direction that the others had been traveling.

One thing he noted aloud to the others was that the creatures were pretty methodical about going into the buildings to search them, yet none had even thought to stop at this home. Maybe Brell's ward worked so as to make this place invisible. Regardless, it did not put anyone at ease yet.

An hour went by and Lancelot introduced himself and his brother. He explained why they were here and how they came to be at Sir Brell's home. They found that the tall dark-haired man was Folgrum, one of the town's blacksmiths. His two sons were Jerrod and Mica. Mrs. Haddy Gray was the wife of Henford Gray, of the town council. Her son was Gregory. When the monsters attacked, she explained, she remembered the tales of Sir Brell and how he had supposedly saved the town on more than one occasion. She normally was not on this side of town, but had made an early morning shopping run for some wooden shoes Gregory desperately wanted. He loved to wear them while she gardened.

It was another two hours before Sir Brell stirred. By then, Gregory was in the other room and slept on the bed. His mother lay next to him for comfort. Folgrum sat huddled with his two sons. They planned their route out of town should things still be dangerous. Tristan listened in on their conversations for anything he could pick up in case their survival depend on it. Lancelot sat patiently and waited for the ex-demon slayer to come-to. He had a cup of water ready and gave it to him as he woke.

Brell gave his thanks. He took the cup and downed the water as if he had not had anything to drink in days. The old man looked very tired, but he stood with a renewed vigor. All traces of alcohol had left him. This man could truly be a demon slayer as he said he was. The armor made Brell look even more impressive. It shone brightly in this dim light, almost as if it lit the room itself. He tied his hair back in a ponytail then moved to the window where Tristan still sat.

"Have things quieted down?" he whispered to Tristan.

"I haven't seen anything in the last half hour or so. No monsters. No people."

"They are still there. I can sense them. This is their favorite time. They like to lie in wait for people to think they are safe and that the danger has passed. When people start to emerge, they will take them as slaves and incubators."

"Incubators?"

"You don't want to know."

"Maybe you're right." Tristan went back to watching out the window.

As if on cue, somewhere off in the distance, a scream was let out, then another, and another. "Isn't there anything we can do?" Lancelot asked.

"Yes, wait," was all Brell could answer.

When night fell and several hours had passed since the last scream or hive devil had walked down the street, Brell confided to the group, "Our best chance for survival will be to head north out of town. I have no food or water left here in my home, and the wards I have created are soon to expire."

"Can't you just make another ward? I do not want to risk my sons' lives out there," Folgrum said in a panic.

"Unfortunately, even in my youth, I would have had to get several hours of rest to recuperate that kind of power. I would like to use what little reserves I have left to get us out of here." He continued with his plan, "We should stay close together and move swiftly but quietly. Once we are clear of the town we should be relatively safe. The Codrugon spawn will be maintaining supply and slave lines and so will be sticking to roads and heading straight to settlements. It is possible that their numbers are vast though. They tend, or at least used to tend to build their numbers like locust before going out to harvest."

Sir Brell went into the bedroom and waked Haddy and Gregory. He sent them into the front room with the others. After they left, he called Lancelot into the room to help him move the bed. Underneath, he removed a loose floorboard and produced from an open space a large, long bundle. "Carry this to the other room," he ordered Lancelot.

When they were all together, Brell unfolded the wrapped

bundle. Within were several magnificent weapons. Each had gilded inlays and were studded with small ornate gems. Folgrum gasped, "You could buy a small town with what those are worth."

"Perhaps, but they have held some sentimental value to me. Nothing now, if we are all killed. I offer these to you for our protection." With that, Brell handed weapons to everyone.

To Tristan and Lancelot, he gave a pair of swords which could be mistaken as twins except that the one given to Lancelot was shorter than Tristan's. Each had three small emeralds in the pommels. Golden runes emblazoned the blades.

Brell handed Folgrum a serrated sword. Its blade was black as night. Folgrum tried to show that his hammer would be good enough for him, but Brell convinced him that the magic in the blade would be necessary to harm devils and their spawn.

He gave each of Folgrum's sons a short sword that matched what he gave Lancelot except that these had a single large ruby in their pommels. "'Fah Ve Rah' is the command word that shall allow them to burst into flame. The same command will allow them to extinguish," he explained. They were flaming blades.

To Mrs. Gray he handed a short bow made of red ash. He explained to her that any arrow fired from it would be enchanted. They could affect demons, devils, and elementals alike.

He even gave a small curved dagger to Gregory. The gems alone in it could secure a small castle.

"What about you?" Lancelot asked. Sir Brell had saved no items for himself, and carried no weapon at his side.

"I shall lead us from this darkness," was all that he said, then swung the front door wide open and stepped out into the night.

3

Cloud cover made it nearly impossible to see. The group found some comfort that the carnage which must have occurred earlier in the day was not visible. There was a deathly silence and the band of survivors walked as softly as they could. They paused at every crunch underfoot to see if the world had heard their escape.

Sir Brell focused on a building somewhere to the north that was still smoldering from an earlier fire. His plan was to go from point to point. Each success moved them closer to freedom and their lives. He felt good. Even with this danger, he felt alive, the poison of the alcohol had been extricated from his body when he performed his warding ritual.

He hadn't told the group why he was so taxed though. He had used a great deal of his power when he tried to contact other demon slayers, and he could only find one. Two demon slayers were good, but not enough to stem the tide of this evil. He did not want to raise false hopes; especially when it was likely that some or none of them were going to live to see another sunrise.

Sir Brell looked back from time to time and worried that this was going to be an impossible task. He had led groups of adventurers before and on far deadlier missions than this, but more than half of this group was made up of children. He was certain that the only one here who could fight was himself. Sure, Folgrum was well built, but he was not bred for fighting. Also, the man worried so much about his two sons that it clouded his judgment. Haddy was also in no condition to fight. She constantly shivered from cold or fright and the way she held the bow it was obvious she possessed no skill with it.

Each person who stumbled through the dark worked to face their own fears. Things were certainly never going to be the same again. Everyone had gone from living comfortably to who knows what horrors. Tristan and Lancelot followed the group from the rear. Tristan gave reassurances to any stragglers that it was going to be okay, and that they needed to keep up with Sir Brell. Lancelot focused on the unseen. He didn't want any nasty surprises.

The group reached the burning building with great effort. Brell watched as each person sat or found a place in the shadows of the gutted home. They sweat not from great exertion but from straining every fiber in their body to avoid detection. The embers crackled, and the youngest three of the group huddled near a still lit fire to collect its warmth.

Tristan and Sir Brell went to each person to give encouragement. Haddy still shivered violently. She looked as if she were going to be sick. Brell rested his hands on her shoulders and chanted. His hands turned a soft blue. Her shivers left and her color returned. Then Brell went to the north side of the building to spy out his next target location.

Standing near the fire, Lancelot looked at his other two companions Mica and Gregory. He smiled when Gregory looked back up at him. "It's going to be okay. We're going to get out of here," he told the youngest. He turned his head sharply when he heard the familiar crunching of the street gravel. He knew there was nobody from this group between him and the darkness.

It moved lightning fast. Molted green and red carapace, the creature was easily twice as tall as Lancelot. He barely got his sword up as it rained down two blows in quick succession from its second and fourth arm; both wielded swords of their own. Gregory yelped as the creature snatched him up with its two right arms.

Mica reached up and hoped to grab Gregory in a tug-of-war,

but the creature moved so fast. In one motion, it tossed Gregory back into the darkness where the dim outline of another creature caught him. Then with two arms, the first creature pulled a half-spear from its sheath and impaled Mica through his stomach. With a garbled scream, Mica was lifted up over the beast, whereupon he slid down the shaft of the spear to the creature's claws. It then released its spear and used its claws to rip the boy in half.

Lancelot cried out and wanted to run, but he was backed up by relentless swing after swing. Twice already, the devil's blades had found his arm, and a steady stream of blood dripped and oozed from its wounds.

Haddy was the first outside the fire to notice and respond to the threat. She screamed loudly and then called out after her son. Her hand gripped tightly the bow, but she had no concept of its use or even that she had a weapon in her hand. She took several steps toward the fighting. Her screaming was replaced by silence as a whirling set of three blades spun out of the darkness and lodged in her face and neck.

In a rage, Folgrum arrived. He dropped his blade and released his hammer from a strap on his belt. In a sweeping motion, the creature both continued its assault on Lancelot and retrieved its spear. Folgrum stepped forward and blindly received the spear in his leg while he gave a swing of such force that the hammer knocked the mandibles up through the creature's skull with a sickening crunch. The blacksmith then fell to the ground in terrible pain.

Tristan followed up and stood over Folgrum as two more of the devils appeared out of the darkness. Each possessed a veritable arsenal of weapons. They moved with deadly elegance and speed and descended upon the two boys.

From out of the corner of his eye, Tristan caught Sir Brell. The demon slayer met the creatures at the brothers. His hands glowed a deep blue and then purple fiery blades of light appeared in each. He moved like no man of middling years. The first devil barely got its blades up before it was cut into three pieces. The second immediately sensed the real threat here and moved on the offensive. It launched a wave of swings upon Brell, but each was deflected by his flame-blades and retaliation was swift and fatal.

Tristan sheathed his sword and then pried Haddy's fingers from her bow. He collected her arrows and then with Lancelot, helped Folgrum to his feet. The three of them headed around to the other side of the house where Brell had herded them. "We must start running now," Brell barked as he used his magics to mend Folgrum's leg.

"What about Mica?" Jerrod asked.

"We must run," was all that his father could muster.

Brell caused his hands to glow and then with a word, the glow became an enveloping light. They used the light to navigate the streets at an all-out sprint. From behind, the clattering sounds of pursuit followed. Blackened tri-blades whizzed and whirled through the air at them and stuck into walls and dirt alike.

When they could feel the creatures breathing down their backs, Sir Brell spun to meet them. His violet blades appeared again and he deflected, parried and attacked the creatures ferociously.

Jerrod also turned to fight and he had the sense to ignite his sword. The devils oddly did not trust the flame, and their attacks upon Jerrod were unsure and lacked the speed as before. He used this to his advantage, and before long, two of the beasts had already fallen to his swings.

Brell recognized that Jerrod had some schooling with the blade and he breathed a little easier. The two hacked and hewed their way through a half dozen of the creatures before there was a lull. They turned and ran to catch up with the others.

"There is no way we are going to be able to outrun those things," Tristan noted. "We need to find a place to hide."

Folgrum responded, "If we stop, we die. We need to keep running."

"The boy is right," Brell retorted as he and Jerrod caught up. "Those flying blades will eventually hamstring us, and we will be cut down. They are much faster than we are."

"Not you," Lancelot quickly interjected.

"Actually, I am not all that fast. I have fought these things before on many occasions, and they are predictable. They know only one fighting style."

Lancelot looked baffled. "Are you kidding me? Those things seem to have no end to the ways they can kill people."

"If we live long enough, I'll show you the differences....Over here." Brell had found an intact two story building.

Inside, it became obvious that they were in a general goods store. They entered a large room that had shelves lined with goods. In the back, behind a door, Brell found what he had looked for. Often, because of space constraints, the larger shops used basements to store extra inventory. The lock on the trapdoor remained unmolested and Brell cut it easily with his summoned blade. "Quickly, down the stairs," he commanded. When all were down below, he closed the door from beneath and hid it with his magic.

For several minutes after, they could hear crashing from above as their pursuers ransacked the store. Shelves were overturned, glass broke, and scratching noises constantly scraped at the ceiling above. After, the noises faded until again they sat or stood in complete silence. Tristan realized that he had forgot to breathe and had to take in a big breath of air. At the sound of his exhale, others let out either sighs or sobs.

They waited without word for several hours. Tristan in the meanwhile had found some dried fruit and meats and silently passed some out to the others. Lancelot took extra and stuffed it into his leather pouch. Everyone ate while Brell contemplated their next move. It was quite possible that those things would be out there upon their exit.

Sir Brell was the first to make a move for the stairs. They creaked under his weight. Lancelot raised his arm as if to try and stop the demon slayer, but Brell continued to the top. He listened for a while with his ear pressed against the trap door. When he was satisfied that nothing lie-in-wait right above, he slowly raised the door so he could peer out from underneath.

Brell's eyes scanned the aftermath of the Codrugon spawns' making. Nothing stood. The shelves had all been destroyed, the windows shattered, and even the door was broken off its hinges. Still, there were no creatures in the shop. With one arm, Brell beckoned while he slowly lifted the door all the way open. The others hesitated at first, but slowly, one by one, they followed Sir Brell up into the shop.

Weapons at the ready, the group fanned out and kept their backs to each other. As much as they had suffered, Brell was pleased that those remaining learned fast. It would be a long time before they could be taught the subtleties of fighting with a blade, but Lancelot certainly could defend himself. Also, Brell reminded himself how much he underestimated the strength of Folgrum and the skill of his son Jerrod. He was very pleased with that mistake. Tristan, though helpful, had shown no aptitude for fighting. He would stay close to him when they next engaged the devils.

The group did their best to extricate themselves from the shop quietly, but the mess of it all made it very difficult and slowed their progress significantly. When they were clear, they hugged the walls of the buildings and moved as one when they crossed the streets. Brell refrained from lighting the way, and there were no good landmarks to gauge their progress.

As the light from the sun crept over the horizon, Sir Brell realized how vulnerable a position they were in and had everyone pick up the pace. They ran between two buildings and stopped for a breather. "That's odd," noted Lancelot.

"What is?" asked Tristan.

"This dragonfly here. It seems to be following us, and ignores me when I try to shoo it away."

"We are discovered! Run!!" Brell yelled. There were no devils in sight, but the group believed him nonetheless and everyone took off as fast as they could go. While running, Sir Brell huffed out between breaths, "The spawn use insects as scouts and spies. They will be on us in no time."

As if on his cue, two huge chitinous beasts appeared around a corner in front of them to bar their way. The one on the left spun twice round and released two of its tri-blades at the group. The first was thrown wide, but the second spun into the air and found its mark. It took Folgrum's left arm clean off at the elbow and left two large gashes in his side. He went down to the ground hard and spun and writhed from the intense pain as blood spurted from his stump.

There were still several paces to cover in order to reach them, and the devil on the right had started to mimic the first's actions. While in its spin though, an arrow pierced its face and caused it to release its blade prematurely. The tri-blade stuck into the neck of the first devil which exploded in a shower of gore.

Jerrod bent over his father and tied the arm off with the part of the shirt that was removed when the arm was amputated. "We've got to help him. He is not dead!" he exclaimed. Barely finished with the tourniquet, he stood as a dozen more of the beasts came from behind and sprinted toward their group. Even with everyone healthy, they would not get far before they were overtaken.

"Leave him there. Fight or we all die Jerrod," Brell explained. He already had his violet swords at the ready and even used one to cut down a tri-blade in midair.

With a word, Jerrod's sword was aflame, and he turned to face the attackers. Lancelot had his sword out and charged the creatures. "What are you doing!?" Brell yelled, "You are going to get yourself killed!"

Lancelot paid no heed to the warning and answered only with a war cry as he picked up his pace. The first devil to stand before him skidded to a halt and looked at him in surprise. As Lancelot raised his sword, an arrow punctured the creature's chest. It grasped for the arrow while the boy's sword cut a diagonal path from its left breast to its right leg. Lancelot kept his momentum and continued the charge. Two more devils took up defensive stances against him and the one on the right fell to an arrow in the brain. The devil on the left began its deadly attack routine and stopped the boy in his tracks. Lancelot had de-ja-vu as he reeled back from the whirling blades. Two more devils circled around to finish him.

Brell and Jerrod met the flanking devils with their blades and the battle was on. Brell was fully capable of taking on two or more of the beasts at the same time, but Jerrod, even with a flaming sword found it hard to keep the enemy off of him. His parries stopped far too few of his adversary's swings and his legs and arms started to bleed freely from his wounds.

From behind them, Tristan rained down arrows as fast as he could draw them. By his twentieth shot, he not only grew tired, but he grew short of ammunition. Tristan did what he could to even the fight that Jerrod was in, but he worried about Lancelot's ability to take care of himself, especially acting so reckless. Six more devils had reinforced the fight, and even though he was able to drop three of them, the other three would tip the balance of the engagement.

Lancelot tripped. He should have been at a disadvantage; he was able to roll under the creature. In an instant his blade was thrust up through its abdomen and the beast fell.

Two creatures simultaneously speared Jerrod through the chest and abdomen. The boy clutched at one of them as he curled down, lifeless. Tristan fired and hit one of the devils in the shoulder, but that only got its attention. The two devils scrambled to cross the battlefield and set upon him. Brell hacked down on one of them from behind and took its leg off at the hip. It flopped like a dying fish on the ground and it swung its blades in a fury, but to no avail. As the other charged Tristan, he calmly drew an arrow back and took aim. It dodged at the last moment but he followed its bobbing head and released. The arrow pierced the top of its crown and disappeared into its body.

There were five devils left. Lancelot had not yet regained his feet and Sir Brell stood over him. He was surrounded. The creatures agreed that they would kill this one first then finish the two younglings off. Brell knew it was only a matter of time before they found their way through his defenses. Tristan had two arrows left.

Brell used his power to create light to temporarily blind his attackers. Lancelot used this instant to roll out and up. He was able to pull one of the devils off of Brell and force its attention upon himself.

Tristan fired his last two arrows into another of the devils and wounded it enough that Brell was able to easily finish it off, but there were still three creatures on Brell and the demon slayer was doing everything he could just to keep their blows at bay. Lancelot was in full parry mode, and although he did well to ward off the swings, he got no attacks in himself.

Tristan reluctantly drew the sword at his side, and as he took his first step toward the melee, a large hand came down on his shoulder to stop him.

"Folgrum, you are in no condi…" his words were cut short as he turned. He thought Folgrum was going to give it his last, but behind Tristan stood Trazk. The orc's scimitar was covered in bluish devil blood.

"I've got this," the orc explained, and he calmly walked over to finish the devils off.

4

The small group huddled around Folgrum. He had both lost a lot of blood and poison coursed through his veins. Trazk had carried the man the rest of the way out of Porterstown, and had just laid him down so that Brell could administer to his wounds. The two brothers returned from burying Jerrod and cleaned the sweat and dirt from their faces.

"I don't know if I have enough left in me to repair him," Sir Brell conceded. His hands already glowed their blues and whites. "His wounds are grievous, and I have had no time to recuperate my power."

"You have to try," Tristan urged.

"Don't think that I won't. I'm just saying…don't pin your hopes on a dried up old man."

Lancelot jumped in, "Sir Brell, what you have done for us, and you too Trazk, cannot be repaid, nor forgot."

"Well, enough dwarven ale, and anything can be forgot." Trazk favored humor over decorum. Everyone left Brell to work his magic.

It was already night again, and Trazk had been away for some time with Tristan. They looked for branches and saplings that would be good for making arrows. The orc had arrived at the earlier combat in time to see Tristan was indeed accurate with a bow. He was not going to let that resource be wasted.

Lancelot watched over Brell and Folgrum. It looked like the blacksmith was going to live. He would be without his good arm and was going to either have to learn to smith with his off-hand or find a new trade all-together. While the boy watched over the two, he cleaned the sword that Jerrod had wielded. Trazk had collected it after the fight and pointed out that any blade that can ignite into flames must be a valuable tool in a fight.

Brell had fallen asleep almost as soon as he had lain down. He didn't stir. For an old man that went from being drunk to fighting off over a dozen devils and healing people on the verge of death, he both needed and deserved this rest. Lancelot found he admired Brell very much. There was something about wielding magic to create swords and light and wards of invisibility. There was certainly an appeal to killing devils and demons and evil monsters. He considered what it must be like to fill such shoes.

Tristan and Trazk returned with bundles of wood in their hands. Trazk explained to Tristan the importance of covering tracks. Tristan listened intently and took both mental notes and asked questions in kind. Lancelot still found it hard to understand half of the words that came out of the orc's mouth, but Tristan seemed to absorb everything he said.

The two sat down near the dwindling campfire. Lancelot walked over and placed more wood on the flames. Trazk pulled a knife from his belt and slowly instructed Tristan how to cut and carve the wood to make arrows. He explained that they still needed to add fletching to the arrows when they were done, but they didn't have the materials.

"Thanks for coming back," Lancelot interrupted their work after they had been talking for some time. He looked right at the grimy orc who was quite intimidating with those large tusks protruding out of its mouth. "Without your help, we'd all be lying dead in that street back there."

"I wasn't going to come back, but something in the back of my brain kept itching. The only thing that made it stop was coming after you. I figured I would get to the town and then come to my senses. Anyway, the itch is gone." Trazk gave a huff, a grunt and a smile and went back to watching Tristan. He had given him the knife and let the boy learn through practical application.

Folgrum started to moan and Lancelot went over to him. He had been applying a damp cloth to his forehead to keep his fever down, and continued to do so now. Tears streamed down the blacksmith's cheeks and he tossed and turned. His life had changed in the worst of ways. It was going to be difficult for him to adjust.

After some time, the two brothers and the orc agreed upon a watch schedule. They would let the demon slayer and blacksmith continue to sleep and would take turns patrolling around the camp while the other two got some rest. Before starting, Trazk explained the subtleties of standing guard, maintaining cover, and being alert. Then he promptly volunteered Lancelot to go first and went to sleep.

Except for tricks of the light and imagined shapes in the shadows, nothing eventful occurred the rest of the night. Tristan worked on arrows while he 'watched' and finished with all the wood they had collected. Trazk made sure the camp was not easily discernable as he covered the outside tracks and dispersed the remnants of the camp fire.

One by one they awoke. Sir Brell checked on Folgrum's arm and noted that it had closed and healed well. Folgrum was definitely weak from the ordeal, and Lancelot volunteered to be his crutch as they set off to the north. By this time, the Hive would already be well on its way and it was probably best now to just steer clear and find some place not in danger of being attacked. Brell knew of a port town some days distance. They could all catch a boat to the island kingdom of Valencia. Brell assured Trazk that he would not be attacked when they arrived at Ferrickport. It was a fairly progressive port with a number of different races coming and going.

"I know your business is in the killing of demons and such,"

Folgrum said to Brell, "but you said you were an agent of the church. Could you please say some words for my fallen sons before we go? It would mean more than you know to me."

"Absolutely," Sir Brell responded. "It is in my purview to perform such rites and services. Gather round everyone. Let us begin."

While Brell said a prayer for those who had fallen, his whole body glowed. He explained after that he had used some magic to prevent the souls of their recently departed companions from being tampered with on their journey to the afterlife. Folgrum appeared to take comfort in those words.

The group made sure they had all of their belongings and filed north in silence. By noon, it started to rain. Lancelot longed for his leather overcoat. Trazk pulled a large, dark grey hooded cloak from a pack on his back and put it on. Sir Brell basked in the rain, not having bathed in longer than he could remember. Tristan and Folgrum plodded on as if the weather made no difference to them.

There were no paths and the group moved for much of the day through tall grasses. Whenever they spotted a copse of trees, they headed for it; not for the shelter, but to minimize the chances of them being spotted. As the day wound on, the grasses became thick with streams. Soon, the group waded through a bog. They constantly found their boots mired in sloshing mud. The wind from the north was cold and biting. It brought with it the smell of the sea.

The clouds grew darker and the rain came down in a torrent. Although barely evening, it was dark as midnight. Brell used his power to create light and they stayed close together lest someone slip into the bog and be lost forever.

"I see a path of righteousness fraught with danger!" a high pitched female voice challenged from ahead. Barely visible in the rain, a tall, frail-looking woman stood boldly before them. There was a palpable sense of danger and everyone could feel it. She was not what she seemed to be.

"I come to offer you aid, for you will need as much help as you can get. I am Halkana, a merchant of sorts. I believe that I can help you." Even with the downpour of water, it was easy to see she was clearly too tall for a normal woman, who stood at almost seven feet. She wore rags, tattered and torn. She had mud up to her knees, and her black sopping hair covered most of her face. The woman had an empty sack tucked in a crude belt made of vines or twine.

Sir Brell stepped forward, "We don't seek trouble! We are just trying to survive on our way through this miserable bog! What help can you offer, and what is your price?!" He had to yell just to hear himself over the pouring rain.

Her voice cut through the torrent, and even at a whisper, she was clearly heard, "I know of your recent loss and your plans to travel to the library of Palladius in Myurondy. Your path though will take a different rout and I only ask for a simple thing before revealing this to you."

Lancelot was lost, "Myurondy?! Palladius?!"

"She's a witch!" Trazk yelled. "She can see into the future! She is trying to sell us information that may not even come to pass!" Lancelot only made out parts of what Trazk explained.

Sir Brell cut them off, "What do you want?!"

The witch smiled, her eyes firmly on Folgrum. Her whisper was as loud as thunder, "I am a purveyor of fine potions. For my latest creation, I need to collect the sorrows of your loss."

"Nooo!!" screamed Folgrum as he charged her. "You will not take all that I have left!" He stumbled through the mud toward the witch. The lanky woman laughed and raised her arm nonchalantly, one finger crooked toward the blacksmith. A wave of power washed over the raging man, and he froze in his tracks.

"Now what to do with you," she ruminated.

"Let him go!" barked Brell, but she ignored him. Halkana slowly circled Folgrum with her outstretched hand to keep him at bay, and as the group caught up, her other arm rose. They felt the wave of power that poured from her outstretched hand. It nauseated and paralyzed them. The group was helpless. No amount of straining could break the grasp of her magic. They could only watch as this horrible scene played out.

Halkana whispered something into Folgrum's ear and his eyes bulged. She stepped back in surprise then appeared to focus more of her effort on him. Tristan felt a tingling through his body. He was disappointed that he still could only stare forward, his body locked in this position. A splash sounded behind him. If someone else had fallen over paralyzed, they would drown in this bog.

Tristan continued to look straight ahead and observed Folgrum shake further. The witch was in front of him. She was desperate in whatever action she took. Then he moved. Folgrum was in slow motion at first, but then his arm came up like lightning, hammer in hand, and he slammed a blow up into Halkana's face. Amazingly, she shook it off.

The visage of her whole body flickered then changed to what she must really have been. She had the relative lankiness that the woman possessed, but her skin was green not unlike Trazk. It had black patches and oozing pustules. Her nose was long, like a rotted carrot, and her fingers were even longer. Each twig-like finger ended in sharp blackened talons.

Folgrum hammered the witch again twice more and she staggered back. Now she showed needle like teeth in a grin that meant all business. She released her grip on the rest of the group and raised her hand to stop the blacksmith. Folgrum ignored her and took the hammer to her gut. When she buckled forward, he cracked a heavy blow into the side of her head. All of this appeared to break no bones or even draw blood, but Halkana was frightened. She hacked out a black cloud from her mouth that set Folgrum to retching and she turned and sprinted deeper into the quagmire.

Folgrum recovered fast and took off after her. "Folgrum! Wait!" Brell screamed after him. Trazk helped Lancelot up. The brother coughed the dirty bog water out of his lungs. Tristan looked between the two groups and decided that Trazk could help his brother. He loped after the demon slayer and blacksmith.

Tristan didn't think it would be so hard to keep up with an old man and one recovering from having his arm hacked off. Maybe it was because he was shorter and the bog was harder for him to move in, but he actually lost ground as he ran. The rain made it very difficult to see Brell's light, and only after he listened for Folgrum's cries was Tristan confidant that he headed in the right direction.

The bog turned more to swamp and Tristan found that things other than water brushed up against his legs. The farther he moved, the more alive his surroundings became. Gnats or mosquitoes buzzed constantly around him, and the sounds of crickets almost became deafening. The light, which he lost sight of on a half dozen occasions, became brighter and he grew excited that he was gaining on them. "Slow down so I can catch up Brell!" The light danced out of view. He heard the yells again from Folgrum, but they sounded distant and in a different direction. This was not good. He paused and listened. After waiting a few seconds for Folgrum with no luck, he stalked after the direction that the light went.

Lancelot recovered quickly and he and Trazk ran after the others. "We are never going to find them," Lancelot lamented, "There is no light to see by, and the rain is making it so we can't hear more than a few feet in front of us."

"Who needs light? Hold on to my cloak. We are going to run as fast as we can…or as fast as you can." Trazk had a special kind of vision that let him see in the dark as good as if it were day. The colors were off a bit, but he could easily make out the matted path the others took, and they followed.

The boy and the orc continued to where the bog became swamp then slowed down some. It was a little more difficult to find the path the others took, and at one point, it even looked as if one of them went in a different direction. Trazk chose to follow the more trodden route. It snaked through the swamp and their surroundings became denser with trees and overgrowth.

Eventually, Trazk saw Brell. The demon slayer stood at the entrance to a cave. A ball of fire erupted from within and Brell dodged at the last moment to avoid being barbequed. Lancelot nearly jumped at the sight since he ran blind until the explosion on a nearby tree lit the whole area.

"You're gonna want to stay back for this one," Trazk warned. The orc sloshed forward to where Brell stood. At the cave, the ground rose slightly, and Trazk was relieved that he could walk on solid ground.

Brell was also relieved he had some reinforcements. He brought the orc up to speed, "Folgrum is in there. He took a direct blast from one of those fireballs. I think he is still alive, but he is in bad shape. That bitch has a lot of tricks up her sleeve."

"Good. So do I." Trazk ran into the cave. Sir Brell didn't even get to protest when a ball of fire engulfed the orc. Amazingly, the orc continued to run through it with no sign of burns. Somewhere inside, female cackling turned to a scream. Lancelot and Brell ran into the cave.

Ahead, Trazk traded blows with the witch. Her talons were as hard as steel and she was able to defend herself from most of his swings. Some of her attacks pierced orc flesh, and Trazk grimaced but made no other complaint. The witch finally bled at least.

Brell instructed Lancelot to flank the witch on the left and he would go right. As they moved around the melee, two large pythons appeared from deeper within the cave and set upon Trazk's allies. Brell was able to carve his attacker with his summoned blades, but Lancelot found it hard to land any good blows. The snake's scales were like metal armor. With its large size, it was able to get itself between Lancelot and the others, and forced the boy down the hall where it had come from.

Lancelot was starting to get used to this defend retreat and he did not like it one bit. He could barely see in this part of the cave. He only had Brell's bladed light to see by and with the distance, it was fading fast. He did recognize the wall that was going to end his retreat and before he reached it, he decided to make a stand. Swinging the sword violently and in wide arcs, he forced the snake to pause. Three swift swings and Lancelot realized he only made the thing mad. Emboldened by the lack of pain, the snake struck out at the boy. A fatal strike for the snake. Lancelot quickly learned what a combatant with a short sword is supposed to do, and by luck, he had his sword pointed at the Python when it attacked. The blade punctured through the creature's open mouth and up into its brain cavity. It went limp immediately.

When he returned to the main hall where the other fight was, it wasn't. The witch had plead for mercy. With her life, she was required to give up her secret, and Trazk had added that they get to peruse her hovel for any treasures that were due a victor.

The witch's eyes rolled back and she divulged what she knew, "Your journey takes you directly to Ferrickport. A man, or rather beast, will seek out your aid and employment. You must accept this task, or more than one of you will die for it. You will attempt to expedite a ship across the Strait of Kollune. Before you board though, seek out the priest named Lareth Corwellyn. Explain the dilemma that you are in, and he will assuredly offer his assistance. You must not let him journey with you or he will suffer a fate worse than death. He is needed elsewhere. Upon rejection, Lareth will offer a different type of succor. It will come in the form of a prayer necklace. Place this around your employer's neck and the sickness which is going to overcome him will be delayed…perhaps even long enough." After offering her divination, the witch slumped down against the wall, defeated.

Lancelot watched Halkana while the orc looted her home and Brell tended to Folgrum.

When he was satisfied with his spoils, Trazk returned to fetch the others. Although badly burned, the blacksmith was alive. Sir Brell's magic was able to reduce his wounds to mild sunburns, but the man's hair and clothes had burned away. After leaving the cave, Trazk gave Folgrum his cloak. All they had to do now was find Tristan.

Tristan closed his eyes. It was dark, but the shadows still distracted him from gaining his bearings. He listened intently. There were no sounds of combat. The buzzing things of the swamp were happy to make noise though. Tristan thought he heard a faint humming somewhere off to the left. When he opened his eyes, he spied the light in the opposite direction of the hum. He splashed off in the direction of the faintly glowing orb. It was hard to tell if it was light from a lantern or torch. It was very uniform in shape and bright in the center. Whatever it was, it was also hard to tell the distance. Whenever Tristan thought he was right on it, it felt like it was another thirty paces away.

Tristan realized he had the bow out, but that was going to be useless without arrows. He replaced it with his sword and for an instant felt at ease as if he were near his father's farm with his brother. The feeling quickly subsided as he continued to focus on catching up with the light. It grew harder to follow as the swamp water became deeper and more underwater snags impeded his progress.

It also became apparent that the light Tristan followed was not coming from Sir Brell. Panic nearly overcame the boy as he fully realized this. To make matters worse, he could not shake the feeling that something either followed him or watched him from close by. The swamp grew deathly silent. Tristan only heard his own breathing and the splashing of the water at his waist.

The light turned and moved toward him. He tried to get a good read on what the light actually was. There was nobody carrying it. It was too big to be a firefly, and had no shape other than being a lighted orb. When it got right up to him and he felt the light blinding him, it winked out.

The water behind Tristan erupted as something large emerged. The only thing that saved him from a swinging claw half the size of his body was that he instinctually dove into the water in front of him. Another claw reached down into the swampy froth and grabbed him by the ankle. Its grip was iron tight and Tristan could not struggle free. The hand lifted him out of the water and held him upside down. Rancid fish breath assailed Tristan's nose as the creature brought him close to its face.

At first Tristan thought the creature rubbed him against its cheek, but then he realized it kept sniffing him. "Let me go," he pleaded. The creature gave no response.

The light blinked back on. Tristan finally saw what was holding him and he wished he didn't. A giant blue creature, lanky for its size, but very muscular, sized him up. It did not look unlike the witch from earlier, but this thing was far larger and definitely uglier. It shared the pustulating skin which gave off its own brand of rot. The eyes on this creature were two black pools that gave no indication of intent or intelligence. Stringy long green hair like seaweed fell down over its shoulders. The thing that bothered Tristan the most though were its teeth. They were the size of daggers, and they were serrated. Between them, he could see long ago eaten food that sat rotting and black.

The light began pulsating. Then the big creature talked, "No," its voice boomed at the glowing orb. The light pulsated more. Tristan thought that he was starting to get what was going on here, and his suspicions were confirmed when the creature answered again, "Mine." It started to lift him higher and it crooked its neck in. The creature's lower jaw disconnected and its mouth opened wide enough to drop the whole boy in.

Tristan realized he still had the sword in his hand and thanked anyone who would hear him. As the creature started to lower him into its mouth, he jack-knifed his body and with both hands swung his blade as hard as he could. The monster bellowed out in pain as its hand was removed from its arm. Tristan rolled off its chin and into the water. The angle of its face allowed him to come down on his feet. Tristan used his momentum to swing the blade hard and his sword connected with the glowing orb. Whatever it was, it was made of flesh. It gave out a high pitched scream and winked out forever.

Keeping his bearings, Tristan swung around and let his sword lead the way. He felt it carve into the beast behind him and it redoubled its howl. Unable to see again, and not caring to find out if the creature had any fight left in it, Tristan ran.

He used the beast's cries to gauge the distance he gained and to help him keep moving away from it. Several minutes later, there was just the sound of the swamp again. Tristan found himself weary from the encounter. At the first tree that he came upon that was climbable, he scaled it. He ascended to the widest branch that he felt would support his weight and just held on. It was not long after that the boy fell asleep.

5

Tristan awoke to pains from his head. Those below had been throwing small rocks at him and laughed when the last had hit him above the ear. Annoyed and relieved, he climbed down and greeted his companions. "You looked so funny trying to brush the rocks away like insects," Lancelot tried to say seriously but couldn't get the grin off his face.

"I'm so glad I could amuse you."

Trazk handed Tristan some ripened apricots while they walked and ran his hand once through the boy's hair to let him know he was glad to see him.

"How did you find me?" Tristan asked, "I was completely lost."

Lancelot answered, "Trazk is an amazing tracker. I couldn't even see the signs he followed. In fact, I didn't even believe we were tracking you until we found that Troll you had gutted. We nearly missed you as we passed under this tree, but you make a funny sound through your nose when you sleep."

He continued as they walked through the swamp, "Also, I noticed while I was holding my sword that I could sense you as I grew closer. Sir Brell said it was likely my mind playing tricks, but I could have sworn I was able to use the sword to find you too."

At the sight of Folgrum, Tristan demanded to learn how they

defeated Halkana. Lancelot explained and grew excited when he concluded with how Trazk took a half dozen potions and a sack of gold coins from the witch.

They walked the whole morning, and eventually the swamp was overtaken by the bog which soon after became grassland again. The salty air revealed their proximity to the coast and eventually the group spied gulls that flew in circles not far to the north. Before Ferrickport came into view, they encountered the road and stopped to camp. Evening had crept upon them and Sir Brell said they had a full day of walking before they would get to the city.

That night, everyone slept a little easier. The devils and the swamp were behind them, and the smell of the sea air instilled some hope for better change. The relief did not prevent the group from setting up their watches and Tristan volunteered for the first so he could craft more arrows.

They woke to light fog and some rain. Trazk divided the gold among them in case they were separated again or just found it best to go their separate ways. Lancelot put his thirty seven golden coins into his pouch. That was just about thirty seven more gold coins than he ever held. He imagined himself buying a suit of armor, a horse, a castle, and maybe a small country.

On the final leg of their journey to Ferrickport, Tristan and Lancelot walked in the back of the group so they could evaluate their situation. It was bad enough that they had lost their parents, but losing new friends, fighting devils, witches and trolls, and leaving the kingdom was a lot to absorb for two so young. Tristan asked, "How are you holding up? It has only been a couple of days, but I miss mom and papa a lot."

"I know. I do too. I have been pretty scared since the cave. I am glad you are here with me. You make me feel like I can keep going. I mean it."

"We are going to have to start a new life. I don't know about you, but everyone else here seems to take it in stride that our kingdom is being overrun by devils. Maybe we should do what that witch said and head to the great library. I wonder if it holds all the answers to what is happening here."

"Actually, the witch said we had to go a different rout. At least to start, we have to be hired by someone and then find someone else and then go somewhere or something."

"That explains it all," Tristan laughed.

The two boys moved from serious conversation to their gold and what they should buy with it. Tristan suggested that they pool their gold together and maybe buy a farm and everything that goes with it. Lancelot felt their days of homesteading were over and that they needed to adapt to this changing world that required the warriors and wizards that they were not.

"Trazk can't take care of us forever," Lancelot explained. "We have to learn to take care of ourselves."

"Of that you are right," his older brother answered. "Maybe you have not noticed, but I have learned to make arrows, cover our tracks, make and break a camp, and am now learning to follow tracks. Maybe you should stop lolli-gagging and figure out what you want to do."

He did not mean what he said as a jab at Lancelot, and the younger brother did not take it as such. "I will do just that." Lancelot jogged up to where Trazk and Brell were conversing about religion and interrupted them.

"Excuse me Trazk. Excuse me Sir Brell, but I have been meaning to ask," he directed his question at Brell, "Can you to teach me everything there is to know about becoming a demon slayer?"

Flattered, the old man put his arm around Lancelot's shoulder. "Well son, becoming a demon slayer is no easy task. It requires years of training. You have to dedicate your life to your craft and your church. You have to teach your body the art of combat, but you also have to exercise your brain. You must become an expert on cosmology, lore, and histories."

"I can do all that," Lancelot said easily.

"Oh, I am sure you can, but it will be slow-going. This old man lacks patience and I have not had a student for some years. And then there was the drinking…" Brell frowned. He certainly did not like what he had become. "Yes," he continued, "I will be honored to have you as my student. Tonight, when we are safely in the Hall of the Fallen Giant, I will start you on your first lesson. You do well enough to keep those eyes and ears open, and that is very important to a demon slayer. You also will learn and need to keep your other senses sharp and aware. Like right now. Did you know there was an evil orc nearby?"

Trazk looked at the two and growled. He then moved back to where Tristan was so the two demon slayers could talk secretly about the arts of outer planar war. Tristan welcomed the orc's company. He immediately peppered Trazk with questions about living outdoors, how to fight, and what the orc knew about making other weapons or armor. The orc positively glowed and did his best to answer all the boy's questions. Teaching this young human pup was going to be fun.

In all this, Folgrum observed. He was torn inside. For the two boys, he was happy that they had credible and experienced warriors to look up to in this time of war. On the other hand, he had nothing and nobody. A fire burned inside him. He would get revenge on the devil creatures. They took his wife, his sons and his life. What good was a one armed blacksmith missing an eyelid and all his hair? He brooded. The storm clouds over his head were much darker than the ones throwing rain down on the land.

The road north was littered with gravel and small stones. The area was accustomed to the rain and Ferrickport's inhabitants had laid the flag beneath the gravel to keep the roads from washing out. It was not comfortable on a traveler's boot, but wagons and horses traveled faster and easier.

About midday, a patrol of riders from the north ran into the bedraggled group. The patrol consisted of about two dozen soldiers mounted on lightly armored steeds. Each wielded a long spear and shield, the twin ship emblem of Ferrickport emblazoned on it. The lead rider raised his arm as the riders approached and the patrol slowed to a halt.

Sir Brell was first to speak, "Hail riders of Ferrickport, we are refugees come from Porterstown. A host of devils rightly named Codrugon spawn have descended upon the land from the west. These boys here and this orc, Trazk, heralded the devils' arrival after their villages had been destroyed. If you do not know already what you are heading into, be warned now. The creatures are dangerous and their numbers are too many to count. We humbly seek sanctuary in your city and passage out."

The rider looked the group up and down, "It is a welcome sight to see more survivors. We had the first arrive yesterday on horseback, but they said the devils were quick on their heels. I am Sir Allenor. My men and I are the eleventh wing to foray south to meet the invaders. Mostly, we have been ordered to harass and deter the enemy from traveling north. Scouts have returned with word that our plan has been a success. The devils continue to travel east toward Malistair and Falconshield's lands. Somebody is going to be in for a surprise."

"Thank you for the news soldier. And it is good to hear that your city is prepared."

"I would not say that we are fully prepared. Some of the gentry are being evacuated as we speak. If what people are saying is true about the size of this horde, should they turn their attention toward Ferrickport, I doubt the city would last long. You are welcome to enjoy the safety of the city. It is most unfortunate that so few have arrived from your town, as that could only mean ill tidings."

The rider raised his right fist to his chest in a salute. He then ordered his wing of riders on, and they circumvented Brell's group and continued south along the road. Brell in turn beckoned for the group to continue and turned north and west toward Ferrickport.

They trudged for less than two more hours in the rain when the port city came into view. Like Porterstown, Ferrickport had a large wall. Interspersed every hundred yards was a tower that overlooked the lands to the south. Unlike Porterstown, the wall and towers were made of stone. Soldiers patrolled reinforced battlements and looked south for any signs of trouble. Behind the wall, buildings large and small stretched up a hill. A Bell rung in the distance. It signaled as a ship left or entered the port.

The gates to the city were open. Although there was nobody outside, a throng of people either loitered or conducted business right inside. The guards in the towers watched the group approach and enter but asked nothing of their identity or intent.

Lancelot held tightly to Tristan's sleeve as they intermingled with the crowd. Tristan did his very best to be aware of both Trazk and Brell's location at all times. Brell knew exactly where he was going and led the others down a long and winding street. Away from the gate, the number of people thinned out and many kept to the left when walking along the cobbled paths. It moderated the traffic flow and made it easier to navigate the city.

Their route wrapped to the left around the hill, and after circling it, they came into the port side. The sight of large ships held Tristan and Lancelot in awe. Tristan found himself holding Brell's sleeve as they continued so that he and his brother could continue to gawk at the wooden behemoths. Lancelot counted fourteen ships along the various docks, and two more ships approached. The bells rang out their arrival.

All thoughts of the busy gate disappeared when they viewed the large number of people who worked on and around the ships. Goods were loaded or unloaded and crews of workers brought large boxes to and from huge warehouses situated across from the ships.

The demon hunter led them two more blocks and then stopped at a tavern. Above, the image of a dancing wench offering a frothy brew adorned the tavern sign.

"Do you really think you should be stopping for a drink?" Lancelot asked.

"Oh ye of little faith," the old man replied, "I am here to secure passage to Valencia."

"What about the witch's words? Shouldn't we be trying to find the man who is going to hire us?"

"Well first, we don't know if the witch was lying. Second, if it's going to happen, it will happen. We need to assume she was just looking for her next good meal, and be about the business we need to be on. The temple of Chess in Myurondy is where you need to go to start your training. It is where I began mine."

"Then it's true? You intend to flee?" Folgrum asked. He appeared to be more depressed than ever.

"I would rather think that we are leaving to prepare," Brell answered him sternly, "We cannot just lead two young boys to their deaths against that horde of devils."

Dejected and angry, Folgrum stormed off down the street, "Fine. I will do this on my own."

"Wait!" Tristan yelled, but Folgrum already decided he would have none of it and disappeared into the crowd of people. The others watched in stunned silence. Brell snapped them out of it and led them into the tavern. First the boys and then the orc followed.

Inside, the tavern was packed. People stood or sat where they could, and everyone drank or waited for a drink. Brell inquired at a few tables and let the answers lead him to the bar. He got into an animated conversation with a large man sitting and nursing an ale. The man turned and looked the boys and the orc over then continued the conversation. After some time, Sir Brell took a coin from his belt and handed it over to the man. Satisfied, both men shook hands and Sir Brell ushered the group out of the tavern.

"Well, I reserved us a spot on the *Wind Charger*. We have until tomorrow evening to meet on board or she leaves without us."

Tristan asked confused, "You mean you just paid that man a gold coin and it did not cover the whole journey for the four of us?"

Brell and Trazk laughed. Then with a more serious tone, the demon slayer answered, "No son, it will cost us eight gold coins for the nine day journey. It does include our meals, and we don't have to help clean the ship. Sounds like we are getting a good deal."

The brothers both realized they overestimated the value of their coins, or at least its value in these big cities. They were going to have to down-size their dreams. Dejectedly, they followed as Brell took them to the Hall of the Fallen Giant. It was not far from the docks, but far enough that the noise did not carry so loud.

Brell explained, "This is where we will stay the night. It is not yet dark, so we should try to procure any traveling equipment that we can tonight. Tomorrow morning may get busy. Trazk, why don't you head out with Tristan? I'll take Lancelot. We should be on the look-out for packs, dried rations, good traveling clothes and a sturdy lantern. Go on ahead while we secure our rooms."

Inside the inn, four older looking men sat at a table and played cards. They were there more socially, as they barely looked to the cards in their hands. When Brell and Lancelot entered, the men looked over. One of them raised his hand in hesitant recognition and then embarrassingly lowered it. Then they went back to their game.

Brell walked to the front desk and cleared his throat loudly so the woman sitting half asleep in the next room knew he was there. She bustled out like she had been busy all along and didn't notice them. "What can I do for you sirs?"

"There are four of us, and I need two rooms for one night."

"Very good, that will be two gold coins per room. So, four gold please." She reached her hand out.

Brell counted out the coins then reached to give them to her. Before dropping them into her hand he asked, "We have an orc with us. Is that going to be a problem?"

She hesitated, "Does he bathe?"

"I'll make sure he does. Other than that, he is no trouble."

As she nodded, Brell dropped the coins into her hand. She quickly put the money into a small wooden lock box. "Very good. We serve breakfast at sunrise and for two hours after. There is one bathing room on each floor. The tavern is there in the back, through those doors. Entertainment should be good tonight, so get there early for seating."

At that last, Lancelot perked his ear and heard people having a good time beyond the doors. Seeing his quizzical look, the innkeeper explained, "Those doors were taken and modified from a giant's home. They are double thick which keeps the inn very cozy and quiet, even on the busiest of nights in the drinking hall."

The two thanked the matron for her help and went out to find their companions.

Trazk and Tristan walked back toward the docks. Their logic was that with all the activity there, they should be able to find anything they wanted. Trazk constantly found he had to grab the boy and steer him away from a collision. With his small village lifestyle, Tristan was overloaded with the sights and sounds of the big city. It was an odd sight to see an orc apologize so much.

The two wound into and out of shops. Tristan was amazed at some of the things he had never heard of. There were clawed boots for climbing and things called light-rods that ignited with magic and gave light brighter than a torch. Adventurers used them to explore underground. They went into a weapons shop and saw repeating crossbows that fired bolts rapidly and caltrops which were small four sided points, one always sticking up, to aid in running away from enemies. Trazk bought some arrows for Tristan and a small sack filled with fletching for the arrows they would continue to make.

Afternoon turned to evening, and things around the docks appeared to get louder and more boisterous as workers from the ships found their way in and out of the many taverns lining the main thoroughfare. Lancelot and Brell caught up with the other two and they compared their list of things shopped for. They had everything covered and even bought two extra leather packs.

The rain picked up and the small group worked its way back to the Hall of the Fallen Giant. Marylinne, the innkeeper, cheerily cleaned up in the main room when they arrived. Music and laughter escaped from behind the large wooden doors. The four went up to their two rooms and got situated. Then they went back down into the drinking hall to unwind.

6

Many of the patrons within the tavern sung to a tune led by a bard on a small circular stage. They clapped and cheered as the minstrel inserted well-placed jokes and jabs into his lyrics. Four barmaids moved from table to table. They often stopped to sit on a lap or chime in with the chorus of bad singers. A rotund middle-aged man stood behind the bar and filled mugs about as fast as his hands would allow.

Brell had his companions stand by the door and he went to a table to have a word with the patrons who sat there. After what seemed to be a polite exchange, the men got up and moved to share tables with others. Brell motioned the other three to come and sit. One of the barmaids came and made herself comfortable at their table to take their order, "I'm Margaret. I'll be your server. You all are new here," she noticed. "Are you staying at our comfortable inn, or do you live in town?"

Brell answered, "We are refugees. We come from Porterstown."

Margaret looked both shocked and saddened. "First drink is on the house. What'll it be?"

The four ordered their drinks and she moved off to another table where a half-drunk customer caught her attention.

"We should not stay up too late," Trazk voiced. "We have a lot to do tomorrow before we get on that ship and I would rather not lose our deposit."

"Agreed," Brell concurred. "Let us unwind for a bit. I would like to get the rain out of my bones before we retire, and the fire from that hearth is doing just the trick."

Margaret returned with their drinks and then returned a little while later with some complementary snacks cooked up by the owner. The four kicked their feet up on the table and enjoyed the remainder of the bard's performance.

After, a small wizened gnome got on stage and introduced himself as Zerral the Magnificent. He was barely three feet tall and it was almost entertainment enough to watch him move around on the stage. That was before he started to wow the audience with a repertoire of magic tricks. He made fire dance from one hand, across his shoulder and to his other hand. He made bubbles the size of his head rise out of a nearby patron's ale glass.

Zerral was in the middle of making a glass of ale sing when a side door to the tavern swung open. A tall man in a wide-brimmed hat stood in the doorway and held a box or small chest in his arms. The only reason the patrons paid any attention was because cold and rain whipped its way into the tavern until the man could get the door secure. He then looked around from table to table. He searched for something or someone. There was something about his gaze that made those who met it turn away, uncomfortable or in fear.

When he looked over at Brell's table, he appeared to be satisfied with his search and headed straight for the four.

The man stood at the table between Lancelot and Brell. The stranger cut right into their conversation and Trazk shrugged with his hands up and gave a 'who in the Hells are you' look.

"Hello, I am Leopold Gambaldi," the man introduced, "and I am in dire need of your service."

The orc responded, offended by the intrusion, "And?"

"You see, I have not much time remaining. I have been afflicted with a serious and incurable disease. At least I thought it was incurable until now." He shifted the chest under one arm and produced a tome from under his coat with the other. "Within these pages I have found hope, and now in your hands I place my fate." His fast talk cowed the group and he continued.

He swung the chest up and it gave a loud thud as it landed on the table. "Please, open it." Tristan reached for and opened the chest while the man pulled a parchment from his jacket pocket.

"May I?" He didn't wait for an answer and slid two of the drinks out of the way. With a flick of his wrist, the parchment unrolled onto the table. It was a map. Brell, Tristan and Lancelot watched as Leopold used the drinking glasses to anchor the map while Trazk kept an intent eye on the man. Then all eyes went to the chest as the light caught the glitter of its contents. Within, gold, silver and gems filled the container to the brim.

Leopold gave the four a moment to take in the wonderful treasure. He then lifted off his wide brimmed hat and bent over to reveal his round bald head, and more importantly two pin-prick marks on his neck. "I have been afflicted with vampirism and I need you to destroy the one that has done this to me." The boys flushed at the revelation. Even Brell was taken aback. Trazk started to rise and half drew his scimitar, but Brell's hand stayed him. Trazk sat back down, but it was obvious he watched and listened with even more skepticism as Leopold continued, "Until last week, I was a proud and prosperous merchant dealing in the sale of finely crafted wood art and the occasional painting. I traveled far and wide to bring my wonders to and from other lands and have made many acquaintances in the process.

"A little more than a fortnight ago, I was enthralled to meet a customer who had many entertaining talents and more importantly, great wealth. This man, Dellan Zhukovich, invited me to stay at his mansion in the mountains," he paused and tapped his finger on a location on the map, "… so that we could discuss all of the facets of my work and which would possibly conclude in a magnificent purchase. Dellan had other ideas, and upon my arrival, I found myself trapped within his home, surrounded by the other inhabitants that resided there. I was able to escape from his Château. I fled back home, but to no avail. Dellan followed me, and in spite, made me what I am and left me to my fate. Well, I still have a hand in my fate, and I wish to entwine Dellan in its final nights."

Tristan was about to ask what Leopold thought they could do, but waited in case Brell or Trazk asked it. Leopold looked each of the four in the eyes before he continued. Lancelot and Tristan both could not keep his gaze and looked away in trepidation.

Leopold tapped a finger on the tome as if he could read the boy's mind and said, "Within these pages, there is a ritual that can purge this sickness from my body. But it requires the blood of the creature that made me." He opened the book and flipped through the pages. For a moment, he searched for the proof, but paused and realized he might lose his audience. As he closed the book, he explained the last, "These are my conditions of payment should you help me. I must go with you. I could become too dangerous if this disease were to take hold of me and if there was nobody around that could put me down. Regardless of my status…, live, dead, or undead, you must agree to kill this vampire that has done this to me, and I am certain, countless others. I have paid you in advance, for I understand the chances that I have. My final condition is that we leave tonight…"

Before anyone could answer or rebuke Leopold, the same door to the Hall of the Fallen Giant swung open with a burst; the loud screeching wind bit at everyone's flesh and knocked over drinks. Even a few of the flames in the room went out. A large burly half-orc struggled out of his surprise, and with a little effort, shut the door.

"Tsk. Tsk. Tsk. Leopold." Everyone's heads suddenly turned to the center of the room, chilled to see a ghostly figure of a man standing upon a table. He had the posture and mannerisms of an aristocrat. His features were chiseled and lean. Muscles were sculpted and taught. Everything about him screamed he was a predator.

His eyes fixed clearly on Mr. Gambaldi. "You seek others to help you kill me? Or is this merely your first dinner? Either way, you have been speaking ill of me Leopold, and I cannot have such impertinence." With that, he drew back a great breath and circled as he released grey brown fumes over the crowd. Many of the patrons reached for their throats then keeled over dead. A man to the left of Lancelot who appeared to be going for his sword, fell face first onto the edge of the table, and his teeth flew as he rattled out his final breath. A wave of nausea passed over those who survived the deadly cloud. Tristan and Lancelot doubled over and grabbed their stomachs as if to retch. Brell and Trazk overcame the urge and stood ready to battle.

As the boys steadied themselves, they realized that those freshly created corpses started to rise and chaos erupted. Those patrons who survived the fumes of death panicked and the general din of melee ensued. The ghostly Dellan commanded, "Feed my children... upon this undeserving flesh."

For some, death came quickly as their zombified companions turned on them without a second thought. Tristan's whole table was lucky that nobody was harmed by the vampire's magics and Trazk had already jumped on the table and circled defensively. He created a perimeter with his scimitar that easily decapitated the first two zombies that encroached.

Tristan came to his senses, "Don't kill them Trazk! What if they can be saved?" Trazk only had to answer with a cocked head and one eyebrow raised as the zombie nearest Tristan lunged forward to take a bite out of his neck. Tristan pushed the zombie back on its heels and it toppled over.

"Get under the table boys," Trazk ordered. "I'll keep them at bay." The orc then kicked a zombie barmaid square in the face. She fell backwards and disappeared into the rest of the chaos.

Brell and Leopold moved to the table where Dellan's ghostly form stood. Leopold reached out with a clawed hand and took a swipe. His hand passed right through Dellan's legs. Dellan started to chuckle, but his smirk turned to a grimace as white light erupted from Brell's hands and visibly impacted the vampire lord's chest.

Dellan shot Brell a look of utter contempt and faded out. He left his newly created zombie corpses to their task. Another bolt of light passed through where the ghostly form once stood.

Brell quickly diverted his attention to the fight at hand. "You two!" he directed a couple of armed patrons, "Help that woman in the corner before she becomes a meal!" The demon slayer's violet swords appeared and he immediately began cutting down zombies where they stood.

With some effort, Brell directed the combat in such a way that living patrons were on one side of the tavern and the zombies were hemmed in on the other. He remembered what Tristan had said, and an idea came to him. "We need to stop killing these folks and subdue them. This effect could be temporary. If so, we want to save as many people as we can…living or dead."

With one hand, Leopold reached into the mass of zombies and plucked one out. It was hard to imagine that someone of his stature would have such strength. He casually pinned the zombie's arms to its side and another patron rolled a table cloth to form a rope. It was easy enough to tie the creature up as it made no real intelligent effort to escape its bonds.

One by one the group grabbed the zombies. When they ran out of things to tie them up with, Leopold whisked them out of the tavern and up the stairs of the inn to empty rooms.

"We are going to have to guard them closely," Brell explained, but Leopold interrupted.

"I was serious when I said we needed to leave tonight. This town is big enough to take care of its problems. We have done enough here."

"What about Lareth Corwellyn?" Lancelot asked. "We need to seek out his aid. The witch has been right so far, so I suggest we do not ignore her words."

Brell stared at Leopold for a moment, and without taking his gaze away, answered Lancelot, "The captain of the *Wind Charger* said we had until tomorrow evening. There is no way that we are going to be able to secure a boat tonight." He directed his second thought at Leopold, "Unless you can fly us there."

Leopold's anger was evident, but so was his frustration with the truth. He nodded and stormed out of the room.

Brell looked over at Lancelot and continued, "It looks like there is time to help with these zombies."

Sometime between the first and second hour after the vampire ghost visited, the patrons that had been turned into zombies transformed back to their normal selves. Unfortunately for many, they had been killed when they turned, and their lifeless bodies had already been dumped in the back by the stables. Those lucky enough to survive the ordeal could not remember anything that happened after the unfortunate visitor arrived.

By early the next morning, the most disturbing of the messes in the tavern had been cleaned up. It was closed except to those staying in the inn or those patrons who most frequented the place. A service would be prepared for the recently fallen.

Brell and Lancelot determined to find Lareth while Trazk and Tristan sought out the *Wind Charger* to ensure they still had passage that night. Leopold took to sleeping under the bed. Even though it was overcast outside, the day made him sweat profusely as if he were being baked over a slow fire.

The path to find the young priest took the demon hunter and his charge out of the docks and into the wealthier district of Ferrickport. Those that the two passed on the street did their best to keep from meeting their gaze, and the few who did make eye contact betrayed a look of disgust at two so dirty gracing the richer side of town.

"Why are we here again?" Lancelot asked his aged mentor.

"The greatest concentration of churches resides in this part of the town. We do not know where Lareth lives or which church he belongs to. The best place to look for him would be here."

"Yeah, I get that part. I'm just uncomfortable with all of this." Lancelot waved his arm toward the latest stares of disapproval from a young lady walking toward them from ahead.

"I rather like this. Beats having your brains eaten by ravenous zombies or your arm cut off by some devil's weapon."

"Well, if you put it that way." Lancelot smiled at the lady contemptuously as she passed.

A short while later, the two arrived at the first temple. Lancelot gawked at its size and gaudiness. A large garden preceded the white marble church. A path to the large wooden double doors was flanked on either side by newly planted blue jacaranda trees. The windows to the temple were multi-colored stained glass. The left window displayed the image of the sun rising over a hillside. The right was that of a large stag standing with the moon behind it. The building itself looked to have battlements that reached skyward and two large flowing green pennants blew in the wind. A yellow stag's head emblazoned each of them.

Brell explained some of the symbolism, "This is the church of Bremmen. He is the creator of good, truth, and justice. The adult male stag is his chosen animal. Since the creation of the other good deities, he has relegated himself to the spheres of Peace, Law, and Truth. Hopefully your parents schooled you on the pantheon?" He eyed Lancelot to see if he had a lot more explaining to do.

"Yes. My mother taught us much about the three children of Gaea."

Brell nodded approvingly.

Lancelot continued, "Bremmen is the twin god-child of Gaea, brother to Damiel and Namrhyth. Where Namrhyth is the balancing scale, Bremmen is a god of righteousness and good, his twin sister the polar-opposite."

Sarauna had taught what she knew to her two sons, having been raised in a church herself. Many of the teachings she had imparted on them shown in their actions. Brell had noticed that right away, even when he was too drunk to stand.

He looked down at the boy now who may one day be his protégé. "Lancelot, I want you to let me do the talking when we go in. We are already not dressed for the part on this side of town, and I do not want to offend anyone with bad etiquette. Also, you may learn a thing or two."

Under his breath, he let trail off, "Blessed am I to be in your company, young demon-slayer." Then Brell and Lancelot waltzed up to the great double doors of the church and went inside.

Although the doors to the temple were broad and heavy, they swung open easily. Light from several large stained glass windows illuminated the expansive sanctuary. The towering windows were flanked by flowing green drapes held open by golden chords. Alternating shades of grey colored the floor tiles, and although no definitive pattern could be discerned, the warmth of its layout comforted them. The pair was greeted by the fragrant smell of jasmine. Three green robed men busied themselves about the perimeter of the room and replaced or lighted candles that were out. Finely decorated pews formed a loose 'C' around the pulpit. A green carpet decorated with golden stag heads led from the central entrance doors straight to alter steps at the other end of the chamber.

One of the robed figures took notice of the two as they entered and approached. He greeted them with a warm smile, "Welcome to the Temple of Bremmen. Are you here for prayer, or is there some other help I can offer?"

Brell gave what Lancelot thought was the most gracious bow he had ever seen, and then gave the robed man an unfamiliar hand sign greeting. The same hand sign was returned and the two men began to walk away together, shoulder to shoulder in hushed whispers. Brell looked back and saw that Lancelot still stood dumbfounded, and motioned with a finger to follow.

The acolyte led the two through a draped doorway and down some stairs. Candles inside small alcoves gave off barely enough light to see the steps by. The stairs wound down far below the church and emptied into a large gallery. Two closed wooden doors led out from each the left and right walls. The pair were led into the second door on the left. Beyond was a small room.

Inside the room, the three took seats around an old rickety wooden table. "I have heard of this Lareth whom you speak of," the robed man continued so that Lancelot was now included in the conversation. "He is a priest of Chess, the goddess of battle. He is a rising star in the city here."

"What was it that the witch said about finding him?" Lancelot looked to Brell.

"Just that. She said find him." Brell turned his attention to the acolyte, "Is he to be found near here?"

"Very near. The temple of Chess is only the second street over. Her symbol is that of a large sword, and will adorn the front of the building to either side of the front doors," he described more for Lancelot's benefit. "When you leave here, go left, and take your first right at the street intersection. The temple will be on the right."

The acolyte rose and continued to speak, "Please stay here while I inform the high priest of your presence. He will not want you to have left without imparting a blessing." He then left the small room.

Lancelot looked around for a couple of minutes. They appeared to be in a storage room also used for clandestine meetings. There were boxes stacked around the room, labeled only with painted numbers. Two wooden cupboards stood on the opposite wall from the door. Everything was dusty except for the table and chairs.

"You must be pretty important for that man to bring you here and then ask you to see the high priest," Lancelot noted.

"We are demon slayers. Any church would be foolish not to recognize us. Especially with devils running about. I wouldn't pin too much on 'important' in the way you are thinking Lancelot. I am a tool of the church, and I worry that they will try and make me go off on some errand or another before we can get back on track."

A man cleared his throat as he entered. He had obviously overheard them and responded, "I have learned that your current mission is important enough that I should not be interfering." He motioned with his hands as Lancelot and Brell tried to stand, "No need. I will sit. I am High Priest Gorm Darburrow."

Gorm was dressed in fine clothing from head to toe. He had the same green and gold that the acolyte wore, but it adorned silken fabric rather than wool. Gorm sat upon a large wooden box rather than the empty chair by the other two.

"This tide of evil must be stopped. Your instincts are not that far off Sir Brell, and although it would be my decision to reinstate you here in Ferrickport, our divining has foretold of your coming and going. Bremmen is hinting that there is something bigger going on and your journey is integral to stopping it all."

Brell replied, "Well, I don't know what you have heard, or

divined for that matter, but across the strait of Kollune, a vampire sits in his castle. I can't see that he has any connection to the Codrugon spawn that have infested these lands."

The wizened man was about to say something but looked over at Lancelot and saw him for what appeared to be the first time. "Who might this be?" he changed the subject.

Lancelot stood and bowed while Brell introduced him, "This is Lancelot, son of Amroth. I met him in Porterstown where he and his brother saved me from myself."

Gorm reached out and shook Lancelot's hand while Brell continued, "We have traveled here with an orc and a blacksmith. The latter lost both his sons to the spawn. I have taken Lancelot as my apprentice. When he is ready, I will bind him to me and the church."

Gorm nodded approvingly as he studied the young man before him. "What of your parents Lancelot? Did they perish?"

Lancelot nodded yes.

"So sorry to hear that." Gorm was sincere in his condolences. "I will put in a special prayer for them in our morning gathering."

The old man stood and paused before he turned to walk away. He looked at Lancelot one more time then shook his head and took his leave.

"What was that?" Lancelot asked.

"He probably has a lot on his mind, and you just happened to be the object of his lost thought," Brell answered thoughtfully.

The two waited a couple of minutes in silence and then left the house of Bremmen.

The dock traffic and noise never seemed to let up. Sailors and merchants gave Trazk and Tristan a wide berth as one look at the orc was all it took to intimidate passer byes. It was no easy task to find the *Wind Charger* though.

The docks were glutted with small ships and sailing vessels that looked for safety from an off-shore storm. Workers swarmed over gang-planks and ship decks like scurrying ants. Everyone wanted to have their ships unloaded or ready to set sail before the torrents of rain found their way to Ferrickport.

When at last they located the *Wind Charger*, the two were relieved. The ship was no less busy than any other, but the confidence and determination with which the crew worked alleviated the chaos that other ships shared. A deck-hand stopped what he was doing long enough to direct the pair toward the captain's quarters.

Before Trazk could knock, the sturdy oaken door swung wide. The captain, although surprised, barely showed it. "What can I do for you? Passage? We're all booked up."

Trazk answered, "Passage it is, but we should already be on your list. My companion, Brell, secured our spots last night. I'm here to make sure we still have them."

A light of recognition lit the large man's face, "Ah, right. There are four of you. I should have remembered you orc. Too much to drink I suppose. I remember now. You have about five hours and we are leaving. Follow me and I will show you to your quarters."

The captain led the pair to the left side of the deck and through a low topped doorway. "I'm captain Graelgos. You can just call me Captain." Graelgos led them down a narrow stair and turned a corner. The hall had three doors on each of the left and right sides. Tristan was amazed that this large man even fit below deck. The Captain led them to the second door to the right, opened it and let the pair inspect it to their satisfaction.

"This is where you will stay," he motioned with his head. "There are cots under the bed there and you can set them up using those hooks up there." The captain then produced two small, green painted stones from his dark maroon jacket and handed them to Trazk. "Take these. They are your get on the ship free pass so I don't have to be bothered. Just make sure you are here before we leave or you don't go."

The captain turned and left without another word. Tristan went into the cabin and pulled one of the cots out. It was a musty, hard black canvas with metal rings punched in the corners. "I think I'll take a bed if it's all the same." He already imagined how comfortable he would not be, as he swayed on the water in this old cot.

Trazk let out a low growling laugh then spun Tristan by the shoulder. "Let us go. We don't have a lot of time and we need to collect the other two."

7

Brell and Lancelot found their way to the church of Chess. Not unlike the house of Bremmen, the church dedicated to the lady of war was large and opulent. It shared many of the same architectural features such as the battlements and clean white splendorous marble walls. The area before the front entrance also had a garden, but this one kept seasonal flowers and low lying bushes. The overcast sky and light drizzle washed out the colors that must have made this a most beautiful place to behold. The pennants at the top of the temple were red with a common sword pointing downward, etched in white or silver. It was hard to tell from where they stood.

Within, they found it to be a far different view. The features were Spartan. A single monochromatic red carpet covered most of the floor. There were a dozen plain wooden pews. The stone floor itself had no pattern or color other than the drab grey of stone.

The temple was devoid of people, but the pair heard noises that came from somewhere down another hall. It sounded like steel on steel. Lancelot looked at Brell with anticipation but the smile Brell returned said that there was no danger here.

The two went through a red curtain that revealed an archway that led to the rest of the church. The sounds of combat, grunting, laughter, and determination grew louder as they walked down a hall into a well-lit room.

Inside the arched chamber, Brell and Lancelot watched with curiosity and amazement. A young man, who could not be much older than Tristan, sparred with four temple acolytes. The four were armored in heavy chain shirts with large wooden shields and wooden cudgels. Each of the four took turns to advance on the man swinging low or high. Occasionally two would come at him from opposite sides. Every time, the young man deftly parried their blows and counter striked with a pair of maces he himself wielded. The grunting came from the four as they were pummeled by the large metal balled weapons, and the laughter came from their wielder. It was obvious the young man did not put everything he had into his swings, or these men would not have survived his expertly landed blows.

The curly red-haired man with a light complexion, and lighter disposition stopped abruptly when he noticed he had an audience. He raised a hand and smile to greet the demon slayers, but one of the acolytes did not recognize that the sparring session had ended. A stern swing of his cudgel landed across the back of the man's skull and sent him sprawling head first into the stone floor.

Lancelot saw the horror on the assailant's face as everyone realized the mistake. Brell rushed to the young man's side. Wet crimson matted his hair and Brell observed aloud that he was unconscious. One of the men rushed out of the room, apparently to seek some help. Brell's hands were already aglow and his healing energies coursed through the young man.

The matted blood remained, but the wound closed and the young man stirred. Brell rolled him over into his lap. When the young man's eyes opened, he smiled, and all he could say was, "Oops." Everyone laughed at this, although the man who had clobbered him could not hide the nervousness in his.

Lancelot gave the man a hand up then helped Brell to his feet. "We are so sorry if we were the cause of this. You awed us with your ability to fight so many at once, and for so long. We did not mean to interrupt." Brell beamed as he saw how eloquently Lancelot engaged the young man in conversation.

"Oh, we were just finishing up when I noticed you. It was a most spectacular conclusion, I must add." The red haired man straightened his shirt and bowed to the three armored acolytes.

Just then the fourth ran in with two priests in tow. They stopped suddenly, confused when they saw nobody lying on the ground.

"Friends, don't look so astonished. Are we not in the house of Chess? Should she not look favorably upon those who do combat in her name? It is fortuitous that these two were here, and I can only thank the Goddess of combat for making them available to help me while practicing my charge."

He looked over at the pair and said, "I am Lareth Corwellyn," and shook their hands. "As much as you think this could have been your fault, your timing and abilities were impeccable. Without you, I could have just as easily been hit, and lay there bleeding now."

Lancelot tried to run any alternate scenario where that could have happened and gave Lareth a dubious look, but left it at that.

The two priests inspected the young combatant, and were reticent to let him alone. Only at his insistent shrugging them off did they take their leave.

Brell introduced himself and Lancelot and went through the motions of deference afforded to a priest of Chess.

After, Brell got to the point of their visit, "As you may know Lareth, there is a very serious incursion into the material world. I suspect it is from the Hells, but can't fathom how such a large number have gotten through. There must be a gate somewhere."

"Sit," Lareth replied and motioned to chairs set against the wall, "I hear Duke Emil has sent his army westward. But nothing more. It is so business-as-usual here and I am at a loss for the inactivity."

"Unfortunately, that is not why we are here, although I get the feeling somehow they are related." Brell took the seat closest to a window and furtively glanced out while he continued.

"We encountered a bog witch two days back. She 'offered' us information that it appears we must now act upon. Our journey will take us across the narrow sea to face a mature vampire. The word of the hag had us looking for your aid." He then described the event at the Fallen Giant and his conversation with High Priest Darburrow.

Lancelot listened intently. Lareth also took this information in and thought at length before he replied, "Surely, there is a connection. And surely I will aid you. You booked passage on a ship? Well, I hope they have room for one more. I will postpone my pilgrimage to Peorn."

Lancelot got the nagging suspicion that there was something further about this, but Lareth and Brell had already shook on the new arrangement and walked from the room. Outside, the rain pounded on the window and it seemed to grow just a little darker.

Trazk and Tristan found their way back to the inn. The clean-up had intensified so Marylinne could be open for tonight's crowd. The mood was still somber, but there were a couple of ex-zombies there who gave their gratitude for not being killed. Someone pointed to the pair and said, "They are the ones you should be thanking."

A dirty man with salt and pepper hair and two-day-old stubble crossed the lobby and pressed his hand into Tristan's. "Thank you. Thank your friends." He looked at Trazk nervously. "May Bayoric bless you." He started to sob, almost uncontrollably. "Without you, we…we would have surely perished."

The man jumped when Trazk put his clawed hand on his skinny shoulder to comfort him. "It will be okay human. Just take care of your friends there. We all have to come together when an enemy is banging at our door and when death is creeping into our homes." Then the man slowly backed up in fear as the orc continued, "We have to join together when war is on the horizon and the crows are in the air, waiting to pick at our entrails."

The man almost fled from the inn as Trazk trailed off.

"You could have just said that it's going to be okay," Tristan scolded him. "The man is scared of you as it is."

Chortling, Trazk replied, "I know. I always seem to get that reaction."

The pair ascended the broad, carpeted stairway up to their room. Inside, not only were the drapes closed, but a Mahogany wardrobe had been pushed in front of the window. The room was dark except what the hall light allowed. From the door, Tristan saw the red, glowing eyes of Leopold as they looked up at them from beneath the bed.

A chill ran down Tristan's spine. "We, um, we could go in the other room," he spoke to the bed.

Leopold's raspy voice whispered in response, "Wise."

Trazk steered the boy away from the door and closed it. They headed over to Brell and Lancelot's room. It was locked. "Great. I guess I get to teach you some drinking games. Let's go."

"Really?" Tristan asked.

"No, not really. Let's go wait outside. We can talk in peace and keep an eye out for the others' return."

The two left the inn and took care to avoid any more thankful patrons.

―――――――――――――

It was sometime after noon that Brell and Lancelot showed up with their new companion. They came upon Trazk as he told Tristan how to pick targets out of crowds. The orc acknowledged them with a nod, and the group moved back into the inn and up to the room without the vampire.

Inside, even with the rain and overcast skies, the mood was bright and cheery, a far contrast to Leopold's darkened chamber. "This is Lareth Corwellyn. He will be traveling with us," Brell introduced.

Lareth showed deference to both Trazk and Tristan as he shook their hands. "I only hope that I can be of good use," he injected humbly.

In short order, the priest learned what had transpired from the time the boys had left their farm to meeting Trazk and Brell, until now. He wanted more than ever to be a part of the success that would follow, and it showed in his eyes.

The group laid out on the bed what they had collected through the day. It was prudent to make a last minute check, and Brell took the time to explain to the boys the significance and use of their cache of items. Lareth also surrendered his belongings to the pile. He had a sizable pouch of coins which he added to the large amount from Leopold's chest. His two maces looked far less menacing when he was not swinging them around. He placed down a fiery red necklace beside his silver holy symbol, then the others looked to each other with sparked recognition.

Tristan pointed to it and directed at Lareth, "The witch said that was important. You were supposed to give it to someone."

Trazk helped, "Yes, to Leopold I believe. He is the one who approached us for aid."

Brell wriggled his nose as if it itched. But it was something else they were supposed to remember that itched his brain. He scratched his nose and left it at that.

Lareth nodded in acknowledgement, "Great. I almost didn't bring this. I was supposed to wear it to my wedding."

Like branches breaking, all heads snapped up at once, and in unison, the other four blurted, "You're getting married?"

"In Peorn. I am betrothed to Kerina Felworn, daughter to the High Prelate. I was supposed to leave in eleven days for Bastipore. Frankly, because of the importance of this wedding, I did not think I would be able to argue my way to help you. It took my superiors all of a minute before they were practically helping me pack. Something bigger is going on here that we do not yet know."

That knowledge did not sit well with Brell and his face betrayed his thoughts. "I was given the same send off from Darburrow at Bremmen's Hall. As usual, they know something and we only get to find out what it is by doing it."

"Isn't that the truth?" Lareth laughed.

Brell got back to business and divided the items into five piles. He then packed them into the leather backpacks in a way they could be easily retrieved should the need arise. After, he laid out their plans and roles.

"It is important that each of us does what we are supposed to, when we are supposed to do it. Lancelot, you will always stay close to me. If ever the group separates, I want you at my side. The same goes for you and Trazk," he nodded at Tristan.

"What will we do?" Lancelot asked.

"Just that," the old man continued, "You are our shadows. We don't know what kind of trouble we are getting into, but we do have an idea of what we are facing."

Brell looked to Lareth, "Your roll here is a little foggy. I think for the time being, you should do your best to watch after our benefactor, Mr. Leopold. His condition can change at any time, and especially while sailing we will be most vulnerable. If what the witch said is true, you should give him that necklace as soon as he is up."

Tristan shivered when reminded of the eyes under the bed.

Lancelot still had more questions, "Brell, we hired the ship to take us to Valencia, but that is not where the Vampire wants us to go. What will we do?"

It was obvious Brell had already thought of that. "Leopold is going to have to wait. Part of our preparation is to get into the Great Library of Myurondy. There we will find the knowledge to defeat our foe. I have fought many a devil, and twice that in demons, but I have not faced a vampire."

The orc and priest both nodded their approval on this course of action.

The rain outside stopped. Trazk opened the window to let the breeze in. Sounds of work and the bustle of business droned. "It looks like we have a couple of hours left before we need to head to the docs. Not sure the captain is going to be happy that our head-count has increased by one…or two."

Brell smiled, "The captain is very fluent in the language of coin. And we have enough to talk sense. We will be fine." He looked to the young priest, "Lareth, have you the time to talk religion to my apprentice here? I am certain he has learned a lot from his mother, but I would like to formalize his road instruction."

Lancelot perked up with excitement, "Yes, please. I am sure I did not listen half as much as I should have when my mom was talking to us."

"That's no lie," Tristan added as he punched his younger brother in the shoulder.

"Hey…." Lancelot wanted to fight back but caught himself and sat to listen.

Lareth nodded. He thought for a minute and then started, "Well, I may be young, but I have traveled. And I have spoken with many priests, wise-men, and oracles. What I am going to tell you may not be church sanctioned talk, strictly being, but it is the best of the truth that I know.

"Gaia created Jhenna, our world. It was a world dominated by a single landmass. The oceans were only lakes and rivers. There were no animals, or people, or other deities. Then Gaia grew lonely. She longed for company. To satisfy this need she bore a child. She named him Namrhyth and watched him grow to be tall, strong, beautiful, and intelligent.

"For hundreds of years they conversed and learned, but Namrhyth was boring. He spent more time alone, contemplating, ignoring. Gaia grew tiresome of his solitaire nature and decided to have another child. She thought long before doing so, and decided upon a new course of action. She would bear two children and instill a sense of freedom in each.

"She bore one son, Bremmen, and one daughter, Damiel. Bremmen and Damiel each had a fire in them that Namrhyth never hoped to equal. They had spirit and passion, and unfortunately, also a deep seeded hatred for each other. One grew from love and compassion, while the other, Damiel, grew from hatred. They fought all of the time, and at first, Gaia was happy. She had children who displayed a great deal of emotion. Both children gave and required much attention.

"Centuries went by, and the fighting did not cease. Even Namrhyth could not contain the two. Gaia grew weary of their antics, and decided enough was enough. She sundered the planet in one mighty blow, splitting the continent into three. Seas and oceans filled in the gaps between the continents, and the three were separated.

"For a time after this, Gaia ignored her children. She had new creations in the form of animals, and the elements. It was a consuming task to watch over the ecology and the growth of her new world. Bremmen and Damiel, seeing what their mother was doing, used the trick to make creations of their own. In this, many of the other deities of the world were created.

"This was not enough though. For the oceans barred passage to the other continents, and there was a great deal to do if the two were going to reach each other. It was far less energy to create humans than more gods. They could be made in plenty. They were used to create great ships, and erect towers and castles. And what was more, the worship from these humans gave the gods even more power.

"It was not long before the first ships sailed across to the other continents, and not long after that before the world was at war. Battles raged in open plains, in forests, mountains, and underground. The planet was in chaos.

"Even Namrhyth and his followers, for he could surly not sit idly while his brother and sister destroyed the planet, as well as the animals, were not immune to the destruction that was taking place. This turmoil lasted for hundreds of years. In that time, fell creatures and magic arose. The gods took on portfolios to strengthen their hold on their worshipers.

"Trenia, goddess of virtue and wisdom was slain by an assassin's knife. In her death, an entire city was destroyed; for the blood of the gods is so volatile as to be made of the stuff of Jhenna.

"Gaia grew wearisome of her children's fighting and finally let her fury be seen. She let Jhenna do her work; volcanic eruptions, floods, earthquakes, and violent storms rent the surface of the world, thousands upon thousands of mortals were slain. All of those gods created by her children were unaffected, and this made her all the angrier. She gathered them together, and with the fire of the sun and the depth of the sea, her voice rang of the doom these creations of her offspring were to see.

"Only Namrhyth could stay her hand. His soothing voice was enough to instill calm in Gaia. It took a lot to convince her to spare the immortal creations and the mortals of Jhenna. After ten years of negotiating and tact, an agreement was reached. The immortal creations were allowed to continue existing, but all of them, including her children were forbidden to step upon Jhenna in immortal guise again. Of course Damiel eventually circumvented this with the advent of avatars, human embodiments of the gods themselves.

"Mortals were allowed to exist on Jhenna, but they would now be watched. Gaia created from Jhenna the Watchers, immortals devoted to her and tied to Jhenna. They rule over the elements and guard against the unbalance that the mortals create and the immortals exploit. Some mortals saw the benefit that these new gods represented, and began worship of Gaia and the Watchers. In this, Druids were born.

"Four thousand years have gone by. Gaia's realm has over this time become exposed to other pantheons. To keep their power, the deities have only admitted non-human gods. Elves, dwarves, halflings and more now populate the world. Good, neutral and evil gods and mortals have added both to the heavens and to Jhenna. Dark lords and righteous kings have dominated the continents, never quite able to unite the entire world. Prophecies abound as to what will happen when this one-day is accomplished, and many more of who will succeed in this task."

Everyone had taken keenly to Lareth's story, and all attention was on him when the door to the bedroom burst open. Leopold Gambaldi stood in the doorway. Smoke rose from his shoulders and exposed flesh. He did not look happy. "You have to go. They are here."

8

Leopold was visibly pained. The skin on his face looked like it boiled in places. "Allies of Dellan are here. They seek the destruction of this city."

"Do you speak of the Codrugon spawn? Or is this a new threat?" Brell was confused.

"The devils are working with Dellan. I saw them consorting with one another. It is one of the reasons I fled from his Chateau before he came after me."

"And how do you know they are here?"

As if on cue, panic and screams dominated the daily sounds of the city outside the window.

"I can smell them." Without missing a beat, Leopold continued, "You need to get to your ship. I can't leave this building yet. I can catch up with you, but you need to move now. I don't know how an alarm wasn't raised."

Each grabbed their pack and headed down the stairs. They were greeted by bewildered stares from Marylinne and other patrons who either had not heard or did not comprehend the chaos outside. The vampire donned his overcoat and wide-brimmed hat and followed them down the stairs.

"Board the windows and doors," Leopold barked out. Nobody knew what to do. Their dumbfounded looks spelled that out for him. He grabbed the front-desk with both hands and ripped a whole section from the foundation. The patrons panicked.

Trazk shook his head as the frightened humans moved for the door, then whispered to Tristan, "And you said I was scaring them." The orc bellowed a deep guttural laugh.

Loud shouts and screams came from just beyond the door. Brell cracked it open to make sure the way was clear and two clawed feet kicked the door open. It knocked both him on his back and the air out of him. Tristan saw that the devils were flying in on the backs of very large hornet-like beasts. They had flown in under the cover of clouds and rain. That particular bit of knowledge did not matter at this time, for there was an insect devil standing in the doorway, claws and weapons at the ready. Two more stood behind it.

Lancelot noted they did move predictably, but their speed and strength would still be an obstacle to overcome. He drew his sword and readied for the onslaught that never came.

Leopold tossed half of the front-desk at the lead creature; it splintered upon impact, and knocked the devil off its balance. The vampire was a blur and nearly beat the desk to the target. He had claws of his own, and icy, iron-like nails ripped into the spawn's chest. The other two moved to surround Leopold, but he moved so fast, he appeared to surround them at every instance instead. They swung. They missed. He swung and insect body parts flew. It was over before it really began. Three dead Codrugon devils lay in their own gore.

More came to the door. Leopold turned to the others. Insect ichor streaked across his face, "Go out the back. You need to get to the ship. Get out of here!" He turned back to meet the new attackers.

Lareth helped Brell to his feet, then the group fled out through the tavern. Those others who could shake off their horror haphazardly followed after them.

The side-alley was about the sanest place to be. Screams and combat came from every other direction. Above, devils flew in formation on the backs of large, hairy creatures with ten legs and two sets of wings. If they were the same things that Tristan saw outside the inn door, they had long, wicked stingers protruding from their abdomens. Four huge compound eyes lined their heads and the beasts had foot-long, serrated mandibles.

Brell led them to the alley entrance but kept them back with an outstretched hand, finger raised. He watched while two more spawn dropped from the backs of their mounts and entered the inn through the front. Sounds of combat continued with Leopold. When the devils entered, the demon-hunter motioned for his companions and the stragglers to follow.

Across the street and back opposite the way they moved, two giant beetles, both the size of castle towers, laboriously landed. The larger came down in the middle of the street. Its head twisted to the right and its maxilla manipulated plasma-like fire before it released a swathing gout of flame upon the nearest buildings. One man, caught in the flames erupted into a screaming mass of melting flesh and expired as he was washed to the ground with the sticky burning sputum.

The second beast unceremoniously crashed down upon three tented shops and collapsed half of two other wooden structures. It struggled to stand and then began its rain of destruction.

It was obvious the group could not escape past the beetles. Brell led them the other way. He kept as close to the shops and taverns and also used as many tent canopies for cover as he could find. There were hundreds of giant, flying insects in the air. They landed to attack anything that moved. Brell could see that the largest concentration of the attack force was focused on the docks. The devils tried to keep anyone from escaping.

The group continued up the street. Three buildings ahead, the city watch attempted to make a stand. They had archers at every window and on the roof of a stout two-story structure. It looked to be an inn. The roof on top was flat, and bags of grain were stacked as makeshift bulwarks. Two armed men with shields, chain shirts and coifs stood at the front door. Their tabards identified them as city watch. They did not look happy to be there, but a dead devil in the doorway pointed to their competence.

The demon hunter paused and let the others catch up so he

could confer with them. Trazk was of the mind to circumnavigate the building. He rightly pointed out a flight of devils that took notice of the top-side guards. Lareth wanted to help before they moved on. Brell had a third idea which the other two agreed to.

Tristan and Lancelot did their best to keep the inn-patrons who had followed them from The Fallen Giant calm. One was the old scraggly man who earlier had thanked Tristan. They all watched as Trazk scurried forward, composite bow out, eyes scanned the sky. Every five or six paces, he notched back and arrow and let it fly at a mount that got too close to the front guards.

When the orc was about half way to the inn, Brell motioned to go. Everyone went at a sprint behind him. Four mounted Codrugon wasps landed in the center of the road, the mounts immediately took flight and the eight insect like riders descended upon the party. Brell and Lareth turned to meet the monsters. Trazk had reached the two guards and exchanged words at the same time he offered cover-fire to his companions.

Tristan and his brother led the other seven people to the front door of the inn. A barrage of tri-blades whizzed and whirled into the pack. The two guards did their best to block the incoming group from the attack, but it could not stop a blade that severed one woman's leg at the knee or another that disemboweled a man.

Trazk's arrows worked in tandem with Lareth's maces and Brell's blades. The Codrugon spawn were fairly easy to take down, but brute force did not work so well against the hornet creatures. The arrows pierced their hide, but barely stuck. Mace blows glanced off ineffectually. Only the purple blades of Brell's summoned swords had any lasting effect. They cut through mandibles and legs effortlessly. One hornet dropped under his onslaught.

The ferocity of Brell's attacks caused the other three hornets to avoid him. Lareth used this to his advantage, and ducked down behind the demon hunter.

The door to the inn opened and Lancelot ushered the survivors from The Fallen Giant inn into this one. He spied that an officer of the watch had set up an impromptu headquarters within who barked out commands to other guards. The door shut and the demon hunter in-training spun to face any new dangers. His brother had just replenished Trazk's quiver and also fired arrows at the hornets. Trazk told him to aim for the eyes.

With a word to Brell, Lareth stood up and his companion swapped places with him. Words of power were unleashed by the young cleric and a ball of coalescing fire formed as his hands spun and molded it without actually touching. The ball grew. Unsure of how to deal with this new threat, the insects moved to engage the archers and shield guards.

One hornet reeled in pain as arrows found two of its four compound eyes. Another hornet got in close. The taller of the two guards stepped in to meet it, shield raised high. With an unknown agility, the beast landed in a crouch and snaked its head under the shield; its jaws snapped tight. At first it pinned the guard's legs. He let out a blood-curling scream. Then his legs severed at the calves. Chunks of flesh, ripped by serrations, dangled from the wound. Blood spurted out of both stumps in tune with his heart as it pumped the life out of him.

The other guard mashed his shield into the side of the beast's face. The creature's left compound eyes softened the blow, but the shield burst one of them. Yellow-green ichor oozed from its face. Razor-sharp mandibles grabbed onto the shield and splintered it. The guard fell backward. He scrambled on his hands and feet like a crab back to the shelter of the front awning.

Lareth unleashed tendrils of fire from his globe, like whips or snakes that looked for their prey. The ball between his hands had grown to nearly half as tall as he was. It floated in the air, hungry. The whips of fire latched onto the third and second hornet by their legs. Whining screams pierced the air as the creatures were held and began to burn. A third tendril wrapped itself around the near-blind insect and tightened. The globe pulsated once and then disgorged a flaming missile into the back of the pinned creature. It burst into flames upon impact. Acrid smoke spilled from the open hole it created.

One hornet yanked hard enough to pull its body free from its leg. It immediately took flight. Trazk, Tristan and several archers on the roof peppered the creature with arrows. Wounded and discouraged, the beast flew off and away over buildings until out of sight.

The other hornet enjoyed the same fate as the first. One, then two pulses of fire rocked the outer shell before a third decimated the thing's side. Lareth let the ball of fire between his hands fade and then wink out.

With a brief respite from combat, the survivors dragged the shinless guard into the inn and barred the door. Brell spoke with the captain about the dire situation outside. Lareth glowed a soft white and pressed his hands to the stumps that were moments before attached to feet. The bleeding stopped, and although the man was passed out, he would live through this injury.

The captain had an underling take the wounded and non-combatants below into the cellar. The main room was cluttered with bodies trying to make themselves useful. 'Reports' were hastily scrawled. Everyone knew this situation was untenable, but the captain was unwilling to give up this currently defendable position.

Brell assessed the situation as it stood, "Captain Erris. I know you feel safer here than on the street, but this may be the best time to high tail it out of here. From what I can tell, this is a very small force, scouts if I may call them that. The larger army will be swarming the city soon. Now, for all we know. Your best bet would be to get these people to the docks. Get them on a ship and get as much distance from here as you can."

Captain Erris was certainly conflicted, "I can't. We can't leave. People are counting on us to keep them safe. I have a duty." He didn't sound as sure as he tried.

"We can't stay here with you. We have obligations that may shape things to come."

"Understood. Look. There are only so many windows to point our bows out. You should go now while things are quiet...."

The inn shook with loud thuds from somewhere above. Sounds of combat rang out all around. Shouts of confusion and panic were the loudest. Several men with short spears crammed up the stairway. Moments later, the shouts grew louder. The combat had breached the upper levels of the inn.

Erris finished his statement, "Get out now while you can. Either that, or I am going to conscript you for this fight."

He turned to follow the others up the stairs, sword out. Lareth chanted a few indiscernible words and the captain's sword began to glow. Erris turned back and mouthed a thanks before he disappeared into the melee.

"Now is the time to go," Trazk stated with urgency. He had already opened the front door. There were no guards standing out front this time. The captain and his small force of city watch were going all-in on the second and third floor of the inn.

Brell was the last one out. He had just finished the familiar protection spell that he had used back on his house in Porterstown. Maybe it would help those in the cellar should the defenders fail.

Outside, the only activity in the streets was further back. One of the huge beetles lumbered in the direction of the group. It stopped twice. The first time to unleash its flames onto a wine shop. The flames from the store gave off hissing purple and orange flares. The second time, the beetle rammed a two-story building. Wood shattered and the upper level collapsed onto the beetle. It shrugged the construction material off like a dog shaking itself dry.

Tristan spied multiple hornet creatures on the roof, their riders fought somewhere in the building. The giant insects had cornered a group of the archers near the front edge of the inn. "Trazk, is there something we can do for them?"

Trazk's reply was a command, "Take us to the other side of the street."

As they made for the safety of the building walls across the way, the orc fired arrow after arrow into the fleshy, less-armored faces of the hornets. Two of the beasts were confounded by his accurate missiles. The men began to scale down the corner edge of the building.

The humongous beetle from down the street approached closer.

One man lost his grip and fell. Brell, Lareth, and Lancelot continued up the street, but Trazk, and now Tristan who followed the orc's lead, continued the covering fire for the men in such a vulnerable position. One of the hornets raised its upper body high and its abdomen slid under its legs driving a spike like stinger into the last man who tried to screen the others' descent. Poison pumped into the man as if the stinger was not enough to kill him. He changed a ghastly shade of brown and then collapsed with a summersault backward over the ledge.

Three last arrows focused on that horrid wasp-like abomination. The remaining men made it down and sought cover. Trazk and his charge sprinted through the street to catch up with the others.

On the roof, Captain Erris led his men out to fight the hornets. They had been victorious inside, but at a cost. The hornets, heavily wounded, moved to engage the human meat coming to fight them. The melee was short. The captain raised his glowing sword in triumph.

The beetle in the street reared itself up, its tarsal claws gripped the top corners of the inn. The large protruding abdomen pressed in on the third floor and chunks of stone and wood fell to the street below. Erris saw his doom. He commanded his men back down the stairs and ran forward, his sword swung on high. A swooshing sound preceded the ignition of the beetle's internal plasma. The fire caught Erris straight on. His flesh melted from his bones even before he slammed headlong into the beast. The sword released from his skeletal grip and clattered down off the building; its soft glowing light faded out.

Tristan looked back one last time to see the creature ignite the whole of the inn. Screams petered out as lives inside extinguished. He cried as he ran. Anguish and anger filled his soul.

The way forward had become less dangerous. Devils were either already inside the surrounding buildings or were involved in the assault on the docks. The demon slayer took no chances though, and they used as much cover as possible to stay hidden while they ran.

Lancelot had to stop the group twice. The running had taxed his endurance to the limit. "We need to rest," he said the second time. "I can't keep running."

"Remember this?" Trazk asked, and lifted him with one arm onto his back. "You need to eat less and run more human." The orc was not slowed as he carried his new baggage.

9

The group continued until it crested a slight hill and the scene on the docks below unfolded. The devils had dropped down all along the waterfront. Sailors formed pockets of resistance and fought as best they could. Fires burned everywhere, most likely caused from a third beetle that even now devastated a warehouse. Some ships burned. Some had begun to sink. Other boats had whatever sails they could unfurl and made for the sea or straights. Hornets, some rider-less, hovered above, circled, and dropped at opportune times to strike down city defenders.

"Our chances don't look good," Brell commented.

Trazk responded, "We still have to go down there. Find out." He let Lancelot down and readied his bow.

"I know," Brell conceded. He led them down a winding street straight into the devils' playground.

When the fighting drew close, the group used as much of the burned out and ruined buildings for cover as they could. Twice, they encountered lone Codrugon spawn that picked through rubble or tried to get in through a door at unseen prey. They were dispatched easily with sword and arrow.

The group drew closer to where ships were or had been moored. Dead littered the ground like snow-cover. There were mostly humans, some dwarves and elves, and very few devils.

Trazk crouch-ran to the first ship that looked serviceable. The small galley listed slightly and he noticed water had penetrated a large hole caused by what looked to be an outward explosion.

When Trazk turned back, he spied a half dozen hornets swoop down. Four had riders. His arrows indicated to the group that they were under attack and from where. It gave Lareth time to conjure up a force shield that stopped a triblade just in time. Tristan followed Trazk's eye line and fired at the approaching enemies. He focused on the riders, as he knew full well he would do nothing to the mounts at the current distance.

Three riders remained after the volley of arrows. The devils dismounted from the air so the hornets could hover and attack from above. One swung two hatchet-ended staffs in unison that formed deadly arcs as it focused on Brell. He easily parried both, and smoothly arced his own blades down in a circular spin. The demon hunter's blades severed the devils spine at both its waist and neck.

The second rider moved purposefully at Lancelot. The boy charged the devil. In mid-stride, he scooped up some dirt from the side of the road and tossed it into the creature's face. It was enough to distract the devil while he leapt into it. Two hands on his pommel, Lancelot drove his sword down into its thorax. He then rolled off and away from the monster. Even in death it swung wildly as it tried to kill anything it could reach.

Trazk and Tristan kept the hornets at bay while Brell took care of the last devil. Lareth summoned up his ball-fire again. After the first of the hornets succumbed to its cleansing flame, the other five flew off for easier meals.

The group continued further down the docks. They hoped that a functional boat still waited for them. Even better would be the *Wind Charger*. Two more engagements similar to the last played out in the death-filled streets. Lancelot received a terrible gash in his back in their final encounter. Brell got to him in time to administer his magics that both removed the wound and the poison within.

Night came and darkness deepened. Everyone knew that meant the danger would multiply. Their chances hinged on that one ship, elusive as it was.

The rain started again and quickly became a drenching downpour. It made it easier for the group to keep hidden and allowed them to continue their search unmolested for a time. The fires were also affected, and their spreading slowed and eventually stopped.

Late into the night, the sound of the rain drowned out any remaining screams or combat. There was still palpable danger in the air, but the group was blind and deaf to their surroundings. Through it, they kept searching. They were more than half way along the wharf before they found their first survivors.

Five men huddled on the deck of the scuttled *Maidenhead* under a collapsed mast and sail. Three looked to be sailors. They all wore the same drab white shirts over dirtied, black truffled pants. A very large copper-skinned man, stubble the only hair visible on his head, sat uncomfortably on a wooden box. He wore a tattered apron over a deep blue long-sleeved, woolen shirt. An old scar that run down the left side of his face hinted there was a story to be told. The last was a halfling of middle years. His clothes were of much finer quality than the others, but just as dirty and tattered from the recent attacks. He was the only one of the five that was armed, and his weapon was a short dagger, the tip broken off. All looked beaten and broken, and were too tired to show how scared they were.

"You are not here to kill us are you?" was the first question the balding, dark-skinned man asked. He didn't even rise from his seat.

"Do we look like monsters?" Trazk replied. The rain hid his smile, and only the more cruel features of his face shown.

It frightened the men more. The halfling, shaking, stepped forward dagger ready for use.

"Stay your weapon little one." Brell diffused the situation. "We, like you, are stranded here. We were on our way to the *Wind Charger* when this all started. Have you any word? Are there any ships left?"

One of the sailors, curly red hair and a round nose just as red, grimly answered, "Aye, she dropped sail at the first sign of death arriving. Her captain had that ship out of here faster an any other."

Brell listened on with displeasure. The man continued, "The

bug monsters dropped down on other boats as they turned to sail. I'll guess that only a handful made it out of here in working shape. If there were light, I would point out the spots where boats went down with their crew."

A leaner, dark-haired sailor with a greasy, wiry goatee jumped in, "Them things trashed all the ships up and down these docks. If you tried to sail, you were fight'n for your life. The bugs are hard to kill, especially the flyin ones."

The last sailor just nodded confirmation that his ship-mates were telling it right.

Red-hair piped back in, "They aint just hard ta kill. They are damn near impossible. We fought em on our ship. I didn't see a one of em die. Royce and me and Will jumped over the side before our ship got sunk."

Brell didn't lighten their spirits, "I'm afraid gentlemen that this is not even close to over. Those were only scouts. Their mission was probably to slow any escape before the main army arrives. They will be taking slaves and food-stock if they haven't started already."

"Do you have a plan to get out of here knowing what you know now sir?" the halfling spoke formally and concisely. "My name is Sir Thelband Highfellow," he pointed to the aproned man, "and this is my new friend Ardus. He is a butcher. Now Ardus and I prefer not to become someone else's breakfast. I would kindly ask that you include us in your plans."

"Us to," Royce with the goatee chimed in.

Brell nodded to the group, then looked back for confirmation from his companions before he spoke, "We will take you. I guarantee no safety. But staying would surely spell your doom. We will need to find a ship, but right now, I would be happy to find a long-boat and we could paddle our way out."

The mood of the five changed. They were now among friends. Best friends as far as they were concerned. Especially if it meant them getting out of here. Will even volunteered that he was a good rower. Everyone laughed at that. "We may find out soon enough," Lareth said and patted Will on the back.

The group size had increased, but the plan remained the same.

They used the rain and darkness as cover. From ship to ship they went; they searched for something that could help them to evacuate. Royce did find one small row-boat. He and Lem carried it along. Will and Lancelot carried the oars.

Thelband stayed close to Brell. He wanted to hear any tidbit that would determine the outcome of his survival. He and Ardus were quick to point out any detours. They knew the streets well, and the group started to see more signs of Codrugon spawn activity.

Not long after finding the boat, the group encountered the unavoidable and unmistakable sounds of combat. Before they could investigate, the melee came around the corner to them. Four city combatants, all had shaved heads and wore loose-fitted clothing, were engaged with a dozen devils. They fought with no crafted weapons, but used their hands and feet to parry and attack. All moved with mesmerizing grace and leapt about, vaulted off objects and walls to gain advantages against a foe that outnumbered them three to one. It was apparent that three of their group could not penetrate the chitinous hides of the devils, but they were effective none-the-less. Off-balancing attacks, leg-sweeps, pressure holds, and aerial maneuvers confounded their foes.

The fourth was different. Her whole body glowed a hazy orange. Her hands delivered strikes using her finger-tips as thrusting weapons. They cracked and punctured the devil skin. The blows themselves were not fatal, but in combination with three more like them, and tremendous kicks to the head and neck, the insectile creatures were slowly brought down.

All of the combatants were cut and bruised, but none were slowed by the poison dripping from the various tools of war wielded by the Codrugon spawn. Brell recognized them for who they were, or rather what they represented. He would share when this was over.

"Let's help!" the demon hunter yelled as he charged. His purple blades appeared in his hands. Tristan fumbled for some arrows while Trazk had already unleashed two. Behind them, the two sailors carrying the boat, dropped it down on top of them like a turtle in its shell. Lancelot led the others into the nearest shop through a broken out window. The door had been blocked and boarded off in an attempt to slow down an earlier assault.

Devils tried to peel off from the melee to engage the new attackers, but the acrobatic fighters kept them hemmed in. With the arrival of Brell, the acrobats redoubled their efforts and brought the creatures into an even tighter circle. The demon slayer started off by low sweeping as one man circle kicked high. Two off-balance devils lost their legs. Two more had already gone down from an overabundance of arrows to the head and neck. The orange glowing woman delivered precision coup-de-grace upon any of the enemy laying on the street.

One of the devils was able to grab a man by the leg as he cartwheeled. Two more devils speared him through the chest, and all three, frustrated with their previous lack of success, tore into him with their mandibles and claws. He punched and jabbed at them again and again, but it was too much and his body finally gave out. The orange woman descended upon the three devils with an unmatched ferocity. Chunks of back and brain scattered from the spot where they all now lay. She turned with fire in her eyes. Her remaining two companions bounded away. Brell took this as a sign and with a final thrust through an abdomen, he kicked his foe away and rolled backwards.

The orange woman, in one motion smashed one foot forward, and yelled a word of power into a thunderous clap from her hands. The sound could be seen as a blur of motion and it overwhelmed the remaining devils. Of the seven left, four exploded into a shower of fragments, ooze, and indiscernible body parts. The remaining three were so damaged and disoriented that they fell to arrows, blades, and orange-glowing hands without a struggle.

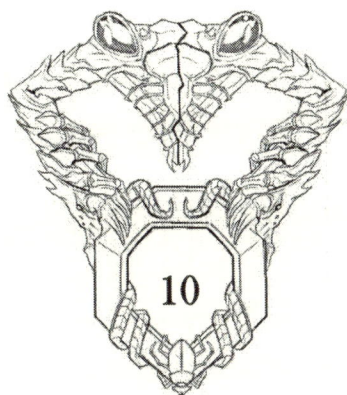

10

Everyone filtered into the same building as Lancelot and the others, then caught their breath. Brell made introductions, although Thelband had to correct him on his name. Of course, Will also felt the need to inject a little trivia too, "We have been traveling for about an hour with Mr. Brell. Me and Royce and Lem. And of course the short fella and Ardus."

The woman, who no longer glowed orange, smiled. Her body was slim yet muscular. She was bald except for her eyebrows which were trimmed to look like hooks over her emerald eyes. Her nose and cheeks were angled over thin, creased lips. With her sleeves pulled up, her toned forearms each displayed tattoos of unknown red and blue flowers. Her tanned, loose fitted clothes looked like robes that had been tailored into pant-bottoms. She, like her other two companions stood barefoot.

"We are Peacekeepers, diplomatic security assigned to the embassy of Tamm," she explained, "I am Tara." Her arm made an underhanded waving gesture, "and this is Edge and Mark. They work with me." Each of the robed men bowed slightly as they were recognized.

The two men appeared to wait for something from Tara, and she finally acknowledged them with a nod. With lightning speed and elven grace, they disappeared through the open window.

"They wish to retrieve our fallen, Gerick, Dario, and Skar. They will return their bodies to the embassy for proper burial. When they return, we will continue our search for survivors."

Lancelot asked puzzled, "What is an embassy?"

Again Tara smiled, "Many of the major cities in the known world, at least those populated by humans, contain embassies. They are neutral ground. Not just for enemies, but for places of differing political philosophies to meet without intimidation or reservations. As long as feuds are not brought within the embassy walls, we respect all-comers. Our primary mission is to ensure foreign dignitaries are safe. Trade agreements and treaties are often signed there. We also make it our mission to assist those in need and those less fortunate than others."

Her tone grew more serious, "We do not interfere with the laws of the lands that we are established in. To do so would damage the trust that kingdoms hold in us." Brell noticed that Tara was pained to say this last part, almost as if she held something back.

Brell was the only one who actually knew of the Peacekeepers and the function they performed in society. The others listened with great interest.

Her expression lightened again though and she continued, "We have varying roles within each embassy. Mine is that of diplomatic security. Those under my charge travel with foreign officials, be they diplomats, kings, scholars, or other valuable personages. We keep them safe to prevent incidents that can often lead to war or trade disputes. Others of us go on missions to help the poor in each kingdom, country, or empire where we are established. Many in the embassy are normal, everyday people keeping the embassy maintained and our records straight. Often there are whole buildings dedicated to the storage of important documents."

Brell decided Tara had given enough lessons on embassy knowledge and interrupted, "Are you aware of the danger this city is in? I know you have seen terrible combat here, but I believe it is only a precursor to a full size army of devils on the horizon."

Tara showed her concern, "This attack alone has crippled the embassy's ability to help Ferrickport. Our plan was to round up as many survivors as possible and flee east. The first of the great Morkroth fortresses lies about twenty leagues east of here, but through the mountains. Without an operational port, I fear we will lose many, if even we can get out of the city. I have heard news that the city of Rosewood to the west fell to the devils already. Our chances are not great, but they beat holing up here and waiting for the hammer to fall."

With all of the information he had, Brell nodded his understanding. Her plan, although not sound, appeared to be the only plan.

"Have you coordinated with the city watch?" he asked, "We ran into a Captain Erris, but he and his men were isolated and trapped in an inn. They didn't make it."

Tara nodded, "No. Those creatures did a very good job of separating us from anyone. The embassy was hit at least a half dozen times. We encountered giant beetles that could breathe fire as well as devils that could make themselves invisible. Only after we were sure the embassy was secure did we start foraging out for survivors. I fear people are either too scared to come out, or worse, there are not enough left to save."

They waited in silence for a short time until Edge and Mark returned. The two brought with them a small sack and passed food from it to each in the room. Tristan found he had no appetite, and handed a small loaf of bread to his brother. He then just watched the others eat while he took in his surroundings. They were in a fairly large room. This was a shop that sold leather goods and rope. Straps, armor, and canvases hung from hooks and sat on shelves. Piled against the front door were a couple of tables and broken chairs. The group sat on work-stools and long benches. Curing and leatherworking tools hung on the wall behind the shop-owner's counter. He recognized a mallet, awl and edger. There was a sack beside them that probably contained other tools. Sadly, blood stains and splatters spelled out the fate of the previous defenders.

A strange light filtered into the window. It appeared to come from the north, out over the water. Brell and Tara went to the window and observed. The light was high in the sky and moved over the city out of their view. Even the heavy rain outside did not obscure it.

The pair quickly exited and jogged out onto a long wharf for a better view. Others trickled out of the shop and caught up. The sailors decided their cover was plenty good, and the light could only mean trouble, so they stayed behind.

The light continued its path further over the center of the city then stopped. It loitered high above, other motes of light began to dance around it.

Trazk let out a guttural warning and motioned for everyone to duck. The buzzing of wings alerted them to several hornets above that flew in the direction of the light. Devils chattered on their backs. Other Codrugon spawn came out of nearby buildings and broke into a run down the street, again in the direction of the mysterious light.

Lightning flashed and revealed a humanoid where the light was. "This is going to get good," Brell grinned.

Lancelot put his hand over his eyes to block the rain, "What is it? I couldn't see."

"Oh, they're in for it now. This is a rare sight. That, my friends, is a druid."

Almost in response to Brell, lightning and thunder played out a song of doom and death. Streaks of arcing energy sprang from the heavens. Tiny explosions in the sky indicated where hornets had been.

"You see, there are two kinds of druids in this world, neither of which you want to mess with. The first," he incorrectly stated, "are followers of Namrhyth, the god of balance between good and evil. They work the world politic. A bunch of kendrungian asses if you ask me, but powerful none-the-less."

Fire spat into the sky but could not reach the druid who rode higher on the wind. More lightning disintegrated even more hornets and their riders. The flashes though revealed there were a lot more than anyone thought.

"Now there is another kind of druid, much rarer. I have only seen one in my life in-fact. These are followers of Gaea herself. They harness great elemental power. They do not abide by intruders such as these devils infecting our home with their unnatural presence."

Something happened and the light dropped suddenly, almost halfway to the ground. Fire once again ignited the sky and engulfed the druid. It washed over him or her, and burned the clothes from their body, although no other apparent damage was inflicted.

For an instant, it appeared all of the rain in the city fell in the direction of the druid. Then crashing sounds heralded jets of waves and flooding further down the dock. The sea swallowed portions of Ferrickport. It looked localized now, but…

Tara suggested, "This might be a good diversion and time for us to leave the city."

Brell nodded in agreement, "Our path takes us across the sea, so we will continue our search on the docks. Gaylen light your way."

The two shook hands then the warriors from the embassy turned and sprinted off into the darkness.

Tristan went into the shop and let the sailors know of their decision to move on. Before he left, he collected the pouch with the leatherworking tools, then climbed out the window to catch up with the group.

Brell risked lighting a covered lantern. He wanted to increase their odds of finding a workable boat that could fit them all. As he surmised, they were unmolested while they combed the docks. The tide appeared to rise and swells crashed harder against the pilings and the shore.

"This can't be good," Brell decided.

A light suddenly appeared from the water and a voice called out, "Hello! Hello! If you can hear me, come out on the wharf! We have a boat!"

It took no goading and the entire group broke out into a sprint. The small rowboat was abandoned on the spot. Further down, they saw two large longboats. They were half-filled with rowers. A man stood on the front edge with a lantern up. "I saw your light! If you want out of here, you better hurry! Something is wrong in the water." He didn't yell the last, but everyone heard it. One of the longboats pulled up next to a pier down below the wharf. A short flight of stairs led down to where the boat waited. A loose rope connected a series of poles and formed a safety rail. Everyone had to use it as they hastily boarded.

The man directed, "Your gear will fit under your seats. Sit on it if you have to. If you are injured or cannot row, move to the front of the boat." Nobody did. "If you are not injured, sit facing me and grab an oar. You'll be needed. We must make haste."

As if they needed to be reminded, the water raised suddenly, and the second longboat careened toward them. It almost collided.

"Get that thing back to the ship! Go! Now!"

The other boat immediately changed direction. Men skillfully manned their rowing stations. The boat slid off into the darkness.

"Now get us back to the ship. There is no more saving to be had here." The man sat himself down at what was now the rear of the boat. Another, stronger man pushed off from the pier with a boat-hook to give the others room to row. First paddles, then oars went into the briny sea. The longboat picked up speed as it cut through the violent waves.

Tristan heard Will repeat to himself, "I can row." In sync to each forward motion of their oars.

Lightning struck more violently. It even hit some of the taller buildings. Back all along the dock, the tide cracked and splintered wood with each hammering wave.

Somewhere off in the distance, a voice was heard, "Lift anchor, I see them!" The man with the lantern slid a shutter and the light became a focused beam. It revealed a large ship that bobbed like a small toy in the ocean. It was the *Wind Charger*. Tristan was sure of it. Men were on the deck. They had just helped those from the other long boat to board. The boat was cast adrift. It would take too long to bring it up.

The men on Tristan's boat deftly brought them up against the ship. He didn't know why, but he was proud of the three sailors he had met, as if he didn't believe they had these skills. They worked with the other crew as if they had known them all their lives. Ropes were tossed down from above. Lem and an unfamiliar man secured the ropes to either side of their longboat. More ropes dropped. These had knots tied in them, and those in the boat, from front and back first climbed up to the main deck. Sailors there dragged each man aboard as he climbed to the outer rail. Some were dumped unceremoniously onto the deck. This was not about finesse though, but speed.

Tristan and Lancelot hit the main deck at the same time. Lancelot grinned from ear to ear. Lareth and Ardus followed, then two sailors. Last to climb over the rail were Brell and the lantern-man. The secured ropes were cut then dropped into the longboat and it was left to its demise. Tristan saw the fat captain as he stood in the rain. His tight maroon dinner jacket was flapped up and rain washed his giant exposed belly. Although a humorous sight, he was all business. Captain Graelgos knew exactly where his men should be and what they should do, He called to them and orchestrated the withdrawal of the *Wind Charger* from danger.

The rescued survivors stood by at first, amazed at the amount of activity that swelled on the main deck. Graelgos had to contend with torrential rain, darkness, and an ever-swelling tide that fought to drag the barque into the wharfs and rocks of Ferrickport. Brell thought to volunteer their services when a large wave covered the ship. Everyone lost their footing, and two sailors were washed overboard. A quick rescue attempt proved futile, and the crew was forced to abandon their fallen comrades and continue the struggle to get the *Wind Charger* safely away. Trazk led the group below decks. Royce, Lem, and Will stayed above and integrated themselves seamlessly into Graelgos' command. They took over the duties of the lost crew. Graelgos identified them by their hair color since he did not yet know their names.

Below, and inside the cabin reserved for them, they found everything had been stripped away to make room for as many people as possible. A large group had already been in here, evidenced by discarded, soaked-through blankets, used bloody bandages, and bits of vomit that could not be fully cleaned. It smelled most unwholesome.

Everyone stripped off their soaked outer lairs of clothing and tried to make themselves as comfortable as possible. The ship rocked and bucked. Water from somewhere else drained into the room from under the door. Tristan's head began to spin, and he put his hand to the wall. It only made it worse and he ejected the contents of his stomach in a spray. He tried to keep it in, but that only made it worse. He smelled the bread from the earlier meal. He dry heaved again. His younger brother, influenced by the sound his heaving gut made, also let loose his meal. Brell directed them both to a bucket that hung from the wall, "You should have told me you were sick. Hurry, in here….That's better." It wasn't.

Having nothing left to give to the bucket did not make things better for the boys. They had turned pale-white. All of the energy had drained from their bodies. The only respite came when they lay on the floor and just closed their eyes. Exhausted, they fell asleep.

The boys woke to conversation. Lareth and Brell talked with unfamiliar faces. "…don't know how many." It was a tall, raven-haired women who replied to some earlier, unheard question. The cabin now had four additional occupants. Everyone stood from the lack of room except for the brothers, who got up from the damp wood floor.

It must have been Lareth who asked, as he followed up with, "Well, do you know where they were dropped?"

The same woman replied, "I believe there was a Valencian merchant that took on the refugees. It gave the captain the needed room to come back and rescue you and me."

Lareth looked to Brell. They both nodded, probably agreeing that this was good news.

A shorter woman, hair rolled in buns, who was probably the sister of the taller, added, "We did see more ships, but were told they were war-ships. The captain wasn't sure if they were going to assist Ferrickport or settle some old scores with Morkroth. They made no effort to contact us when they sailed by.

Trazk noticed Tristan and Lancelot now stood awake, "Come with me boys. Let's get some fresh air and something in your bellies."

Tristan put his hand up to ward off any food, but Trazk just turned and left the cabin. They were compelled to follow. Topside, the clouds were only visible in the distance. A clean, cold wind washed across the deck. The smell of salt and brine refreshed their senses. Sailors busied about their responsibilities, but it was a calm busy. The captain was not on deck. *Wind Charger* fully had the wind in her sails and cut through the narrow sea, no land visible in any direction.

The boys took some time to absorb the sights and smells. Then, after they were sure they would not give it back up, they ate some hot frothy stew brought out by a halfling cook. The little man, skinny by halfling standards, let his light brown hair grow down to his shoulders, and had a matching beard, flecked with red. He wore black leather boots that went over his tan pants and up the lengths of his legs. He tapped his foot and waited there until the boys had tasted it. He would not leave without their opinion. Onions, carrots, potatoes and celery were mixed with just the right amount of beef and spices. The deep mmm's of satisfaction were what the tiny chef wanted to hear. "I have more if you're still hungry. Just ask for Charlie." With that, he disappeared through a door under a stair.

Trazk noted, "He likes kids, otherwise he would not have offered you seconds."

"I am nearly an adult," Tristan protested.

Trazk answered only with a shrug, and then turned and went below deck.

Tristan turned to his brother and asked, "I don't look like a kid, do I?"

Lancelot laughed, "I'm the one who should be offended. I know I'm shorter, but I don't have your red spots."

Tristan punched his brother in the arm, then turned to explore the deck of the ship. His brother was going to stay where he was, then thought better of it and followed. There was power behind the wind. They felt the *Wind Charger* force its way across the water. Tristan noted that they had never traveled this fast in their lives. They steered clear of the sailors and found their way around the perimeter of the ship, up to the large captain's wheel on the aft castle, then down below to explore the galley and cargo hold.

A day went by, then another. Exploring the ship grew stale. Moods soured. Brell, of everyone, was in the worst disposition. Captain Graelgos informed the group that he would not be able to take them to Valencia. He would take them north and west across the straight to Timbershaven. Brell protested, but the captain said that all, non-military, vessels would be subject to long waits, while others may be taken by the navy for military operations.

On the fourth day, the northern shores of the Strait of Kollune were spotted. Shortly after, the *Wind Charger* disgorged its passengers in Timbershaven's port. The sailors were off the boat first to secure supplies for whatever journey they would take after. The docks were small, and their ship could only be moored along the largest wharf.

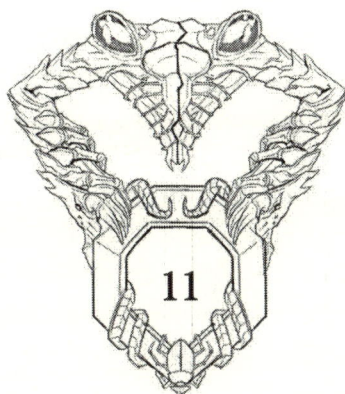

11

Timbershaven was by no means flat. It was built up a steep sloping hill, easily mistaken for a cliff. Wooden stairways snaked up between buildings and decks, all constructed out of the hillside. The shops and homes were hard to distinguish. All were whitewashed and had high steeple roofs. At the bottom of the town, the small warehouses and other buildings were built right on the water, secured by thick pilings and connected by wooden bridges and piers.

From any one location, you could not take in the whole town. Outcroppings of rock and thick stands of pine trees upset the line of sight. It gave it a quaint, secluded, if not creepy feel. Sounds around the wharf were no different than those in Ferrickport. The refugees filed off the ship. Captain Graelgos stood above and watched as they left. It didn't sit well with him to dump these people here, and it was obvious. He watched as they somberly marched to the end of the wharf and broke off in different directions.

Brell knew this place like the last, and after he directed another four refugees to the nearest inn, took a long flight of wooden stairs up to a large flat deck. Before them stood an indistinct building except for a sign with a picture of a seagull standing on a pile of snow and the establishment's name, 'The Frosty Gull'. Like the window shutters, the double doors to this establishment were painted green.

Inside, six or seven townspeople sat throughout the pub. It looked to be lunch time as everyone ate some bowl of this or that. The men wore conspicuous leather caps with bills over the front and back. Every one of them had a beard at least long enough to touch his chest without looking down.

The floors, counters, tables, and chairs were made of dark pine. There was little ornamentation inside except for two stuffed seagulls hanging behind the bar, near the kitchen door. A one-armed man worked behind the bar. His beard was disheveled and was the only hair on his face. He had a twisting scar on his upper lip where a mustache would be, underneath a nose that had been broken on more than one occasion. A lithe, curly-haired woman came out from the kitchen and helped the man with something and then returned to her duties in the other room.

Brell made eye contact with the man behind the bar and followed his gaze to empty tables off to the left. "Let's sit over there," he said. Thelband and Ardus were still with the group, and they all sat where he beckoned. The other patrons paid them little notice which Trazk took as a welcome change.

Lareth remarked, "I have never been to this town. It is rustic and quiet."

"Quiet here, by the water," Brell corrected. "Timbershaven is a lumber town. Further up the mountain above us, they work the trees into planks and other wood-stuffs and sell it to the nearby kingdoms. Now that can be quite noisy, day or night."

He continued to enlighten the group on the town's history, "There are no kings and princes here. They are led only by a mayor. Fiercely independent, Timbershavens like to avoid the politics of…well, of everywhere else. They keep their port small, one big ship at a time, and have an insignificant militia. They don't want to rouse any neighbors into thinking they want more than they have."

The curly-haired woman from the bar came back out during Brell's oration and stood behind him. She put her arms around his neck and reached around to kiss him on his cheek.

"I stand corrected," He sheepishly admitted, "There is one

princess in Timbershaven."

"Uncle Brell!" she exclaimed, "I am almost twenty and eight. You can't keep calling me princess in front of the patrons. It's embarrassing."

Brell stood to give her a proper hug and introductions after looking her up and down. He laughed and smiled. He had not shown this side of himself to the group. "Elle, these are my friends and traveling companions. Traveling companions and friends, this is my beautiful niece Elle. She is daughter to my sister Becca. That old wounded fart over there," he pointed to the man behind the bar, "is Samuel."

The man grinned, but it did not look pretty. Everyone waved, some with hesitation.

Brell sat back down and Elle plopped herself on his lap as if she were just a little girl. "Tell me of your adventures Baba."

The demon hunter turned pale. Trazk repeated, "Baba?"

Elle laughed. "Oh, I'm sorry Uncle Baba. I didn't know that was not your traveling name." She laughed again and then leapt from his lap. "I'll just go and fetch some drinks, then I'll get started on something to eat." She went through the motions of mentally counting the seats around the two tables.

Brell quickly changed the subject, "Elle is a great cook."

Everyone else just stared at him, then the whole room broke out in laughter. Some patrons overheard and laughed. Some had no clue, but laughed all the same.

Soon after, a minstrel found his way into the Frosty Gull. The rest of the afternoon was spent singing, eating, drinking, and catching up. Samuel was not as scary as he looked. It was obvious Brell was very fond of him, and in-fact, they had fought together in the Darsican wars. Samuel had lost his arm, and a mace had nearly cratered his face in that ill-fated war. The group also learned that Brell and his sister were born in Timbershaven. Fate took his sister Becca almost a dozen winters ago to sickness. Elle pointed out that Brell had not always been an agent of the church. He and his father had built the Frosty Gull when the demon hunter had not yet joined the church on his holy calling. She loved that her father took over the place after grandpa died and has happily helped him since.

The latter half of the evening was spent describing what was going on across the sea and what was going to happen from here. Someone had summoned the mayor to come and hear of the devil incursion and what that may mean to the town. The mayor insightfully decided that ship-building was going to become very popular. He ordered some of his underlings to start the planning and then thanked Brell for coming here to warn them.

Brell spent a good amount of time entertaining people he had known in his past life. They were very cordial and forthcoming with things they knew about the area. The most important information involved Dellan, the vampire. Grewell, a wood merchant, had tried to visit Galagburg, a hamlet three days north. He was turned away by another traveler who warned him that a local lord named Dellan terrorized the region, and that he had an army on the march.

Ardus and Thelband showed little surprise that they were talking about vampires and devils. The halfling offered, "Ardus and I would like to continue with you, wherever it may lead us. We are now homeless, and this problem is not going to go away without someone doing something about it."

Brell worried, "Do you understand the danger that we are facing here? This is not a decision to make lightly. Have you the skills to keep yourself alive should you find yourself alone with the enemy?"

Thelband assured the group that he, like most halflings, was perfectly capable. When the others looked to the butcher, Ardus just shrugged, "Give me a sword and shield, and I'll have your back." He was big, and the statement was hard to refute.

Everyone nodded a silent agreement, and Brell shook both of their hands, "Welcome to the fold."

The group discussed their options. "Lareth, it looks as if your suspicions about a connection might have foundation," Brell conceded.

Trazk added, "The army could be insects. I would bet a dozen human teeth on that..." He looked up a little embarrassed, "I, um mean halfling teeth."

Irritated, Thelband corrected, "Try again."

"Argh. You know what I mean. They are connected," the orc said with finality.

Tristan asked, "Are we still going to try for the Great Library? Do we even have time now?"

It was Brell's turn to look annoyed. "Good observation Tristan. It looks like we have gained some good information that puts us in a bad spot. On the one hand, it is in our best interest to journey to the library. There, we may find all the answers we need to prepare for a confrontation with a mature vampire. And by mature, I mean powerful. On the other hand, if Dellan is indeed working with the devils, then we have no time. We have to face him now before another series of towns are overrun."

"Do you think they are coming through gates?" Lareth quizzed, "If so, do they have more than one? And if that, what is to stop them from popping up anywhere and everywhere?"

Brell let his fingers play with his beard. "Hmmm…again, another good observation. Gates are very difficult to open. I mean very. There is a lot of preparation that goes into creating them and preparing the way for those who would come through. I have to think, if there were more than one gate, they would not be opening it in such a backwoods place as this. No, you open something like that in a city where your hordes don't have to walk a fortnight to encounter resistance, and more importantly your goal.

"I think…" he continued, "I think that this is either an over exaggerated army, if it is indeed devils, and that they may just be more scouts. We would have to deal with them regardless, as they are very dangerous. But, on to your other point Lareth. Let's go off my assumption that there is a gate and it could only be one gate. That means there IS a gate somewhere, and it needs to be closed. We have been running so much, we didn't stop to think, and maybe we can do something about it."

Trazk looked around then added, "Or we can ring the vampire's neck and make him talk. He is probably connected, so he probably knows what we can do to stop his friends."

It was agreed. A little more planning, and they decided they would leave tomorrow for Galagburg. They were going to fight a vampire.

At first sun-up, Brell took Ardus and Thelband to get outfitted. Elle convinced him to leave Tristan and Lancelot with her. She wanted to fill them up before they set out, or at least that is what she claimed. Lancelot was happy to be off his feet. Brell liked to talk, but he liked to walk more. Trazk had been gone by the time everyone woke. Only Lareth loitered for a bit. Even he decided he had something to do and asked Samuel for some directions then disappeared.

When she brought the first bowl of hot oats and honey, Elle innocently asked, "Do you really think you should travel with Uncle Brell and the others? They have many years of experience, and there is only danger and death where they are going."

Lancelot tried to figure out a way he could sound brave before answering. Tristan sighed and fielded her question, "We understand the dangers. We do. And we are scared."

"I'm not," his brother said with certainty that showed uncertainty.

Tristan hit him in the arm then continued, "But this world is changing. We lost our family before we even knew they were gone. When I am with Brell and Trazk, I see hope and I feel safe, even amongst the fighting and danger. But they can't fight this evil alone, and they certainly can't fight it forever. They have both said we have potential. I don't want to sit around hiding all my life, waiting for the things in the dark to take me away from those I love. I want to face them. I want to beat them."

"Me too," Lancelot joined in.

Elle looked on both of them with a little pity and a lot of worry. "But it takes years of training to be as skilled as either of them. I know a few things. Maybe you can stay with me a while. My father and I will teach you all the basics. When my uncle returns from killing the vampire, which he will, I promise, maybe you can travel with him on less dangerous journeys?"

Lancelot looked dejected. He had heard this kind of talk from his mother. Tristan though, looked suspicious. "Did Brell put you up to this?" he asked through narrowed eyes.

Elle looked both surprised and embarrassed. "No. Of course not. He does think of you boys as family, and so do I. We want what is best for you."

"I'm not buying it," Tristan scolded. "You want to train us? I think you have about an hour."

Samuel laughed. He walked around the counter to the boys and stuck out his one good hand. "Offer accepted." Both boys shook on it.

The first thing the ex-soldier taught the boys was how to stand. Both had an awkward, 'want to run away' way of placing their feet. "A good soldier stands to meet his foe, both with balance, and intelligence. Watch. If I turn sideways and plant my feet like this, I not only make myself less of a target, it also keeps my balance in relation to my foe, and my sword arm is all ready to deliver the hardest impact." He made both the boys mimic his stance and take some practice swings.

Next, he showed them how to drive a foe back. "Look how my swing has given me the momentum to bring my foot forward, and with a backswing and movement like this…" he followed up his backswing by bringing his other foot forward, "I can keep my foe on his toes, drive him back, and deliver the most swings."

Elle brought out three bucklers. She strapped one to her father's arm. Then she helped the two brothers to strap and hold theirs properly.

"A good shield, especially a buckler," Samuel continued, "is an excellent versatile tool. It does not get in your way, can be used for defense, and can be used to strike a foe. Look at this strong backhand motion. Even with little momentum, I can use it to smack my enemy in the face. When you use a bow or crossbow, it can still be worn, and will do little to disturb your shot, especially if you practice with it."

While they trained with their wooden swords and bucklers, Elle studied the boys' swords given to them by Brell back at his home. She found something curious about the gems, and how the swords hummed when she held them both in her hands at the same time. Lancelot spied her use some sort of magics while she sat there behind the counter.

An hour went by and both boys sweat profusely from the exercises they were put through. The barkeep was just showing them some side-step maneuvers when Brell and company returned.

The demon hunter looked on at what had unfolded, annoyance written all over his face. He looked first to Samuel, who either didn't notice him, or chose not to, and then to Elle. She made eye contact and then quickly turned her focus to the swords. He walked straight to her and gruffly whispered words of displeasure. They moved what was to be a heated argument to the back-room.

Tristan and Lancelot stopped practicing as Ardus walked in the door. He was unrecognizable. Head to toe, the giant man was encased in brightly polished plate armor with dark blue details. He carried a large, steel shield on his left arm. It was insignificant in his grasp. His head was shrouded by a helmet with its face-plate down, crafted to look like a bear's snarling face. Strapped to his belt was a long, broad sword in its sheath. In his right hand, he carried a thick hafted spear. It was tipped by a twin-fork, barbs at the ends, like double-fish-hooks. On his back was attached the largest two-handed hammer that anyone could have seen or made.

Thelband Highfellow trailed in after Ardus. He was not nearly as conspicuous, although that might have been the idea. The halfling wore black leathers from top to bottom. Even his belt and pouches were stained a deep charcoal. Strapped on either side of his belt were two daggers. Around his neck was a dark colored kerchief. Thelband's step was noticeably bolder than before.

After he knew his appearance had the desired effect, Ardus pulled his helmet and shield off and placed them on a table, then took a seat. Thelband sat down beside him. "Barkeep, a drink for my thirsty warrior friend and me. We are in need of sustenance before our big adventure."

Samuel laughed as he poured them his darkest brew, "Well, in your case, you mean little adventure don't you?"

"Har har. Those jokes do get old, you know?"

"Of course they do, little master. But not to me." Samuel placed the drinks before his new friends. "On the house, of course."

"Well, if you are trying to buy my silence with free drinks, it worked." The halfling took a long drag on his ale.

Tristan was at the table too. He studied the helmet that his head would certainly bang around in were he to put it on. "What made you choose a bear face?"

"It was the only helmet I could fit my head into," Ardus answered with amusement. "I wanted a skull mask to scare my enemy, but it squeezed my ears and nose."

Tristan looked at him, then the helmet, then back to him. "I don't think you need the skull to look the part."

Unintelligible arguing persisted from the kitchen.

It was Lancelot's turn to ask a question, "Is it hard to walk in all that armor?"

Ardus laughed, "To be honest, I am, or was used to wearing a lot less armor. I have not fought in a long, long time. I think I could use the extra protection so I can make a few mistakes while I get back in form. It's not too heavy, but I won't be jumping around in combat. That is certain."

Tristan and Lancelot got back up and practiced their newly learned stances together. Samuel yelled out corrections from behind the bar. Other patrons, who had now filtered into the tavern sat and watched while they ate or nursed their early morning medicine.

An hour passed. The arguing in the back had died down to a low droning. At one point Elle came back out and grabbed the boys' two swords, then turned back into the kitchen. Trazk returned from his mysterious duties. It did not appear he had done any shopping. He had no extra gear with him.

He sat down at the table with Ardus and Thelband, and watched the boys curiously. "Tristan, come over here." Tristan did as commanded. "I know it's a hard nut to swallow, but are you taking the news okay?"

"What news?" Tristan asked.

"About not going with us?"

Tristan grew angry and was about to chastise the orc when Brell came in, "They are going with us."

"But I thought we decided…" The orc cut himself off and looked guiltily at Tristan.

The older brother became red with anger. "Thanks for your confidence!" It was the only thing he could think of.

Brell salvaged the orc's embarrassment, "Somehow, these boys have Elle and Samuel on their side. They won't take no for an answer."

Lancelot tried to put on an angry face, and nodded his agreement.

"The best we can hope for is that they will prove useful on our perilous task."

Trazk shook his head, "But…"

Tristan cut him off, "But nothing. You got me and my brother into this mess. You are not going to discard us now. You are stuck with us. And I was told never to leave your side. So you are double stuck with me!" He wanted to storm out, but just stood there and stared down the orc.

Brell cut the tension with a laugh. "Ornery." He ran his hand through Tristan's hair and then shook his head about. It eased the boy's anger. "Go in back," he commanded. "Elle wants to talk to you. Both of you." The boys, used to orders now, did as he said.

The kitchen was large, about half the size of the dining area. Two long tables stretched down the center. The far wall was lined with shelves from floor to ceiling, stocked with innumerable spices, sacks, jars, and books. To the left of the entrance, against the wall that divided the cooking area from the sitting area, two large stoves remained heated. A large pot sat on the wider of them. Utensils hung from the wall above the stove. Even more hung from the ceiling over the tables.

One table had various cooking ingredients and dishes. The other, Elle sat at with the two swords. She beckoned for the boys to take seats opposite her. Stools were tucked under the table for easy access and to keep the isle clear when someone was busy back here with cooking.

"Meet Grace and Hope," Elle said as they were seated. Both boys looked thoroughly confused. "That's their names."

"Girl names?" Lancelot asked.

"They are feminine swords, so yes."

"What? We are using girl swords?" he said distastefully.

"Don't be so quick to discard them. They like you." She smiled.

"This is getting weird," Tristan chimed in.

"Let me remove your doubts and fears about these swords. Listen to what I have to say, then decide if you think you can handle them." Elle squinted her eyes at the boys in mock annoyance.

"These swords are sentient, they have souls. In fact, like you, they are siblings. They were born together and have traveled together all of their lives."

"How do you know this?" Lancelot looked like he didn't believe her.

"They told me so, and they can tell you too, if you would only listen. Hope is the longer one, and she was the first one forged by her father, many hundreds of moons ago. Grace came shortly after, made from the same enchanted metals from a long-forgotten source."

Elle picked Hope up and tilted the sword downward so the boys could see the blade. These three emeralds represent their connection to one-another..."

"Why are there three?" Tristan asked before she could continue.

"There was a third blade made, but it was separated from these two long ago. The sisters have called out to it, but have not heard a response."

She slid her index finger down the middle of the blade over the golden runes. "These are runes of invoking, to be used by the wielder of the blade. They are the same for both sisters."

Lancelot squirmed at all of the female references. He was trying to understand.

Elle continued, "The four runes are *Pel*, *Mora*, *Fin*, and *Mira*. You need only invoke them while wielding the blade to gain their benefit. *Pel* means protection. *Mora* is strength. *Fin* is to find. And *Mira* is for agility."

Lancelot, the angry curious one, asked, "You mean if I say

Mora, I will become stronger?"

"Yes. The rune will glow for a short time, activated. You will gain strength for the time that it is glowing, and then it will need to rest. I don't know how long before you could use it again, but the more you exert, the longer between uses. That is all I gathered. Each rune works the same way."

"What is find?" Tristan was also curious.

"*Fin. Fin* is to find. If you say find, nothing will happen. Hold the blade and utter *Fin* and you will know the location of the other sword owner. I believe if the other blade is being held, you can even communicate with him or her."

Lancelot did not give her a chance to continue. He snatched up Grace and bolted for the door. His face could not hide his enthusiasm. "Wait a minute and then find me!" He was gone in the next instant.

Tristan looked to Elle.

"Go ahead," She said with a pleasant smile.

Tristan counted to thirty aloud then gripped Hope. "*Find*....er *Fin.*" He rolled his eyes at his mistake while the sword rune glowed a dim white. His face quickly changed to shock and then determination. "He is outside. Are you outside?"

"*I am behind the tavern,*" his brother's voice revealed in his mind.

"He is in my head talking," Tristan explained to Elle excitedly. He ran out the door.

Tristan found his brother hiding exactly where he was told, and even better, exactly where Tristan had pictured him being. They talked to each other for a minute through the swords. Elle came out to check on them. Lancelot handed her Grace while the runes still glowed. Elle was able to immediately communicate with Tristan. They all laughed together at this shared moment, then went back inside. As Tristan showed Brell his sword, the rune light faded out and the gold turned silver. "Hmm," the boy pondered out loud, "I think we can't use the rune again until it turns gold."

Lareth announced, "I spoke with the mayor and was gifted horses and two carts. He said the road out of Timbershaven had not quite washed out from the rains, so it should be a manageable journey to Galagburg."

Brell divided up money into pouches, and passed them out to each of the group, including the two boys. He gave them disapproving looks as he placed a pouch in each of their hands, then a smile.

"Let's ride," the demon hunter said with aplomb. He hugged his niece and brother-in-law, and then led the way out of the Frosty Gull.

Lancelot ran over and gave Elle a hug too. "Thank you for everything. Especially with the swords, even if they are girl swords. How did you do all of that stuff with them? How do you know magic?"

"Having a rich uncle to pay for the best schooling has its advantages," she replied. "Good luck on your journey young demon slayer." She held him tight and for more than just a moment. "Look after my uncle please. He is the only one I have. And thank you for bringing him home to me. I missed him dearly."

Lancelot teared-up, but wiped them away so Elle did not see. Samuel did though, walked over, and gave him a big hug too. "You are brave young sir. But it is okay to be afraid. It keeps you on your toes. Don't ever let it beat you and you can use it to your advantage." He then held him at arm's reach by one of his shoulders and said, "Tialar be with you, son of Sarauna."

"Did you know my mother?" Lancelot was shocked.

Samuel only smiled and put his arm around his daughter's shoulders as they watched Tristan hurry his brother out the door.

The group was already far ahead up the stairs. Tristan and Lancelot ran up after them. When they reached the top, they were out of breath. From where they stood, they looked out over the sea. Small specks, which Brell pointed out as ships, moved slowly from west to east on the water.

Behind them, a little further up the hill, the horses and wagons waited.

Tristan was impressed. There were enough horses for everyone to ride. Trazk opted to drive the wagon Ardus rode in. Ardus was too big and heavy to be on these horses, and Trazk knew how to handle a wagon.

Thelband drove the second wagon and had three additional mares tethered to follow behind. Each of the wagons were filled with barrels of water, dried foodstuffs, blankets, and other equipment and tools.

All of the horses that were not pulling the carts were saddled and ready to ride.

"I guess I should have asked earlier, can you boys ride?" Brell addressed the late-comers.

Tristan answered while Lancelot nodded affirmation, "We lived on a farm and had plenty of occasion to ride."

"Good. Get on."

Everyone with a horse mounted up, and Brell led them north out of Timbershaven.

12

A light fog conspired to mask the way to Galagburg. There was a dirt road that led away from the coastal town, well maintained and used by the lumbermen who worked nearby. Small trenches were cut alongside the road and lined with small rocks to drain the frequent rains and occasional snow melt. The trees grew almost right up to the road and there was just a thin view of the fog-laden sky above.

Brell and Lancelot rode abreast in front of the first wagon. Tristan trailed behind the second. Trazk made the older boy ride with his bow out. Both knew he could not use it from horseback, but the orc wanted him to become familiar with its feel. Training would come soon enough.

Sounds of axes on trunk, trees falling, and men yelling to each other permeated the wood. It dominated the conversations in the group, something other than the gloom of what was to come. Brell admitted that he almost devoted his life to lumber cutting.

Three times on the first day of their journey, they ran into tradesmen who brought their cut lumber back to town. The first encounter, Brell was ready to divert the group off the road, but the ditches were too steep for the wagon-wheels. He just watched helplessly as the wood-cutter reared up. The man rode with two younger men, probably his sons. They waved and jumped out of their cart. The two boys each pulled a plank from the back and laid them diagonal from the road, across a ditch, into the grassy dirt on the other side. Their father deftly guided the horses and his cart across. Once the way was clear, he waved Brell's group by.

Brell rode up next to the man. They conversed for a minute and then the demon slayer reached into his pouch and paid the man some coins. He waved over Tristan and Lancelot to help him move two planks from the tradesman's wagon to one of their own.

"He says it is generally the courtesy of the north-facing travelers to give right of way to the lumbermen bringing the good back to town," Brell educated the group, "I should have remembered. It has been so long."

The planks worked like a charm the second and third time they met wagons of lumber. The lumbermen showed their appreciation with waves and nods.

Throughout the ride, they intersected several paths that led off to the left or right. Brell explained that many of the townspeople lived out here for convenience, seclusion or both. The lumbermen operated large machines in or near their homesteads that could be used to split the logs and cut planks.

Night crept up on the companions faster than they anticipated or wished. They steered the carts off the road, unhooked the horses, and tethered all of the animals to a thick pine. Lareth pulled a dozen thin, wooden poles from a cart and set them in rings secured around the wagon's walls. A leather canvas, with pre-sewn hooks looped over the poles and created a roof over the carts. Trazk and Lancelot set up a campfire between the two carts that had been parked to form a 'V'.

"Let's pair up for watches. I don't want to spend too long, so I suggest we sleep six hours and take two-hour watches? Everyone agreed. Ardus took the first watch by himself. The night passed uneventful and the group was awakened to the sounds of axes chopping trees.

Ardus cooked the group some boiled pork and potatoes for breakfast. It tasted very bland, but hot food more than made up. The wagons and horses were inspected for damage or injury, and the group mounted up into the familiar column from the day before.

The fog returned, and a chill frost on the ground heralded colder weather to come. That morning, everyone kept a blanket wrapped around them while they rode, save Trazk who 'didn't need such things'.

The sounds of the lumbermen diminished as did the frequency of side-tracks the further north they moved into the wood. The road veered west and they found that they were tracking into low foot-hills with very gentle slopes. It wasn't until late in the afternoon that the fog finally left them alone. The thick trees did not reveal any more than the fog had. The sun was missed as it sailed overhead, and the shadows from the late afternoon laid long in their path.

Camp the second night was similar to the first, except that wolf howls replaced the sounds of woodsman axes. The horses remained skittish throughout the night, and Lancelot awoke to find they had been moved to within the limited protection of the wagon 'V' while he slept. During both nights, the boys had been paired up with their respective trainer. They spent time learning about their new craft, and discussed with each other what they had learned over breakfast. While the adults packed the gear, they were given some time to practice what Samuel had taught them.

Throughout the day, Tristan and Lancelot fiddled with Hope and Grace and used the *Fin* rune as often as they could. The swords only required about ten minutes of rest to give five minutes of mental communication. Lancelot even discovered that if he held Grace and focused on Hope, he could tell its location without activating the rune. They also found they could double the time communicating because one could activate a rune for the roughly five minutes, and then the other could activate his rune.

"*Look at Trazk. I think he is asleep,*" Lancelot channeled his thoughts to Tristan.

Tristan replied the same way, "*Don't be so sure. I think he does that on purpose. He cocks his head like that when he first sits down to sleep. And did you ever notice, he doesn't lay down? He is always sitting when he sleeps.*" The thought was barely audible. They had expended their time for this chat. Tristan rode up next to Trazk. He received a shifty, eyes-kind-of-closed look. That made him laugh and he fell back in line.

A woman's scream jolted all of them out of complacency and almost out of their saddles.

Brell instinctively looked back to make sure they were all there and unmolested. Trazk already had his bow in hand and scanned what little horizon he could.

A second scream, this time from a younger girl, materialized from somewhere off to their left, ahead.

Thelband rolled off of his seat to the ground. He sprinted off toward the shriek. Brell tried to stay him, "Wait!" It didn't.

"Stay close," he commanded to Lancelot and the pair rode after Thelband. The halfling had the advantage even with his short legs. Branches whipped and slapped the two riders and forced them to slower than a trot. Thelband only need avoid the trees' trunks. Whimpering came from ahead. They went the right direction.

A clearing opened up. The scene was grim. Three grey wolves fought over the remains of a human. A fourth circled Thelband. It limped with a dagger in its foreleg. Behind all of them, a large, black-furred wolf stood on its hind legs. It stood more like a man than a beast. Its muscular arms ended in deadly claws which it used to rip the arm from a woman who had just lifted a child into a tree. Her golden dress stained dark as she bled out.

The hungry wolves noticed new prey when they heard the two panicked horses enter the glade. Brell and Lancelot dismounted with weapons at the ready.

Dagger wolf lunged at Thelband. The halfling dodged one way and slashed the snout of the snarling beast. It retreated in pain and continued its circling.

Brell slapped his horse on its flank, and the two mounts fled back the way they had come. Three wolves, hate in their eyes, moved to encircle the demon slayers. Lancelot instinctively tightened his grip on Grace. He felt her grow warm in his hand. *"Pel Mira,"* He sensed her instruct him. He did not know but he mouthed the words from her thoughts. Two runes glowed bright.

The wolves pounced. One at Brell, two at his smaller companion. Brell's wolf used a controlled lunge to force him off balance. He didn't budge. Then the large wolf chose to dive at his legs. Brell drove both force swords down through its skull. It did not even yelp before it died.

Lancelot crouched as the two beasts sprang. The first went high. The boy's back arched and twisted. The wolf missed and only caught the backswing of Grace. Its leg severed at the knee. The second wolf went low. Its bite found an ankle and dragged Lancelot to the ground. It shook violently at first. He screamed out. Then the ravenous canine pulled him back toward its other kill. The pain was immense, but Lancelot did not lose sight of his target. He bucked and swung. His sword found the tip of the wolf's nose and pieces flew from its face. The dog let go and sprang back with a growl.

Lareth and Ardus arrived. The man-wolf's attention was now on the new group. It loped toward them. Its front claws dragged on the ground, but it didn't use them for locomotion.

Ardus moved between Thelband and his wolf. When the wolf did not charge him, he charged it. Snapping jaws were met with a steel gauntlet and bits of wolf teeth scattered from its face. The butcher's other hand grasped the wolf by the neck. The creature's body convulsed and it tried to loosen his grasp. Ardus squeezed, drew his sword and thrust it through the wolf's stomach. It went limp and Ardus tossed it aside.

The bipedal wolf howled at the death of its comrades. Its nostrils flared and eyes shone red. It was focused on Ardus, for he was the last to kill a wolf. Ardus' attention was not fully on the beast. It sprung into the air at him. In an instant, a dagger pierced its hide, through the breast. Simultaneously, Lareth slammed into it from the side. Both went down in a tangled heap.

Claws gripped the young priest and he had no good space to strike with his mace. Lareth did everything he could to hold and squeeze the snarling monster. It was too easy for the wolf man to twist in his grasp and it brought its gaping jaws down on armored shoulders. Straps, flesh and sinew snapped under the vice-like bite. Lareth screamed out in agony.

An arrow pierced the high sloping back of the bipedal wolf. It winced, but did not let go of its prey. Then a glowing purple blade cut deep into its side. The creature gave up its bite and rolled away, flesh encrusted bloody teeth bared against the demon hunter.

"Silver!" Lareth cried between pained breaths. "Use silver!"

Brell moved to strike the beast again. It made one last lunge at Lareth but the purple sword came down hard on its left arm and severed it mid-bicep. The wolf-man howled in pain and ran off into the wood, faster than a horse.

The demon hunter immediately administered to the priest before he bled out.

The last visible wolf took two arrows, and the sight of Ardus baring down on it intimidated it enough that it ran off with its tail between its legs. The wolf with the missing leg had already managed to slink off. Trazk followed to make sure none would return.

Lancelot raced to help Ardus with Lareth. It was then that he realized the wound on his leg was completely healed. It had closed on its own while he and his wolf had circled for openings in the other's defense. It felt tender, but did not hurt. Only his pants were ripped.

Lareth wheezed, "Help the little ones. I'll be fine when I have caught my breath. Your magics have stopped the bleeding."

There was a boy and girl who still climbed in the branches and who had watched on in horror as the combat unfolded. They cried but were grateful as Brell coaxed and then lifted them down from the tree. Unfortunately, it was their mom and dad who lay dead in the clearing. The mom had sacrificed herself for their safety.

The children described how the chilling encounter started.

The boy started, "Pa told us that our home wouldn't be safe no more be'in there was a madman takin over."

His sister helped between sobs, "We were traveling on the road with my daddy's wagon and our ponies, Sara and Rose." She was too frightened to continue.

Her brother finished, "The large wolf attacked us with a whole pack of smaller ones, but they was just as vicious and mad. Rose and Sara was trapped while those monsters ate 'em." He paused and almost lost it as he thought back on it.

"Go on," Brell urged. He had his arms around the kids to give them safety.

"Pa yelled out it was our only chance to get away, so we jumped down and ran for our lives. I heard the big wolf yell 'No!', and it and some of the smaller wolves chased us down to here. They were so fast and mad."

"That's enough," the demon hunter whispered. "We will take you home. Do you have any relatives where you live?"

The girl answered, "Only Aunt Sara, but she is mean."

"Where does your aunt live?"

"In Galagburg," the boy responded, "Not too far from our house."

"Okay. Let's get you back there. The roads are not safe, especially with these wolves roaming around," Brell spoke softly and he empathetically held the children to assuage their fears. They went back with the group. They would not let go of Brell's hands until they were safely in a wagon, hiding under some blankets next to Ardus.

Tristan waited with trepidation for their return. "Is everything okay? There was a lot a screaming over there." He blanched when he saw his brother's ripped pants and then Lareth's bloody tunic and shoulder.

"They are fine, but we need to get these kids home and ourselves out of danger." Brell already directed the line forward.

Tristan looked around then asked "Where is Trazk? Is he okay?"

Ardus answered from the back of the wagon that Lareth now drove, "He took off into the wood. I think he can handle himself."

Lancelot rode down one side of the line and up the other to make a quick welfare check on both the group and the wagon-wheels. It would be a terrible time for a mishap. When satisfied, he returned to the front alongside his trainer. Brell and Lancelot rode two of the extra mares. The two they had ridden into combat on never found their way back.

The road bent slightly to the left. Ahead, the carnage of the family wagon came into view. The wolves were no longer there, but the guts and detritus of the fallen ponies painted a picture of what had clearly happened. They stopped to clear the wagon off the road. When Lareth saw how much of the family belongings were within, he made the argument that it should be brought back for the children. As quick as they could, Brell and Lareth hooked up Tristan and Lancelot's mounts to the forward wagon. Tristan volunteered to drive it, and he and his brother jumped in. The caravan crept forward again toward Galagburg.

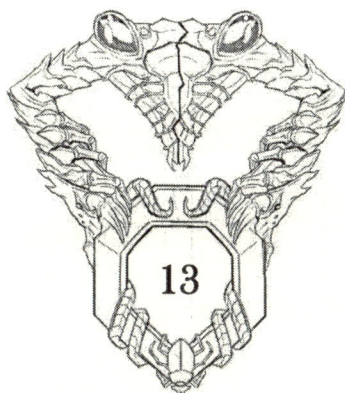

13

It was a long two hour ride. Nobody spoke. Worry highlighted every brow. The children whimpered under the blanket, and all Ardus could do was lay a gentle hand on each. Three riders in the Red and Black colors of Galagburg rode out from the town to meet them. On the tip of one spear, a pennant with a tower aflame fluttered above the riders.

"Have you injured?" the lead man yelled forward before the riders had caught up. They slowed at Brell's raised hand, then stopped before the caravan. Upon seeing Lareth, he asked again, "Have you injured? It appears you have been through a lot by the looks of your driver there."

"Wolves." Brell's admission told the men everything they expected to hear.

The soldiers rode alongside Brell and led the group through the main street of Galagburg. A large gaggle of citizens crowded the road but parted as they drove past. The lead soldier tried to add insight to Brell's account, "The wolves have become a big problem of recent."

"That is an understatement. It pains me to say, but we came across some of your people back in the woods. A family. The mother and father were slaughtered, but we managed to bring back their children unharmed. I'm sorry, but I didn't get their names."

The man perked up. Surprise, and then sorrow played across his face. "You must have Lensa and Bjorn. This is very sad. They only just left town."

A second soldier added, "It is true then. We cannot leave, even if we wanted to."

Brell found that comment curious, but kept it to himself.

Overcast skies and trickles of ground-hugging fog magnified the gloom that penetrated the town's atmosphere. Like Timbershaven, Galagburg's buildings had steeple roofs. The similarities ended there. Black tarred roofs sat over gray-painted wood structures. The roads were muddy from the week's rain, and large puddles obstructed pathways through the town.

The people who walked through the streets were quiet and morose. Their attire reflected the general attitude of the town, and many wore gray, brown, or black cloaks and shirts over even more drab and worn pants. A small number of soldiers kept their appearances clean and professional, but the majority wore used and irregularly fitted uniforms. Brell wondered if there was a rash of conscriptions.

His suspicions were confirmed when a foppish-looking overweight man, gussied up with wooden shoes and a ruffle sleeved azure shirt, stepped out before their caravan. What little grey hair the man had was greased over an odd, egg shaped head devoid of half of his lower teeth. "Greeetings." The man bowed awkwardly. "I am Mayor Silas Bettencourt. I see you have met members of our newly formed *Guard de' Force*. Galagburg welcomes you. Please enjoy the hospitality and safety of our town."

The man sidled up to Brell and placed a hand on the demon-hunters tan tarpan so he could walk with his neck crooked up. The caravan started slowly down the street again. "Are you traders? Have you come here with business? I can assure you that Galagburg is very safe."

It was hard not to laugh at how hard Silas tried to cover for the fear and danger that permeated the town. "We are here on business of a personal nature. We could use accommodations for ourselves and our horses if you would be so kind as to point them out."

"Oh." The Mayor was dejected. "Yes," he said with far less enthusiasm, "we have an inn and stable. You can stay there. It's the Bear Trap Inn and Barn. I am sure one of these fine soldiers can lead the way."

The youngest of the soldiers leaned down to whisper, but if it was a secret, Brell heard it plainly, "These folks here saved the Winthrop kids from wolves, sir. Might'n be the wolves are running with the Beast." The mayor nervously looked up at Brell and then back at his companions as the soldier continued, "They say Emily and Rork were killed. Bjorn and his sister are in the back wagon."

The mayor looked back to Brell again, "Oh, um, well...As you may have heard, um, we have a problem with wolves. It is important that we look over young Bjorn and Lensa Winthrop."

Brell tried to assuage the Mayor's worries, "Our priest looked the children over. They had little more than bumps and scratches. Shock and loss are what they need recovery from."

"Yes, um, well...I will need to speak with them. I want to send out some hunters right away to deal with um, these, um wolves."

Nobody mentioned the wolf-man, but Brell knew it was on the Mayor's mind. He wasn't sure yet why the Mayor did not reveal it.

They took a side-road and quickly found themselves in front of the inn with the stables. Mayor Silas gave an excuse to leave and asked a soldier to escort the children to his house so he could figure out what to do with them.

Lensa was wrapped around Ardus and would not let him leave her side. She cried and would not go with the soldiers, not without Ardus. He warmly obliged her, "I will go with them to see the mayor." The hulking warrior had become her comforter. Ardus picked her up and stepped out of the cart. He walked down the street after the soldiers. Lensa was on his waist and Bjorn tightly held his hand.

"Ardus will do right by them. He is a good man." Thelband did not need to explain.

Brell nodded both his approval and agreement before he addressed the more mundane matters, "Okay. I'll get us some rooms. Can you all please bring the gear in? We don't need it left in the rain, or worse, ransacked by wolves."

Tristan, Lancelot and Thelband unloaded the carts. Lareth went around the side to get the horses stabled.

The Bear Trap Inn was a spacious hall with thick wooden posts that supported the rooms on the floor above. The dining area looked all the bigger by the lack of people and furniture. Two small tables and thrice as many chairs were situated near the bar. Brell sat at one of the tables and watched the others finish. When the gear was in the front, he beckoned for them where a pitcher of milk and sliced cheese waited to be ravenously consumed.

"What?" Thelband asked. "No ale?"

Brell smiled, "This is better for you. But if it's ale you want," he thumbed to the bar, "then Edrigar can get you one."

The halfling eyed the demon slayer suspiciously, but drank the milk anyway.

"So, this is the life of adventure boys," Brell directed at the brothers, "We travel from one inn and tavern to the next. Death is our mistress and loneliness often our companion. Our days and sometime weeks are littered with boredom followed by intense negotiations or battles. You sure this is what you want to sign up for?"

Lancelot laughed. His older brother nearly choked on some cheese and coughed out, "Is that all you've got?" He cleared his throat with a glass of milk, a little sour for his taste, "We are stuck to you like this town's mud on my damn boot." He tried to rub it off on Lancelot's leg under the table.

Lancelot jerked back and up out of his chair. It caught everyone else off guard. Tristan finally got his laugh out. Both boys received shifty-eyed looks from the other three.

Lareth brought them back to the here-and-now, "How long do you think Trazk will be?"

"It depends if he was trying to lead the wolves away from us or if he's hunting them. I suspect it was the latter," Brell reflected, "I think we would have seen him by now if it was the first. Maybe he will be here soon."

Tristan worried and it showed on his face. "Maybe we should

go look for him. We don't have the wagons to slow us down."

Lareth put his hand on Tristan's shoulder. "But we don't know where he went. I'm sure he is fine."

It settled the boy, some.

A little over an hour went by. The traveling equipment had been put up in their rooms and the group, minus the orc and butcher sat at a table and played a dice game. The innkeeper, Edrigar, sat at the second table and watched them. Lancelot explained to everyone the rules and strategies while they played. Tristan already knew how to play, and only Thelband appeared to master it.

"You have to select three of the dice..." Lancelot explained when the door to the inn creaked open. The Mayor and two of his red tabarded soldiers entered.

Edrigar quickly jumped to his feet. "Oh Mayor, come sit over here. What can I get for you?"

Silas' gaze followed the innkeeper, but he walked toward the seated group. "I'll have my wine Edrigar, thank you, but I am here to talk to these good folk."

The mayor pulled a chair from the empty table, spun it around and sat. He faced the back of the chair with his arms draped over the top. Although he was happy, he smiled and his missing teeth made him look more disturbing than jovial.

"I had an interesting talk with the Winthrop children." The mayor's previous speech impediment had washed away. "It looks as if you have single-handedly saved our town by scaring off the Beast of Galagburg. He popped out of his chair with energy. He couldn't tell if he wanted to sit or stand. Silas then reached over the table and shook each and everyone's hands, his own were clammy, but his grip was backed by the warmth of his sincerity. "The town is going to love you. I love you. In fact, we will have a feast tonight in your honor."

Brell protested, "We only scared it off from one fight. It is still out there."

"Oh the Beast never runs from a fight. I am certain you are heroes."

Brell and Lareth exchanged cynical looks but kept it between themselves.

The mayor continued as he sat back down, "It has been nearly a month now that we have been plagued with these wolves and reports of the Beast. Word to Lord Zuchavich was met with silence, so we necessitated creating *Guard de' Force*. I thought that up. It sounded better than town militia. You see? We have been losing all of our trade business. Ships are sailing around and north of us. They brave the sea over the Beast. Without the traffic, fine establishments like this one will fall into disrepair, and then poverty.

"We sent out patrols to cull the wolves, but could never find them when we searched. Twice, the Beast was found, but on those two times, the patrols were wiped out. Only one man ever returned to testify to the beast's actual existence.

"All that is changed now. Thanks to you. I have sent riders out on every road to report that Galagburg is open for business once again!" The mayor jumped out of his seat at this last. "We shall ring the church bell twenty times in your honor!" Without further word, the mayor and his two red tabarded soldiers left.

"A reward might have been nice." Thelband was half-serious.

"Good deeds are reward enough for Demon Slayers." Brell chided.

"And that is why I am not a Demon Slayer. And it is probably why most Demon Slayers are poor." The halfling tried to get the last word.

Brell mused aloud, "Probably true....Probably true."

14

The he group finished their rest. Lancelot asked, "Can we go out and explore the town?"

"No," Brell said as he tried to figure out something in his head. "We can go out, but I think we need to get some questions answered."

Lancelot was puzzled, "Isn't that the same thing?"

Brell shook his head and led them out of the Bear Trap. Outside, they were met by a drizzling rain and more than a few waiting townspeople.

The group of people backed them up against the double doors of the inn. Each reached in to touch one or another of their saviors. Tristan turned red from embarrassment. So did his brother. There were thanks and crying, and a pent up relief from these people. Brell tried to humbly deflect them, but they were having none of it. This made things harder to get done. A man even offered his daughters hand in marriage to Lancelot. He thought Brell was his father or grandfather. Again, Brell respectfully declined.

Their pace was a crawl. It took nearly ten minutes to get beyond two buildings. More people found their way to the crowd and the street swelled with the tumult of bodies and the buzz of congratulations. They received vests, flowers and food baskets.

Lareth leaned in to Brell, "The Mayor better be right about the

Beast being gone." Brell just nodded.

A very tall, skinny man with long dusty hair and a booming voice cried out to the crowd, "Make way for the heroes of Galagburg! Out of their path! They have important business here, and you all are keeping them from it!" He forcefully, yet respectfully pushed people away to the left and right in front of the group. The crowd gave way, but did not leave the street.

The tall man came in close and put his arm around Brell's shoulders and led them further up the street as if he knew their final destination. All the while he shouted for others to keep out of the way.

"Thank you," was all the demon slayer could muster and allowed his escort to continue. It was obvious the tall man had sway with the crowd.

"I assume you are looking for the Mayor." He was mistaken, but before Brell could correct him, the man continued, "He is with Markos the moneylender. Markos was also out today, and before you ran the Beast off, Markos was attacked by it. He got away, but his arm got taken."

Lareth poked Brell in the back to which the demon hunter replied, "I know."

The man looked at him confused, but Brell ignored that and directed at him, "Yes. Please take us to see Silas right away." He then turned back to his companions, "Don't draw here, but be ready to. I think we are in for a fight."

"Clear the way!" The man let go of Brell and started off at a jog. "Clear the way!"

The house must have been clear on the other side of town. It took what Brell felt was wholly too long to reach Markos' home. The two story house doubled as a business. An orange lettered sign out front, 'Markos Coinage', prominently hung over the front window.

"Here it is. Would you like me to announce you?" the tall man asked.

"Yes, please." Brell had his hands ready to summon his swords.

Tristan grabbed the hilt of Hope and activated *Fin*. His brother came into clear focus in his mind. *"What do you think it is?"*

The tall man opened the door and led them inside. The room was dark except for the light that came in through the open door and filtered through the gray curtains. Stairs were off to the right.

"Brell cut off the arm of the wolf-man....I suspect we may have found him in his other form."

They went up the stairs. At the top was a door, partially open. Voices conversed. The tall man pushed open the door. "Hello Mayor. Hello Markos. The heroes wanted to..."

The mayor sat in a chair over Markos who was bandaged and laid in a bed. A wash basin rested in Silas' lap. The man had thick sideburns and a mop of hair. It was obvious the bandaged arm was not all there. The drapes in the room were drawn, and the only light came from a lamp on a dresser behind Silas.

The mayor started to stand, and Markos was all smiles until his eyes met Brell's. There was instant recognition. In a moment, Brell's twin swords appeared in his hands. He used his shoulder to knock the tall man back into the corner of the room, away from Markos.

Markos was fast, and in one motion, he had transformed and was out of the bed. His arm that had been severed had regenerated to the wrist. He was almost fully recovered. The man was big. The wolf was bigger. Markos had to crouch within the confines of the room.

Mayor Silas, a wolf-man behind him, faced the group unaware, the wash basin tucked under one arm and his other outstretched for a shake. He had not even registered the combat initiate when a claw erupted from his chest. Chunks of heart and chords of intestine wreathed Markos' claw. In the next instant, the hand was removed and Silas fell to the floor. The wash basin splashed and bounced out of the mayor's arm. The tall man screamed in horror. Markos' attention snapped to him, and he crouched to strike.

"Pel Mora Mira," the two brothers incanted in the doorway.

Brell dived to the right and intercepted the springing Markos. This time the wolf man was ready. He ducked under the first blade and parried the second with Silas' chair. His half-healed stump slammed into Brell's chest. The old man flew across the room, his back and flanks crashed through the upper-floor window. His head left a red skid mark against the window frame before the demon hunter disappeared with the shattered glass and shredded drapes.

There were startled screams outside.

Light poured in and highlighted Markos' muscular physique and distorted features. His hackles were up. Red eyes bulged from a lupine face. His snout bared enormous canines that dripped saliva mixed with some other darker black material. A tattered shirt and pants half hung from his fur-matted body.

"Get around to the other side and attack him from there," Tristan commanded his brother as he feinted a lunge at the beast. It kept Markos's attention away from the tall man who had curled up in a ball and whimpered.

Lancelot pivoted into the room along the window-side of the bed. He kept his facing toward Markos.

The wolf-man punched at Tristan with his stump as he had done to Brell. Instinctively, Tristan met the arm with his own hand. The boy was almost blinded by a flare from his sword as the Mora rune burned bright. He felt the force of the attack, but his hand met the swing with equal force, and the blow was stayed.

Lareth followed into the room behind Lancelot and mimicked his movements, eyes on Markos.

"Now!" Lancelot screamed into Tristan's mind. The younger had leapt the bed and was in position. Both brothers thrust their swords at the same time into the chest and back of Markos. Tristan did not let go of the stump and it pulled the wolf-man further off balance.

The creature's hide was thick and the swords did not penetrate far. It hurt Markos though. The beast reeled back and up. His head smashed through the wood ceiling. Dust flew out, and Markos went into an involuntary coughing fit. Tristan slashed down on the wolf man's legs while Lancelot used both hands in a second thrust. The younger brother's blade found a soft spot under a rib and Grace slide into Markos to the hilt.

Again the money lender lurched back and up. This time though, he toppled backward, the wall was the only thing that kept him from falling over.

"ARGENTUS HELIOFAUS!" Lareth incanted. For an instant, the runes disappeared on Hope, then the steel sheen of the blade turned a polished silver. The runes bled through the surface and burst with brightness. "Strike the beast now Tristan!"

Tristan moved out toward the bed and then used the end of it to spring back. Markos made one last defensive strike against him. It was easy enough to avoid the low swinging claw and Hope made the perfect level swipe at the base of Markos' neck. The lupine head sat for but a moment, then rolled off the front of Markos and landed with an unceremonious thump on the wooden floor.

In the next moment, there was a fervor of movement as Tristan looked after the tall man, Lareth started a spell of consecration and Lancelot moved to the window.

Brell lay below in the street, unconscious or dead. Two men struggled underneath him. They must have broken his fall. Three other townsfolk also strived to help extricate the downed men. A woman in a muddy dress lay nearby, having fainted at the sight of the encounter.

Without thinking, Lancelot vaulted through the window. His hand caught on broken glass, but the Pel rune prevented injury. The boy cleared the remainder of the roof and he landed square in front of the downed men. The crowd gasped then backed up at the sight of his sword.

Realizing he made the wrong impression, Lancelot sheathed Grace and helped to get Brell off the other men. He sat and rested Brell's head in his lap. The demon hunter had a large gash above his right eye, and a goose-egg formed next to that. Lancelot heard steady breathing and he heaved a big sigh. "Help that woman," he directed the men who had just aided him with Brell.

The crowd still looked on dumbfounded. They had no clue what happened until the tall man came out of the shop with Tristan, Lareth and Thelband. "Good folk of Galagburg, the Beast of Galagburg returned to get his revenge on us, but these brave men killed it."

The crowd cheered.

"People! People!" he yelled, but had to wait for the fervor to die down. "People. Poor Mayor Silas was killed by the Beast. He tried his best to fight the creature off," he lied. "After he fell, these warriors stood in my defense, in your defense, and finished the job." He made no mention of his role in the fight.

The crowd let out a collective moan. Some women cried. "What of Markos?" someone yelled out.

"Alas, Markos was also slain by the evil Beast," he lied again. Nobody refuted his account.

Lareth had bent over Brell and his spells worked their healing magic. When the demon hunter opened his eyes, the cleric smiled and whispered, "Not only do you know how to make an exit, you make my braining look like child's play. We are even old man."

Brell would have laughed, but his mind was still foggy from the fall. His lips only parted slightly. Lancelot let him lay there a few minutes more until he felt the unsteadiness leave his muscles.

The priest moved to the woman who had been helped up and offered her a small prayer in lieu of healing she didn't need.

The crowd has swelled since the fight, and news spread through the town of the final demise of the Beast of Galagburg. The tall man formally introduced himself as Zed. He was a carpenter. "I knew Silas well, I can't leave him upstairs like that. Could one of you help me in there?"

Tristan offered with a raised hand and followed Zed back into the building. The carpenter went up the stairs slowly. They creaked under foot and made him want to change his mind with each step. He wanted to turn and flee this macabre place. Tristan sensed his fear. "Let me lead."

Zed looked back down at him. His eyes showed gratitude and he nodded at the boy's suggestion. He knew he was not brave enough, and this would be the only way he could finish what needed to be done. Tristan squeezed by the tall man. Hope was out, and under his breath, he whispered the words, *"Pel Mora Fin Mira"*…. Only one rune glowed. In his head, he heard his brother.

"What is it? Are you in danger?" Lancelot's tension permeated the link.

"No," Tristan replied. *"Just playing it safe. It is too short a time to activate the other runes."* He held Hope tighter as if she would offer him more security.

"Okay. Let me know if you need me to run in there."

Tristan found he had not moved on the stairs, and Zed made no comment on his hesitation. The boy willed himself forward to the landing. The door was half open and from the top of the stairs he could see blood was everywhere. Sticky crimson had even pooled outside the bedroom in the hall.

"Here goes." He pushed the wooden door open. To his relief, the scene had not changed much. Where the wolf-man had lain, now was Markos, headless and in human form. Both he and Zed sighed audibly. "Zed, why did you not reveal Markos as the Beast? I understand you making Silas a hero. I would have done the same thing. But Markos…he killed friends and other innocent people."

"I know." Zed paused. "I know. Markos was my friend too. I have to believe this was some kind of curse. He has always been a kind man. His business is not the most well- loved profession, but Markos treated people proper. It just wouldn't be decent to blame him for all of this. And what would it achieve? They are dead. He is dead. The mayor is dead. We have to pick up the pieces. We have to move on."

Tristan thought on it and understood. "You did right by him Zed. I will not reveal what happened."

"Thank you."

The two wrapped the bodies in blankets, then sat for a long while on the end of the bed. Zed just cried with his face in his hands. Tristan sat silently and contemplated what this all amounted to. He had more questions, but he just put his arm over Zed and offered him what comfort he could.

The bodies of Silas and Markos were brought out into the street. Zed went next door where he lived and returned with some boards and tools. The carpenter nailed the boards over the front door and the downstairs windows. A cart was brought over and four somber soldiers loaded the bodies in. Zed directed them, "Take them to the church. I will speak with Father Neirul shortly." He then turned to the crowd, "Do not enter this shop! It is off limits! The scene inside is too horrid for innocent eyes to endure."

15

Word spread quickly through the town. The church bells rang seven times for the fallen mayor. The group was escorted back to the inn by an even more exultant mob. When they arrived, they were joined by Ardus. Bjorn and Lensa were under each arm. The children were still scared, but they understood what had happened and the excitement was contagious.

Someone had run ahead with the gifts that had been previously lavished on the group, and there was even more stuff on the tables in the eating hall. Activity around the inn picked up throughout the afternoon. An odd assortment of chairs and tables were brought into the dining hall. It was as if these people could not quite believe it was over, and they felt secure just being around their heroes. A cornucopia of emotions ran through the inn, feelings that were probably mirrored throughout the town. More people came in. A pair of musicians sat in the corner and eased the crowd into a comfortable atmosphere.

The group sat at the original tables. The gifts, although most had been brought upstairs, still trickled in. Various dishes of food filled the table, and everyone ate or drank something.

"You should take over as mayor here," Lareth urged Zed. "These people really like you, and you have leadership qualities."

"I don't know. Really. I was a scared child in Markos' house.

How could I ever expect to be able to lead?"

Ardus, who sat there and fed Lensa on his lap, chimed in, "Mr. Zed, fear is something every one of us possesses. You were in an impossible situation. I could not have killed Ma…the Beast… without Lareth's magics. I would have been as useful as you in that fight. Outside though, I hear you controlled that crowd like no other. There is no way I could speak to that many people without pissing my pants. You've already made big decisions. You closed the money shop. You sent the mayor on to the church to be prepared for burial. You have given the people hope through our actions. We are just tools. You are a carpenter. You should understand that. Tools are only as good as those who know how to handle them properly. You, sir, are a craftsman."

Zed blushed but soaked the compliment in.

Brell shifted the subject, "Zed, have you a library, hall of records, or sage? We came to Galagburg looking for information."

"We had a sage, but the years got to him. He passed earlier this summer. The other things, this town is too small for. What are you looking for if I may ask?"

"Lord Zhukovich." Zed paled as Brell mentioned the name. "We need information on Dellan."

"You are asking for trouble. That bastard ignored our plea for assistance with the Beast. He has some damned army with him now too. Who, what or why, I don't know, but it is scaring people trying to get into the town. Aside from the Beast and all."

Lareth leaned in and asked, "Has anyone seen this army?"

"A patrol. They had come from the high hills, just under the mountain. They saw formations training off in the distance. Silas assumed he was going to send some our way, but weeks and now a month have gone by with nothing. Before that, Lord Zhukovich was down here requiring workers. He offered good money, but the way he was asking, it was more than unnerving. I think six or seven people volunteered, but they aint been seen since."

Brell played with his small beard as he often did while he contemplated. He looked around to the others, "This may be a different threat. It doesn't sound like the Codrugon spawn, so that lessens the chances we are worrying about a second gate. Troublesome though."

Lareth added while he scratched his healed wound, "You know, I was thinking about the Beast. There is too much coincidence. I know it has been a month....but so close to Dellan? I think he put it here to keep this region ignorant of his other workings."

Zed could not believe this talk. "You think Lord Zhukovich would do this? He may be a little demanding and strange, but has not threatened the town before."

Lareth educated the carpenter, "There are things you don't know and probably would not want to know about your Lord Zhukovich. He is not a man. He is a creature of the undead. A vampire."

Brell took over, "I know, we would not have believed it either, except we saw it with our own eyes. Across the strait of Kollune is a port-town, Ferrickport."

"I am familiar."

"Well, while there, we were hired to find and kill Dellan. Of course that is not evidence, but Dellan actually appeared to prevent us from even starting our journey. He killed half the patrons of the tavern we were in. Turned them to zombies."

Tristan shuddered at the memory, "He is telling the truth. My brother and I were there when it happened. The vampire made no attempt to hide his nature or intentions. He is pure evil."

"I will not doubt what you say," Zed whispered. "What can we do?"

Brell answered, "I don't think Dellan has any grand plans for Galagburg. We believe he is in league with something far more sinister. Their plans are yet unannounced. All we know is devils have been released south of here and this part of Jhenna is in immense danger."

Zed stood, "A lot has happened here in town, and it looks like a lot is happening around us. Let me organize a council to review where we stand. If I learn any more information on Lord Zhukovich, I will share it with you." He looked over to the innkeeper. "Edrigar, these people are honored guests of Galagburg. Please refund them payment for lodgings and food. I'll make sure you are reimbursed."

Edrigar merrily acknowledged and immediately did as asked.

"Thank you. The town thanks you. I thank you." Zed shook their hands and then left.

The sun had gone down. Townsfolk had filtered out of the Bear Trap. Tables and chairs were left behind. It looked like business might pick up again. Three other patrons remained. They all sat at a table, drank ale and reminisced about some-such. Occasional laughs burst from their table.

"These old bones have had enough falling out windows for one night," Brell said as he pushed off the table with both arms to stand, "I think it is time to go recuperate with some sleep."

It wasn't a command, but it was what everyone else had waited to hear. The others stood with Brell and either verbally concurred or yawned their agreement.

"I'll take these little ones to their aunt." Ardus cradled a sleeping Lensa. Bjorn kept rubbing his eyes. "I may not be back until the morning." It was obvious how attached to these two he was.

Pleasantries and good nights were exchanged and the group dispersed. Upstairs, Brell paired with Lancelot while Tristan, Lareth and Thelband opted to share a room. They had three rooms, but left the third vacant.

The rooms were small. Two beds were aligned side-by-side in each. Small shelves hung about shoulder height to place personal belongings. A single window with moth-eaten drapes filtered the only real air and light in. Dust had settled on shelves and sills, and there was an old musty odor that had no apparent origin. The Bear Trap Inn had not seen guests in some time.

16

In his room, Lancelot unpacked as little as possible so they could make preparations for sleep. Brell had just unbuckled and kicked the first boot off when a sharp rap on the window startled them. Half-booted, a single purple blade formed in Brell's left hand. He looked to the window, but their blade and lamplight only offered them reflections of themselves.

He moved closer to the window and squinted. Lancelot, behind him, had Grace drawn and already alerted his brother to the potential threat. Movement could be heard from the adjoining room.

"*Don't be surprised when Lareth comes in,*" Tristan warned.

Lareth opened the bedroom door just as Lancelot said, "Lareth is coming."

With a quick glance over his shoulder to confirm Lancelot's proclamation, Brell moved so that his face was against the window. The sword in his hand dissipated and he opened the window. "Was wondering when you would arrive. Come in."

"I have been here for two days." Leopold floated outside the window and squeezed himself into the tiny room. "You took long enough to get here."

"Sorry, but we don't fly," Brell retorted.

The vampire was not in good shape. He looked shriveled and

gaunt, more so than before. Small bits of dirt fell from folds of his clothes and he patted himself down to shake it all out. "Troublesome having to sleep underground." The only thing that wasn't dirt-stained was the large brimmed hat he put on his head.

Tristan came into the room and Lareth motioned for him to close the door. The two boys sat at the foot of a bed to make more room for the other three to stand.

"You made it out of Ferrickport," Brell observed. "We did not make it out until nightfall, and our knowledge of events were limited to the activity on the docks and the path that took us there. Have you any other news?"

Leopold was less focused on the past, but humored their questions so he would not be pestered later, "Yes, Ferrickport is no more."

The group let out a concerted gasp.

"A great and powerful druid thought to rid the land of pesky insects. He found their sting to be too much even for him to bear. In his dying breath, or at least that is how I pictured it, he pulled the ocean in like a blanket and covered the city in water. It had little effect, other than to save the citizens a horrible death, or worse, a horrible life of slavery."

"How did you survive?" Tristan asked without thinking.

Leopold laughed, "I was covered by the sea, just like all the rest. Let's just say I could hold my breath longer. Lucky for me I can swim, oh and fly."

Lancelot followed up on his brother's question, "Did anyone else make it out?"

"I still have a heart. I plucked four or five lucky floaters and dropped them on rooves still visible above the waves. My focus was not on Ferrickport though. I needed to get across the straits fast, or I would perish under the light of day."

Done with answering questions, Leopold got to the point of his entrance, "I have not fed since the transformation, and I grow less capable of holding that off as each hour passes."

As if he had anticipated this insight, Lareth opened his fist to reveal his ruby charm. It was attached to a golden neck chain. "You must wear this, or so we have been told. We probably should have given it to you sooner."

Leopold eyed the necklace and Lareth warily, then looked at Brell.

"He speaks true. Please, trust us," the old man said flatly.

Leopold reached for the necklace, hesitated, and then snatched it out of the priest's outstretched hand. He hesitated one last time at the moment before he laid it around his neck. He looked to each of the others, then let it drop against his skin. The vampire stood taller briefly and inhaled a huge breath.

"I am invigorated," he exhaled. "You are right. This will help…for how long though, I know not. We need to strike Dellan now, before it wears off, or before he catches wind that we are here. He has agents everywhere."

"That is not good," Tristan posited, "Didn't you say you thought Markos might be connected to him?" He looked to Lareth.

"Only a hypothesis, but it does make sense, and if there is more than one agent of Dellan, I can't believe he doesn't know we are already here," Lareth answered.

Leopold interrupted, "Another reason to leave right now."

"What of Trazk?" Tristan asked. "We need to wait for him or find him before we go."

Brell fielded this one, "I'm afraid Leopold is correct. Time is now a factor, for more reasons than one. We should get some rest though. Can you wait four hours?" he directed the last at the vampire.

"Yes. Hurry. I'll scout the north road." The vampire tilted his body near horizontally and glided rather than flew out the window, as if he floated on the wind.

Tristan looked flustered, "We aren't really going to leave without Trazk are we?"

"Let's see where we are in four hours," Brell tried to offer assurance. "Everyone to bed. I doubt we will sleep, but try."

Lareth ushered Tristan back to their room. Lancelot and Brell dimmed their lamp and got on the covers. Brell laughed, "Yeah, I was not going to sleep under these blankets either. They smell older than me."

The hours passed much too quickly for anyone's liking. Lancelot went downstairs to leave a note from Brell to the innkeeper, but Edrigar still entertained patrons below. "Up for a midnight snack Young sir?" the owner asked.

"Oh no, um we thought you would be asleep and Brell asked me to leave this here for you." Lancelot handed the innkeeper the note. "It just says we must leave on business outside town, but would like to keep our stuff here. I think we are just using the two rooms, so you can rent out the other if you need to."

"Ah, courteous. Thanks. I hope I'll be needing it soon, but the locals won't be staying here. In fact, I'll be kicking them to the street soon enough. Excited as I am for the business today, it has been long. Very long."

Lancelot turned to go back up the stairs and Edrigar called after him, "Safe journeys young sir. To all of you. Bayoric grant you his blessings." The young demon hunter waved and sprang back up the stairs.

When he came in the door, everything was ready to go. Brell handed Lancelot his backpack. Lareth tromped down the stairs to get the horses. Tristan helped his younger brother with the straps on a pack that was a little oversized for him. Luckily, they would only need to wear them when they got to the vampires manor.

It took some time to get all the traveling gear back downstairs and loaded into the wagons. Edrigar and the stable boy, Ned, helped them.

"Will you be long sirs?" Edrigar asked.

Brell spoke down to him from his horse. "I hope not. Thank you again for your hospitality."

"Where are you headed off to?" the innkeeper could not contain his curiosity.

"East." Brell lied. Edrigar was nice enough, but, as they knew there may be more spies in Galagburg, it was safest to minimize word of their actual destination.

First, the caravan drove to get Ardus with direction from Thelband. After the blacksmith had finished the arduous process of putting on all of his plate armor, Brell did indeed lead the group out the east road but quickly took the first clear path north. Leopold met them shortly after they were out of Galagburg, and easily navigated the off-road areas to get them back on track. He had to distance himself from the group because the horses were unsettled in his presence. Once out of the trees and brush, the group stopped long enough for Lancelot to inspect wheels and hoofs by lantern-light. He gave the all-clear, shuttered the light, and they caravanned on.

The sky was overcast and blocked out the moon. Pitch blackness blanketed them from sight. Brell lit three candles. One he placed on the back of each wagon, and the third he carried himself. "When the candles have run their course, we should be far enough from town, and more importantly, prying eyes, that we can use the lanterns to light our way." he surmised.

Less than a mile into their northward journey, Brell's mount elicited a loud neigh, and reared up on its hind legs. The demon hunter only escaped being pitched with a tight grip on the horse's mane. His candle extinguished and he was blind. It took everything the demon hunter knew about riding to keep the horse from bolting off into the darkness. Then in an instant, a beam of light shown from behind. Lancelot had the wits to lift the shutter on his lantern. It was Leopold, he was on the road ahead and running toward them. The vampire was fast. Brell hoped he was not attacking because Leopold was way too close to defend against.

The vampire stopped just as he reached the caravan. He stood nonchalantly, "You need to move faster. This pace is too slow."

"You didn't need to run up on us like that. You scared my horse," Brell scolded.

"If you can't handle your horse, how can I expect you to handle Dellan?"

"Did you just come back here to hurry us up, or is there more?" Brell was less interested in the answer and more annoyed.

"There is more. Look." Leopold didn't point. He stood and watched Brell for a reaction.

The shadows created by the lantern offered a hint of movement to both the left and right of the road. Lancelot at first turned the lantern to the left. It didn't immediately reveal anything. He then lifted the shutters on the other sides of his lantern. They could see now. Everywhere were animals. Deer, bears, foxes, ermine, wild pig and more all moved purposefully south. None feared the other. Something else drove them. The group watched in awe for several minutes. The parade of animals continued unabated, oblivious or uncaring of their humanoid audience.

"This is not good," Brell muttered, "What more do you know?"

The vampire was satisfied to receive the question he expected, "I have traveled several miles to the east and west. It is the same everywhere. Something big is coming. I suspect it is Dellan. It looks like we will not have to hunt him down after all."

"Is this guy for real?" Lancelot sent to Tristan, *"How does he think we can fight someone that can do this?"*

Leopold interrupted the thought, *"I wonder the same thing pups. You all had better prepare yourselves for the worst. I only need you to live long enough to get me close. I fear it will be upon me, and me alone, to finish this."*

The brothers simultaneously took their hands off Hope and Grace to break the link. Leopold ignored that, and continued, *"Best you be careful when you send your thoughts out like that. You never know who can hear them. Worse, you never know who or what you will let in."* They felt the vampire leave their minds, but he left a slimy, nauseating feeling. Both wanted to vomit.

Brell sat and contemplated. Then he conferred with Lareth, Ardus, and Thelband. Not wanting to be excluded, Lancelot rode in closer to hear. Tristan stayed near the back and used what little light he had to watch the road behind them.

"...strategic positions anywhere around here." Lancelot only caught the end of Brell's point, but his trainer continued, "So I think we either send the wagons back, or we abandon them here."

"How about both?" Thelband offered. "Let's pack everything from one into the other. I'll bring the load back to town. It is only a mile or two. I can also warn Galagburg in case this is bigger than us." The halfling looked around for Trazk and was satisfied he was not about to be hit with some kind of height joke. "Halfling teeth," he mumbled under his breath.

"A sound idea," Brell agreed. "Maybe we can send the boys in your stead."

Lancelot was about to protest, but Thelband rejected Brell's suggestion, "I am Sir Thelband Highfellow, highborn to the Highfellow family in Wellinghill. I think I can use my status to influence things in Galagburg should they not be receptive to the news. I love the boys here, but I am not so sure they would have the same respect, sway, or experience to follow this through."

Not insulted in the least, Lancelot nodded his agreement. Brell also grudgingly acquiesced, "Okay then. Let's get the wagon packed with all haste. You will take a horse with you. You don't need to lose time trying to remove the wagon harness from that one."

17

Once Thelband had the wagon turned south rolling toward Galagburg and Ardus had been helped up onto a mount, Leopold led the group toward Dellan. He slowed his run so the horses could keep up. It had only been about two hours since they left town, and it already felt like they would be overwhelmed with trouble.

It started to drizzle. The wind picked up and the droplets felt like tiny needles against their faces and hands. They moved with the full lantern light. At their pace, it was necessary to see both Leopold and the dirt path.

Brell reined up when he saw the vampire slow. He didn't need a repeat of earlier. Leopold put a finger up for them to remain and ran off to the right in a blur.

"Do you hear that?" Tristan cocked his head as he asked. A dull 'Bum, bum, bum' sounded far off in the distance. "It sounds like drums," he finished.

The horses all became skittish at the same time. "Hold your reins tight," Brell commanded.

Leopold returned, but from the left side of the road. "The army moves toward us. They are pretty spread out. Let's follow the road straight ahead. We can break through. Dellan is sure to be on the road. I can feel him straight ahead of us."

The vampire led the group forward once again, but this time at a more guarded pace. Except for the lantern light, it was still dark as pitch. As they rode, they could hear the thumping of the drum beat. It was exactly what someone would use to keep a marching army in formation. It got loud enough that they could feel the sound reverberate through their bones.

Rain soaked the dirt road, and as the packed dirt turned to mud, it slowed the progress of the riders. "I worry we are going to hit this army head on. What if our mounts are too tired to get us out should we encounter insurmountable odds?" asked Ardus.

Brell replied, "I don't think Leopold plans on retreating. Slow it down some more."

"No. Stop." It was Lareth. His face drained of color, "They are close. Very close. And they are no devils or men. This army is an army of the dead. I don't know how, but I can feel their souls. Tormented." The group did as he commanded.

Leopold came back to where they huddled. "Why don't we press forward?" His eyes glowed a sickly red.

Brell tried to point out, "We can't hit them straight on. There is undead within that army. We don't know how much or of what type."

"No matter. He is so close." The vampire leapt into the air and out of sight.

While they had deliberated, the marching army came out of the darkness and into view less than one hundred paces away. A horn blared from behind the front rank and the whole formation stopped. Helmets and shields did not hide the disposition of the troops. Even in shadows, the group could see some soldiers had flesh torn from their faces. Some showed no skin or muscle at all. Dark magics compelled these lifeless beings to animate, and an even darker magic controlled them now.

The soldiers in the road parted and made way for a single rider on a skeletal horse. He looked no different from the foot troops in that life had left him long ago. The similarities ended there. The rider sat rigid on his undead mount. Blue flames flickered within his eye sockets. Chunks of skin hung from his face like a beard. Maggots animated the flesh as they dined on rotted bits. Roaches and other small crawling things emerged and skittered across his face or shoulder to disappear into another unnatural orifice. He wore a great helm accentuated by basilisk horns and a large emerald above the brow. It was collapsed in from some past combat having made it a permanent fixture on his head. Grey strands of patchwork hair loosely peeked out from under the helm. He exuded command even though his azure cloak was moth eaten and the rider should have been buried in a grave or tomb, not sitting there upon a horse. Across his lap, resting under one skeletal hand, laid a black sword. Red glowing runes creeped up the blade and made it look as if it were lit by an unearthly fire. The mount he sat upon bore patchwork, rusted armor. An ancient, long forgotten insignia etched on its caparison identified his ages-past allegiance.

The rider bellowed, "Enemies of Dellan, I am general Zumathash." His voice was gravely and unwavering. "I lead this fine army in the name of Lord Zhukovich. Have you come to surrender? I am sure I can find room for you in one of my many units. We are legion, and no force living or dead will impede our march."

Lareth had already dismounted and had conjured up his ball of flame. He released it. The ball floated head-height off the ground and sped toward the general. The half-skeletal rider watched in amusement as the ball slowed, then stopped in front of him. Its fiery tendrils elongated and whipped out. Two soldiers exploded like dried tinder. When the general was hit, a green-hued shield lit and deflected the lash. Unflinching, he observed the display with pleasure, almost as if he wished a defiant response.

The general backed his mount up and laughed, "They are ready to join. Archers…"

"Dismount! Dismount!" Brell yelled out as he slid down the side of his horse. Most of the others mirrored his actions. Nearly twenty rotting soldiers, crossbows already loaded, stepped out between gaps left by their comrades. They brought their weapons up to aim and fired.

Some quarrels zipped by. Most found a target. Horses screamed out in agony and either died instantly or disappeared off into the wood to bleed out their last minutes.

The group was in the open now. They could lay down next to the fresh corpses and be slaughtered, or they could run. Brell chose the latter option for them. "Quick, use the woods as cover!" he yelled.

Tristan and Lancelot helped up Ardus. The giant warrior had been thrown from his horse and found it difficult to rise with so much armor. His shield, that had just saved him, proudly displayed three bolts.

A second line of archers fired their volley. Brell had already taken shelter behind trees. Ardus used his shield to block shots that would have hit Lancelot. It left him exposed and he caught two bolts of his own. The metal plates, although strong, could not fully protect against the power of the crossbows and he bled from two wounds in his side. Tristan had dived down behind a dead horse. It shuddered as it absorbed a number of hits. The three used the pause and ran for safety.

A third barrage fired. Whizzing sounds went overhead or behind. Thumping and cracking noises signified where the quarrels hit trees.

Brell took them south and kept the road in sight, but they stayed off it. Lancelot still carried the lantern and was their only light source. They heard the horns then the marching of the army resume, but it quickly faded as they made distance against it. Tristan yelped in surprise as a horde of undead charged them from the left. While they had parlayed with Zumathash, the flanks of the army must have kept marching. Trees and darkness had obscured their presence. The disturbing silence of the marauders was unnerving.

Two naked pale humanoids, red glowing eyes as big as saucers, led their zombie handlers by chains secured around their neck. When the ambushers were close enough, the zombies released their grips and the ghoulish attackers sprang to engage. Behind them, armored in chainmail with shields and wielding an assortment of weapons, two score or more undead plodded forward.

Lancelot was the first to be attacked. He held up Grace to

defend against his assailant, but the creature deftly knocked his hand away and landed on him. It wrapped its legs around the boy's torso and bit off a chunk of his face at the cheek. The young demon hunter started to yell, but it was cut off by some paralytic affect. Something in the creature's bite was poison. His arms and legs went rigid and he fell over. The creature's victim lay there while it tore another bite out of his shoulder.

Dirty claws reached for his older brother. Only because he tripped backward did he avoid them. Tristan used the momentum of his fall to roll into a somersault and got back on his feet, Hope at the ready. Before the ghastly monster could reach him, Ardus had it by its neck chain. "No you don't!" His two-handed grip slid down to the end of the chain and he swung it in circles. It brought the creature around twice and he generated so much momentum that when the creature hit a tree, its neck cracked and its head flopped down unnaturally onto its back before the thing slid down the trunk. The tree was left with a large red stain.

The other undead were not fazed by the morale-breaking kill. They pushed in to attack. Brell and Ardus met the zombies with glowing swords and spear. The large warrior took two quick thrusts and then discarded his twin forked pole-arm in favor of his broad sword. The enemy lacked vitals vulnerable to thrusting blows. The two were driven back by the sheer number of foes. It was obvious this was going to be short fight if they didn't do something fast. A dozen zombies were about to envelope them on either side.

Tristan grabbed an arm of Lancelot's ghoul. The creature gnashed at him with short needle-like teeth. Its corpulent skin tore away as he pulled on it. The ghoul's leg's wrapped tighter around its prey. Putrescent ooze leaked where the skin tore, and Tristan began to lose his grip. Ardus stepped in and directed his angry rant at the creature, "There is only one way to kill a foe that does not want to die." He shed his shield and sword and used both meaty hands to grip the monster, one hand under the chin, the other at the back of its skull. The armored warrior laid his knee into its back and twisted with all his might. The cadaverous head made a 'splooch' sound as it, and half the creature's spine, disconnected from its body.

Two zombies slashed their swords repeatedly across Ardus' back. The warrior purposefully turned on them. He grabbed each zombie by its helmeted head. With an angry bellow, he mashed the two heads together. The helmets crushed and crumpled under his vice-like grasp and the zombies dropped to the ground.

"Lareth, use the Light of Gaylen to burn away our enemy!" Brell yelled out. The demon hunter made a slow, fighting retreat back to the group. He looked over his shoulder. "Where is Lareth?"

"I don't know. Maybe he ran to the other side of the road when we fled." Ardus used his sword to slice off legs and arms from zombies that had come on their flank. Although his blows were strong enough to cut through limbs in one swing, Brell noticed the warrior slowed. The wounds in his side hampered him and Brell wondered how much blood Ardus had lost.

Tristan sat over his brother. He held a cloth to his shoulder to staunch the bleeding. *"Answer me Lancelot. Can you hear me?"* he pleaded into his mind to no effect. "Brell, Lancelot can't move. His eyes are open, and he is breathing, but that is all. Help him!"

"I'm afraid we can't do anything until this is over. Sit tight with him. We are doing our best."

They had killed less than a quarter of the zombies, and a second wave could be seen coming into the light of the lantern.

Leopold landed near Brell. "You won't be able to get through this. You need to get back to the town." The vampire had already destroyed three zombies in the time it took for him to convey his message. "Go, I'll hold these off to give you time. We will meet again in the inn tomorrow night if the town still stands." Leopold was a blur. He went from one zombie warrior to the next. Before one had hit the ground, another was dispatched.

Brell turned in time to see Trazk step from the shadows. His scimitar was out; black ichor coated the blade. The orc scooped up Lancelot and turned away as Tristan followed.

"We have a way out. Quickly!" the old veteran yelled.

Ardus finished with his respective foe and hobbled after Brell. Back on the road, Trazk was on a horse with Lancelot splayed over in front of him. Tristan stood by anxiously. There was one other horse. These were the ones Brell and Lancelot had lost in the first fight with Markos. On the ground, several wolf pelts had been discarded to make room for riders.

Brell beckoned Ardus over and helped him up onto the remaining mount. "Tristan, you and I will jog back. We are faster than the zombies and we're not wounded." He slapped a mare on its flanks and yelled, "Go!"

The riders took off at full gallop while Brell and Tristan ran after them.

Ahead, zombies closed in from either side to intercept them. Tristan handed Brell his brother's sword and invoked the *Mora Mira* runes on his own. Brell followed his lead, and the two used a burst of speed and agility to navigate the narrowing gap and leave the enemy behind.

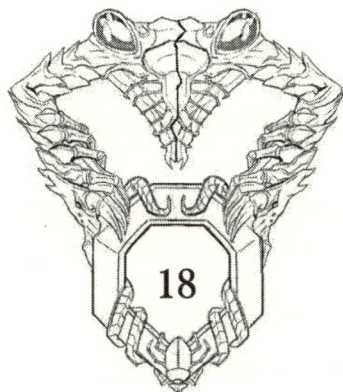

18

The runners found that the earlier detour around Galagburg took them further out than they realized. It was well over three miles back to town. Brell was impressed with the magical endurance the swords had bestowed upon them. The two ran on in silence until their destination came into view. Thelband waited for them with four militia. The men were armed with either bows or crossbows. As they slowed to catch their breath, more archers appeared in windows and on rooftops. "Great! You made it back!" the halfling exclaimed.

Tristan walked off the run, hands on hips. Even with the power of Hope, he was exhausted. Brell was worse off. He was bent over, hands on knees. Sweat dripped down off of his pointed nose. He could still talk though. "You need to fortify these buildings." His head cocked to assess the state of the town before he continued, "Better yet, this town needs to be evacuated."

"Sir, there would be no time to evacuate everyone. There are nearly three hundred people in Galagburg and its outskirts." It looked like the eldest man spoke to him, although none of them could be over twenty.

"Is Zed in charge?"

"We think so. There has been nothing formal. Zed is with Friar Mark and your friends." The young man was visibly shaken and just wanted some orders to take his mind off what may be coming.

"Take me to them," Brell said, then directed at the other three, "You get crates, boards, wagons and anything else you can. Board up the lower windows on any building facing north or east. You pile as much stuff up between buildings. If there is too much space to do that, you either fill the gaps with soldiers, or you evacuate everyone beyond protecting back into the town center."

The three stared at him, hesitant. "Now!" Brell barked, and they scrambled and sprinted off to obey. "Take me to Zed now," he said to the fourth a little too testily.

It was still a few hours before sun-up. Townspeople already scurried about. Lanterns sat on window sills. Torches sat in sconces on poles placed regularly down the two main Galagburg roads. Brell did not sense the urgency required, but hopefully that would change. He stopped men in red tabards at every opportunity. The command was always the same, "Get to the edge of town. They are reinforcing it. Help them." Nobody questioned his authority.

The three were led to a house next door to the church. It was a small building with a fence and gate at its front. Brell's last command was to a pair of militia trying to hurry by, "Get some help. Come remove this fence. Keep it as whole as possible and take it to the north edge of town. They are reinforcing against attack. It could be used to bolster the defense." The man who had escorted them went with the last group of soldiers.

Inside, the home had been set up as a make-shift hospital. Folded sheets were stacked with rags and large bowls of water. Hanging from the front room wall, a large holy symbol of the gods was prominently displayed. There was no flurry of activity, but it looked like someone got the message, and preparations had been made.

Brell called out, "Excuse me. Hello?"

"Back here," came a voice. Tristan didn't recognize it from any of the people he had met. Brell led them around the side of a long table and through a doorway off to the right. A small hall bent around and opened into a brightly lit room. Lancelot lay on a table wincing as a bespectacled man in a green shirt leaned over with a needle and thread. He was stitching his brother's face. Trazk stood over his shoulder and watched with concern.

Ardus sat in a chair nearby. His armored breastplate lay on the ground next to his warhammer, his top-clothes strewn over that. The large man looked half asleep. He was bound in bandages around his midsection. Two red spots bled through and marked where the crossbows had hit.

Brell walked over and inspected Lancelot's shoulder through a ripped shirt. The wound was closed and was healing. Most importantly, he was conscious. The paralysis had worn off. Friar Mark must have access to healing magics. Mark spoke as if he could read Brell's thoughts, "The wound was festering. I used what reserves I had to cleanse it. Sorry I could not do anything for your friend there, or this face here."

"He is a skilled surgeon," Ardus attested. "Magics were not necessary."

"They may be needed before this is over." Brell was serious and determined. "Does anyone know where Zed is? I was told he was here."

The man with the needle answered while he threaded Lancelot's cheek, "He left with Father Neirul minutes before you arrived. I think he said he was going to the town hall."

Brell assessed the situation here then made his calls to action, "Okay, Ardus, I put the care of this boy in your hands. Thelband, find Zed and coordinate with him. Whatever you do, emphasize evacuation and defense. If we can deter the zombies and force them to go around, we will have won here." Thelband nodded and left. "I will supervise the defense of the town. Trazk, take Tristan with you. Can you scout out the best path for women and children to evacuate if need be?"

Trazk grunted an affirmation.

"Good. We converge on the inn should trouble force our hand." With the last, Brell squeezed Lancelot's hand then left the church.

"Let's go boy." Trazk was ready to leave too. "Thank you priest. You have our gratitude." Mark smiled after the two as they also exited.

While they mounted upon the two horses, Tristan said to the orc, "It's good to see you are not wolf food. What happened to you? Brell and the others came back after the wolf fight. But you didn't."

"The wolves were not acting naturally. They were under someone's control, probably the werewolf's. Normally, you can just scatter animals off and be done with it. I sensed they would have harried us all the way to your human settlement. I had to finish the job. I was pretty proud of myself. Those pelts were pristine. Too bad I had to leave them on the road."

"Yeah, but you saved us," Tristan pointed out.

"I guess so."

Tristan followed up, "How long did it take you? We spent all day and most of the night in Galagburg and you never showed up."

"Are you scolding me boy?" Trazk laughed. "I'm an orc. I know, you just think of me as your tusked, ugly friend and brilliant mentor, but did you see those flesh-bags in the settlement? They are afraid of me. If I went there on my own, they would have attacked me first and asked you questions later. I waited at the north side of the settlement for you to come out, but Brell though, he could be tricky by going out east."

"How did you know to come north after us."

The orc just smiled and put his finger to his nose.

"No way." Tristan didn't believe him. Trazk just laughed again and they rode west and south out of town. The orc was right. They received plenty of fearful stares on their ride out.

19

Back in Mark's house, Lancelot sat up in a chair. The friar had given him a blanket and a cup of hot water. The boy was still a little groggy from the paralysis. The effect had come almost instantly when the teeth ripped into his cheek. "It was the most horrifying thing I could imagine," he explained to Ardus.

"What's that?"

"The monster that bit me. The one that made me freeze. I could feel the pain. It hurt more than anything I have ever felt. But I couldn't move. I could hear everything. The combat. Yelling. But I couldn't do anything."

"We call those sarcophagus thieves. In the desert where I am from, they raid burial grounds and eat the dead. Here, they are called ghouls. I don't know why they have that effect. I mean, everything they eat is already dead. Why need something to stop a dead person."

"I think they use it to more easily make things dead. Then they eat them."

"Hmm. Makes sense. No more questions son, I need to catch some winks."

Ardus moved from the chair to a floor so he could sleep. Mark had brought a pillow and then went next door to make preparations in the chapel of the church.

"Good idea," Lancelot agreed with him. "Do you think Lareth is dead?"

"What makes you say that?" Ardus was ready to sleep.

"Well, his horse fell down on him. "

Ardus sat up at hearing this. He stared at Lancelot for a good minute. "I hope not. We need him."

"I know. He is my friend." Lancelot cocked his head up. "Ardus, why don't you use your hammer?"

The warrior laughed. "Oh that. I forget I carry it. I use it more to keep my stamina up. Also, it's impressive to behold. Make em piss their pants imagining what it could do. It's too slow though. Heavy as it is. Ornament really."

The two tried to get some sleep. Lancelot kept replaying the fight in his mind. It was very scary knowing there were 'things' that could do that to a person. "Ardus? How did you survive? I mean, not today. But every day. What did you do before you were a butcher?"

Ardus resigned himself to getting no sleep. "I was a butcher of men," he whispered at first. "I fought in slave pits. When I was younger than you, my mother was killed. My father, two brothers and me were sold off to slavers. I was told I would fight for my freedom. That was enough to give me the will to live. My first day of training, I was dropped in a hole with a wild dog. If I could kill it with my bare hands, I would get to fight again. The betting on my life had already started. When you are faced with your imminent death, you learn really fast what you are capable of.

"It was a cruel life, but my master was good to me, at least when he was certain I was not going to keel over anytime soon. I was trained in the use of most weapons. Early on, I had it in my mind that I would break free and rescue the rest of my family. Years went by and the fighting took us across the continent. I fought against men, centaurs, goblins, and many forms of beast. My master became rich on me. One day, after I had become accustomed to my life and resigned to spend the rest of my days in the pits, I found myself facing off against one of my brothers. I conspired to end the fight, but my brother was no longer inside him. He, like me, had spent his entire life in battle. Something had snapped and drove him mad. He did not recognize me."

Ardus paused at the painful memory. "Our fight was the bloodiest and longest lasting fight I ever had to endure. In the end....well, I am here. My master saw what that fight had done to me, not just physically. He handed me a large purse of gold and my freedom. I never looked back...even to look for my father and my other brother."

Sadly, he looked over to find Lancelot deep in sleep. Ardus shook his head and closed his eyes.

20

"Okay, this is going to be the rally point." Trazk was pleased with the off the road clearing he found. His torch had revealed a barely perceptible break in the underbrush and trees. A small path led them to a dimly lit circle of grass, big enough for two score people to stand, cramped, shoulder to shoulder. The orc dismounted and grabbed a large stick he eyed. From his saddlebag, he produced a worn shirt and tied it to the stick. Then he drove the stick into the center of the clearing. Next the orc fished a blanket out of the same bag. He used his belt-knife to cut the blanket in two.

"What are you doing?" Tristan also dismounted and followed.

Trazk walked the short distance back to the road. "I would make hard to see signs, but average meat...er townsfolk find it hard to spot subtle." He took the two halves of the blanket and tied each to a branch that overhung the road. "I don't think zombies will understand the significance of these, at least not until something with some brains is with them." Trazk didn't look that pleased with his handiwork. "Normally, I would be teaching you to mark the trees or spot other signs, but we don't have time for that. Just know, this is not the way we normally work."

Tristan liked to hear Trazk include him even though that was not the intention of his instruction. "What do we do next?" He asked.

The orc stared at the boy for a long moment before he answered, "The road here leads to the town where Brell's niece lives. One of us should travel back there to warn them of the zombie army. The other should head back to the town up the road there and let them know of this rally point. I expect most people to just keep running, but the soldiers need a place to gather their wits if they are to keep their town."

"I would like to go back to Galagburg," Tristan volunteered.

"It is settled then. I ride now. You should find Brell and Zed. Let them pass along the information. Red blanket, rally zone." With that, Trazk mounted his horse, turned and rode hard along the southern road.

Tristan looked around. Darkness seemed to close in on him now that he was alone. He put his hand on Hope for comfort. "*La*" he felt in his head. He repeated it aloud. His sword gave off a soft glow. Something Elle had not told him about. He drew his sword from its scabbard and the blade increased the output of light. There was now a fourth rune on the blade, on the opposite side from the other three. The entirety of the glade was now visible. "*What other secrets are you keeping from me?*" Tristan thought to himself really.

Hope heard though and the boy nearly jumped out of his britches when she responded. Her voice in his head was a musical sound that flowed like water, "*I don't wish to keep secrets from you my young companion. I have only been operating on your desire for my use.*"

Tristan thought back, "*Can you talk all of the time? What else can you do?*"

"*I do not know the limits of my powers. And I can communicate only about the present, my ability to aid you, and my understanding of my environment.*"

He pressed her further, "*Why do the powers you give me last only a short time?*"

"*Each time you invoke my powers, it makes me tired. I must rest. I signal this through the runes. Once you are more attuned, you will know when the power will fade.*"

"*How do I attune myself better?*"

"*Simply, the longer you hold me, the more attuned we become. If you* hold any of my sisters, and are attuned to them, I believe we can magnify our output."

"You mean Grace and the other one? What is her name?" Tristan liked that he was getting somewhere. He had already given his horse the simple nudge back toward Galagburg and they slowly traveled while he continued his conversation.

She seemed hesitant to answer this last before finally confiding, *"There are seven sisters. We were forged by Tharkus Threll, long ago to face the mighty Gormanthrazomere. Alas, the warlord defeated the armies of my maker. We were scattered to the winds. I don't know how far my seeking works, but at one time, I knew where Patience resided. Grace and I were found by a young man named Brell. He saw us more as tools, which of course we are, and used us to defeat Krebdulas the diamond eyed beast. Although this Brell had a good heart, it was hardened. Something inside him prevented us from making any meaningful contact. It is kind of embarrassing to be used as a hammer when we are so much more."*

Tristan was sympathetic to Brell and the swords, *"Brell is good. I have never met someone who wanted to do so much right. I'd go easy on him. But my brother and I are different. We will pay attention to what you tell us. That, I promise. We need all the help we can get."*

The boy and sword both rode silent the rest of the way back into town under the glow of Hope.

21

A scream. A moment later another scream. Lancelot shook off the sleep. Ardus was already in the chair, strapping his leg armor.

"Looks like it's begun," the warrior stated matter-of-factly. "Grab your sword. Let's try to find Brell."

Lancelot waited patiently for Ardus to finish armoring up. The warrior made sure everything was secured and his shield sat balanced on his arm. He hefted his heavy broadsword and looked to the boy, "Open the door for me." Lancelot did as asked and stepped aside. Ardus was huge. He barely made it through the door with his armor. Bear visor glared as he made his presence known.

It was still dark, but the clouds had mostly cleared and a fine orange glow heralded the rising sun. A torch in sconce lit the scene. Four townspeople ran past. Behind them, a unit of zombies marched as well as could be expected down the street. They clanked from ring studded leather and haphazard banging swords or clubs. It looked to be about a dozen of the enemy.

Two of the town guard, further down the street, beckoned for everyone they saw to follow them. Their arms waved urgently and they showed no more courage than those fleeing by. No effort was made to hide their fright and they fled along with the civilians.

Ardus moved to interdict the undead. He showed no concern for their deadly disposition. Zombified walking corpses attempted to keep in line as the shield crashed into their ranks. Their attempt at remaining in formation hampered their efforts to kill Ardus. The big man easily fought three soldiers at a time.

Half of the unit had been cut down when a shrill voice commanded the dead, "Don't stand in formation when you are engaged! Surround your foe and chop him to bits!" It was a wiry man, grease and dirt glazed his skin and hair. He wore a patchwork leather coat too large for his frame. In one hand the man carried a lantern, and in the other a serrated short blade. From the looks of it, he commanded not only this unit, but another ransacking a home. A dead woman lay in the front entry, her entrails spilled.

The zombies did as the dirty man said and they surrounded Ardus. The warrior ignored their ineffectual blows and steadily destroyed them, one by one.

Lancelot easily skirted around the melee and, with Grace in hand, sprinted toward the dirty man. The scoundrel noticed Lancelot's charge and called to his zombies. The boy was far too fast by comparison, and before any had come out of the house, dirty man had to defend himself. Confident, Lancelot feinted a strike to the man's head, and when the blade was raised to defend, Grace cleanly cut low. She sliced just above his pelvis, his paunch bloated for a moment before it disgorged his intestines and other unidentifiable parts.

The armored undead came out to follow their last living order. They descended upon Lancelot in the chaotic manner with which was their norm. Ardus was quickly at the boy's side, and it took mere moments to be rid of the remaining walking corpses.

"I wish the whole of this army was this easy to fight," Lancelot hoped aloud, but memory of the ghoul quickly sobered his thoughts.

"Let's find the others," was Ardus' only reply.

The pair wound their way back toward the center of town. Twice they stopped to help others who either tried to carry away too much of their belongings or had hurt themselves hurrying to escape the attack.

A horn sounded in the distance. The direction placed it out of the town to the north. Lancelot recognized the horn. Tristan connected with his thoughts, *"Did you hear that? It sounds like the army might be near the town. I am riding as fast as I can."*

"We have already been attacked. Ardus and I fought off twenty or so zombies. Well, Ardus fought them. I helped. We are looking for Brell now."

"Stay safe little brother. If you need, your sword can light. Use the La rune."

Lancelot could see Brell up ahead, *"Wait, there is no La rune. Oh, my sword just lit up. I see the rune now. How did you know that?"*

"I'll tell you later. Keep your eyes out for danger and listen to Brell. Tell him that Trazk went south to warn Elle and Timbershaven. Tell him that the rally point is ready. Down the southern road they will see two red blankets hanging from branches. Take the path on the right to a clearing. They should be safe there."

"Will do. Get back fast. I'm worried." The boys went silent but did not sever their connection.

"We encountered zombies by the church," Ardus reported to Brell. "I think they have human handlers. They only fight like soldiers when told." Brell nodded that he understood.

Lancelot spit out almost all at once, "My brother says Trazk went south to warn your niece and the others. Tristan is riding back. We can send people south. Look for blankets or something hanging from trees and there is a spot to rest down a path."

Brell chewed on the information. "Good. Hopefully we see Zed soon. Help me with this." The demon hunter looked to have been breaking apart a large wooden table. He crouched to get his arms under the pile of planks at one end. Ardus got on the other side and they moved the wood between two of the houses. Other men already hammered boards up as a makeshift barrier.

"Follow. I need to run up this line and check the work." Brell led the others around homes and up the street. Zed and Thelband were near the end of their inspection. Six militia stood by. They appeared to be waiting on instruction.

Zed asked, "How goes the defenses?"

"It's shoddy, but will have to do." Brell was obviously not happy with what he saw. "Zed, can you start placing men between each building? If you can spare two with crossbows in every gap, that would be the best I could ask for. I know you are not going to like it, but the town has already been breached near the church. I think we should put those houses to fire. It will form a barrier and funnel the army's efforts here." He gestured to indicate the makeshift walls. "You ought to start evacuating people now. Women. Children. Men with injuries. They can head south. There are blankets hanging from trees to let them know when they can stop."

"Evacuations I can do, but burning down the town is like killing your hens so the fox can't get them. I would be willing to have men in place to start the fires should we become overrun there. Otherwise, I'd prefer to leave troops to fight any more small incursions."

"Your men are cowards." Ardus didn't mince words. "Let me lead them and the town would stand a better chance." He looked to Brell.

The demon hunter tugged on his beard. "Okay. It doesn't make much tactical sense, but your argument is sound Zed. If you agree that Ardus leads the men to defend the east side of town, I'll try to make-do here."

Of course Zed agreed. He turned to his most senior man in a red tabard, the one who looked least scared. "Go with Ardus here. Round up ten men. Set up fires in preparation. Defend the town. Don't burn the houses unless you have to. Please."

Ardus and the man left. Brell put his hand on Lancelot's shoulder to keep him from going too. Zed turned to the next red tabard and commanded, "Go to each section leader. I want one man from each section to round up the civilians in their area and go with them when they leave the town. Have the sections report back here, except Vargos. Tell him to watch the southern road out and then have him reinforce the men at the eastern buildings. I don't want undefended townspeople being slaughtered on the road. If they are attacked, I expect no militia to take flight until the safety of the citizens has been guaranteed." The man hesitated then ran off to do his duty.

"Okay Brell. When they start trickling in here, the men are yours. Please save this town. I'll go assemble more people to help. Is there anything else you need?"

Brell thought for a moment then answered, "Food and water. We will need enough that these posts can be manned throughout the day, maybe two. Weapons. Crossbows are likely to only slow down zombies. I was thinking they would be used against the ghouls. I will need swords, clubs and spears. Everything you can spare."

To the last of his soldiers, Zed gave his final command, "You heard the man, scour this town for all of the weapons you can find. Empty the armory. Bring weapons and food back here. I want all soldiers that are not helping with the evacuation here on the double." The men at his command took off running in nearly every direction. "At least they understand the urgency. I just hope they are up to the task. Okay. Now that that is taken care of, I am a carpenter. Let me stay here and help you."

"Much appreciated. Hand me that hammer there. We can pull boards from the front of this home..." Brell led Zed around the corner. Their hammering picked up where their conversation left off.

Lancelot was left alone with Thelband. The halfling noticed they had been left to their own devices. "I know what we can do."

"What's that?" the boy was intrigued at the diminutive man's smile.

"We can scout. Not the dangerous kind." Thelband pointed to a balcony on the second floor of the home. It looked out in the direction of the approaching zombie horde. "Come on, I'll help you up. It will be more fun than going inside and climbing the stairs."

22

Tristan saw townspeople before he saw the town. He kept directing them back the way he came. By the time he entered the town, he was certain that way more people were on their way to the glade than could hide inside it. Hopefully it wouldn't matter. There were no signs of the undead here. Maybe they limited their excursion to the other side of town. Better yet, maybe the 'army' was smaller than everyone thought. Spread out, it could appear pretty intimidating. It would be a useful tactic.

Thrice, Lancelot had contacted Tristan. He was apparently sitting on a balcony somewhere. The enemy had not made themselves visible except at the first, near the church. He thought how nice it was having a horse. It was like a security blanket. If he had to, Tristan could bolt out of harm's way and off to safety. Of course, that wouldn't help his brother. He worried; and he hated being separated. Lancelot was always at the forefront of too many fights. Way too close for comfort.

Tristan found he had turned onto a familiar road and stopped in front of the Bear Trap Inn. Edrigar boarded up the windows. The innkeeper did not see the boy watching him. Tristan turned his mount and continued on eastward. He wasn't sure where his brother was holed up, then he had an idea, *"Hope. Take me to Grace."* He felt the subtle tug of instinct lead him down this street and that.

"Almost forgot you could do that."

Brell was in the middle of a conversation with Zed when Tristan rode into view. Seven or eight militia stood ready behind makeshift barricades and fences. They were armed with various missile and melee weapons. Almost to a man, they stared out past the town into the dimly lit wood. The small path north out of town was barely visible from this far left. A palpable unease permeated the area.

When he was in earshot, he overheard the tail end of Brell's conversation, "…should be secure enough. Those zombies must have wandered in ahead of the rest of the army, or failed to follow orders. You see anything yet Thelband?"

"Nothing!" was yelled from a second story porch.

As Tristan reigned up, Brell welcomed him back, "Good to see you made it okay. We received your messages." He looked to Tristan's waist. "Handy thing those swords. I'm glad they found their way into your hands."

"You gave those to us Brell," Tristan replied then laughed.

"I know. Luck though. I could have just as easily handed those to someone who fell." He changed the subject, "Did you see anything unusual riding through the town?"

"No. People were leaving is all. I heard a horn before I got into town."

Brell said, "We heard the same and thought that was going to signal an attack, but nothing has happened. I am sure they are here, just keeping out of sight. Maybe they are worried about the limitations of their troops. Maybe they will go around. Who can know the mind of the undead?"

Almost as if on cue, Lancelot yelled from his perch, "They are coming. On the road. It is too far for me to see who, but it looks like a rider and people….things…on foot."

Everyone waited. It seemed like an eternity. Brell was about to go see what was going on when a red tabard soldier rode into view. He came down the street from the direction of the sighted enemy and pulled up in front of Zed and Brell. The man was pale and sweating. His words stammered out, "S..sirs. The army at our front is s…surrounding us. We have…we have until…" he gulped, "until nightfall to turn over the vampire and his mercenary friends."

Brell answered the puzzled look on Zed's face, "That would be us. We only just learned of the zombie army." He felt he had betrayed the trust of the town's hospitality and tried to explain further, "Dellan Zhukovich is a vampire. The general who leads this army appears to be a free-willed undead zombie. Possibly a death knight. He is in league with Dellan. We were tasked by a man, turned to vampire by Dellan, to kill the creature that made him. It looks like our quest has put your town squarely in Dellan's sights."

He looked down at his feet while Zed distilled the new information.

"What's your name soldier?" Zed asked the militia-man in the red tabard.

"Bill sir." He responded.

"I assume they are waiting for a response?" Zed waited for Bill's nod of affirmation. "Okay Bill, I want you to make sure this message gets to them. The people they are looking for were here, but they left. We believe they are traveling to see Dellan right now. Can you do that Bill?"

"But sir…"

"Just relay the message I gave you. Nothing less. Nothing more. Do you understand?"

"Yes sir."

"Good. Thank you Bill. Get back there. Please return with their response."

Bill rode off. Zed looked at Brell who was astonished by his reply. "Don't look so surprised Brell," the carpenter said, "they were coming whether you were here or not. You don't amass an army within days because you just learned someone is coming to kill you. They have been building this army. You may be an excuse to unleash it, but I doubt that too. Come, let's go find out our fate."

Brell motioned for Lancelot and Thelband to stay put. "Come with me Tristan. You can stay in contact with your brother. Zed, you speak with the wisdom of a true leader."

As the three walked, Bill rode back and met them half-way,

relief painted his face. "Sirs, we told the rider what you said. The rider asked us when they had left. Sergeant Nord told them this morning. The rider looked satisfied by the answer and told us his army would move around the town."

Zed scratched the rider's horse behind the ear. "Thank you Bill. Return to your post. Inform us if there is anything new."

As Bill rode back, Zed turned to Brell and said, "I suspect they will attack. We had better check the men." Zed led the three back to their spot and stopped at each gap to ensure the readiness of the militia.

"Zed thinks they are going to attack. Keep a sharp lookout," Tristan warned his brother.

"Thelband sees movement beyond the tree line. They could be coming right now."

"Lancelot says they see movement. Watch for a possible attack," Tristan relayed the information.

"They won't attack quiet yet, but there may be some anxious handlers or maybe unruly zombies," Brell postulated, "We should get to our positions none-the-less."

The sun rose. Clouds dotted the sky and cold wind drove through the town out of the north. Everyone was thankful for the rations. Nobody was allowed to leave their post. Boredom set in. Soldiers wondered why they were still guarding when it had been said that the army circumnavigated Galagburg. After hitting its zenith, the sun crept downward. It was nearly hidden behind the mountains when the drum beats started.

Three horn blasts blared, followed by scattered yells and commands. Line after line of armored zombies breached the tree line and marched toward the town. Lancelot and Thelband had the best view, and no matter, left or right, they could not see the end of the formations as they bore down on the town defenders.

"Only shoot at fast moving creatures or living targets!" yelled Brell. "Your crossbows will do little, if anything against zombies."

Some soldiers fired anyway. Their bolts whizzed across the open space between the trees and where they took cover. As told, bolts that hit the zombies penetrated armor and flesh, but did nothing to slow the advance.

Row after row of rotting corpses shambled out of the wood. Fires sprung up on the eastern side of town. Between the formations of dead soldiers, fast moving ghouls appeared. These had no handler or chains. They used their hands to help propel them through the uneven grass. Crossbows fired, but the monsters deftly avoided the deadly bolts. There were about a dozen of the ghouls spread out in the visible line. When they reached the barrier, they jumped and climbed it easily. It was meant more for the slow-moving zombies. Panic could clearly be heard everywhere. Brell cut down the single ghoul that made it between his buildings.

"Stand fast!" he rallied the near fleeing militia. "Use the barriers to fight the zombies. Stack them up here. Do not let them through!" He beckoned for Lancelot and Thelband to come down. "Thelband, take Tristan around that way. Help kill the ghouls. Keep going until they are gone. Let the militia fight the zombies. Lancelot, with me." They went along the easterly buildings.

There was no ghoul behind the first barricade they passed, and the second had already killed theirs. It was beyond that where they found huge problems. Large groups of militia were routed and running their way, a half dozen ghouls were on their heels. "Turn and fight!" Brell commanded. His spectral swords raised, he sprinted in to turn the tide.

A ghoul had just jumped a soldier from behind and was eating into his back. With one swing of violet justice, the ghoul's head was split like a melon. The other ghouls took notice and slowed their chase. Some soldiers also gained their courage back and filed in behind the demon hunter. "The creatures can paralyze you with a bite or claw, but they can do little more damage than a man. Fight them as a group and you can overwhelm them."

Lancelot relayed the information to his brother through Grace and then joined a pair of soldiers who approached the carrion creature on the farthest right. The ghoul was very quick. It took a swipe at Lancelot, but was parried with the flat of his blade. It then drove its nails into the neck of the man next to him. The soldier froze in his tracks and then toppled over sideways. Lancelot gave the creature no more time to act. He swung grace ferociously. "Get him!" he yelled to the other man. They stabbed and slashed at the ghoul. It could not defend against both of them, and succumbed to their blows.

Each group of soldiers faired similarly. Three ghouls were left. The militia consolidated into two groups. Four, including Brell surrounded two, while Lancelot and his group charged headlong into the last. It was over fairly quickly. Seven militia lie paralyzed. Only one looked to have mortal wounds. "Quickly now. Let's move these men into that building over there. We have to get back and help fight off the zombies," Brell explained.

When the paralyzed men had been situated, Brell left the oldest soldier to bind their wounds and help them back into the battle when able. He looked around and saw that they were close enough to the main road in to town. "Let's help over there." He pointed and led the group to reinforce. More of the routed militia found their way back having witnessed the success of Brell's group. They followed around a large wooden building into a bloodbath.

Zombies were crouched over soldiers, eating flesh, internal organs and bone. Moans escaped from the last of the militia as they lay there being eaten alive. Across the road, Ardus had just arrived with a group of men. He and Brell made brief eye contact and both knew what had to be done. Two dozen men and boys charged the zombie invaders. At first, the killing was easy, but the undead numbered in the hundreds. That, coupled with slick, blood-soaked ground, blunted the attack. Zombies still marched in from the woods. Six soldiers fell to grasping hands and snapping jaws. The zombies forewent their weapons to just pull their prey apart. Defenders were overwhelmed faster than they could kill the horde.

An aging militia man, grey hair streaked with red called for a phased withdrawal. Brell agreed. First they commanded the youngest to fall back. Lancelot was with the first group and encouraged them, "Don't run. Stay together. Don't panic. If other's see us running scared, they are going to run scared too. Zombies are slow." He led them in an orderly retreat one building back in the middle of the street. "We wait here for the adults. When they get here, we will move a couple more buildings back." He counted the heads. They were down two boys. "Ready!" Lancelot yelled.

Brell and the others sprinted around the corner. The men were far less organized than the boys and terror was in their eyes. Brell used both hands and made a shooing motion. "Go! Go! Go!" The last man around the corner was jumped by a ghoul. His gurgled scream turned into bone crunching sounds as the monster chewed on his spine. Everyone turned to run. Ardus, slowed by the armor, was now the rear-guard.

A large cracking sound was followed by earth-shaking to the right. Brell urged everyone to run faster. A house exploded in a shower of beams and splintered boards. Inside, a humanoid, tall enough for his head to poke above the roofline shrugged his way through the broken home. It had arms and legs sewed on from various, unknown animals and creatures. Only the head looked human, but even that was the size of a small child. It reminded Lancelot of the beetles back in Ferrickport, and he shivered at how small they were in this world of giants.

The group was large and loud enough to steal the attention away from any fighting they passed. Militia from between each of the buildings joined them in their rout. Further ahead, another patchwork giant smashed through a home. He had a lifeless man in one hand, and held him like a child's doll. The creature kicked and batted his way through the wooden building and parked himself out in the middle of the street to face the fleeing militia.

Patchwork would be an understatement. The arm that held the lifeless man was oversized and green with bursting pustules. The creature's right arm was a giant fiery red claw, not dissimilar from a crab. It stood on two distinctly different legs. The left, a tree-trunk like grey. It was big enough to crush a man under. Its right leg was more a tentacle that writhed and folded under it, but surprisingly supported the giant's weight. Even its face was a mold made from an unknown amount of sources. A single tusk protruded from one side of its face. Greenish scales surrounded an eye that blinked through a nictitating membrane. All this sat under a molted fur mane with various horns and bone protrusions.

Brell huffed to Lancelot, "Use your sword, you have to get by it. Warn the others. Get to the inn. If that has fallen, get on the road south." He then waved to those behind him and turned right between a fenced home and a bakery. The line of retreat, except Lancelot, followed him.

"Will do!" Lancelot yelled as he ran toward the giant. He invoked Grace, "*Pel. Mora. Mira.*" The golem eyed him as Lancelot approached and then bobbed left. It used the dead man as a club and swung at the boy. Lancelot easily dodged the swing and rolled down and through the giants outstretched legs. He smiled at the power Grace bestowed upon him and even took a swipe with his sword as he passed under. Black blood spilled from the grey trunk. He was already on his feet and moved away. The body of the man plopped down in front of him, hurled by the beast. Lancelot was deft enough to rear back and stop before it hit him.

His pause was enough for the tentacle leg to wrap around his waist. Lancelot looked terrified as he was lifted off the ground, up toward the creatures face. His sword arm was pinned by the tentacle. He could do nothing, even with this strength, to break free. This leg would literally squeeze the life out of him.

Just then the creature was rocked by crashing plate armor. It was Ardus. He threw himself headlong into the golem and knocked it clean off its feet. The tentacle loosened enough for Lancelot to free Grace and he swiped and stabbed at the leg. The creature rolled onto its side and used its pincer to grab Ardus. The sound of bending metal and bones snapping preceded a howl from the warrior. Blood trickled out of his mouth.

The zombies clambered toward the brawl.

No matter how many times he slashed, the tentacle would not let go of Lancelot. "Toss me your sword boy!" Ardus squeezed between gritting teeth.

"But I have already activated the runes!"

"Just do it!"

Lancelot used every ounce of agility granted to him to fling the sword to the pinned fighter. He could see why the man wanted his blade. Ardus' sword arm was pinned and hanging loosely. The claw had split through some tendons and sinew. The man made a herculean effort to move the claw just enough so that he was in the path of Grace. He caught the sword with his off-hand. The shield had been crushed and lay useless on the ground. With one more great effort, Ardus drove the short blade deep into the face of the golem. In an instant it released both opponents. Feeling the speed ebb away, Lancelot didn't waste time rolling out from the legs and into the open.

Zombies were nearly upon them.

Not opting for self-preservation, Ardus rolled to bring himself closer to the creature's head. He used Grace like an axe and repeatedly chopped down on the golem's face and neck. Within moments the decapitated head looked more like puree than a body part.

"The zombies! Come on Ardus," Lancelot urged.

Ardus looked up in time to see two zombies bite into his exposed leg and side. Grunting, he brought Grace down, pommel first into their skulls. Bone and flesh caved into the brain cavities and the zombies fell motionless. Others reached and grasped for him. Lancelot was back at Ardus' side, and helped him limp away. They barely outpaced the walking dead.

"I wish I had time to strip off some of this armor. It's slowing us down." Ardus had already abandoned his helm and bent shield. "Not sure I'm going to make it kid."

"We can do it," was all that Lancelot could manage. He gave everything he had to support Ardus. They had gained a few paces on the zombies, but breaking glass ahead to the right hinted they might be cut off soon. It gave Ardus a boost of adrenaline and he hurried his limp.

"Just a little further. They are coming," Lancelot huffed between labored breaths.

"Who?" Ardus forgot Lancelot could converse through his sword. As if to answer him, Tristan and Thelband drove a wagon around the corner. They drove at them fast, almost too fast. The wagon's left wheels lifted off of the ground as it made the bend. While Thelband made to turn the wagon around, Tristan leapt from his seat and bounded over to help. He got his shoulder under Ardus' other arm and together they were able to double-time it to the back of the wagon.

"Hurry. They are right behind you." Thelband had climbed over the back of the seat and pulled on Ardus the best he could while the boys tried to lift him. They struggled and failed to get the big man into the wagon.

"It's no use," Ardus stated the obvious. "Climb in boys, we are going to do this the hard way." Thelband understood and handed each boy a coil of rope as they got into the wagon.

"What is this for?" Lancelot asked.

The halfling had already tied one rope around the front corner of the wagon and under the driving seat. He quickly worked the second rope. "Tie those around Ardus' wrists."

"No time." Ardus knew the jig was up. "Toss me the rope. Hold on to my arms." He leaned forward in the wagon so that only his upper torso rested in the open backed wagon. Each hand held tight to a rope. Tristan and Lancelot did as he asked. "Get your footing if you can." The wagon lurched forward. Zombies reached for Ardus' legs. Instinctively he kicked at one and knocked it onto its backside. The lone horse struggled with the wagon and its new cargo.

Zombies appeared through the doors and alleys ahead and spilled out into the road. Thelband directed the horse and wagon down an unoccupied street and they picked up speed. It was two more turns before they stopped the wagon to get Ardus all the way in. His hands bled from the burn of the ropes. Both boys sweat profusely from holding him as long as they did.

"Thanks. Find Brell if you can. I am going to be useless until healed." Ardus rolled onto his back and closed his eyes. He bled from more places than the boys could count.

23

Thelband kept the wagon at a slow pace. He had to avoid panicked soldiers and miscellaneous debris left out in the road. The din of the undead faded the further they moved south and west in the town. Tristan looked back and saw that the entire east side of Galagburg was on fire. "I don't think we can save this town," he voiced his thoughts.

"It sure doesn't look like it. We need to find Brell and get out of here." Thelband looked over at Tristan and asked, "You said Trazk is already out of town, right?"

"Yes. He went to warn Elle. He is probably not even there yet." The horse and wagon turned a corner, and they found themselves outside the Bear Trap Inn. Noises escaped the open door. People hurried in and out of the building.

Lancelot hopped down from the back of the wagon. "Get Brell," Thelband told him, but he already knew that is what he was after. The boy disappeared through the door.

"Should we help Ardus out?" Tristan asked. He looked back at the large unconscious man.

"No. Let's wait and see. I am hoping we can leave the big lug here. Maybe we can go in and pack our things and ride on out of town." The halfling went back and checked on Ardus' bandages. Lancelot had done a pretty poor job of patching the warrior up.

Thelband doubled up two bandages on his leg, tightened another, and then removed his jacket. This he folded and placed under Ardus' head. "Can't believe how thick his skull is. He was bumping around in this wagon with nothing to protect that fine brain of his."

Lancelot returned with Brell. The demon hunter's arms and hands were covered in blood. He wiped them with a reddened cloth. "We turned the inn into a hospital. Soldiers are coming in from everywhere. Glad you brought Ardus here."

Thelband hesitated, "I was thinking we could just heal him in the wagon here and get out of Galagburg. The zombies broke through everywhere. I doubt the inn will be here when morning comes."

Brell pondered his words then walked around to inspect Ardus. "Some of these are deep. I don't have much magic left." His hands glowed the familiar light as he used his holy powers to heal some of Ardus' wounds. Lacerations closed. Teeth ejected themselves from bites. His chest became fuller as his ribcage mended. "That's about all I can do for him until morning. It looks like the serious ones are closed. He won't be able to fight until I get a chance to heal him again, or until he has rested for a few days, maybe even a week." Brell took in the view outside the inn. His remaining friends were all in or around this wagon. Aside from the bright glowing to the east, the town was only lit by a few torches. Clouds had rolled in and redoubled their efforts to blot out the stars. Cold winds from the west threatened to bring snow. "You are right Thelband. It is time to leave. All of you, come help me pack our things."

Inside, several men lay unconscious in a row against the side wall. Edrigar did his best to assist Friar Mark and Father Neirul as the priests bandaged a man who had lost his arm. The man must have been a veteran. He was still awake and wouldn't even wince as Mark tightened the tourniquet around his stump. Zed sat in a chair. He sweat profusely from some unknown task. Brell went right up to the default leader of Galagburg, "It's time to evacuate your town. There is no way you will survive this onslaught if you stay."

Zed looked up, resignation in his eyes and replied, "Yes, I agree. We probably should have abandoned the town outright." The tired carpenter gestured for a soldier to come over and he directed at him, "Find the squadron leaders, we need to retreat. Tell them to move as orderly as possible and head south, toward Timbershaven. Maybe they will be better prepared to defend against this unholy army." He looked back to Brell. "Will you be traveling with us? Your martial expertise is most welcome."

Brell nodded, "I am sorry. We still have a task to perform. Possibly cutting the head off the dragon will dissipate this army. Although I fear Zumathash has more free-will than we could hope."

"Zumathash?" Zed was very interested.

"He is just another one of those monsters. He leads this army in the name of Dellan."

"I knew of a Zumathash when I was a child. It was said that a hundred or more years ago, he was convicted of murdering several children in some ghoulish ceremony. He escaped the hangman's rope and fled into the woods. I wonder if some darker power has rewarded him with…well with whatever he has now. Anyway, he became the favorite boogieman of bedtime stories and fables to threaten unruly kids."

"It doesn't really matter now Zed." Brell moved toward the stairs. "You have to get your people to safety." Tristan followed the demon hunter up to their rooms to get their belongings.

While they packed, Tristan asked, "Are we going to be in the rear-guard?"

Brell could tell he was nervous. "We are not leaving with Zed and the others. We still have a job to do."

"But we are missing Lareth and Trazk. Ardus is badly injured."

"I know Tristan. This task has been most perilous. Now you know why we tried to get you and your brother to stay behind. Our chances didn't look good then. They look worse now. I would not be opposed to you and your brother going back with Elle when we depart."

Tristan looked at Brell for a long minute. He noticed how old and tired the demon hunter really was. "How do you keep going? I mean, you know this is an ill-fated quest. You know our chances are slim at best. What drives you to continue?"

"Duty, moral obligation. I don't know, stupidity. Maybe all three." Brell put his hand on Tristan's shoulder. "You are young yet. Nobody expects you to throw your life into a cause. You are supposed to be exploring an innocent world still. The gods are not affording you that comfort. I fear though, Elle is as safe as we. The zombie horde will be there within a week. Across the sea, devils march upon ill-defended towns and cities. There may be no safe place to hide."

"We are not looking to hide. We might have been when we first met you, but we want to make a difference. Lancelot looks up to you Brell. He admires who you are and what you can do. We both know that with training, we will have to rely less on others. I know things have been tough, but if we were not at your side or Trazk's, in all likelihood, my brother and I would be dead. We are going to stick this out. We live or die fighting alongside our heroes."

"Let's not talk about being dead or dying. There will be plenty time for that some other year," Brell smiled with his response, "This looks like it. How about we get the others? Hopefully, it's not too late."

"Too late for what?"

Brell already walked out the door. His voice carried back, "Too late to make an end-around."

Downstairs, Lancelot and Thelband watched as the others carried the wounded outside into the wagon.

Guilt in his voice, Lancelot said as if being accused, "We tried to help them, but they said it would be faster if taller, stronger people were carrying them. And 'The door is too narrow for all us folk to be going through at the same time'. We tried."

Brell chuckled, "If they only knew." He pulled a hood over his head and gently commanded, "Follow."

Outside, Brell made quick talk with Zed. They shook hands, then the demon hunter beckoned the others after him.

"So what's the plan?" Thelband asked as he hurried to keep up. "I take it that we have no horses?"

"West." Brell led them between abandoned buildings. None of the militia had been stationed on this side of the town. "Just outside, the terrain drops precipitously. There is a narrow valley below. We can climb down and follow it for a time and then climb back out, hopefully behind Zumathash and onward to the vampire. Ardus will go with Zed. Possibly he can meet up with Trazk. Hopefully that orc finds us before we get where we are going."

"You healed Ardus," Lancelot said, "why couldn't he travel with us?"

"His wounds were deep, and infected by those unholy creatures. My healing only mended some of his bones and flesh. He may be strong, but those were serious injuries."

"Strong enough," the deep, hard voice of Ardus trailed from behind them. They paused as the warrior lumbered toward them, huffing. "I'm coming with you."

Brell protested, "You should rest. You imperil us all. We might be climbing sheer cliffs."

"I nearly bloodied Zed's nose when he said something similar. Don't make me hit an old man too. I'm coming with you. Thought you could leave me unconscious in a wagon." Ardus caught up and fell in line with the others. Brell sighed but thought better of further argument. Lancelot just smiled to his brother.

24

The group marched in silence. The hard packed road of Galagburg ended abruptly at the edge of the last buildings and they padded through a soft open field of grass and dirt. The field quickly gave way to brush and trees. Flat, soft dirt turned to uneven, broken stones and boulders.

Brell led them single file as the ground sloped abruptly. "I wish we had some rope to tie to each other. This is going to get dangerous," he said from ahead. They skirted a non-existent path along the top of the darkened gorge. Tristan looked below but could see nothing further than a few feet. The edge wasn't sheer, but it was easily a broken neck with one wrong step.

Crickets chirped below. Their calls echoed eerily off the canyon walls. Thelband noted, "As long as we can hear them, I bet we are safe from the undead. Maybe we can stay up here."

The halfling caught Brell's gaze and followed it back to Ardus, who was laboring behind with Lancelot's help. "I hope so." The demon hunter whispered back.

They snaked north. The air held a fine mist that painted the rocks with a slick sheen. Clouds prevented the moon from helping the group to see the perils that lie ahead. Only a single, flickering torch assured any form of safety. Brell led them slightly away from the edge of the gorge. Too many times already someone slipped or caught themselves from sliding over the ledge. They stopped on more than a dozen occasions to help Ardus climb over rock curtains that blocked their path.

Eventually a river, swelled from previous rains, blocked their progress and they followed it north and west. Before they saw the river dump over into the ravine, they were warned by its swirling splashes and then the crashing against rocks and shore below.

"Our hand is forced," Brell conceded, "I see no other choice than to go down."

Tristan asked, "Couldn't we follow the river back and cross somewhere else?"

Thelband answered that, "No. The river would be too dangerous and cold for us to cross. We would have to strip down Ardus and swim him across. His armor is too heavy. We might even be forced to leave it behind." As if reading Tristan's mind, he answered his next question too, "And if we followed it back far enough for a bridge, we would surely encounter the undead army first."

"We will rest here first," Brell instructed, "No sense in testing our endurance."

A cold voice startled them all, "You should have started down already. Your progress is pathetically slow." Swords were drawn or summoned as the group readied for an attack that did not come. It was Leopold. He was drenched in sweat as if he had been in the river. Water dripped from his chin and nose. "Wasting your time trying to save that town may have cost us all dearly. And now this traipsing around."

"We have injured and we are blind." Brell was annoyed. He obviously was either tired of being pressured or didn't like Leopold and it was finally starting to show.

Leopold ignored him. "I will ferry you down below. There is not much time. Scouts have followed you and are almost here."

Tristan looked at his brother worriedly. "Can we fight them? Are there too many?" he asked.

"We could fight them, but there are too many to insure someone doesn't find their way back to tell their general. They are tracking survivors, not you in particular. If word got back that it was you traveling north here, the entire army would come down on you. Stealth is your only hope."

Brell was still annoyed, "By all means. Get about it then. Take Ardus first."

The vampire walked over to the warrior. Ardus watched him warily as Leopold circled around behind him. "Do you mind?" The vampire hesitated until Ardus nodded his approval and then slipped his hands into the warrior's underarms. His grip was vice-like.

Leopold lifted off the ground, floated rather, and his arms strained at first when lifting Ardus, but they both went into the air and over the ledge. The two drifted down into the darkness smoothly and silently. As the vampire came back into view, a torch from below revealed Ardus' location, less than a hundred feet down. He stood with his back to the cliff wall, near a large pool fed by the waterfall.

In the same manner as the first, Leopold ferried each of the group to the bottom. When Lancelot had arrived, Brell and Tristan had already come before him. Only Thelband was left. Brell and Ardus watched the darkness a little too intently. "What is it?" Lancelot asked.

Tristan put his finger to his lips then shrugged. Lancelot gripped Grace and activated *Fin*.

"Okay. I'm quiet. What is going on?" He asked his brother again.

"We heard the weirdest sound coming from over there." Tristan pointed away from the wall. In this darkness, and with all of the underbrush around the pool, it was impossible to see anything beyond a few feet. *"It sounded like metal tapping on stone. It seemed to stop when it got our attention."*

"I don't see anything," Lancelot said nonchalantly.

"Nobody did!" Tristan stressed, *"That's what put us on edge. There is definitely something there. It must be invisible."*

Both boys heard an unfamiliar chuckle in their minds and they both looked at each other, worried and confused.

Then another voice entered their head, this one sounded or

thought like Leopold, *"What is this about something invisible?"* The vampire landed with Thelband in front of the boys, his back to where the mysterious noise came from. He gently placed the halfling down, but his gaze would not let the brothers go. *"I don't sense anything there in the brush. Tell me what you h…"*

The chuckling interrupted his thought, but it also had a voice, deep and ancient, *"It looks like we have a full-blown party in your heads. Too bad the gift I offer is not going to sit well with you."*

Both Tristan and Lancelot saw the horror on Leopold's face. Others were not privy to the conversation in their heads and studied the bushes for signs of movement.

Leopold leapt into the air. He was panicked.

Behind, water exploded out, spraying everyone except the vampire already in flight. Those able to react could only spin to see a massive glinting form emerge from behind the waterfall. It stretched itself upward and almost jumped, but its body and arm were long enough to swat the fleeing vampire just as he crested the gorge. Leopold spun haphazardly back to the earth and smashed into the rocks on the edge of the pool.

Brell, the first to recover, yelled, "Kromax, no!"

To call Kromax huge was an understatement. He was a dragon of epic proportions. Only the front half of his body was visible this side of the waterfall. Hindquarters remained hidden in a secret cave while the cascading water washed over and reflected on his coppery silver scales. Kromax's head was adorned with a crown of horns. They resembled spears set as a defensive perimeter and attached to a bone plate that curved back over his brow. Not nearly the same size, but more intimidating to say the least, were Kromax's teeth. Each as big as a small sword, any bite from his house-sized jaw would be fatal.

"Please!" Brell pleaded.

His enormous claw had pinned the vampire to a rock. Leopold lay stunned and unmoving. Kromax's long neck swiveled downward so that his face was level and square with that of Brell. He looked at the demon hunter as if to measure him.

All others stood frozen. Lancelot wanted to run, but terror had gripped him. Only urine and feces escaped. He could not even call out to his brother in their thoughts.

As Brell raised his hand and tried to speak, Kromax's head swiveled up, then down, and his massive jaws clamped down on the hapless undead. Leopold's upper torso disappeared with a loud slurping sound. The dragon then raised his head up high and roared so loud and long that it nearly deafened the group.

"Vinwangher Draconis!" Kromax's roar turned to a yell. "Why have you brought this thing here?" His claws had curled up, and one of them flicked out at Leopold's legs, scattering them like twigs several yards into the underbrush. His attention was fully on Brell. "Are you so addled that you cavort with vampires now? Give me reason not to eat you and your friends. You. You of all people should know better than to bring undead filth to my doorstep."

A greenish gas escaped from the dragon's nostrils as it snorted. Brell broke into a coughing fit and had to cover his mouth and eyes, then stepped back to get fresh air. When he looked up at Kromax, his face was red with burning welts and his eyes watered profusely.

Still, nobody else dared move. Nobody else could move.

The dragon's tone lightened from outright anger, but shifted to scolding, "The Brell I have known would not willingly travel with a vampire. Did he compel you into this?"

Brell, the only one who had not soiled his pants, stood defiantly in front of the dragon. He started to raise a finger but thought otherwise and put his hands on his hips. "Leopold was no ally, and even gave us the authority to kill him IF he were to turn against us. We were hunting for the master vampire that turned him. Leopold had a book which may have been able to reverse the process. You just thought it was okay to go ahead and snuff out his existence."

Kromax's attitude turned to one of indifference. He lifted a claw and looked at the nails uninterestedly. "Well, I suppose I did you a favor then." He almost yawned.

Now Brell did raise his finger and his face turned red while veins bulged in his neck. "Don't you try and turn this into 'Brell owes Kromax one'! You may very well have doomed our quest! I'm thinking 'Kromax owes Brell one' for a change."

Kromax shook off his apathetic tenor, and like silky lightning, the rest of his body slithered out from behind the waterfall. He reared up, and his wings and head disappeared momentarily into the darkness above. Then, just as quick, he was nose to nose with the demon hunter. He had fire in his eyes and his tone was all business. "Don't presume to demand from the great Kromax puny human! What kindness I have shown in the past is no reflection of my future actions. I should eat you right now!"

Brell's hands were back on his hips. He made no retreat and only stared into the mighty dragon's eyes.

"Try it."

The dragon growled, and the growl turned to a gurgle, then to a laugh.

"Brell, you really do have no sense. You have not changed a bit since we met." Kromax looked around as if noticing everyone else for the first time. He smiled, or at least it looked like a smile. "Clean your friends up and bring them inside." The dragon turned and his twisting body followed behind his head; eventually it disappeared back behind the waterfall into a well camouflaged cave.

25

Nobody but Brell had yet moved.

"It's okay. He is not going to eat you. You can move." Brell went to the water first, before it became dirtied, and splashed it on his face. The welts from the dragon breath oozed puss. The demon hunter winced as he cleaned out each swelled bump.

Ardus was the first to break from the terror that gripped them. He disrobed and then waited patiently for Brell to finish before he cleaned his own britches. "In all my life, I have never seen something so terrifying. And I thought I feared no death."

"Don't be hard on yourself," Brell consoled. "A dragon's fear is amplified. Yes, a hundred foot long fire-breathing beast is terrifying enough to behold, but Dragons are beings infused with magic. They exude fear as an unbathed man stinks. It is a magical fear that emanates from the dragon's body. Even while it sleeps, it gives off an aura. Maybe it is a natural defense mechanism."

"You know a dragon?" Tristan finally asked with astonishment. He still shivered where he stood.

"Kromax and I go way back. At least way back in my life. I think he is several hundred years old. Maybe more. He has laid waste to castles with me on his back. We traveled together through time once." Brell stopped and stared off at the thought then shook his head. "He sure can be a headache sometimes."

"He was noticeably angry at you. Did you do something to him in the past?" Ardus quizzed.

"Aside from the argument that caused us to part ways....and it was less an argument than me being angry at him for being...well, being him. I have to think it was Leopold."

Thelband helped the brothers to get their limbs moving again. Lancelot shook like a leaf. Brell paused to help him undress, then continued as he washed the boy's clothes for him.

"Not long before I left, Kromax and I went after a lich who was the exarch of a minor demon lord. On that quest, we stormed a tower looking for information where we both became cursed. We didn't know at the time, but it left us practically blind to seeing undead. The curse nearly got us both killed in the final confrontation with Azar, the lich. We didn't see him until he was already upon us with his cohort of wraiths and specters. In the final battle, Kromax was battered and weakened. He never felt so vulnerable. I have to think the scars run deep. I just didn't think he would react so negatively to Leopold."

Surprised, Ardus questioned, "You knew Kromax was here? Why didn't you say anything to us?"

Brell replied, "To be honest, I only speculated he was in this gorge. I had no clue where."

"We all crapped our pants," Ardus changed the subject. "How did you avoid making such a mess Brell?"

"I think it is just that I have spent so much time with that Dragon that his fear has no effect on me. Maybe I just built an immunity to it. Maybe I am just too old and too stupid to care. I remember the day I knighted my pants with my own shit. If you meet more dragons, I suggest having an extra pair of pants.... Every time."

After cleaning themselves, the group checked their weapons and supplies. Brell gave a small prayer and apology to Leopold.

"So what does it feel like to be cursed?" Thelband pondered to Brell.

"Scary actually. You don't know you are cursed. It took me more than a year to find the cure, and even that doesn't leave some cheery feeling to let you know the curse is lifted. You just have to go on with your life and trust in the magic."

The old demon hunter led them around the pool and into the waterfall. Hastily, the rest followed.

"This reminds me of the cave back home," Tristan reminisced to his brother.

"Yeah, but this one has a REAL dragon. I never thought we would see one. And now we just watched one eat a vampire while we ran away from an army of zombies on our way to fight another vampire. Wow," Lancelot replied.

"Wow," his brother's thought echoed and then trailed off.

Both boys were speechless. Beyond the falls the cave widened and descended natural stairs. Torches had been recently lit by another and revealed a cavern that easily matched the size of their farm fields back home. Bats flitted about in the upper reaches, hidden by jagged stalactites. Although the torches on the other side could be seen, something in the air slightly distorted the view. At the foot of the stairs and covering the floor from wall to wall several feet high was the true breath-stealer. A treasure undreamed of welcomed the adventurers into the hall. Gold, silver, platinum and mithril coins abound. Items protruded from the piles, for it was several piles of treasure melded into one. Weapons, armor, and other less discernable things just lie about, as if for the taking.

Brell looked at the boys and sensed the treasure-lust that was coming over them. "Do not take anything. Kromax, like any other dragon in the land has some genius ability to know exactly how much treasure is in its hoard. We do not want to be accused of thieves. Think of Leopold before you try anything foolish here."

That snapped the boys' attention away from the glitter and to Kromax. But the dragon was nowhere to be seen, and there appeared to be no other exits to this massive chamber.

Brell immediately led them over a pile of coins that shifted under their feet like sands from a dune. He determinedly wound through Kromax's hoard and crossed the chamber to the far wall. It was rough-hewn with the sporadically lit torches offering their patterned light. The demon hunter searched, first with his eyes, and then with his hands against the wall.

Ardus, tired of waiting, finally asked, "Do you need help? What are you looking for?"

"A secret way in to Kromax's inner chamber. They are always very hard to find and well-guarded. I know it is here somewhere. Maybe we should start in the center here and work our way out each way. Look for anything odd about the wall such as imperceptible door lines, or odd feelings which might be an illusion."

Lancelot offered, "How about there, above?" He pointed to a ledge, maybe a foot higher than Ardus' head. It ran the length of the back wall.

Brell turned red at missing what now seemed so obvious. Annoyed, he commanded Ardus, "Give me a boost."

The burly warrior cusped his hands together like a stirrup, and heaved Brell up with a pained grunt. Brell rested his elbow on the ledge and used his other hand to shield his eyes from the torch light. "This is it. Push me up further."

Once Brell was up, Ardus helped everyone to climb the ledge. He then stepped back and took a running jump up the wall, and easily slipped and slammed against it. All of the wind was knocked out of him. Tristan and Lancelot had to climb down and it took all of the companions from above and below to haul the massive warrior up.

Everyone sat down and strained to catch their breath.

About twelve feet back, the ledge met another wall that sloped up and back over them to connect to the ceiling. A grey painted wooden door seemed oddly out of place here.

"What do you think this means?" Tristan puzzled as he stared at the door. "You don't think the Dragon could fit through that door do you?"

Brell smiled the 'I know something you don't know' smile, and failed to play down his obvious excitement of recovering from not noticing the ledge. "No, not in their true form."

"True form?" This time Thelband asked.

"Yes, true form. Dragons of a certain age can master the ability to shapeshift. And Kromax is very old. He may even be able to take more than one form. As far as I have seen, Dragons are limited to humanoids. You know, orcs, dwarves, humans and the such. They prefer elves. I'll never understand why."

"It is because elves, like ourselves, are a long-lived race." Kromax was among them, and had come from somewhere other than the door which they all faced. He stood taller than Ardus, more fit and lean. He was shirtless and his muscles were toned. His skin was dark bronze, like Ardus, the same as humans that lived in the lower latitudes. The dragon, now man, sported a pony tail of golden yellow hair. "It is a deference we pay them. Well, I don't. But you know what I mean." He walked toward the door. "Come, sit with me. You have much to tell."

Everyone followed Kromax through the molted grey door. Beyond lay an entry hall far unlike the treasure chamber they left behind. They stood in a trapezoidal hall, two bronze statues of unfamiliar human females stood nude in dancing poses, their index fingers nearly touching as they each reached over the single exit leading from the center of the hall. The walls were smooth and worked with intricate circular designs. The floor was tiled with reflective marble.

Kromax walked ahead leisurely and glanced back only once to see that everyone followed. A dim light, which originated nowhere but seemed to be everywhere, bathed the area in a soft glow.

A short distance away, the hall opened into a comfortable looking sitting room. Large, and very expensive carpets covered the floor and even hung from the wall. "Take your shoes off," the dragon warned as they were led in. Large pillows of all shapes and colors littered the floor. A single gilded divan was situated further back, center-lined to easily take in the whole room. "Have a seat anywhere." And by anywhere, he meant 'go ahead and sit on the floor or the pillows.' Kromax lay on the sofa and propped his head up with his hand.

Tristan took his boots off and helped his brother remove his water-logged footwear that seemed too tight to remove. The others already sat and faced Kromax by the time the boys were done.

Hurriedly, they sat behind Brell and took in the rest of the room.

There were two other exits, both hallways, curtained with thick brown tapestries. Each displayed a symbol of religious significance. Tristan thought it might be dwarven by the hard lines and bold, runic features. On either side of the room were dark stained teak tables with petite drawers. They could not quite be classified as desks.

"Convince me," Kromax said vaguely.

A long silence followed before Brell cleared his throat. He looked at the bronzed man laying so laissez-faire, but certain that the answer he gave could spell the end of this quest in a most unsatisfying manner. He swallowed one more time before he responded, "Kromax the Resolute, Harbinger of Fate, Master of the Five Ways, and Bringer of Justice…" Kromax smiled ever so slightly at the formality. "I have spoken true of our association with Leopold Gambaldi, the vampire. It was our intent to destroy his maker in hopes of returning Leopold to his human form. We harbor no evil in our hearts and had not known that…"

Kromax cut him off, "No, no. I get all that. Convince me why I should be helping you. And I don't want to hear, 'because oh great and wonderful master of the passing wind, we have traveled together and kicked some serious demon-tail together…blah blah blah'. Tell me true or I'll have to eat one of your young." He looked right at Lancelot who turned sheet white.

Brell let slip, "You are still an ass." Then pursed his lips as if to catch what had already been said.

Kromax burst into laughter, "Haaa! Not the truth I was looking for, but it's a start." He looked beyond Brell to the rest of his audience and more specifically at Lancelot, "Fear me not human child. I know Brell inside and out, and he would not be traveling with those I would eat. Well, maybe rip in half, but certainly not eat. I'll get to the point. Brell, you are old. What was so important to get your brittle and crumply bones moving again? Why are you here?"

With new understanding, Brell sighed and turned, his hand offering the boys. "These two. I blame these two."

Tristan looked offended and wanted to protest, but Brell

continued, "These boys were made homeless by an army of devils. They found me and then brought me back to life when I thought I was done giving. Tristan and Lancelot have instilled in me purpose and hope. Their quest is now mine. Helping the vampire was secondary. I have a sense that his creator has a hand in the larger picture." Brell stood and walked over so he was between the brothers. He kneeled and placed a hand on each of their shoulders. "I sense greatness in these brothers. A lot to learn they have, but I see myself in them. They would benefit greatly with the patronage of one so mighty as yourself."

Kromax's eyebrow rose, "Go on."

Brell changed his tack, "The lands to the south are now overrun with Codrugon spawn. I fear all of Tamm is now gone. And you and I both know Tamm is the only duchy in Morkroth worth giving a damn about."

"I guess that changes my summer plans." Kromax's interruption was met with a furrowed brow.

Brell continued, "And now these lands are infested with an army of undead. Its leader allies himself with this very vampire that we seek. My niece may be dead or dying as we sit here on pillows and chat about the weather. The world is going to shit. This is not the time to lay back and, and well do whatever it is you do these days."

"To be honest," Kromax sat up and sighed in tune with a shrug, "I have not had the luxury to lie around. This is the first time in a month that I get to relax and entertain. An old friend even. I have spent my days collecting bribes from the snow goblins to the north; and have been counting, counting, counting all the coins. You know they pay in coppers? It's the same price everywhere, and the fetid blue-skins pay me in coppers! Where do they get that? Robbing poor farmers? They seriously mess with the beauty of my hoard. Faraxus is going to think I'm a hobo dragon." He looked around to each of the group, pleading in his eyes. "Would any of you be willing to exchange gold for my copper? I'll give a good deal."

Brell erupted, "Why are you always so flippant?!" He moved toward Kromax, one arm on his hip and the other with a finger in the bronze man's face. "You do this every time! I thought at first, you just had a way of trying to make light of heavy situations. Why do you think I dodged out of the Smoky Grind Tavern those years ago? I couldn't stand your immaturity and jokes! You make my blood boil!"

He turned and started to storm out of the room. Before reaching the exit, Brell spun, his finger still in its accusatory pose. His mouth opened to sling one last jab, but he was too angry to think of anything else to say.

Kromax tried to look serious, but took advantage of Brell's pause, "Don't try to catch flies with that mouth open."

Brell spit out an angry "Gah!" and left, red-faced and defeated. In a panic, Tristan rose and followed him out of the waiting chamber.

Kromax looked innocently at the others who were more stunned than he at this unfortunate turn of events. "Oops. Do any of you have questions for me?"

26

Brell left through the grey door and after the two had put their boots back on leapt from the ledge as he ignored its height. He kicked a small gem out of his way on his b-line toward the waterfall. Tristan struggled to keep up.

"Slow down Brell. I understand you are angry, but I think you are going way overboard here. Kromax could really help us." He clumsily climbed a mountain of gold.

Brell put a hand out and helped Tristan crest the pile. Then his hands went to his hips. He was ankle deep in gold coins. The demon hunter took a breath to say something, then took another to say something else. He paused, then aborted his tirade with a sigh and conceded, "You might be right. That dragon infuriates me. I thought it might be different, but he has not changed."

A shadow over Brell's shoulder caught Tristan's attention, but it was fleeting, and he was not even certain he saw something.

Brell put his arm around Tristan's shoulder and they continued toward the exit. "I think some fresh air will calm these angry nerves. Kromax has not kicked us all out, so there is hope yet to parley his assistance."

Another shadow, then another. Just beyond the waterfall. Or were they in the waterfall? Brell noticed it this time. He halted Tristan and with an outstretched arm behind him commanded him to wait while he investigated. The spots of shadows became a blanket of darkness in the water. Tristan thought he saw arms or legs.

The old man's wizened hair disappeared beneath the hill of coins they were on and that is when Tristan saw a wave of zombies pour into the cave.

In Kromax's audience chamber, the group had no questions they were willing to ask, and the dragon digressed to jokes or lamented his failed friendship with Brell. Not much of it made sense. They had no point of reference; for they lacked both worldly experience and all of them had not yet recovered from the dragon fear. After much self-aggrandizement, Kromax realized he had lost his audience.

He stood and said, "It looks like our meeting is over. I had hoped to hear much more of your quests and adventures." It went over his head that he couldn't very well learn of their adventures with all of his bloviating. "Brell needs to lighten up. Always so serious."

Lancelot looked to Thelband and they followed Ardus' lead to quickly stand and back out of the room. He was last to leave. Before he did, he put his hand to Grace. *"I would have traded you your coppers if Brell didn't get so mad."*

Kromax just stared at him as he left, still as a statue.

When they arrived at the grey door, they found it open and heard combat beyond. Ardus ran forward. Thelband urged Lancelot to draw his sword and follow. The two moved in unison into the great treasure hall. Already several paces ahead, Ardus disappeared over the ledge in a single leap.

Combatants, or more correctly invaders overwhelmed the far side of the chamber. It looked as if the whole of the undead army was here. The flicker of twin violet blades signified Brell's location in the melee, and he was surrounded by walls of enemies. The majority were the slow moving zombies, though their sheer number was dangerous, especially since they packed the entrance, or more importantly, the only exit to the chamber. Ghouls pranced about, their neck chains rattled. They looked for openings and generally acted erratically. A lone shadowy figure hovered near the waterfall and commanded the troops to act. The numbers continued to swell. They were almost twelve deep when Ardus rammed into their flank.

"We need to get down there and fast!" Lancelot worried for Brell and Tristan's safety. He panicked when he could not see Tristan and he prepared to make the leap into combat.

Sir Thelband put his hand on Lancelot's elbow to stay him, "No. We don't stand a chance against that horde. You will only get yourself killed if you climb down there."

"*Tristan! Where are you?*" he reached out for his brother. He was met with silence.

The din of combat echoed off of the chamber walls. It was deafening. Below, they could see where each of their companions fought. Brell's blades were a blur. He was swinging them incredibly fast, and it looked as if he were stepping on the bodies of the fallen, for he rose higher as he whirled and slashed. Ardus was a brute. Even as wounded as he was, he smashed, slashed, punched and threw anything near him.

Grey smoky fingers clawed the ledge then pulled a rotting, near-fleshless ghoul up to face the boy and halfling. Lancelot spun in with his sword and the ghoul deftly arched back to avoid its blade. Then Lancelot used his momentum and swing to kick the ghoul square in the chest as it rose back. The creature flew down into a swell of zombies.

Thelband called out to him, "Lancelot! Duck."

Lancelot instinctively obeyed. A solid bolt of lightning streaked over his head. His hairs raised and he felt a warm tingle pass through his body. It came from behind and streaked forward with a crackling whip-like sound. A score of zombies and even a couple of ghouls caught the impact of white hot tendrils. They either caught fire or exploded where they stood.

The bolt originated from the fingers of Kromax. He had been in his human form, but now was mid transformation. It looked as if his human form flew, but it more expanded and by the time he was fully dragon, only his tail remained on the ledge with Thelband and Lancelot. Even that wisped and whipped upward to avoid crushing the pair.

"You have entered the house of Kromax unannounced and uninvited!" the dragon's voice boomed above the chorus of moans and clanking weapons. "And you stink of unwashed bodies. A crime far greater than the trespass!"

The dragon finally descended from his transformation and his front claws trampled down upon several of the undead. The great chamber shook from his titanic landing. Ardus stumbled and then uncomfortably continued to fight his opponents even though he found the dragon's chest to be right above his head.

Kromax craned his head around and down to be level with the gladiator, "Inspires you?" then snatched a half-dozen zombies up into his mouth. He quickly spit them up and out. "Gack! You taste worse than you smell!"

The horde refocused toward Kromax, but ghoulish claws nor zombie blades could penetrate his hide.

Bronze talons reached down and around Ardus. "Sorry about the zombie sludge. Anyways, this is now not your fight, so why don't you sit this one out?" He lifted the warrior up and unceremoniously dropped him back onto the ledge. Chunks of zombie body parts rained down on him as Kromax shook his claw off.

"What about Brell and Tristan?" Ardus yelled back, "Help them!"

"Like Brell needs, wants, or even deserves my help." Kromax sounded hurt.

The great bronze dragon's body swiveled up and then took a belly flop down onto the largest swell of zombies that he could without crushing his old friend. Again the chamber rocked. More than not toppled off balance and fell to the ground. For the zombies, it was not an easy task to regain their footing. Brell, who had also fallen, was quick to take advantage. He lifted Tristan from the spot where he fought and tried to make for the ledge, but soon found himself surrounded again.

Kromax, belly to floor, scooched his body forward, and like an eel cutting through water, used his head to part a path of gold to the demon hunter. This time, he kept his great jaws sealed. He was not about to eat any more zombies.

Brell cut down a leaping ghoul just as the path offered his freedom. "Thank you Kromax," he said between labored breathes. He stumbled as best he could back to the ledge, Tristan over his shoulder. Ardus laid down and lowered an arm to easily pull the boy and then the demon hunter up. Brell sweat profusely from his exertion.

There they sat for nearly an hour while the Harbinger of Fate cleaned house. On two more rare occasions, a ghoul made it to the ledge. One was brained by Ardus' backhand, and the other met several slashes from Thelband's dagger before falling back into the room. Lancelot sat with Tristan. He poured water over his forehead, then noticed blackened marks on his arm and neck.

"What happened to him?" he pleaded to Brell.

"A shadow had drained him of all his strength. One second he was ready to fight, the next I was killing the thing that was trying to gain entry into his body. He will recover, but he will hurt for some time."

"What happened here?" Lancelot asked.

Brell answered, "We were followed. These things were led by some dread knight. I spied him trying to escape when Kromax came to our aid."

"No worries," Thelband excused, "I think it had better hurry if it is going to escape the wrath of Kromax."

"That's right," The dragon interjected, "I think this undead problem has just become my problem." Kromax was nestled near the ledge, his eyes level with the group. "You can rest here if you like, then continue on your journey. I doubt you will be molested by the likes of them again."

"Why?" Brell looked at Kromax suspiciously. "I can

understand you killing these undead because they violated your home. But why continue to help us?"

Kromax stared down Brell for what seemed an eternity, then looked at Lancelot and winked, "I'm in it for the money. Call me a mercenary." He laughed then turned to the exit. His wings gave just enough lift that he glided out through the waterfall graceful and silent.

Brell threw his hands up, "What was that all about?" Lancelot thought it best to let Brell wonder away and kept quiet.

Ardus gave direction, "Let's take Kromax up on his offer. I will be needing your healing hands Brell." It was now obvious he limped even worse than before. A large dark spot was evident on his left pant-leg and he had other scratches, bruises and cuts on his arms, back and chest. Lancelot rushed to help him walk, but the warrior shrugged him off, "I can walk. Help Brell with your brother." He also appeared irritated, if not for another reason.

The group returned to the sitting chamber and decided it was as good a place as any to recuperate. Brell stacked nearly half the pillows together so that Ardus and Tristan could rest comfortably. Ardus looked like a small child as he sunk into the fluff, and Tristan disappeared altogether. Brell's hands glowed their healing white and the large wound, now visible on the pantless warrior, closed up, along with the other, smaller injuries.

Thelband went through the packs and gathered what rations he could. About half-way through, he gave a sigh of dismay, "Folks, we may have a problem. We are looking at about another day and a half worth of food here. It's gonna take us longer than that just to get to the vampire's house." He looked at Brell for approval as he asked, "How about I go look for something to eat? Kromax did say to make ourselves at home."

Brell's eyes made a juggling motion as he contemplated the ramifications of ransacking the Dragon's home. "I don't see any other option really. Just be careful, and don't touch anything you don't have to. Dragons are quirky."

"Can I go with him?" Lancelot asked.

Brell shook his head no, "Why don't you stay here with me and watch over these two? Maybe we can start you learning your healing craft."

Lancelot was both surprised and pleased to hear this. "Of course." He said as businesslike as he could, but a creeping smile betrayed his enthusiasm.

Tristan sat bolt upright and rammed a jumble of thoughts into Lancelot's head, "*We are under attack! Warn Kromax! Zombies! Argh....*" He grasped his arm and neck.

"*Relax brother. Kromax saved us. He must have heard my calls to you when I could not see you in the treasure chamber.*" Lancelot calmed his brother down.

27

Thelband delayed until Brell had inspected Tristan and made sure he was indeed going to be okay. The color returned to the boy, and Tristan claimed he needed a walk to shake the cold off.

"You can go with Thelband," Brell allowed, "but don't do any heavy lifting, and stay close."

While Brell and Lancelot cleared out a space near Ardus, Tristan and Thelband emptied two of the packs which they strapped to their backs.

"Left or right?" Thelband asked.

"Let's try the left curtain," Tristan said as he walked over and parted it. He put his hand on the corner of the hall to steady himself. Standing so suddenly gave him the spins.

"Take it easy," Thelband cautioned.

Tristan waited for the nausea to pass then led the way through.

Beyond was a hall with floors and walls that matched the foyer into Kromax's 'human' lair. About mid-way, three steps descended, and beyond those, the hall dead-ended. Two plain wooden doors faced each other, while a third, ornate, and rather gaudy bronze monstrosity lie straight ahead.

Tristan was drawn to the decorative, dragon-headed handle. The door itself was rather plain actually, pressed bronze with iron nails to secure it. The frame exploded out around it. It looked as if

216

someone crafted all manner of scenes and designs out of support beams used in mines. Nothing made sense in the frame, although figures were recognizable as humanoid or animal. It was so offensive, Thelband jokingly suggested they light the whole thing on fire.

Tristan laughed and approached the door. "Should we?" He asked as he reached for the handle.

"Better not," Thelband cautioned, "I think this may be the Dragon's personal chambers. We are just looking for food. Not loot."

"I know," Tristan hesitated, "But aren't you at least curious?"

"Curious killed the gnome. I'm no gnome, and I am not looking to get myself eaten."

Tristan diverted to the door on the left. Instinctively, he knocked. Then they both laughed. At least until the door opened.

"Can I help you?" a very old looking woman with onyx skin and deep emerald eyes asked.

Both Thelband and Tristan tripped over each other trying to back up in their surprise.

The woman just looked at them without cracking a smile and waited for them to regain their footing. "Do you need something?" She asked.

"I'm sorry. You surprised us madam." Thelband was the first to recover. "I am Sir Thelband Highfellow and this is my traveling companion Tristan. We are guests of Kromax. He, um, stepped out. We were just looking for some food." He bowed as deeply as he could. Tristan put his hand on his belly and crooked over, far less inspiring.

The woman opened the door wider. "Come in." She wiped her hands on a grey apron that she wore over a white dress. Around her waist she had what looked like a workman's belt, but instead of carpentry tools, she had kitchen utensils and what looked like spice containers. Her long white hair was tied back behind her head in a ponytail.

Immediately, the smell of cooking informed them they had found the kitchen. This was a large room with a dining table in the center. Eight chairs surrounded the table, but the woman used two of them to stack crates. Onions peeked out of one of the small brown boxes. On the table were candles, and two place settings set and ready. Near to the crates, the woman returned to her task. She stood at a much smaller table, a cutting board and mixed vegetables, near-prepared, on top. Beside her, a lit fireplace housed a small cauldron of boiling liquid, the source of the fantastic smell. Her back was to Thelband and Tristan.

"Sit," she commanded and used her elbow to direct the two to the table. They did as she said. The lady took a thick cloth which she used to grab the scalding cauldron handle and lifted it onto the edge of the table. "Give me the bowls there." Again they did as she bade. She took a ladle off her belt and scooped two healthy servings of what looked and smelled like lamb stew into each bowl.

Both Thelband and Tristan tasted the stew. Their faces and "Mmm"s indicated they liked what they ate. Between bites, Thelband asked, "Who might you be? Kromax's cook?"

She crossed her arms. "That. And his wife." She watched, amused, as liquid sprayed out of Thelband's mouth and nose.

"My apologies!" he coughed out along with some food. "I didn't know."

The woman looked sympathetically on Thelband. "You walked right into that one Sir Thelband, didn't you?" Then she smiled and said, "I am Magari Sindunu. Maggs is fine."

He still sat dumbfounded. Tristan picked up on his confusion and noted, "I think he is surprised that a human is married to a dragon, unless you are a dragon too. Are you?"

Now Magari laughed. "No. I am as human as you, young man. I had his same look the day I found out my betrothed was a dragon. It sure took some getting used to, but I love my big baby."

"Your cooking is incredible. This looks like any stew I have had at home, but there are so many tastes. And they blend together like…." Tristan couldn't find the right words.

"I think that is why Kromax proposed to me. He sure got cozy the minute he tasted my roast swine. It was a whirlwind romance after that."

Thelband finally regained his senses, "Um Magari. We hate to be more of an imposition, but our other friends are close by in the sitting room. They are recovering from a fight in the treasure hall."

Magari's brows creased and she looked worried. "What happened? Is Melkar, I mean Kromax okay?" she asked as she wringed her hands. It looked as if she were about to take flight to find him.

Thelband stood and put his arms out to stop her, "Oh he is okay. Better than okay. He stomped the enemy good. But he now has a mind to take the fight to the rest of them. You see, an evil undead army of zombies is marauding in the lands above. I think Kromax is going to stop them in their tracks."

Magari looked even more worried than before. "That old dragon shouldn't be out playing with undead. He has a…" she looked at them conspiratorially and weighed their allegiance, "a blind spot for the likes of them. And I don't mean a good one."

"Do you mean he is still cursed?" Thelband asked. It took her by surprise.

Before she could answer, Tristan, who had been chewing on another bit of information asked, "Who is Melkar?"

Magari put one hand on the table to keep her balance. She didn't take well the news of Kromax being in a fight. After a deep breath, she answered, "That is my husband's human name. I forget he doesn't reveal himself to others like he has done for me." She stared off toward the wall for a moment, lost in thought before she continued, "Come. Let's meet your friends. I am sure they need a good meal as much as you."

Thelband bent over and spooned up the last of his stew and finished by slurping the left-over juices. He wanted to finish just in case this was his last chance to enjoy Magari's cooking. She smiled as he hurriedly pushed his chair in and jogged to lead the way back to the group. Tristan fell in behind Magari.

"How long have you been married to Melkar, if it is not too rude of me to ask?"

"It might be if it were anyone but me. I am tickled to have guests. We met shortly after my seventeenth birth year. I am now eighty eight."

Thelband parted the curtain and introduced Magari to the group as she stepped through the threshold. She was received with pretty much the same reaction she received from the halfling in the kitchen. One by one, Thelband introduced his companions to her. When he said Brell's name, she registered instant recognition. Immediately, even before she could catch herself, Magari slapped Brell as hard as she could muster. Instead of retreating, she stepped into his space so she was looking right into his eyes. Of course, she only stood as high as his chest.

"How dare you!" she accused him. She wanted to belt him again, but the greater part of her anger passed.

Brell stepped back and put his hands up to ward her off. "Excuse me milady, and apologies. But what have I done to you?"

"Not me. Kromax! You left him high and dry nearly twenty years ago. He spun into depression. Our marriage was in shambles for nearly three years. How could you do that to a friend?"

Brell became defensive, "I...Look, I didn't know dragons considered anyone friends. He pissed me off. And I don't mean just the once, but time and time again."

"He is right," she affirmed to herself more than to the audience here, "You are a humorless bag of holy wafers."

"I have a sense of humor. Kromax just takes everything too far. The world is a joke to him."

"He is a bronze dragon. What else do you expect? His god and his god alone holds the answers to all riddles and the answers are always a joke."

"That's not true. His god wasn't even here when the world was formed. How could he?"

"Palladius have mercy on me for even bringing this up. You take it up with my husband when he returns. I am not going to get in an argument on religion with a priest."

Brell was already on the defensive, so he couldn't help trying to get the last word, "I'm a demon hunter, not a priest."

"Same thing." She turned to the others, "Let's get some food in you. I'm sure listening to this is not helping anyone's stomach, especially this one." She put her hand on Lancelot's head. "You must be really hungry." He just nodded.

With everyone seated at the table, Magari went around and served bowls of the stew along with a small loaf of bread and a hot mug of hard cider. She whispered in Ardus' ear that she had something to help him heal faster. Tristan took the offered bread, but declined a second bowl. Thelband joyously thanked her. She just winked to indicate their secret. Brell and she exchanged no words, but his face gave away his like of her cooking. He was nearly the last one served, but the first one finished.

They spent several hours in the dining hall, for a single question from Tristan, "What is it like being married to a dragon?" turned into tales of adventure. Magari knew them all even though she took part in none of them. Brell filled in the gaps or chimed in when he thought something was a little different than he remembered, and they warmed some to each other. Nearly half of the adventures had Brell and Kromax fighting alongside wizards and warriors. Magari soured though after relating of the two companions' split. Brell grew quiet hearing how hurt the Dragon was. Of late, the dragon had devolved into a thug who took the money of lizard folk and goblins farther to the north and occasionally roughed up their neighbors.

When the fire had died down, Magari led the group to a series of rooms established for guests. The rooms were astonishingly clean and new looking. Magari admitted that they had never been used but she was pleased that finally they could be.

Although there were enough rooms for everyone, and the place was safe enough, Lancelot found solace sharing a bed with his brother.

"Can you believe Brell adventured with a dragon?" Lancelot could not hide his excitement, even in whisper.

"Yeah. It was sad that Kromax kept the secret of his wife from him. I could tell it really pained him."

"But with good reason. You heard what Magari said. Kromax was worried that someone could use that as a weakness against him. And Brell admitted that he had indeed been captured and

221

questioned on the very matter. Good thing Kromax busted him out."

"I am sad for Magari too. She must be so lonely."

"What do you mean?" Lancelot was caught up in the glory and romance of it all. "She could have him fly anywhere at any time. She could visit countries on the other side of the world or be taken to the highest mountain top."

"But she had to keep her life a secret. She couldn't make friends. True friends anyways. She would always have to worry about revealing who Kromax really was. And I could tell that Brell really thought of himself and Kromax as having been the best of friends. So to have a secret kept from him like that."

"I guess so."

The boys thought silently to themselves until they drifted into sleep.

28

By the time the boys woke, everyone else had already eaten and were helping Magari clean. Two plates of lamb with mixed eggs waited, barely warm. The brothers consumed their breakfast then Tristan asked what they could do.

Magari took their plates and directed them, "Brell told me of your journey and that you are short of supplies. Why don't you head through that door there and help Thelband in the pantry. Take whatever you like. Melkar will restock it when he returns."

Crunching sounds betrayed Thelband's activity before Lancelot had even opened the door. He snacked on a celery stick and contemplated all the combinations of meals that could be prepared with the ingredients stocked in the oversized storeroom. He noticed the boys, "Can you imagine?" He ignored the fact that they were not privy to his thoughts. "I worked in some of the finest dining establishments, and in all my years, I have not seen such a sight." Thelband was clearly in awe.

"Should you be eating their food?" Lancelot asked. He knew they could take it, but it just seemed rude.

Thelband ignored him, "I've laid out three packs there. The last is where the spices go. I can't believe they have adder's salt." He gently directed the boys toward the back shelves. "You will find the dried stuff back there. Grab mostly fish if you can. Put it in the middle pack. I'll see what fresh food I can squeeze in. We deserve at least one good meal on the road."

The way Thelband kept replacing items between the packs and shelves, they would never leave the pantry. It was Brell who cut the halfling's prefect expedition short, "Hurry up. We leave in ten minutes."

"Oh no!" Thelband protested, "We are not ready yet."

To his horror, Brell strode in and with a sweeping motion of his arm, scooped random food items from the wrong shelf and dumped them unceremoniously on the floor in front of the packs. "Done," the demon-hunter said with finality, "Ten minutes." Then left.

Eyes wide with anger and a hint of tears, Thelband looked to the boys. He already put some of Brell's pile back on a shelf. "Go. Gather your things. I will finish here." Brell's demonstration certainly added tempo to the final packing.

There wasn't much for the brothers to do but loiter until everyone else was ready. Ardus looked well and healed. Brell kept pacing back and forth to check each pack or weapon. Thelband finally emerged from the pantry about four seconds before they left. He was not happy, but said nothing.

Magari led the group through the great gaudy bronze door, and as suspected, they were led into and through the master bed chamber. Tristan noted that Kromax was given little in the way of pomp. His door-frame the only extravagance allowed by his wife. The room itself housed a large, simple bed, without posts or headboard. Silk blankets hinted at the richness of it. Around the windowless room, bright pictures of outdoor settings brought light to the drab greys and browns of the stone walls and simple pottery.

Several stairs and switch-backs later, they were led to a final unadorned room. A metal handled lever accompanied an iron reinforced door. Magari walked over and put her hand to handle then turned back to the companions. "This is it. Beyond you will feel a little funny as you walk through a force illusion, but you will emerge atop the crag. Be careful."

The dragon's wife pulled hard on the handle. A loud click was followed by the door swinging open. Each gave their thanks as they filed out of the small room. Brell was last. He gave a good long look at Magari then hugged her. "Tell him I am sorry Maggs," he whispered into her ear then kissed her on the cheek.

"Tell him yourself." Magari playfully scolded. The tears in her eyes told Brell she was really worried though. "Be well and safe Sir Brell Allencourt, Liberator of Solice, Pathfinder of the Infinite Planes, Demon-Slayer, and Dragon-friend."

Brell gave a solemn smile and followed the others outside.

It was sometime past noon. They had emerged from an outcropping of rocks. The surrounding area was overgrown with bushes and conifer trees. Tristan and Lancelot tried to spot where the rocks gave way to illusion, but it was completely seamless. On top of that, magical force from the illusion shaped itself to the form of the rocks it appeared to be.

"I hate being underground," Brell complained, "I can never figure out when first light is. We have lost half a day already."

"Bright side," Thelband pointed out, "No zombies."

"Little comfort." Ardus took Brell's side. "Just because they are not here, doesn't mean we won't be fighting them in five minutes." The little man shot him a betrayed look.

"No, he is right," Brell corrected. "Listen." He paused and everyone did as he said. "Hear that? Birds. Birds mean no zombies. Maybe this is our lucky break."

"Brell's right. We should eat while there is no danger." Everyone looked at Thelband with their best 'are you crazy?' face. Brell rolled his eyes and led the group north along the top of the crag, his silence Thelband's only rebuke.

The walk was pleasant and uneventful. The forest canopy blocked out whatever sunlight the clouds failed to. They often found themselves skirting alongside the crag. The light of day revealed a lush expanse of shrubbery, streamlets, and wild rock formations below. Squirrels and rabbits frequently burst into view then up a tree or through the underbrush.

Occasionally, a break in the trees revealed high snow-capped mountain peaks. They were not far from their destination and although the surroundings gave no sign, each could feel the palpable danger and anticipation of what was to come.

As the day closed, Brell gave Thelband permission to light a fire and cook up the 'good stuff'. "After tonight," he chided, "we are going to have to be both minimalists and stealthy. We have no idea how long it will actually take to reach Delan's residence, nor what spies he has this close to home." Everyone agreed.

Thelband went all out. He used every trick he knew to make the last great meal before being consigned to a hell of 'the dry stuff'. Nobody complained as they sat around the fire, and the way they vigorously attacked their meals, Thelband was confident he had accomplished what he set out to do.

After the meal, Tristan pulled the leatherworking bag he had taken in Ferrickport. Inside he found the necessary tools to fletch arrows. He asked Ardus to go out with him and look for wood so he could complete the task. Brell reminded them to remain near the camp.

In camp, Lancelot settled next to Brell. He drew warmth both from the fire and from the demon-hunter as he leaned against him. Taken aback at first, Brell rested his arm around the young man's shoulder. He almost forgot how young Lancelot was, and how unsettling this had all been.

Lancelot watched the fire, "Brell, are we going to find Dellan?"

He too gazed into the flames. Fascination delayed his answer, "Yes. Of course we will."

"Kromax killed Leopold. Trazk is not here. There are no roads." Lancelot was worried.

Brell let out half breath, half laugh. "We are lucky." He paused long enough that Lancelot raised his head to look at him. "Magari and I spoke last night while you slept. She has rode Kromax many times in flight. She has seen much and described to me Dellan's estate and gave good descriptions of landmarks. We will find it. We will find him."

Comforted by those words, Lancelot shifted and lay down with his head in Brell's lap. He watched the fire for a bit and drifted to sleep.

Tristan and Ardus returned sometime later. Brell stood leaning against a tree with his arms folded. He looked unassuming, but Tristan knew he was ready for anything. Lancelot was curled up next to Thelband. Magari had not only supplied them with food, but also new woolen blankets. "Get some sleep," Ardus nodded toward Lancelot and the halfling. "They have the right idea." He then walked over to Brell. "I'm sure you've been the only one on watch tonight. Let me take over." Brell gave thanks with his eyes and acknowledged with a nod.

Tristan was sure this was going to be one of the last peaceful nights for some time. He decided to forego making arrows for some sleep. After he lay down, Brell came over from the shadows and checked on the wounds he received from the shadow creatures. "These should be okay by the time you wake, but to be sure, I am going to give it a little help."

Even as Tristan thanked Brell for saving him in the dragon's cave, a soft white light from Brell's hands massaged the tender areas where Tristan had been grabbed. The hairs on his neck and arms raised and he could see flickering blue motes in the pearl glow. Long before Brell concluded his healing prayer, the unnatural wounds faded and Tristan fell fast asleep.

29

Tristan woke to a light rain tickling his face and ears. The rest of the group had risen some time earlier and packed the camp. Lancelot sat nearby with his back to a tree. He sharpened a small blade that was not Grace. "Where's your sword?" the older brother asked.

Lancelot lifted the edge of his cloak that covered his right thigh. Grace was safely sheathed. "I worry I have been relying on her too often and thought I had better have some back-up. And know how to use it. Thelband is going to show me how to throw this thing. It feels so small even though Grace is barely bigger."

Tristan reached for his bow then presented it chest high, "Yes. I agree," he said before strapping it to his back.

The group made an effort to conceal their camp-site. They swept footprints with branches and dispersed the logs and ash from their fire.

Brell led them eastward, away from the ravine. There was no path so he used the natural blockage of brush and rocks to guide him. Always, he pushed toward the left when he could. Already they could tell they were on an incline, and it became steeper the further they went.

The flora here consisted of blackberry bushes and poison oak. Trees were nearly all pine, but larger oaks sprinkled the area. The canopy blocked out the light of day, and even the rain only ran down the trunks of the trees. Brell decided against man-made light sources and they trudged on in shadow.

Tristan watched from the back. Lancelot was directly in front of him. Thelband and Ardus walked side-by-side, and he couldn't even see Brell ahead of them. They all moved in silence kept an ear out for natural noises they wanted to persist. The crickets and birds obliged them through the day and into the night.

By nightfall, the group was seriously tested by the steepness of their path. Brell found a relatively flat outcropping of rocks of which contained a low overhang. "Let's light a fire there." He pointed to the hollow beneath the largest boulder. "We can sleep under the branches of the trees. Watch can use the fire. It looks like this is pretty well shielded from view, if not from the rain." As if on cue, Ardus slipped while bending to inspect where the fire would be. "Careful. It is slippery," Brell deadpanned. Ardus didn't quite get the humor and the look he shot Brell conveyed that.

The group ate dried and salted fish. Thelband was forbidden from cooking it because of the smell. His look mimicked that of Ardus' earlier frown. Lancelot split his waking time between throwing his dagger into tree trunks and tending to wounds with Brell. Tristan was content with making arrows and was proud of the progress he made before turning in. Ardus took the first watch, and had actually been on watch from the time they got the fire going.

———————————

Tristan was wakened by a gentle pressure on his shoulder. His eyes snapped open and he nearly bolted up. It was Thelband. The halfling still had his hand on him and prevented him from hitting his head in the confined space. "Come with me," Thelband whispered, "and bring your bow."

Tristan did as instructed. He looked around. Brell watched him from near the fire but said nothing. Ardus snored under a prickly berry bush, and his brother also lay nearby. It was still dark.

Crickets told him they were not under attack, and he wondered what was going on. Thelband waited long enough to make sure he had boots on and weapons strapped and then darted off, up and away from the camp.

With longer legs, Tristan was able to catch up to Thelband who slowed to use cover as he continued up the side of the steep hill. Tristan took a moment to look over his right shoulder and realized they were above the tree line. It was open sky to the right and mountainside to the left. The clouds had scattered and a crescent moon illuminated the ground just enough to prevent the two from running into boulders or off a cliff. Tristan found good occasion to stub his toe or slip on loose rocks. He did his best to keep his pain to himself.

The pair moved through the landscape for an hour or more. Tristan wanted to ask what was going on, but he both had to spend his time focused on where he stepped, and did not want to break the silence that accompanied them.

Tristan nearly tripped over the halfling as Thelband abruptly stopped. They stood amid thorny brush. To their right, a large rock, split down the middle resembled a large, horned demon head and protruded up and away from the hill. Thelband jumped out onto the rock and then shimmied into the crack and away from the safety of the incline. Tristan watched him at first until he saw that he had safely perched himself near the top of the right horn. The halfling only looked back briefly at Tristan then stared off to his left.

Tristan followed the actions of Thelband, and as he neared the top of the horn, Thelband scooched a little and helped the boy into his original seat.

Tristan followed Thelband's gaze and pointing finger. In the distance, he recognized only points of light at first. As his eyes adjusted, he made out the outlines of a small castle. A road below led up to a steep ravine where either a stationary bridge or an open drawbridge gave ingress to the castle.

"That's it," Thelband whispered, "We have made it to the chateau Zhukovich. Let's get a closer look."

"What about the others?" Tristan looked worried.

"They are following." Thelband already climbed off the rock. "Brell trusts us. We are here to get as much information about the lay and report when he arrives."

Tristan looked unsure but followed the halfling back into the brush nonetheless. He drew his bow and kept arching his head this way and that until the castle finally came into view again. They followed along the hillside. The natural flow of the rocks and dips brought them lower as they drew near.

Dellan's home was built right out of the mountainside. The walls melded into the rock of the mountain and gave the impression of an unfinished masterpiece. Open windows, balconies and gargoyles dotted the walls. Twin minarets poked up from the center of the castle. Pennants adorned the conical roofs of the towers. It was too early in the morning to make out the insignias.

On closer inspection, the ravine, although deep enough to harm or kill someone from a fall, was much smaller than when first observed. From here, it looked more like a collapse at some point forced the construction of the drawbridge.

Tristan spotted movement on the wall. Even in the dark, he could make out two figures, one secured under a balcony, the other, which must be using a rope climbed from beneath. Before he could point it out, Thelband acknowledged that he saw.

They moved closer.

The higher figure put his arms out and supported the other as the second climbed over onto the balcony.

Almost instantly, a shuttered door burst open and light spilled onto the exposed balcony to reveal two unmistakable figures. Lareth, the priest of Chess stood above, his arm raised to shield his eyes from the outpouring illumination. Below him, Trazk who struggled with the ropes, hurried in anticipation of an ambush.

What could only be Dellan, slid to the balcony from within. His strength and speed were incredible. With a single hand clutched to the front of Lareth's armor, he lifted him, arm fully outstretched. The priest recovered and reached for his mace. Dellan easily restrained Lareth's weapon arm with his other hand.

Trazk was still tangled within ropes but still tried to climb over the balcony to help. Dellan barely took notice of him.

Thelband sprinted and rolled down a steep slope. He moved erratically and with desperation.

Tristan instinctively readied his bow, took aim and fired. His shot rang high and ricocheted off stone framework that outlined the doors and balcony. He was sure Dellan looked to his exact spot.

The vampire lord smiled, then said something to Lareth. Dellan brought the priest close and hugged Lareth's neck with his face. Something happened and Dellan reeled and released Lareth.

The hapless priest tumbled back and over the balcony ledge. Trazk made an ineffectual grab at Lareth, but he was too far. The fall was quick. The echoing crunch and crumpled body offered no doubt about Lareth's final fate.

Above, Dellan raged blindly. He struck twice where he thought Trazk was. Masonry shattered and crumbled. Although he missed the orc hunter, he destroyed the section of balcony so completely, there was nothing left to use as handholds. The orc fell.

Tristan yelped and covered his eyes. There was not the same sound of a crashing body, but instead a muffled grunt. He opened his eyes. Trazk hung there, barely above the ground. The ropes he had hopelessly been entangled in saved him from Lareth's demise. Thelband was already there and cut away at the rope. Trazk fell then recovered. They both began the run back toward Tristan.

Dellan had also recovered and looked as if he cast a spell. He gestured and then pointed down at the two runners. Tristan fired a second, then a third arrow at Dellan. One arrow looked to hit, but the vampire stood unfazed.

Two of the gargoyles perched above the balcony stirred. First, it looked as if they shook off years of slumber. Small rocks dislodged as they stretched and turned. The stone creatures looked to Dellan first, and then to their quarry. Each stood, then dropped from their resting places. A clumsy drop turned to an elegant dive. Momentum brought them up behind Thelband.

Tristan shouted, "Look out!" Thelband reacted as if he knew what was after him and where. He rolled to the right and brought a small blade to bear. The gargoyle flew too fast, and Thelband's swing missed.

The second gargoyle flew up behind Trazk and grappled him around his waist. The orc was shocked as the creature lifted him off the ground and started its ascent.

Thelband's gargoyle could not easily circle back around and chose instead to change targets to Tristan. Two powerful beats of its wings gave it lift and speed and it raced up the slope.

Trazk was already tens of feet off the ground and had managed to spin his body around so that he was face to face with his attacker. He gave out a terrifying guttural yell. His eyes bulged and he began flailing madly. The orc's elbows smashed against stone jaw. It had little more effect than to make the beast snarl in anger.

Tristan loosed one arrow. It missed. He was not going to get time for another. He drew Hope. "*Pel. Mora.*" He felt the power. The gargoyle's flight hugged inches above the rising terrain. It had clearly chosen a trajectory to barrel through the teenage boy.

Trazk knew what would happen if he didn't do something fast. Time was not on his side. He reached around both sides of the gargoyle and grabbed it by the wings. Then, with all his might, he tucked those wings to the side of the animated rock construct and squeezed. The gargoyle clawed into Trazk's back, but lost control of its flight. They spun, then crashed into the side of the mountain. Broken stone and battered orc toppled down to rest among thorny brush.

"*Mira!*" Tristan waited until the last second, less than a second, to shift to the right. A duck, coupled with a high arching swing, cleaved through the gargoyle's wing. Broken rock showered over him. The gargoyle spun out of control and crashed. Dust and granite spewed up. The beast was dazed but rose. In a single leap, Tristan crossed the distance between him and his foe.

Hope sliced down on the arm with the severed wing. It broke into several pieces. The gargoyle raised its other arm in defense. A sideways cut removed its hand at the wrist. Tristan spun with his momentum. A final, diagonal down-swing cut the head in half.

Tristan looked for the other gargoyle. At first he thought maybe it had escaped with Trazk, but his gaze followed Thelband to where they had tumbled. He ran down to help them.

By the way his arm flopped, it was clear that Trazk has broken it and probably his shoulder. He was unconscious but alive. There was little evidence that the chunks of stone and debris belonged to a gargoyle.

"*Fin. Lancelot, are you close?*" Tristan hoped his brother was holding Grace.

"*We are moving as fast as we can. It's not easy finding Thelband's marked path. Are you okay?*" Lancelot's thoughts grew concerned.

"*It's bad,*" Tristan replied, "*Trazk is here and he is hurt. We found the Vampire's castle, but he knows we are here. Just hurry!*"

Thelband put his hand on Tristan's back to get his attention. "You stay here with Trazk. I will find the others. How close are they?"

"They don't know. Whatever clues you left for them, they are finding them, just not fast enough."

Thelband left Tristan with Trazk and scurried up to find the others.

Tristan used Hope to clear the brush from the immediate area, rested Trazk's head on a belt pouch, then picked rocks and thorns out of the orc. "You were lucky my friend," he whispered to his unconscious mentor.

Lancelot relayed to Tristan, "*Brell says that Trazk has some potions he took from the witch. They have healing properties. If you can, make him drink them.*"

Tristan searched Trazk's pack until he found what he was looking for.

Brell complained, "Damn halfling. How am I supposed to deduce that two twigs crossing is telling me which way to go?"

"Keep going straight," Lance called from the back, "We are going the right direction, just speed it up."

Brell's irritation grew. "Get up front here. If your sword is telling you the right way to go, why weren't you in front from the start?"

Lance sheepishly replied when he had moved to the front, "I forgot."

Dawn fast approached and it became easier for them to see the pitfalls of their path. By the time the sun breached the horizon, Thelband had found them. He gave a brief report of what he saw and they hurried back the way he had come.

They found Tristan with a groggy, but now semi-conscious Trazk. The orc mumbled in his own language. His eyes were still glazed.

"I gave him everything I could find," Tristan confessed, "I'm not sure it was all the same stuff."

Brell immediately went to work to set the breaks and then used his magic to mend the bones. After, he spoke, "We should move him. Does Dellan know you are in this very spot?"

Thelband responded for Tristan, "Probably. He was watching us. He knows we can kill his guardians too. Does it matter? The sun is rising."

"No vampire would leave himself unprotected. He will have more minions that can freely roam in the light."

Ardus and Lancelot helped Trazk up and they did their best to move within the cover of foliage without hostile eyes noticing. They spent the morning and early into the afternoon sitting still, watching.

Although awake, Trazk's wits did not return to him until after he had some lunch. He sat up, then nearly passed out from the effort. Ardus helped him to prop against a short spruce tree. Trazk kept his eyes closed as he relayed where he had been up to this point.

"I'll start with, Elle and Samuel are safe. At least they were when I left them."

Brell sighed relief and Trazk continued, "The zombie general is no shambling idiot. He used modern military tactics, shield formations, archer lines, the whole works. He certainly knows what he was doing. They move slowly though. It gave the people of

Timbershaven ample time to escape. Most got on boats. Others got in their carts or huffed it into the wilds, away from the town."

"By the time I had skirted around the army, I have to think they were not even half way to Timbershaven. Getting around the undead horde was no easy task. Zed had given me an escort, but they had both slowed me down and had lost enough men helping me. We got caught up in a few skirmishes. I sent the survivors away after that. They needed to get to safety too."

Trazk went quiet and took a minute to muster more strength. He looked nauseous. "My horse died right as I made it back to Galagburg. It looked as if about a quarter of the town burned down, but the undead were not interested in raiding. Only killing. Most of the place remains intact, should survivors find their way back.

"I picked up our original trail back to where we faced off with the undead archers. One pair of tracks led north."

Brell said what everyone was thinking, "Lareth."

"Yeah," the orc conceded, "He was nearly to the castle when I caught up with him. He admitted leaving him was the right thing to do."

"We didn't even know he got left behind," Lancelot protested guiltily.

"No matter." Trazk had a hundred yard stare. "He said his horse had fallen on him. He laid there until the army had passed. His leg was broken, but he had his own magics to mend it."

"We both figured you had already made it to the castle. To be sure, we decided not to take the direct entrance. Climbing for me wasn't hard, but in order to help up Lareth, I needed to tie myself off to a balcony..."

Tristan interrupted, "I saw him fall. I think Dellan bit him."

Trazk confirmed, "He did. I heard him make some snide remark about coming so far or some-such. Then I heard the vampire choking. Didn't know they did that."

"They don't." Brell had been listening intently. He put his hand to his goatee. "Odd."

Tristan cut in again, "Don't you think we should get Lareth's body? Shouldn't we bury him?"

Brell resigned, "That will have to wait until this task is done."

"If any of us are left to do it," Trazk admitted with no delicacy. Brell shot him a glance, but the orc didn't care to notice.

Ardus passed a wineskin to Trazk. "Drink." The orc gulped down the contents, some of which spilled out on his chin and chest. He wiped what he could with his forearm, then laid his head back and closed his eyes again.

The conversation died there. Brell moved off to a spot where he could recover while watching the castle. The others loitered in quiet contemplation.

30

The demon hunter gave the group two more hours to ready themselves then gathered them around Trazk. The orcs hue looked more orc green than sick green. Brell applied more healing light to his wounds then Trazk stood. He was steady.

"Good." Brell was relieved. "We have to do this now. Dellan knows we are here, and if we use any more light resting, we are going to give him that much more time to prepare. Also, we want this fight during the day. At night, he might be unstoppable."

Thelband pointed out, "We don't have many hours left of light here."

"Exactly," Brell looked to Trazk, "Do you want to sit this one out? I know you are going to be less than healthy in there."

Trazk grunted his annoyance, then replied, "Orcs have far more health than humans. Don't worry about me."

Brell smiled. "I know. I was just asking. Okay. We have to suspect they are watching the balconies and the front door. And getting Ardus up to a balcony might be more trouble than its worth."

He looked around the group then continued, "We don't have a wizard, but we do have scouts. Thelband went out while we rested. What did you find?"

It was Thelband's turn to smile. "If you can believe it, Dellan likes gardens. He has a big one within his grounds. I found a goat trail that passes over the castle. We can lower ourselves right in."

"We will be exposed?" Ardus asked.

"If they are looking, then yes."

"Do we have a distraction planned?" The big man guessed in anticipation.

Brell cut in, "Sadly no. We are going to have to hope his guardians are not so thoughtful or perceptive. We don't have the resources or man-power for such a diversion. And I don't want to waste you on the front door, while we sneak in the back."

"Well, thanks." Ardus said sarcastically.

Brell finished the plan with, "Finally, we need to find and kill Dellan before he wakes."

Nobody had anything better to suggest. They all gathered their gear and, one by one, followed Thelband away from the castle. At first, they climbed up steep, barren slopes of rock, then onto a nearly discernable trail that used switchbacks to quickly rise above the castle.

It took less than an hour to get above the spot Thelband had described. Everyone except the halfling was extremely winded. Ardus even vomited from the exertion.

They waited and watched for several minutes to be sure they were not going to be assaulted from the air or from arrows. Brell secured a silken rope they were given by Magari, then dropped the coil. The end of it plopped down into a gardened courtyard. Again the wait.

Thelband was first, then the boys. Trazk descended as though he had not just recently hurt himself. Brell went down slow and deliberate. Ardus was last and took the longest. Half way he stopped; the others thought he would fall. The butcher looked around while he caught his breath, then descended the rest of the way without incident.

Thelband wasted no time after he had touched down. He scouted through archways and windows that granted access into the castle proper.

When everyone was down he reported, "Either nobody noticed

us, or they are going for reinforcements. Windows look into unused rooms. Doors are unlocked and lead into halls."

Brell studied the two doors for a moment. He half asked and half answered his own question, "This door would lead toward the center of the castle?" He pulled the handle and the door swung open. More than a half dozen skeletal figures charged down the hallway toward them. Each was armed with a different bladed or bludgeoning weapon, but all wore similarly crafted tabards of grey and red. A crimson wolf head adorned the center. Behind them, a man with dark robes and a tall hat incanted, his eyes glowed red under heavy black brows.

Brell stepped back on his heels and managed to deflect the blow from a curved sword. The skeletons spilled out into the courtyard. At first they circled around Brell, but then noticed the others and split off to engage.

Trazk backed across the courtyard to where they had descended, two of the undead followed.

Ardus, completely caught off guard, took a blow to the back from a serrated topped mace. His armor scraped and screeched, but held. Still without weapon at the ready, the big man caught the second blow with his free hand and yanked the mace from the skeleton. Weaponless, the skeletal warrior jumped on him. It scraped at his eyes and ears.

Tristan and Lancelot stood back to back, sister swords drawn. The skeletons were fast, but not strong. It was easier to defend against those using the blunted instruments. Swords and daggers though were quick enough to bypass parries.

Thelband used his height and the surroundings to his advantage. He managed to pull two of the skeletons off of the group. He rolled and maneuvered so the pursuers were never in position to strike.

That left Brell. He found himself alone and unengaged. Twin light blades appeared and he spun to assist the boys. Two good swings though alerted him to the danger they were in. His blades deflected off of an invisible shield around the undead fighters. Untiring enemies would eventually get the upper hand. "Weapons aren't working!" he yelled.

Trazk picked up on the meaning right away and led the skeletons in a dance around the rope. He used their aggression against them and the pair got entangled. He used the slack to quickly wrap and tie them. It was makeshift, and he was going to have to stay here.

Ardus bled profusely from his face and it made melee difficult. He finally got a good hold of his foe. By the neck, he swung the skeleton over his shoulder and slammed him into the ground. It had little or no effect except the loud slapping sound. He used this momentum to then spin and hurl the skeleton against a wall. It hit, fell, then shook off whatever daze was upon it. If skeletons could smile, it grinned at Ardus. It got to its feet and charged again.

The brothers knew something was up when Hope and Grace failed to cut through their opponents. Brell only confirmed it. In link, they agreed to mirror the actions of Thelband. The *Mira* rune gave them the advantage they needed to keep the skeletons off balance and swinging errantly.

Brell looked for the robed figure and found it was still at the other end of the hall. The demon hunter broke into a light jog toward the man and kept an ear for more trouble. More trouble came. Four more skeletons appeared from either side of a 'T' shaped hall at the end of this one. As they stepped in between Brell and his target, the man with the thick brows laughed. It did not deter Brell who continued the final few steps toward him.

Ardus now had his skeleton folded in half, pinned tight near his waist. He grabbed and threw Tristan's opponent, then gave a resigned sigh. His fist was bloodied from use, the mace lay discarded somewhere. The skeleton scrunched up in his arm clawed at his leg and armor.

Tristan used the moment to chase after Brell.

Down the hall, the skeletons huddled tight. These four had shields and spears at the ready. They thrust in unison, but their spears retreated with them. Brell threw his hand up in a swatting motion. The four skeletons flew back against the wall. Two knocked the robed man off balance, his incanting disrupted.

Lance cut a skeleton in half at the waist.

Ardus crushed his skeleton into a ball and discarded it so he could face another.

Thelband slashed this way and that, and two skeletons were suddenly without feet.

Trazk used his strength and weight to crush his captive skeletons against the wall. They sounded like cracking crab shells and it echoed in the courtyard.

The toppled figure in robes kneeled to regain his footing. Brell, who had overrun him to the left, spun right, his violet blade cut deep into the side of the man.

Two of the skeletons nearest the demon hunter engaged him to protect their master.

Tristan sprinted up to the kneeling man and chopped down, both hands on Hope. His head split wide. Brains showered the combatants, walls and floor.

Brell made short work of his two aggressors, then stopped and stared at the brainless man. His blood leaked out like a spilled glass of wine.

"Little help here." Tristan snapped Brell out of his thought. Two shielded skeletons pressed on him. Brell easily cut the skeletons down before they could defend themselves against him.

The others came down the hall. The courtyard garden lay quiet behind them.

31

Tristan willed his sword, "*La,*" and Hope illuminated the hallways. The way back out to the garden was plain stone all around, two empty sconces the only decoration, adorned the walls about midway down the hall.

At the 'T', it was very different. The hall crossing had a fine green carpet that rolled the length of the floor. The walls had wood paneling built over them and gave the feel that this place was anything but a castle. Pictures were hung, spaced evenly along the path. All so far depicted outdoor settings, devoid of animals or people. Like the outer hall, this one had sconces. One contained a candle, freshly lit.

"This will be a problem," Brell said as he took the scene in. He had just finished bandaging Ardus' head. The warrior's face was comically covered. Only his mouth, nostrils and one eye poked through.

The others just looked to him to finish. He did. "All this...." Brell gestured with both hands to the surrounding accoutrements. "This will hide any secret doors or pathways the vampire uses to hide himself during the day."

"*Hope, are you there? Can you hear me?*" Tristan asked.

"*Yes young Tristan. I am here.*" Her voice was soothing in his mind.

"Do you have a way to help us find this vampire? He may have hidden himself within these wooden walls."

She answered in a pained apologetic way, *"Alas, I have a sister who might be able to help, but neither Grace nor I have that rune or sense."*

The others waited at the turn in the hall. Tristan realized they were waiting for him and ran to catch up.

Ardus suggested, "We can always burn the hallways down. That should reveal any secrets."

Brell took the proposition seriously, "Possibly. But Dellan would certainly be alerted. We should think to use that as a last ditch effort."

Trazk lingered in the rear. He took the candle from the sconce and scraped it on the wall. It left a clear white sheen. The orc grunted his satisfaction and followed the others.

The halls twisted and turned. The group checked doors as they encountered them. Door after door only revealed one unused room after another. Except that they did not encounter a wax mark, they could have easily become lost in the sameness.

Finally, Thelband alerted them to a change of scenery, "Stairs. They go down."

Lancelot realized how slack everyone had become when they all readied their weapons, tensed, and slowed their breathing.

Tristan strained to hear any noises from below. He looked to his brother who watched the others for a hint of what they knew. The group thinned to single file behind the halfling.

Thelband hugged the wall as he followed the descending stairs in a clockwise spiral. Half way down he put a hand up to halt the rest of the group, then continued silently down into darkness.

A minute went by. Brell looked impatient, but knew to stay where he was. Thelband returned. He said nothing but put two hands up, ten fingers. Then he closed his hands into fists and raised two more fingers. Brell nodded. Then Thelband closed his hand, let his eyes widen and raised two more fingers. Brell nodded again then backed up slowly so he stood in the midst of the others.

"Looks like there are a dozen more skeletons and at least two priests this time." The demon hunter whispered.

"We need to take the living out first if we want to kill the dead." He put his hands on Tristan and Trazk's shoulders. "You know what to do."

Tristan followed Trazk's lead. They readied their bows and nocked an arrow.

Lancelot watched the pair descent the stairs by the light of his sword. Their shadows stretched up and around the wall. He thought he could hear Tristan breathing, but it was his own breath he let out. He had been holding it.

Brell stood at the head of the stairs, head cocked. "Get ready," he whispered. A moment more went by. "Let's go," he said louder and with authority. The demon hunter hurried down the stairs, both glowing blades summoned.

Lancelot, Ardus and Thelband quickly followed Brell down the stairs. The hallways here were similar to those above, but the rolled carpet was red, and the pictures that hung were of various people rather than locations. Three doors lined either side of a long hall that turned left at the end. In the center, a burned out candle lay next to a dead robed human. An arrow stuck out of his upper torso. Behind him stood an injured priest. His arrow was in his arm. He incanted though; the dozen skeletons stood between him and the stairs.

Lancelot stepped off of the stairs just in time to see his brother slice a skeleton in two at the waist. Black tendrils whisped from the fallen skeleton and enveloped Tristan who staggered back. He was visibly shaken and weakened.

"Get back!" Brell shouted to him. The demon hunter lunged so that he was between the retreating boy and more undead. He blocked two blows simultaneously then let his blades disappear. He used his hands in washing motions to push back the skeletons with an invisible force.

Trazk also backed up behind Brell. He had been parrying with his bow. Brell's tactic freed the orc to use his bow as was intended. Trazk drew and fired three times in rapid succession. The first arrow shattered a skeleton's jaw. The following arrows hit their mark. The priest took one step back, clutched one of the arrows, and then fell over dead.

Brell, who was visibly winded, summoned his blades again and cut down a skeleton, sans the black tendrils.

Tristan backed up further until he was side-by-side with Lancelot. "I felt like a part of me died there."

"Stay here big brother. We can handle this." Lancelot charged up to Brell's side and engaged a skeleton.

Ardus waited for a space in the narrow hall to open up then waded into the remaining skeletons. His fists were more effective than his sword and he quickly dispatched three.

Trazk sidled up next to Tristan and inspected the grey pallor the tendrils had caused. "This will wear off with rest. If you had aimed better, this wouldn't have happened."

Tristan wanted to defend his excellent shot under the circumstances, but Trazk was right. He just looked down. The darkness had sapped some of his will to fight. It depressed him. He loaded and raised his bow to fire, but Trazk put an arm on his and shook his head. "Don't waste your arrows on these. Bows are very ineffective against skeletons." Tristan lowered his bow in further defeat.

Lancelot fell back after killing a skeleton. Brell and Ardus, side-by-side, completed the melee, grace on the right and brute bashing violence on the left.

When they were finished, Brell patched Ardus' bloody knuckles. "Your wrist is swollen. Don't you ever use your weapons?"

Ardus made a peculiar face, made weirder from his bandages; something to replace a shrug. "If they were zombies, be sure I would arm myself. There is just something satisfying about killing with my bear hands."

Brell shook his head then pulled a small vial from his belt-pouch as he walked back to Tristan. "Drink this," he commanded. "I had Friar Mark concoct something just in case we ran into life drainers. It will return some or all of your strength and will to live."

Tristan broke the wax cover on the vial then put it to his nose to smell. His head instinctively backed away from the foul concoction.

"Are you sure this is safe?" he asked as his nose crinkled.

"Perfectly," Brell said both confidently and with a small amount of humor.

Tristan held his nose as he downed the potion. His other hand immediately covered his mouth to prevent from vomiting.

"Keep it in," Brell cautioned. "It won't work if you spit it out."

Tristan was bent over. He put one hand out to ward Brell back. He made small gagging noises, but nothing came out.

"Okay. I feel it working." Color returned to Tristan's face.

32

As Tristan recovered, the group gathered to gain their bearings and catch their breath. Ardus stood while the others sat against the walls across from each other. Thelband hummed a tune. The others felt their spirits rise, if ever so slightly.

"We don't have much daylight left," Brell conceded, "We may want to start thinking of hiding places, or better yet, leaving and coming back."

Lancelot shook his head, "No. I have an idea. At least, maybe we should explore it before we make a decision."

Brell looked at him, impressed. "We are listening."

"Tristan and I have not spoken about it, but twice now, while we communicated with our swords, we were interrupted. Spied upon."

"What do you mean?" the demon hunter asked with a cocked head. He was very interested.

Lancelot answered, "Leopold and Kromax. They both could hear our conversations in our heads. They both could answer and talk to us."

Brell looked concerned, "Maybe you should refrain from using that power here in the castle. It could give our position away."

Tristan's eyes shined. He understood and exclaimed, "Or maybe our swords can tell us where he is too! Maybe we can find him while he sleeps!"

"Exactly!" Lancelot enthusiastically confirmed.

Their exuberance was a little contagious. Brell relented, "At least, maybe we can prevent him getting the best of us if we know where he will strike from."

Trazk caught Tristan's gaze and nodded his approval to the boy.

Thelband looked up the stairs then said, "I hear chatter. Do we wait here and ambush them or press on?"

Brell stood and summoned his weapons. The others followed his lead. The old man said, "We give them a minute, no more."

Trazk tapped Tristan's elbow and pointed further back down the hall. Tristan put Hope away and readied his bow as he moved backwards, eyes on the stairs.

When nothing came down the steps, one by one fell in behind Brell as he wordlessly made his way down the hall and around the corner.

They searched the floor as quickly as they could. Tristan and Lancelot took turns activating their *Fin* rune. Neither could will their blade to tell them where Dellan hid. They kept their telepathic conversations to a minimum, only really wondering to each other if this was going to work and to call out to Dellan.

More stairs. They descended. Everything was the same, except there were blue carpets and the pictures were places. Chambers were laboratories, kitchens, sitting halls.

"I think we are at ground level," Thelband offered, "I spied the bridge from a window. It's starting to get dark." He looked worried.

"That means we have a way to escape if we need to." Brell was also worried. "Let's find the front door."

"Why? Are you planning on leaving so soon?" Everyone froze. Shock. Fear. They knew immediately who said that. As one, the group spun around.

Dellan stood in the center of the hallway. He was tall, taller than Ardus, but wiry rather than bulky. His arms were crossed. The vampire was dressed in plain black clothes, ornate golden buttons secured his shirt and pants. His ebon boots were impeccably polished. The group immediately recognized his snarling face from back at the Fallen Giant. His hair was disheveled though, slick and combed on the right, but haphazard and cut or burnt into odd angles on the left. Half of the left side of his jaw was missing, rotted or burned away. It was hard to tell which. His hands trembled, and it was obvious he forced a controlled interaction with the group. The same fire and hatred burned in his eyes as the first night they saw him.

The vampire's focus was on Brell, but his gloat was for the boys, "Excellent plan to track me. Well, to use your ability to track. For it has given me the time I need to muster my friends all the while keeping track of you."

Dellan's body turned slightly and his arms slid to the ready. His pale hands had black, sharp nails, and he was happy they drew the attention of his audience. He took a step forward. It was enough.

Brell leapt into action, twin lavender blades arced down. Dellan's arms came up as an 'X' and the blades slammed down into the 'V'. Electricity sparked from the blow, then Brell's blades flickered and went out. The demon hunter fell forward off-balance. He still tried to drive his non-existent blades down. Surprise was replaced by pain as Dellan struck Brell in the side of the head. It spun him like a top into the wall.

Lancelot rushed forward to help his mentor. Dellan reached out to grab the boy. Ardus grabbed that arm with two beefy strong arms and swung Dellan back away from Lancelot. The vampire tried to shake Ardus off, but the warrior was having none of it. Ardus stepped in close and then put his elbow into the hole in Dellan's face.

Dellan stepped back and wrenched his hand free. Trazk and Tristan let loose arrows. Both found their marks, but neither fazed the vampire. Dellan looked down at the shafts and swiped his arm in an arc. The arrows snapped off. Trazk let loose a second arrow that Dellan batted out of the air.

Ardus stepped in and delivered a hard downward swing. Dellan easily pirouetted under the sword attack. The vampire, claws like steel, ripped across Ardus' breastplate. Then Dellan delivered and uppercut that not only knocked the large fighter back, but sent the bandages on his head spiraling one way while a pair of teeth dislodged and flew the other. Ardus staggered. His eyes glazed for the briefest of moments before he caught himself and shook off the daze that nearly left him unconscious.

33

Even just awakened, Dellan was too powerful to face like this. Without instruction, the group retreated. The boys and Thelband ran while Brell, Ardus, and Trask withdrew, their faces to the vampire lord.

"It's a trap!" Lancelot yelled the obvious when they had reached a four-way intersection. Dellan's minions were waiting. The left and right sides of the hall were wider than the one they had just come from.

On the left was the end of the wide hall. Open double doors were packed with armed and ready skeletons. Their masters hung back, several rows of bodies deep in a large throne chamber beyond.

Across from where they had come, stood a dozen or more armed and armored humans. At least they looked like humans, until they glared with gleaming fangs and glowing eyes.

Finally, to the right, behind five very large gargoyles was the front gate. The doors were closed behind a curtain of crisscrossed steel. Certainly the drawbridge was also up if not visible. The only other egress were two doors on either side of the gateway. A lone torch gave their shadows an even more menacing look.

Dellan taunted after them, "There is nowhere to go. Your fate is inevitable. Even your benefactor has abandoned you."

"Ardus, we need to do this right." Brell sized up the big fighter for the task at hand. "The gate!" he yelled. His bright blades flared and he shifted toward the gargoyles with a guttural yell. Even with the heavy armor and bleeding chest, Ardus' body responded with cat-like reflexes and muscle-memory. The two bull-charged into the front gargoyles and knocked them off balance. One stone guardian already lost an arm at the elbow.

The rest of the group and the hordes in the halls now reacted. Lancelot and Tristan invoked their swords, though the younger brother's did not impart its abilities. *"Grace has not recharged from the last fight!"* Lancelot frantically thought to Tristan.

"Just fight like you were taught," Tristan urged him.

Lancelot landed a solid blow against the chest of a gargoyle. The blade bit in, but the damage was superficial since the creature did not bleed or have critical organs.

Thelband fared no better although he dodged the gargoyle's claws better than Lancelot could parry them.

As the skeletons charged across the hall, Brell grunted out, "Rear guard." He and Ardus shifted their focus away from the gargoyles and moved back to blunt the attack.

Three of the vampires came around the corner. They hugged the walls and ceiling like spiders and crawled over the melee below.

Tristan had disabled a gargoyle enough to take it out of action. It had lost both arms and its right leg was severed at the knee. Wings flapped, but the creature only spun toward the wall like a broken, fluttering butterfly. He spent a second too long admiring his handiwork. An iron grip locked on his shoulder, claws dug into flesh. He let out a scream.

Trazk answered his call, his shoulder slammed into a stone back and jolted the gargoyle forward. It did not relinquish its hold on the boy. This made Trazk angry. Spittle flew then frothed from his fanged grimace. He hooked his arm to it, then braced against the creature with his left foot and heaved. First he grunted. Then a loud crack sounded. Then the arm split from the gargoyles shoulder; unevenly it splintered.

The grasping claw was still joined to Tristan's shoulder. He cried from the pain. The orc drew his scimitar and bashed the pommel against the finger joints. They broke free from the hand. Trazk then flung the arm at the face of the gargoyle as it tried to recover. In the same movement, he leapt forward as the creature blocked its own limb. An unbalanced kick was enough to send the Gargoyle back, barreling it into and tripping up Thelband's pursuer.

Now two gargoyles turned to face Trazk. He welcomed them through a crusty yellow grin, "A real fight. Good." As the two stone sentinels moved to intercept, Trazk commanded his diminutive companion, "Get one of those doors open. We need a way out."

"Make it fast!" Brell yelled back from the melee in front. He and Ardus were knee deep in skeletal bones. They had destroyed much of four lines of skeletons, but the easy kills were becoming harder to find. The demon hunter was protected by a white light that deflected arrows and spears like an extra set of armor. Ardus had heavy armor, but weapons found the gaps. He was bleeding from several wounds. Brell was amazed at this man's stamina. Fight after fight this bull of a warrior just kept going. This fight was the right time to have him at his side.

Foe-less, Thelband went to work on the door. The lock was not complicated, but he had no tools other than his knives. A stone hand smashed and shattered on the wall next to his head. He sneaked a glance back. A gargoyle had thrown his own severed hand in an attempt to stop him. Trazk kept it from doing more than that. The lock popped. "Got it!" he declared and then stood to find a new opponent.

The three vampire minions dropped from the ceiling. Two were behind the halfling and Thelband swung his daggers at the first to keep her at bay. The two flankers each grabbed and held his stubby arms. Sour breath was the last he knew as the female lunged in and ripped open his jugular with her fangs. Blood sprayed out on Thelband's attackers and the trio went into a frenzy of biting and sucking his life's blood as he slipped down to the floor.

"It is hopeless!" Dellan called out over the fray from somewhere behind the skeletons, "One down. How long can you hope to last?"

"Hold the line," Brell commanded Ardus. The warrior freed the dusty maul strapped to his back and nodded assurance that he would do just that. Muscles grew taught as the heavy warhammer swung across the front line of skeletons. It screamed its purpose as wood splintered and bones snapped. Two skeletons hurriedly took swings that bloodied the warrior. The butcher shook his head. He didn't like how much exertion this thing took, how slow it was and how it left him vulnerable. Brell moved toward the back just in time as Ardus changed his tactic. The big man let loose with another swing. Off balance at first, he let the swing propel him into a spin, and he increased the momentum and force. Skeletons ducked or charged at him, but only met with a final fate from their new iron god. The noise was deafening. Skulls, armor, arms and ribcages smacked off the wall with the force and sound of thunder.

The demon hunter dodged behind where Lancelot fought, but not before cutting the boy's gargoyle foe down at the knee. As Lancelot finished the creature with thrusts to the head, Brell snatched the lone torch from its sconce.

Lancelot put his foot to the gargoyle's face as he struggled to pull Grace out. He watched Brell with curiosity, and as Brell noticed his young charge's observation, he admitted, "You won't be learning this one anytime soon." The demon hunter cupped one hand on the other side of the flame, and he half-whispered half kissed the fire at the top of the torch. It went from a smoky orange and red to a flaring white light. Brell gently walked over to the three crouching vampires who fed on Thelband then blew into the flame.

One vampire looked up toward the annoying light just as motes of white fire spilled out onto the bloodbath. The three screamed in agony as their flesh started to disintegrate. One mote bore a path through the female vampire's head into her eye socket and floated out through her ear. The other two vampires scurried up the wall as they burned. The entire hall was illuminated as if the sun were rising.

Dellan let out a pained howl from somewhere in the mass of bodies. Three other vampires that crawled on the ceiling ready to drop down immolated and fell. They flared up bright on the ground or on skeletons before extinguishing into smoking piles of flesh and ash.

The other vampires retreated. At least one of them was blinded.

Although untouched by flame, Thelband lay bloody and lifeless. His face was nearly unrecognizable. The vampires had cannibalized his neck, jaw, and cheeks.

At the instant that the last flare died down, Dellan tumbled over Ardus' whirling havoc. A blur b-lined for the demon hunter before Brell could unleash more fire.

Lancelot struggled with his lodged sword still and Trazk wrestled with the final gargoyle.

Only Tristan stood by Brell. The boy stepped forward to intercept Dellan. Sharp pain greeted him as the vampire's claws pierced his shoulder like a spear. Lancelot's brother screamed in agony and Dellan shook Tristan off like he was dirt on his fingers. Hope bounced and clanged to the floor. Tristan was thrown back the opposite way, past Brell. He lay sprawled and bloody against the closed gate.

"Tristan!" Trazk cried out. He redoubled his effort against his granite opponent.

Brell spun toward Dellan and the vampire smacked away the torch with one hand and grabbed the demon hunter by the neck with his other. Brell was lifted off the ground and to Dellan's face where the vampire gloated while the old man gasped raggedly for air, "This is the heroes sent to defeat me?"

Brell just stared at the hole in Dellan's face while trying to gulp any air he could. Rank, rotting bile issued from the wound. It was still fresh and wet. Dellan twisted Brell's head to force him to lock eyes, "Oh? Strong enough to resist my charms? No matter fool. I am done with you." Dellan's free hand reached into Brell's belly and pulled out a string of intestines. Brell would have screamed if he could. He only answered with tears and a squirm. Dellan discarded him with a toss to the right. Brell slipped on his own blood and fell down with his back to the stone wall; one hand tried to keep the rest of his innards inside. The other waved back and forth to fend off any more attacks. He had had enough.

Trazk and Lancelot freed at the same time. The vampire saw the orc as the greater threat.

"Don't think you are going to gut me like him," Trazk challenged while nodding toward Brell. "I am going to rip your head off."

Dellan stopped as if stunned. Then he laughed.

Ardus was out of spin. He let his hammer fly and it careened off the wall and into a skeleton or two. He picked up two scimitars that lay at his feet and he drunkenly waded into the skeletons and their handlers. He was both dizzy and drained from dark energies. He let his training take over as he had little sense left of what to do.

Lancelot bent over and picked up Hope. Immediately his mind was flooded with conversation between his swords. They were communicating with each other. "*Stop!*" he screamed to them. He could not concentrate.

Hope silenced while Grace explained, "*Lancelot, give my sister to your trainer. We may be able to help after all.*"

He did as instructed and rushed to Brell's side. Blood had pooled up around where the demon-hunter sat. "Brell. Please, take this." He offered Hope to him.

Brell tried to ward off Lancelot until he recognized him. "We are lost. I am so sorry son." He took the sword from Lancelot and his eyes lit up. "I understand," he said.

Lancelot was confused until Brell was in his head, "*Lancelot, your sword does not have the strength to help you, but I do. Rather, you have the strength to help me help you.*"

The demon-slaying apprentice looked down at his master. Brell's head was slumped over. He continued to bleed out. Hope was in his hand, but lay more on the floor than in a grip. Inside his head, Lancelot could feel Brell's vigor and enthusiasm. "*First we have to give you more time. Put your hand over my stomach and incant Guin Mistra Selmek. Keep repeating that. Focus on my wound. Focus on my life force.*"

Lancelot repeated the words aloud, even as Brell tried to finish his thought to him, "GUIN-MISTRA-SELMEK." His hands gave off a fuzzy glow. He could sense, no feel Brell guiding him though the link. "GUIN-MISTRA-SELMEK." Brell's wound started to close. His guts began slithering back into his stomach. "GUIN-MIS...."

Brell put a hand on his and cut him off. "You can't waste all of your energy on me. It will drain you too much." His voice cracked, and he was visibly drained and weak. You need to turn our magic on them. He nodded toward Ardus who was barely visible in a sea of undead. Then they looked toward Trazk. He was in a desperate fight with Dellan. He spent more time dodging blows than delivering them. Dellan was clearly playing with him. At least his attention was not on Tristan who lay unconscious or worse.

"Help your brother. Get him and go through the door. Get outside to Lareth. It is the blood. Lareth's blood is poison to Dellan..."

The vampire spun on them. He heard and he was going to thwart their plans. Then a chunk of his head splintered off toward the ceiling. Trazk was battering him in the ear and face with a gargoyle arm. Chips and chunks of stone broke off more than the bone fragments Dellan's head gave. The vampire was off balance though and Trazk was not going to let him retake the initiative so soon. "You damn blood-sucking maggot!" the orc yelled. "I told you I was going to take your head off!" Dellan was on one knee. Trazk kept hammering.

"We have to help Ardus too. Quickly." Lancelot's thoughts were urgent but not panicked.

"Hands open. Right Forefinger to left thumb. Counter-clockwise wave. Force your will on them. Step into it. The harder the step, the more force." Brell's instructions were precise.

Lancelot did as he felt and was told. He let anger be his stomp. He let worry for his friends guide his wave. A large 'whooshing' sound followed the foot clap. Skeletons, fanatics and even Ardus were caught together in a horizontal tornado that washed them back beyond the far doors.

"Too much." Brell had nothing else to say.

Dellan had shaken off the surprise assault and was now trying to get by Trazk. The orc threw his body into the vampire biting and clawing at Dellan's face.

Lancelot ran to Tristan. His runes lit up and were ready. "GUIN-MISTRA-SELMEK." He repeated twice before Tristan's eyes opened. It took him a few seconds to figure out where he was.

Lancelot helped him to stand and filled him in, "You have to go. Dellan knows our plan. Find your way out. Bring some of the blood of Lareth. It can help us kill Dellan."

Tristan looked up with fear in his eyes. Lancelot knew.

"*Pel Mora Fin Mira,*" the younger brother invoked then spun. Dellan was on him. Lancelot parried one swipe, then another. As Dellan readied a third, the boy kicked him straight on in the chest and the vampire was knocked back to the T-intersection. Lancelot was already on him putting Dellan squarely on the defensive.

34

Trazk opened the door for Tristan. "Let's go." The bloody orc put an arm around Tristan's shoulder and ushered him out of the hall. Beyond, stairs spiraled up tightly. Trazk got behind his charge and practically pushed him up the stairs as fast as they could go. They stopped once so Tristan could vomit.

At the top of the stairs, a landing looked to go in two directions, one deeper into the castle and one back over the hall. They took the over-hall hall. A series of murder-holes looked out over the front gate.

"This is what we want," Trazk said pleased.

"We can't fit through there," Tristan said incredulously.

Trazk gave Tristan a look as if the boy's words injured him. "You are young yet. So I will teach you now. In the world of many races, you will learn, Dwarves are renowned for building things." He stepped all the way back against the far wall. "And orcs are here to tear them down!" He charged the wall and with all his force, slammed into it, right where a murder-hole was. The wall gave and crumbled. Stone and orc spilled out and onto the drawbridge below.

Tristan looked out and there was no movement from Trazk. He made the mistake of calling down to him, "Are you okay?" Too late. On the road to the right, a gargoyle cocked its head. It had been looking where Trazk had fallen but now looked up at the boy. The stone guardian launched itself into the air at him. It was slow for a flier, but came at him fast enough. As it ascended toward the murder-hole it suddenly descended violently. Trazk was on its leg.

"Get down here and do what needs to be done," Trazk yelled as the gargoyle and its passenger careened out of view. Grinding stone told the boy they landed or crashed somewhere.

Tristan sidled down so he could hang-drop. It wasn't as far as he thought. After he landed, he instinctively reached for Hope. She wasn't there. He looked around in a panic, then decided he had to just go.

Across the bridge was Lareth's body. The gargoyle must have been standing guard over him. He lay exactly as he had fallen the night before. Tristan inspected him closer. Multiple bones had broken through the skin on his arms, leg and chest. The vampire's bite was visible and the blood around it had dried. Very little blood was on the ground.

The sound of Trazk's combat continued. Tristan searched Lareth for anything to store blood in. Nothing. He found one the priest's maces nearby. Lareth had a knife on his belt.

Desperately, Tristan patted down his dead friend one more time. *"What would Lancelot do?"* he thought to himself. His younger brother had a penchant for figuring out lazy solutions when their mother told them to do things. The pain of remembering his mother nearly paralyzed Tristan if he didn't come up with a crazy Lancelot solution first.

He rolled Lareth on his side and raised his tunic. A large dark splotch covered Lareth's back where the blood had pooled. He laid on the ground so that Lareth was alongside him, then used the priest's knife to cut a large incision above and along the spine from neck to butt. The knife rode over ribs but cut deep where there were none. Tristan then half-rolled Lareth onto him. Cold blood poured out unevenly over the boy.

He rolled Lareth back over to preserve blood then went to task of wiping and smearing the blood all over himself. When he was nearly finished Trazk came into view. His arm looked broken. The orc stopped.

"What are you doing?" Trazk asked curiously as he drew his sword.

"There was nowhere to store the blood. We need the blood to kill Dellan."

Trazk did not take his eyes off of the boy as he walked over to Lareth's body. He knelt down, slowly. Deliberately. Then he used one hand to splash some of the blood onto his blade. The orc cocked his head and an eyebrow clearly to ask if any of this registered in the boy's mind.

"Stupid Lancelot," Tristan said under his breath.

After Trazk had stood and walked back across the drawbridge, Tristan hurried to the body and coated the knife. He was about to follow the orc when he remembered he had arrows too. He dipped those then ran to where the orc stood under the modified opening in the castle.

"Would be nice if the ropes were still here," Trazk mused. "Guess you will have to get back there and help."

"What do you mean?" Tristan was dismayed.

"Arm's broken. I can't get up there, even if you pushed me by the ass." Trazk cupped his hands. He winced with pain as he turned the arm. "Foot in here. You are going to get one chance, so don't mess it up." The orc spread his feet and crouched to brace himself.

Tristan put his hands on Trazk's shoulders and then stepped into the make-shift stirrup. With a heave and a yell of pain and effort, Trazk launched the boy high above the gate. It was more than enough. Tristan caught the opening with both hands and even was able to get a foot in. "I'm up!" he yelled as he quickly secured himself inside. When he looked back down, Trazk had sprinted off and to the right.

35

Lancelot struggled alongside Ardus. The big man's shoulder was dislocated and he was fighting with a half-desiccated hand. The negative energy from the magics had drained and emaciated him. The warrior held no grudge from the earlier wind blast and encouraged Lancelot with every foe they dropped. "I don't hear the vampire boasting now," Ardus laughed, then coughed as blood spit out of his mouth. "Just because he ran off, doesn't mean he has left the fight. Let's work our way back to Brell."

Side-by-side, the two fought their way back from the main audience chamber. The skeleton priests were dead. Their magic would have no additional effect. One of them though cast a spell that reanimated nearly all of the skeletons that had already been re-killed. Ardus had counted and pointed out at least three vampire spawn left. The combatants wisely checked the ceiling for any approach.

"Do you think we can do this?" Lancelot asked. He was protected by a softly glowing shield of light, but his runes had been quiet now for nearly five minutes. He was very tired, and he knew Ardus must be beyond exhaustion.

"We do this until we cannot any longer," Ardus said matter-of-fact.

When they reached Brell, the old man looked up with silent

acknowledgement. The demon hunter's breathing was shallow. Lancelot worried he would die at any moment. The two kept the skeletons from overwhelming them in the hall. Lancelot wanted to create another whirlwind, but the last took almost all of his reserves.

Just then, Tristan emerged through the door. Blood dripped off his chin. He held the dagger tightly.

"Impressive big brother," Lancelot called back in awe.

Tristan shot him the look he gave when Lancelot got them into trouble, then scanned the hall until he found his bow. He recovered it just in time.

As the skeletons surged, two vampire spawns crawled over the melee. Tristan fired his bow. The arrow perfectly pierced the lead vampire through the forehead and buried itself in its skull. The creature tried to scream but only dropped from the ceiling in front of Tristan. A hole opened in the back of its head then spread to the neck. Flesh and bone collapsed in on itself around the arrowhead.

Tristan already had another arrow ready and fired at the second vampire. This female undead was ready for his shot and used the corner and ceiling as a vault. She leapt to her real target, Brell. Tristan realized this and in a panic fired a third arrow. It missed the spawn.

"My master wants you all to know you won't avoid your fate," the wiry vampire declared as she reached down with both hands and ripped out Brell's intestines in one wild swing. His eyes went wide, then glassy. The violent motion pulled him over onto his side. Hope rolled from his grasp.

"No!" Lancelot screamed, then spun to face the spawn. Ardus shifted to keep skeletons from pushing in, but the surge overwhelmed him and skeletons toppled the large warrior onto Lancelot. The whole front line collapsed.

Tears in his eyes, Tristan lined up his fourth shot. He put his arrow in the breast of the vampire. She lunged backward, inhumanly spinning and clinging to the wall. Her head shot one last look of hatred at the boy then to her wound. Like the other vampire, the hole grew and collapsed in on itself. She screamed in agony and dropped down, face first. The stench of her disintegrating wafted from the large hole in her back.

Tristan dropped his bow and ran to scoop up Hope, but the skeletons pushed over the fallen group and prevented him from reaching her. He backed up slowly, the bloody knife his only protection.

Lancelot gasped for air. Ardus was in plate armor and already weighed a ton. His body protected him, even as it slowly killed him. The hulking warrior indicated he was still alive with grunts and groans. Those skeletons that were not on top of him clawing to get to his insides thrusted spears down. Some found metal, some flesh.

The skeleton front line pressed toward Tristan who had his back to the gate. He stood to fight and was ready to die. The mass of undead stopped then parted. Dellan walked down the hall toward him. "You have fought bravely young Tristan." He glanced over to Brell. "I am sorry your grandfather had to die, but you don't."

The skeletons filled in behind him. All others were unmoving except those that tried to silence Ardus and Lancelot.

Tristan tightened his grip on the knife. He strained not to scream his reply, "He was not our grandfather. But he taught us enough to know NEVER to side with the likes of you." He stepped forward and hurled the knife at Dellan. The vampire lord nonchalantly swatted the bloody dagger with the back of hand as he stepped closer. Tristan spied that his hand smoked.

"It is sad that you have made this choice. Regardless, you will serve me." Dellan was fast and he was already on Tristan, one arm around his shoulder to bring him in for a bite. The vampire lord immediately realized his mistake, but before he could recoil, Tristan wrapped his arms and legs around Dellan's torso and squeezed. The blood of Lareth transferred to Dellan almost as if it willed itself to.

Dellan's face contorted. He scraped and thrashed. They spun like two dancers before momentum and pain were too much for the boy. He let go and fell back.

"Tristan!" he heard Trazk behind the skeletons who stood silent and still. The boy looked up to see a blade spinning in the air. It clanked across the floor near enough for him to retrieve from where he stood.

Dellan still spun and burned. Lareth's blood was holy acid sizzling the undead flesh. His agony was intense. Tristan walked over to him. The vampire was blind to his surroundings, the flesh on his face had melted down over his eyes.

"You are finished." Tristan said calmly as he took the stance Samuel had made him practice. Then he swung the sword. Dellan's head rolled off of his shoulders. A golden necklace, attached with an iron alien shaped medallion and a single polished emerald, dropped to the floor next to the crackling body.

All at once, the skeletons fell to the floor. Tristan saw Trazk pick a path toward him but stopped at the large pile of bones. The pile shook. Then it lifted like a bubble in a bath. Ardus rose with Lancelot in his arms. Skeletal digits, limbs and skulls rolled off of them like water as he limped out.

They all converged where Brell lay. Ardus put Lancelot down. The gentle impact of the floor woke him from unconsciousness and he gasped for air.

Tristan smiled sadly down at him. "It is done."

Lancelot turned his head toward Brell then began to cry.

Ardus let the boys grieve for as long as he could. The big warrior braced against the wall and Trazk relocated his shoulder, then Ardus set the orc's arm in a sling. After, the two veterans took up positions down the hall, alert to further danger.

Lancelot reflected on the odyssey that brought them to this place. He shook his head at the price as he rose. "I guess that is it then."

Tristan, even without the sister-swords connecting their thoughts shared the same sentiment, "And an iron medallion is our payment for everything we have done."

Ardus and Trazk were ready. The ex-gladiator grimaced. His cracked ribs reminded him he should not be talking. "We are not done yet."

The boys looked puzzled as Ardus continued, "The vampire's rot lies there, but he may be able to reform back at his resting place.

We have to find him and finish this."

Before they continued, the four struggled to get the front gate open. Trazk reasoned that if they needed a hasty retreat, nobody was in any condition to drop swiftly down a rope.

For hours they navigated through rooms and corridors. Often, they found themselves going in circles. It was Trazk's tapping, sharp eye or a combination of both that discovered a secret panel in a non-descript room.

"*La.*" Lancelot lit Grace and led the others down a narrow stair. Cobwebs tried to bar their way and betrayed misuse. Every step, as slow as it was, echoed loudly.

"*Remind me to teach you how to walk quietly,*" Tristan chided his younger brother.

Lancelot braved a sneer over his shoulder. The stair abruptly emptied into a small chapel. Profane pictures lined either wall. Rotted pews sagged or lay collapsed in their own disrepair.

The group walked to the far side of the room where a trick of the chancel wall concealed a sliver of a passage behind a stone altar. Both Trazk and Tristan readied bows and hugged close behind Lancelot as he stepped in. Ardus wheezed behind them. He used the wall for support.

"*If there is a fight, I think it will be just the three of us. Ardus looks beat,*" Tristan warned.

Lancelot responded with a whisper, "Let's hope there is no fight."

The passage wound like an 'S' at first and then spiraled down. Rivulets of water seeped down the wall. Damp, humid, dead air greeted them at the bottom. The stone floor gave way to soft, turned earth. A dozen coffins rested haphazardly and half-buried throughout a fairly sizable chamber. Two halls exited opposite from where they entered.

Eight of the coffin lids were moved aside. Lancelot moved from one to another and braved a look into each. Each time he sighed, it told the group that no vampire lay within.

Everyone knew what to expect for the final four coffins. Ardus moved with strained determination.

"Ardus." Lancelot met his gaze. "We have this."

Tristan dropped his bow and drew Hope, "*La.*" She glowed brightly.

Together, the boys incanted, "*Pel, Mora, Mira.*"

Lancelot flicked his left hand out and a pale purple blade appeared in it.

"*I guess I'll be opening the coffins,*" Tristan said with realization.

The two boys took up positions on either side of a coffin. Tristan counted down in their heads then with one hand slid the coffin lid off. He surprised himself with how easily the hinges snapped and how far it flew and shattered against the far wall. "*Oops! Excited I guess...*" he tried to explain.

Lancelot was all business and ignored Tristan and the coffin lid. Grace and lavender light were a blur as he struck down. The short sword penetrated through a young looking male vampire, his coffin, and down through the dirt. The violence of his blows reflected the rage on his face.

The vampire let out a high pitch gurgling scream.

Three other coffin lids burst from their hinges. Two male vampires stood up in their coffins. A female sprang from the third and contorted as she leapt up to and attached herself to the ceiling.

The first male attempted to soliloquy, probably some threat, but Hope cut out his larynx before repeatedly thrusting though where his heart would be.

Lancelot intercepted the second male who tried to turn on a broken and bleeding Ardus. Both blades came down from behind in an 'X' motion. The vampire was quartered where he stood.

The female coiled and then lunged through the air at Lancelot. Tristan was faster and intercepted her mid-flight with a tremendous punch to the side of her face. Even dried, Lareth's blood remained potent. His hand went through one side of her face and came out the other. Bits of skull and brain washed and sizzled against the wall. An arrow from Trazk's bow then penetrated her breast before her body hit the ground. Even in a sling, the orc was a marksman.

Ardus stood himself up, ready to meet the second vampire. His jaw dropped as he realized how fast this all happened. "I think I am ready to retire."

Lancelot walked up to the big warrior and smiled. "This can be more dangerous than a drug. I think I just got a super charge from Grace." His hands glowed white and he grabbed Ardus. Healing power filled his large companion and healed some of the more grievous wounds.

"Sorry Trazk, I didn't realize how serious Ardus' wounds were," the boy said as he looked apologetically to the orc. "I'll get you on the next one."

"Better we are all alive than..." Trazk cut himself off realizing it came out wrong.

"I know what you mean," Lancelot said a little sadder.

The group inspected the room and coffins more closely. The coffin insides were made of fine silk fabrics. Most of them contained jewels or other personal effects from their dead inhabitants. Trazk set to bagging them. "This is the reason you always check to make sure they are all dead. This is often the only way heroes get paid...when they don't die."

"You called yourself a hero," Lancelot laughed at him.

"You wound me," the orc said sarcastically.

When they finished, Tristan asked, "Left or right?" He indicated with a nod to the two exit passages.

Trazk surprised him one more time. "Center." He used both hands to slide a raised stone door open. "Those other passages," he grunted, "lead up. Probably to other exits used by the vampires."

The door revealed a lavish room fit for a king. This was where Dellan resided. He had a four-poster bed. His coffin was concealed on the far side of it and did not detract from the richness of the room. At first glance, it looked to be just an ornate box. There was a table with papers and maps laid out on it, and a desk with more to investigate. At the foot of the bed sat two large chests.

"Before we start digging, we need to finish this," Ardus explained, "If the vampire lord survived, he will have returned, probably here."

"Our swords are sapped," Tristan interjected.

"Not your training," Trazk chided. "Don't sell yourself short.

And anyways, you want to see a coffin lid fly, I'm sure Ardus can help."

Ardus just smiled.

The coffin was empty.

The four set to looting everything that was not attached to the wall, but before long, everything shook.

"Earthquake?!" Tristan questioned in a panic.

It was quiet.

"Not sure." Trazk was puzzled too. "That was short." He listened then looked to Ardus. "Do you think Delan's castle is held up by magic? Shouldn't it have all come down when Tristan first liquefied him?"

As if in answer, the room shook again.

"Quickly!" Ardus beckoned for everyone to exit with haste. "My limp requires we leave now."

The castle rumbled eight or nine more times as they hurriedly ascended stairs and navigated hallways.

They made it back to the entrance hall and sprinted out through the open gate. Debris tumbled down off to the left.

When they turned to watch the whole castle collapse, they were surprised to see Kromax half- buried in the side of the mountain. He knocked a tower over and his head disappeared into a large hole.

When he drew it out, he scanned around and saw the four down below. "There you are!" He bellowed with a smile. The great beast pushed himself out of the castle. More of it tumbled from above. He let his wings catch the wind and he glided down to greet them. The dragon morphed into his human form as his legs touched the ground.

With hugs and tears, the group caught Kromax up on Dellan's fate, and the Dragon explained the zombie general Zumathash also met a grisly end.

They gathered their fallen comrades and took flight.

36

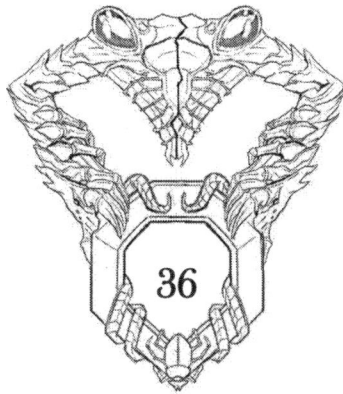

The next day, the group gathered around a familiar kitchen table.

Magari complained again as she served Lancelot another bowl of stew, "How long are those heads going to be in here?"

Kromax gave her a look of mock indignation. "You know what we went through to get these…" Her sour glare cut him off. "Just a little longer please?" he asked sheepishly.

She crossed her arms for a second and looked at the rotted head of Dellan and the burnt head of Zumathash. She pretended to contemplate, then relented, "Ok. But if maggots start growing in either of those, they are out of here." Magari got back to her pot and added some more onion.

Kromax turned his attention back to the group seated at the table. Tristan and Lancelot sat next to each other on one side, both ate and listened. Ardus had more bandages on him than a mummy. Trazk rested his broken arm in a sling.

"Thank you for coming to get us." Ardus was grateful. "I would not have been able to walk much further than the drawbridge."

"You are my friends," Kromax acknowledged, "I could do no less." He looked over at Trazk. "I still can't believe how times change. You guys travelled with a vampire and an orc. Amazing."

Trazk grunted, "Open minds make for open hearts."

Tristan spit out his mouthful and they all laughed. "What happened to eating humans and all that?"

Trazk looked at him hard before answering, "What makes you think I am not going to do that still?"

They enjoyed each other's company, and when the boys had finished eating, they all got up and somberly filed out of the room. Wordless, they walked down the hall, through the sitting chamber and treasure room.

Outside the waterfall, three freshly turned graves waited for them.

Each contemplated or reminisced. Magari broke the silence, "Have you thought about what will happen now?"

Kromax pulled her in close under one arm. "It looks like Ardus and Trazk are going with me. This fight is personal now. We have all lost friends and family." He looked to the brothers and asked, "Are you sure you do not want to come with us?"

Lancelot answered for the both of them, "No. We have to find our mother and father. At the very least, we need to learn of their fate."

Tristan played with the strange medallion around his neck. "Yes. There is so much in this world that needs to be fixed right now. This is the best way. You guys will always be family to us, but we have to do this."

Magari smiled and handed each of them a sack she had prepared. "Go with the blessing of Bayoric and protection of Chess."

Tristan thanked her and each of the others until he got to Trazk. Him, he gave a long hug. "I remember the first day we met."

"Yes," Trazk remembered, "At least you are no longer dumb and deer-eyed. You have a chance now." They both smiled.

Lancelot gave each a hug then said a blessing over the graves. He stopped over Brell's for a long time. "Thank you."

The two brothers gave each other a heartfelt hug, turned, and began their journey back home. They looked back once and waved. Each carried a sack of gold, jewels and more.

Lancelot said with a smile, "We really did get to see a dragon."

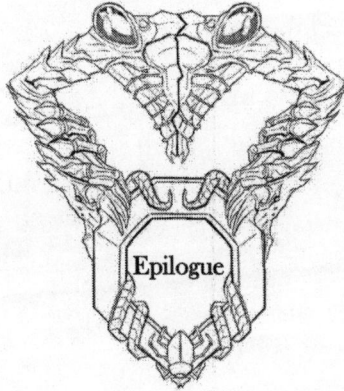

Epilogue

Devin thought that once they were through the mountains, they would be free of their pursuers. He was wrong. Only eleven people of the hundred or so that started out from the flooded city of Ferrickport scrambled down the rocks into the uneven hills below. He curled his arms tight around his daughter Nia as he thought of their harrowing exodus.

Vellina, goddess of luck, had to be watching over them. How else could they have run into Tara the Peacekeeper in all the chaos and tumult from the flooding, the dark storm, and the invading monsters?

Almost three months of perilous hiking and now, it seemed their luck had run out. They still had to make it out of the hills and then it would be no less than a two day run across the open plains to Anvil Point, a military port on the border between Tamm and the Duchy of Malistair.

Behind them, visible in the broken boulders and winding escarpments, fifty or so of the insect creatures came. Tara urged the group on. Devin could see her face. It was obvious, she calculated how far they would get before they were overrun.

"This way!" Tara yelled and she changed direction.

Devin followed, but his gaze ran ahead. Further down the hill, a lone figure, most likely a teenaged boy, waved. Tara made a b-line for the figure. When the entire group began the descent in the prescribed direction, the figure disappeared behind low lying bushes.

The path was steep here and Devin lost his footing more than once. He was able to use his slide and momentum to keep from falling, but he slowed considerably. Thurdron, the dwarf merchant, passed him on the way down.

Nia could see what Devin couldn't. Her father slipped and stutter-stepped much too slowly. The monsters moved differently. They loped and bound down the mountainside as if they were bred for this moment. Their faces grew more discernable the closer they got. Even alien to her, their features clearly gave away that they had slaughter on their minds.

Fifty yards away, one of the monsters let loose some spinning toy. It knew how to use it, and the whirling disk zoomed down at Nia and Devin with deadly accuracy. "Father," she whimpered into his ear. Her word caught Devin off guard and he slipped down onto his hind side. Nia also bounced in his lap, but she held ever more tightly to his neck.

The blade ricocheted off a rock. Sparks flew one way, the blade zinged off another.

Devin required no more encouragement, and let his bounce propel him back up into a sprint. Urgency and reckless panic became his energy. The father weaved, yet his downward pace increased.

Ahead, Tara faced him and waved him toward her. She held a rock in either hand. When she was sure Devin had seen her, she threw her rocks and immediately retrieved more. Up and behind him, Devin heard the stones strike metal. Nia's breathing relaxed some and her choking grip loosened a little. "She hit the spinning toys, father," his daughter exhaled with reverence.

Past Tara, Thurdron dipped behind some rocks and out of sight. The boy that Devin had spied from before was there. He urged Devin his way. When Devin and Nia arrived, the boy said, "Hurry. Down there." The group of survivors huddled between a stand of rocks and the hillside. Several large, dirty leather blankets camouflaged the hiding spot, and when Devin had crawled down inside and set Nia down, the boy closed the flap of the last blanket.

Semni, a skinny merchant complained through labored breathing, "They are going to find us here. We. Have to keep going."

Thurdron, the second to last to arrive, appeared to already have caught his breath. He shot Semni an 'are you crazy?' look, then explained the obvious, "We would never make it to…well, to anywhere. These hills dump into open fields for miles around. Do you think any of us can outrun them?" He didn't expect an answer, nor did he receive one.

Devin risked a look through a gap in the blanket. The boy stood crouched. He faced intently up the hill, a taught chord in one hand.

The sounds of rock on metal still persisted, but the occasional whooshing of the spinning blades also zipped overhead somewhere.

Footsteps caused Devin to look past the boy and he saw Tara somersaulted over and out of view. The boy watched her briefly then back up to the demons. Their path had obviously shifted and they were intent on the diplomat.

Devin watched as the boy crouched further. His muscles tightened, then in one sudden motion, the boy yanked on the chord with all his might. Somewhere in the distance, stone grinded on stone. Then a whoosh. Finally, crunching, crushing carapaces. High pitched screeches rose and fell sharply. The demons could scream. That was good to know. Those caught in whatever contraption was out there gurgled what could only be horrid death rattles.

"Yes!" the boy exclaimed. A Second later, he ducked as a metal blade lodged into the stone near his head. "Oh shit!" the boy said surprised, then rolled out away from the hide.

Tara yelled from somewhere, "Behind you!" then a few seconds later, "Watch out!"

Semni, who someone should have been watching more closely, panicked. He rushed past Devin, and out from safety. The scared man cleared three paces before he was lifted into the air on a demon's pike. It watched with interest as he squirmed and screamed, but Nia screamed louder and its head snapped in their direction.

Devin fought the urge to snatch Nia up and run, and instead stepped out of the hide. The insect-demon was perched on the rock in front of him. Semni dangled lifeless on its crooked spear. The creature stood and swung its pike around to level at the man in challenge.

Devin acted the faster and yanked the metal blade that protruded from the rock at the demon's feet. It cut him. He ignored the pain and fire that shot through his hand and gave a level cut across the monster's knees. The creature buckled. Semni's corpse, still caught on the spear's hook, wheeled the demon off balance and both fell away on the other side of the stone boulder.

Devin saw it was grim. More than a score of demons still ran down the hillside and certainly noticed his action. Beyond the stone where the flopping demon lie, a grizzly contraption had caught between four and six demons in some kind of wooden and steel tenderizer. Another dozen demons either tried to catch the boy or fight through Tara. From what Devin saw, none of them had succeeded.

"We have to go. We are spotted." Devin looked to the others with determination. Nia jumped into his arms. He was careful to keep the blade away from her. Devin only realized too late there was more than just a sharp blade to this weapon.

The others followed him. He led them the only direction that made sense, toward Tara. Vesper, then Kelvin screamed out their last, mere moments after clearing the hide. *"This was it then,"* Devin thought. The group ran toward the Peacekeeper. Her eyes met Devin's and he saw her sigh in resignation. Then she began to glow orange.

Tara's movements became less 'flowing water' to more of a 'jagged lightning swarm'. Her movements were unpredictable as she spun through the air then struck a demon from behind. Parts of something from inside the demon were in her hand.

Her movements brought her closer to the group and the many, many monsters behind them.

Devin led the group past Tara and toward the last outcropping of rocks before the great level sea of land. Two insect creatures were hot on their heels, choosing easy meat over what Tara had to offer them.

On the rocks ahead, a large, half-insect, half-man rose to stand upon the outcropping. Immediately, Devin diverted on a perpendicular path. The man watched them run, his crazed eyes visible from behind a blackened carapace face...or helm...

Devin realized it was armor. The man wore a patchwork of insect armor. More obvious at this distance was that he lacked a left hand. His one good hand, like the boy before, held onto the end of a rope. He pulled it, then leapt from the rocks.

As if in one motion, the man unstrapped a silvered hammer from his belt, the handle found its way into his grip. The arm with no hand appeared to fold out from either side of his bicep and, by the time the man landed, had formed into a wicked black blade where his forearm and hand should be. It ignited.

As if that weren't enough, hundreds of arrows rained up over the man, Devin, his group, the boy, Tara and her opponents. They showered the oncoming monsters that were still back in the hills. Some, hopefully many perished in that volley.

Devin's path changed again. Crazed as the man looked, Nia's father gambled their fate was better off in his hand.

As the group took shelter behind the large warrior, Devin took note that the man wore the chitnous hides of these creatures, but there was gleaming metal weaved into or complimenting the already tough insect carapaces. He was wrong about the man missing only his hand. The unfolded sword that was expertly joined into the flaming blade covered the area where both a hand and forearm should be. Some kind of box that held the sword in place wheezed and grinded as a squirting, flaming liquid continuously coated the already deadly blade. Some of the warrior's joints were similarly encapsulated in metallic whirly boxes. All of it, as piecemeal as it really was, interconnected and left a very intimidating impression.

The only thing the warrior had that was not connected was his warhammer. This, the man threw at the closest incoming insect marauder. The hammer impacted the beast and collapsed its chest.

278

A huge and deafening thunderclap ripped the creature in half and flattened the demon behind it.

A demon that must have tired of chasing the boy arrived from a different direction and leapt at the man. It wielded two spears in its four arms. The man parried two quick thrusts from one spear, but the second sunk into the warrior's side. He grimaced and stretched a hand out, palm open. The hammer, lying almost out of sight, flew back into his grip. He first swiped down and shattered the spear that was still in him, then he swung the hammer up. It destroyed the demon-insect's mandibles, eyes and forehead.

The warrior ignored the demon as it flailed about. Blue ichor and whistling sounds issued from a hole in its face. The man was more concerned with the second half of the spear still embedded in him. He called out to the boy, "David, to me!"

The boy, David, rolled and dodged away from two demon's that chased him. They were quick, but he was both quick and nimble. He must have known he could not hurt the creatures, because he had no weapon drawn.

"Incoming!" David yelled as he led the two demons back toward the warrior. The big man worked faster to dislodge the spear.

Thurdron approached the man. "Can I help with that?" he asked with trepidation.

The warrior looked exasperated. "It's hooked. Push it through."

The dwarf was unsure but took a hold of the shattered haft.

"Push now!" the man screamed. Thurdron put all of his weight into his thrust. He could feel and hear the spear tear more flesh as it exited the other side.

The big man groaned. He swayed for a second then as he steadied himself, he unclasped a small potion vial and drank from it. The blood immediately stopped flowing from the hole in his back. He quickly uncapped another vial and downed that.

Devin watched this unfold and gripped his hand where he had cut it. An intense burning was creeping up his arm.

"Father, look," Nia said with a whisper. She did not want to draw attention from any more monsters. She pointed up the hill, beyond the creatures that still bounded down toward them.

It was hard to follow her gaze at first, for the tumult of battle rejoined mere feet from the cowering group.

"Look!" she said more forcefully.

This time, he looked up the hill. A dust cloud moved swiftly down. He thought at first it was an avalanche, but there were a pair of figures leading the smoky line. It was hard to tell from here, but they must be mounted.

A straggler demon turned back toward the riders and disappeared in their cloud. The 'avalanche' continued to gain speed down the hill.

As the riders grew closer, Tara caught Devin's attention. She no longer glowed orange, but several demon creatures lay dead at her feet. She now moved like the flowing water, as she did when he first saw her. It did not look as if she were injured, but more insect-men surrounded her than before.

David tripped the remaining demon near the group. The large man had already smashed the first. This one found a similar fate. The hammer greedily pulped the creature as soon as it lost its footing.

David came back to the group to check the injured while the large warrior reinforced Tara. "Is there anyone hurt?" Apparently only Devin had a wound, and it was self-inflicted at that.

"I am." Devin raised his hand, his hurt hand, and instantly regretted it. He immediately felt dizzy and fell back against the rocks.

"You are poisoned," David pointed out. "Quickly, drink this." He produced a small vial, not dissimilar from that of the warrior.

Nia took the vial from the boy as her father was too disoriented to grab it. She made him drink every drop from the small ceramic container. David looked to the others, but only Devin was hurt.

Devin immediately noticed the effects of the potion. His hand did not ache, and the dizzy spell ended abruptly. The wound, which a minute ago was festering, had closed up. Only a slight reddening remained.

"Thank you. Is there anything we can do to help?" Devin

wanted to be useful.

David shrugged and answered, "We just need to stay out of Fulgrum's way." He looked toward the warrior who was raging on two more demons. "I'll just get in trouble again if we do."

Devin thanked David and then swooped Nia up into his arms. "Let's get a better vantage." He easily climbed the rocks behind them to watch nervously for the rest of this battle to unfold. Thurdron spoke quietly with David and also watched worriedly as the fighting continued.

The two riders had already reached the largest group of Insects still in the hills. They had moved with unreal speed down the mountain and then rocky hills. Both were more clearly visible now.

The larger of the two was armored from head to foot in gleaming plate armor. He swung a sword down to either side and blocked thrown discs and spears with a blue striped shield. Even his horse was equipped in plate barding. A red plume protruded from the top of the man's helmet.

The rider's companion was armored, but nowhere near the same. She wore a mix of chainmail and small plates over leather. Long, golden hair flowed out beneath an emerald studded circlet. In each hand, the woman wielded what looked like two sticks of purple light. They must have had edges though, because she cut through the insect-demons easily.

A demon avoided her swing and impaled her horse that sent the woman flying. Before the monsters converged on the woman, the male rider sidled up next to her. He threw something on the ground and a moment later, two massive onyx bears materialized at their sides. The rider dismounted and looked to the woman. She appeared unconscious or dead.

The bears had a single purpose and they excelled at it. One swatted demons left and right. The other pulled a demon in close and disemboweled it in its rending paws before it bit another monster's head half off. Neither blows from whirling disks nor pronged spears did anything to slow the bears.

One demon penetrated the defensive circle of the two ursa, but failed to measure the threat from the man's horse. The plated mount rose up and trampled the thing to death as it poised to strike.

The woman rose and the two continued their fight on foot.

The man was a walking bulwark. The rare blow or attack that got past his shield could not find its way through his armor. He always let the demons strike first and hacked them down with the assistance of their forward momentum.

The woman was a blur of purple light. On occasion, a group of demons flew backward after a thunderous noise. This was almost always answered by Fulgrum's hammer, as if the raging warrior felt challenged by its call.

The bears defended their flanks as the two marched steadily down the hill.

A commotion stirred at the foot of the rocks. Devin heard Thurdron inspire two of the remaining group to take up arms with him. They retrieved demon spears and charged after Fulgrum and Tara.

Nia looked up at her father nervously. "Are you going to help them Father?"

"Yes," he answered, "I will stay here and guard my princess."

She sighed in relief, "Thank you." Then she hugged his legs as he watched the battle conclude.

The insect demons knew they had lost the fight, but they exhibited no panic. They did not retreat. They just kept fighting, even when Tara glowed orange again for her final assault.

The two groups met in the middle. No more human or dwarf lives were lost.

The victors walked back in silence. They stopped only to kill a still crawling insect-thing.

Fulgrum lumbered right up to David and ran his hand through the boy's hair. "Good boy." Then he turned to the others.

"I am Fulgrum, blacksmith. This is David."

Tara reached out and shook Fulgrum's hand. "Thank you good sirs. As you saw, we were few and would not have made it further than we stand now without your help." She looked about and took stock of their numbers, then frowned.

The blond woman spoke, "We tracked this scouting party

through the mountains. We knew they were on the scent of survivors from Ferrickport. A ways back, we freed some of your group that had been captured."

The man looked from face to face. It looked as if he were searching for someone. "There are not many of you left. I am sorry to see that."

Thurdron answered that, "There were ninety three of us. Guarded by three Peacekeepers. Sadly, only seven are left under the protection of a single guardian." As his voice trailed off, he mouthed a thank you to Tara.

Fulgrum sized up his new allies and then asked the woman, "Demon Hunter, you know Brell?"

The way her eyes lit up, Fulgrum had his answer before she spoke. "Yes, yes I do. Do you know his whereabouts? He reached out to me as this whole invasion was starting."

The blacksmith responded, "If they are alive, he and his friends traveled by boat. They were making way to the isle of Valencia."

She nodded her understanding.

Devin asked, "Good sir, you were looking for someone? We have all lost many here."

"Amroth," the man said. "I'm Amroth, and this is my wife Sarauna. Yes. We are looking for our two sons, Tristan and Lancelot."

End

Tristan

Trazk

Brell

Lancelot

Lareth

Folgrum

Ardus

Thelband

Kromax

Made in the USA
Monee, IL
04 December 2019